SHERLOCK HOLMES
Cry of the Innocents

SHERLOCK HOLMES
Cry of the Innocents

CAVAN SCOTT

TITAN BOOKS

Sherlock Holmes: Cry of the Innocents
Print edition ISBN: 9781783297160
Electronic edition ISBN: 9781783297177

Published by Titan Books
A division of Titan Publishing Group Ltd
144 Southwark St, London SE1 0UP

First edition: September 2017
2 4 6 8 10 9 7 5 3 1

A CIP catalogue record for this title is available from the British Library.

Printed and bound in the United States.

What did you think of this book?
We love to hear from our readers. Please email us at:
readerfeedback@titanemail.com, or write to us at the above address.

To receive advance information, news, competitions, and exclusive offers
online, please sign up for the Titan newsletter on our website.
www.titanbooks.com

For George

CHAPTER ONE

MARCH COMES IN WITH A ROAR

"I thought it was the end of the world."

"Come now, darling," I said, gently admonishing my wife. "Merely supply Mrs Hudson with the facts. There's no need to over-egg the pudding."

My former landlady peered over half-moon glasses and fixed me with the look she usually reserved for pedlars of dubious merchandise. "Over-egg the pudding? Doctor, what is it they say about men in glass houses? Remember, I've read those stories of yours. As has Mr Holmes." She paused, a mischievous smile playing on her lips. "What did he call them again?"

I sat back in my old armchair and nursed the glass of brandy that Mrs Hudson had pressed into my hand on our arrival.

"He thought they read very well," I lied.

"Really? That's not what I remember. Wasn't it something about 'sensationalised twaddle'?"

"Mrs Hudson," my wife gasped, although I could tell by the amusement in her voice that the reprimand was anything but genuine.

I smiled despite myself. "That sounds... rather familiar."

Mrs Hudson was not about to let me get away with it that easily. "So if the doctor's worried about the pudding being over-egged, maybe we should head down to the kitchen and introduce Mr Pot to Mr Kettle."

I raised my hands in mock surrender. "Like the eggs themselves, I know when I am beaten."

At that Mary laughed, and the sound warmed my frozen bones more than the fire that roared in the hearth.

"I'm sorry, Doctor," Mrs Hudson said, an apology I immediately waved away.

"Mrs Hudson, who else is going to put me in my place while Holmes is on the continent? Now, Mary, please, the stage is yours."

I sipped my brandy as Mary continued her tale. It began, like so many stories told by the English, with the weather. The February of 1891 had been surprisingly mild and March had looked as if it would follow in its predecessor's footsteps. I had been reminded of the old saying that March comes in like a lion, and goes out like a lamb. Little did we know how wild an animal it would be.

The morning of Monday 9 March had started pleasantly enough. The barometer that hung in the hallway of our Kensington home had been rising steadily, promising a fine and pleasant day. There had been reports of a smattering of snow elsewhere in the country, but nothing more than moderate winds were expected. Mother Nature, however, is a fickle mistress. As if to punish mankind for daring to predict her ways, she turned on us, sending a storm to end all storms.

"I was glad when John shut up the surgery," Mary admitted to Mrs Hudson. "The windows were already rattling in their frames, and the snow falling hard."

Mrs Hudson placed a hand on my wife's arm. "I was caught out in it myself. Nearly lost my hat on Bickenhall Street."

"We dined and retired to the sitting room, where John lit the fire. I tried to distract myself with needlepoint, but my attempts to relax were punctuated by the sound of roof tiles smashing on the road outside. John was at the hearth when it happened, adding more wood to the fire. An incredible squall thundered through the house, and before I knew what was happening the chimney stack fell through the ceiling. John was nearly crushed."

Again I felt the need to interject. "I was able to throw myself clear."

"But not before taking that bang to your head," Mrs Hudson pointed out. Instinctively, my hand went to the bandage she had helped my wife apply.

"All that mattered was that Mary was safe," I said. "We couldn't stay at home with a gaping hole in the ceiling…"

"…so you came here," Mrs Hudson said, completing my sentence in a manner she had picked up thanks to years of looking after Sherlock Holmes, a necessity if she wanted to get a word in edgeways. "And I'm glad you did. 221B is a fortress, always has been. You can return home when the storm has passed, and see what the damage is."

My wife made to reply, but the thought made her voice catch in her throat. I put aside my glass and went to her, kneeling in front of the settee where so many clients had revealed their woes. "Try not to worry, my dear. I'm sure it won't be half as bad as we imagine."

As if to contradict me, the sounds of the tempest outside intensified. The journey across town had been traumatic. I had bundled my wife, maid and housekeeper into a cab and we had held on for dear life as the poor horses negotiated the snow-bound roads. The wheels of the carriage stuck fast not once, but three times on the way to my former lodgings in Baker Street. On the third occurrence, I was forced to disembark and help the beleaguered cabbie dig us out. Smashed tiles littered the freshly fallen snow, windows were blown out and gates hung loose from railings. It struck me that the only folk who would welcome the storm were the slaters, carpenters, glaziers and gardeners who would no doubt find themselves in gainful employment for many months to come.

By the time we neared Baker Street, the roads had become impassable. Paying our courageous cabbie, we braved the last part of the journey ourselves, crunching through snow that was already up to our knees. It was slow progress, our extremities chilled and our hearts low. I had never been so glad to see 221B in all my life, although the steps leading up to that well-remembered door were completely covered with snow.

Mrs Hudson had taken one look at us and ushered us in. We were soon ensconced in the cosy sitting room, drinks delivered into our hands and the fire stoked, while our staff warmed themselves in Mrs Hudson's kitchen.

As the flames danced in the grate, Mary glanced furtively at the ceiling, as if expecting 221B's own chimney breast to follow the example of its counterpart in Kensington and come crashing down.

I, myself, had never felt safer. Sitting here, with the paraphernalia of Holmes's singular life all around, made me feel that nothing could touch me. From my friend's eternally chaotic desk to that damned Persian slipper stuffed with tobacco, it was as if Holmes himself were with us, holding back the storm. Little did I know that the events of this calamitous evening would pale into insignificance compared with the perils that lay ahead.

And so we settled in for the night, holed up in these most familiar of surroundings. Mrs Hudson made a comfortable nest for our own housekeeper and maid in her rooms downstairs, while Mary would sleep in my old bedroom, the single bed meaning that I faced a night on the settee. The windows were secured against the elements and the curtains drawn. As Holmes's grandfather clock chimed midnight, I lounged on the sofa reading a long-forgotten adventure novel I had found upstairs, Mary having retired some hours before.

The house was at peace, save for the wind whistling a merry tune down the chimney and the steady tick of the clock. Everything felt so familiar that I half expected the sound of Holmes's Stradivarius to emanate from his empty bedchamber in the adjoining room.

Cocooned in a blanket, I forced myself to turn off the light when I realised that I had read the same paragraph three times. I extinguished the lamp, plunging the sitting room into darkness. Sleepily I turned over, trying to make myself comfortable, when an unexpected sound catapulted me back to my senses. I sat up, eyes wide in the gloom. Where had it come from? Not from the steps that led up to my old room, or from the narrow landing on the other side of the sitting-room door. I was suddenly aware of every creak and groan in the house. What had it been?

As nothing out of the ordinary happened, and the seconds turned into minutes, I relaxed. I lay back, laughing at myself nervously. What a fool I had become, jumping at shadows.

I closed my eyes… and there it was again. A tap, followed by a scrape, metal against wood. I leapt from the settee, nearly upsetting the lantern from the table beside me. I froze, listening intently.

There. It was coming from Holmes's bedroom, not the scrape of horsehair against violin string, but that of a window being opened, followed by a great gust of wind that rattled the bedroom door in its frame.

The blood boiled in my veins. An opportunistic thief was using the storm to invade Holmes's inner sanctum. How dare he!

Not wanting to alert the intruder to my presence, I took up the poker and crept forwards, the weapon raised in my hand, ready for action.

I paused by the door and listened to the creak of the floorboards on the other side of the wood. I reached for the doorknob, but it was pulled from my hand, the door opened from within.

A tall, lanky frame slammed into me and I tumbled back, the poker tumbling from my hand. My already injured head made contact with the floor and stars spiralled across my vision. My arm was pinned to the ground, a grip like iron grasping my wrist. Light bloomed in the darkness and I turned to see Mary rushing down the stairs from my former bedroom, a lantern in her hand.

"John?"

"Mary, stay back," I warned, before I looked up at my attacker and the voice caught in my throat. Sharp grey eyes were staring down at me, thick eyebrows raised in amazement on a large domed forehead.

"What the devil are you doing sneaking around in the dark, Watson? exclaimed Sherlock Holmes. "I could have killed you!"

CHAPTER TWO

THE MORNING AFTER

Those of you who have read my earlier work will know that I previously claimed not to have seen Holmes at all during the winter and spring of 1891. For this deception I must apologise. While it is unlikely that this manuscript will ever see print, I feel now more than ever that I should commit to paper *all* the adventures I shared with Sherlock Holmes. This includes that handful of cases which, due to their sensitive or potentially scandalous nature, I have vowed never to enter into the public record.

Of course, as Holmes helped me back to my feet, I had no idea that the affair in which we would soon be embroiled would be one that Holmes's brother Mycroft would deem inappropriate for publication.

"Holmes," said I, brushing myself down, "I thought you were overseas."

"I am, or rather I was. I have been working in France, Watson, at the behest of Monsieur Marie François Sadi Carnot."

"The President?" Mary exclaimed, recognising the name from the papers.

"The very same," Holmes replied. "Although please do not ask me the nature of my case."

"A matter of national security, eh?" I asked, drawing a look of reproach from my friend. "Sorry. Say no more, old chap."

"The work has reached somewhat of a natural lull, and so I took the opportunity to return to England and deal with several matters at home."

"Your timing could have been better."

"Thankfully the crossing was relatively calm, although the journey from Dover was positively hellish. The thought of Baker Street drove me on, and yet on arrival I found 221B's front door behind three foot of snow."

"Did you not think to wake Mrs Hudson?"

"And face her wrath? Come, Watson. Not even the residents of Bedlam would attempt to rouse our redoubtable landlady from her slumber. I deduced that it would be far safer to shimmy up the drainpipe and enter through my bedroom window."

Holmes's account was interrupted by the sudden appearance of Mrs Hudson at the sitting-room door, and her delight in seeing her prodigal lodger. I could not help but recall the dull October afternoon three years previously when Holmes had occupied his not-inconsiderable mind by attempting to break into every window and door of 221B Baker Street in order to ascertain the security of the house. That was until Mrs Hudson had returned home to find him hanging from the roof. Her expression, and indeed her language, was far more congenial today, although both Holmes and I glossed over the true nature of his ingress.

Energised by Holmes's sudden appearance, all thought of sleep was banished from my mind. The ladies returned to their respective beds while the two of us sat opposite each other by the fire, talking into the early hours. The conversation was as effortless as ever; Holmes sat puffing away at his noxious black shag while I enjoyed the subtle delights of my own Arcadia mix.

Eventually, when our tobacco pouches were as exhausted as our limbs, we retired to bed, Holmes to his room and I to the settee. This time I slipped easily into the arms of Morpheus, despite the valiant efforts of the storm outside.

The following morning saw welcome helpings of Mrs Hudson's renowned kedgeree before Holmes and I braved the weather to scope out the fate of my Kensington home. The wind had subsided although a powdery flurry of snow fell steadily from the grey skies. London was returning to life, the roads already cleared by the enterprising unemployed ready and willing to earn an extra penny from businesses and cab companies keen to get the capital moving once again.

On arrival at my modest practice, I was pleased to discover that the damage was less extensive than I had feared. In fact, I even managed to send a boy to find my usual handyman. Kennet was pleased to raise me to the very top of his list of repairs thanks in part to the chance it offered to meet Holmes. My friend's celebrity had grown much these last few years, not least since the publication of *A Study in Scarlet* and *The Sign of The Four*.

The work in hand, we returned to Baker Street, safe in the knowledge that the house was secured. Mary and I were not homeless, thanks to the generosity of both Holmes and Mrs Hudson, who said we could stay indefinitely.

"Indeed," Holmes said, "I will be returning to Paris on the first ferry so you can have the place to yourself."

It was a prediction that would soon be confounded.

While Mary was understandably concerned to return home, our plight was nothing compared to that of the poor wretches who had suffered most at the cruel hands of the great blizzard.

According to *The Times*, the west of England had been most seriously hit. Devon and Cornwall were cut off from the rest of the country, railway lines buried beneath drifts of some eighteen feet or more. Entire trains had been entombed and were being dug out by the army, the rescued passengers understandably shaken after their chilling ordeal. There were also reports of ships lost at sea, and in the weeks to come the cost to the agricultural community would be keenly felt, thousands of animals lost in one abominable night.

I was reading of these terrible events as there came a knock at the front door. I exchanged a look with both Holmes and Mary as we listened to the stately tread of Mrs Hudson in the hall below. How many cases had begun with a sharp rap on the door such as this? I glanced at my watch. It had just turned seven o'clock and the wind had picked up again. The streets outside were abandoned through fear of another tumultuous night. Who had braved the weather to arrive on our doorstep?

There was a cry of alarm from Mrs Hudson, followed by the sound of someone stumbling up the stairs. Holmes and I were on our feet as the door crashed open. A corpulent man lurched into the room, broad shoulders covered with snow and a gloved hand clutching his chest. He was dressed in the red-lined robes of a Catholic priest, a silver cross around a full neck and eyes so wide that they looked as though they were trying to escape from their sockets. Jowls wobbled as the man gasped for breath, a strawberry-tinged birthmark livid against ashen skin. He looked wildly around the room, his gaze finally settling on my companion.

"*Signore Holmes*," the priest wheezed in a voice barely more than a whisper. "*Il corpe…*"

And without another word our unexpected guest pitched forward and landed lifeless at our feet.

CHAPTER THREE

NEW SCOTLAND YARD

For the second night in a row I found myself buffeted by a cold easterly wind, although this time I was not looking for sanctuary, but being whisked towards the mortuary in a hansom.

I had rushed to our visitor's side as soon as he fell, seeking a pulse, while Mary held his head in her lap. Holmes had raised the alarm as soon as I had confirmed that the man was dead and, thanks to the detective's standing with the Metropolitan Police, none other than Inspector Lestrade had arrived at 221B within the hour. Statements were taken and the body removed, although Lestrade had made it perfectly clear that Holmes was to remain exactly where he was.

"We will be in touch as soon as there is any information regarding the identity of the corpse, Mr Holmes."

"Which information do you mean exactly? The fact that the deceased holds the rank of Monsignor in the Holy Catholic Church, that he has recently travelled to England from the Vatican, or that he suffered dreadfully from gout?"

"I'm in no mood for your parlour games, Mr Holmes—" Lestrade responded.

"Parlour games!"

Lestrade continued as if Holmes hadn't spoken: "—and must insist that you do as I have asked."

Lestrade made his farewells and departed, leaving Holmes to pace the floor and inform all of Baker Street just what he thought of the inspector.

"Holmes, please," I entreated, sitting on the settee beside Mary, her hand held tightly in mine. "My wife is upset."

"So am I!" came the indignant reply.

"I am quite well, John," Mary said, although I believed not a word of it. Holmes, to his credit, deposited himself in his customary chair and made a concerted effort to hide his impatience. We ate dinner in near silence, Holmes barely touching his food, his eyes flitting constantly to the clock on the mantel. It was only after dessert, when Mary insisted that she was over the worst of the shock, that Holmes leapt from his chair and grabbed his long coat, hat and scarf.

"Mary, I—" I began, but she stopped me.

"Go with him. You won't be able to settle otherwise."

Kissing her on the cheek, I grabbed my outerwear and hurried down the seventeen steps to the front door to join Holmes on Baker Street.

Before long we were rattling through the darkening streets of London, our hansom cab swaying in the wind.

Not wanting to prompt another diatribe regarding Lestrade, I returned my colleague's attention to his earlier deductions.

"So, our visitor…" I ventured.

Holmes let out an exasperated sigh. "Please do not humour me, Watson," said he, guessing where this line of questioning was going. "You know my methods better than anyone. That the man held the station of Monsignor was obvious by the red piping and buttons on his cassock."

"But that he had travelled from Rome? Could he not be part of the Cardinal's retinue here in London?"

"Not according to the shoes the unfortunate fellow revealed as he sprawled across Mrs Hudson's carpet. Black leather with gold buckles and red appliqué. According to the stitching I would venture that they were manufactured by Ditta Annibale Gammarelli, clerical tailors to the Vatican since 1798."

I chose not to point out that a London policeman would have little reason to be familiar with the minutiae of Italian ecclesiastical tailoring. At least the diagnosis of gout had been as clear to me as it was to Holmes. The Monsignor's left ankle had been roughly the size of a cricket ball, which, Holmes pointed out, would also account for the choice of Oxfords over boots.

We fell into silence as we approached New Scotland Yard. Upon our arrival on the Victoria Embankment, Holmes marched into the large red and white building. Bustling past the bemused constable on the front desk, we made straight for our mysterious clergyman's temporary resting place.

As if expecting our approach, Lestrade appeared in the dingy corridor and raised his hands in the manner one would use to try to halt a speeding locomotive. Thankfully, Holmes stopped in his tracks.

Lestrade sighed. "I thought I told you to stay put."

"You did," Holmes conceded, "and I ignored you. I will see the body now."

He moved to continue along the corridor, only to be restrained by a hand on his shoulder.

"No, you will not. While you have served us well in the past, Mr Holmes, may I remind you that this is Scotland Yard. You are a guest here, a welcome guest most of the time, but one who should be careful not to overstep the mark."

I decided it was best to intercede. "Inspector, with all due respect, a man died on our doorstep tonight."

"I thought it was your sitting room."

"In Holmes's lodgings then. Is it any wonder that we are curious about what brought him to Baker Street? Can you at least tell us if he has been examined by the police surgeon?"

Lestrade narrowed his eyes, before shaking his head in defeat. "Oh, very well. Yes, he has been examined."

"And has the cause of death been ascertained?"

"Unfortunately, God help us all."

I was tiring of these games. "Then spit it out, man. What killed him?"

"Isn't it obvious?" said Holmes. "The police surgeon believes that the Monsignor died of complications arising from cholera."

CHAPTER FOUR

MONSIGNOR ERMACORA

"Cholera?" came my horrified reply. "Are you sure?"

"The symptoms are clear for the police surgeon to see," said Holmes. "The man had obviously been suffering from some kind of stomach complaint. There were traces of vomit on his cassock, which he had endeavoured to wipe clean. Then there was the smell. Even accounting for the evacuation of the bowels post mortem…"

"Mr Holmes, please," Lestrade said, his discomfort obvious.

My companion raised a disparaging eyebrow. "I'm sorry, Inspector. I thought this was a mortuary. Surely such conversations take place as a matter of course."

Lestrade let out an exasperated breath, and beckoned us over to a closed door on the other side of the corridor. Opening it, he led us into a small windowless room. At its centre were a table and four chairs, although I noticed Holmes's eyes flick towards the modest leather case that sat against the wall.

Lestrade walked around the table and pulled out a chair, indicating that we should sit opposite him.

"Are we being interrogated?" I joked, eager to break the tension.

Lestrade did not smile. "According to the cabbie who brought the priest to your door, the man was feverish, almost beside himself with pain. He doubled over almost as soon as he'd entered the cab, clutching his stomach. As Mr Holmes said, he was… unwell on the way to Baker Street."

"Did the cabbie attempt to clean up?" I asked, concerned for the poor chap.

Lestrade nodded. "Unfortunately so. He's been quarantined, just in case."

"May I question him?" Holmes asked.

Lestrade's lips were tight as he replied, "I assume you know what quarantine means, Mr Holmes?"

Holmes's lips tightened. "Where did he pick up the gentleman?"

"In Tyburnia, staggering down the Bayswater Road." The inspector pulled out his notebook and flipped through its pages. "'At last, at last,' he said, when the cab stopped to pick him up. 'Take me to Baker Street, at once.'"

"I see. And he was carrying that case?"

Lestrade viewed the article with suspicion, as if it were liable to jump up and bite him like a rabid dog. "You can tell from the leather, I suppose? Italian, is it?"

"I can tell from the address label," Holmes replied, cocking his head to read the graceful handwriting from his seat. "Monsignor Ermacora."

"Of the Holy City?" I guessed.

"Quite so."

Lestrade was looking distinctly unimpressed. "As you suggested, the *Monsignor* had also…" he paused, in a display of squeamishness surprising for a policeman, "…soiled his undergarments." He turned to another page in his notebook. "'A thin, watery diarrhoea' according to the police surgeon."

"I would examine the vestments," Holmes announced.

Lestrade looked up sharply from his notebook. "For what reason?"

"Clues, Lestrade. What else?"

Lestrade flipped the notebook shut and returned it to his pocket. "Then you're out of luck. They've already been burned."

"Standard procedure," I interjected, "in cases of cholera."

"*If* this is a case of cholera," Holmes said.

"But you said…" I began.

"I said that the police surgeon believes it to be cholera. Cramps, vomiting and diarrhoea, followed by a heart attack. Am I right, Inspector?"

"You've hit the nail on the head, as usual."

Now Holmes turned his attention to me. "Doctor, tell me – when was the last outbreak of cholera in London?"

"I don't know. Sixty-two? Sixty-three maybe?"

"1866," Holmes informed me, "and almost entirely confined to the East End. Inspector, may I?"

Lestrade's brow furrowed. "May you what?"

"Examine the late Monsignor's luggage? Or is that also due to be consigned to the furnace?"

Lestrade scratched his dark-brown sideburns. "I'm not sure."

"It should be quite safe," I assured the policeman. "The leather itself won't be contagious."

"And even if it were, I still wear my gloves," Holmes said, raising his hands to show the inspector. "You may burn them afterwards if it helps you sleep at night."

Huffing, Lestrade waved Holmes to continue. The detective was out of his seat in an instant. He recovered the case and placed it on the table. I suppressed a smile at the scrape of Lestrade's chair as he pushed himself back an inch or two.

Holmes examined the lock; satisfied, he pulled out his trusty lock picks. The case was open in a jiffy and Holmes was rifling through the Monsignor's possessions as if they were historical artefacts rather than the effects of a man who had recently shuffled off this mortal coil.

The priest had obviously been a believer in travelling light. The case contained only a few items of clothing, a Holy Bible and a small black notebook, fixed with a clasp. The clothes were examined, the Bible thumbed through and the notebook read in silence.

Finally, Holmes uttered two short words: "Saint Nicole."

"What's that?" I asked.

Holmes passed me the notebook. "The last words Monsignor Ermacora wrote before meeting his maker."

"Not quite, Holmes," I pointed out. "There's a number, 930."

Holmes addressed the inspector. "Lestrade, was a ticket found upon his person?"

"A ticket?"

"A train ticket. The Monsignor was picked up while transporting a case through Tyburnia. Surely it is no great leap to suggest that he had recently arrived at Paddington Station."

"Why not hail a cab at the station?" I asked.

"The station, like the rest of the city, is still recovering from the events of Monday night. What was it he cried on finding a cab, Inspector?"

"At last, at last," Lestrade provided.

"Suggesting that up to that point he had been searching in vain. Plus, the poor fellow was running a fever and in great discomfort. He would have been disorientated, confused; lost in a foreign city. But what of Saint Nicole?"

"A study of his?" I suggested.

"Quite possibly," Holmes conceded, taking the notebook back from me. "Saint Nicole; also sometimes known as Saint Colette.

She lived the life of an anchoress in Picardy, France; Corbie Abbey to be precise."

"An anchoress?" Lestrade asked.

"Walled into a cell with only a small window to connect her to the outside world."

"Good heavens," said I.

Holmes continued flicking through the notebook. "While she certainly lived an interesting life, I do not believe she was the subject of the Monsignor's devotions. This notebook contains nothing but dates, times and locations. The Monsignor obviously used it as an *aide-mémoire*, jotting down his appointments as they were made. The entry before 'Nicole' is an itinerary, detailing his journey across Europe. I hope his journey to Dover was less traumatic than my own."

"Does it tell us his intended destination?" Lestrade asked. "When he arrived in England, I mean?"

Holmes shook his head. "Sadly not. Although look at the numbers that Watson so dutifully noticed: 930." He held the page to his nose. "There is an indentation between the nine and the three, where the pen pressed into the paper but no ink flowed. Nine thirty then."

"A train time!" I realised.

"A reasonable hypothesis, Watson. I believe that we are searching for a place bearing the saint's name, an abbey or parish church, located somewhere between here and Taunton."

"Taunton?" asked Lestrade.

"According to *The Times*, the line below Taunton is still impassable due to the snow. Lestrade, have you a register of Catholic churches, primarily in the west of England?"

Like a bloodhound with a new scent, Lestrade vanished from the room to reappear ten minutes later. Panting heavily, he slammed a heavy leather-bound tome on the table.

"Here," he said, opening the book to the appropriate page. "The Church of St Nicole."

"Corn Street, Bristol," Holmes read. "Excellent work, Lestrade."

The inspector positively beamed, like a child praised for tying his own shoelaces.

"We must send a telegram to your counterparts in Bristol," Holmes announced, "to discover if there have been any recent cases of cholera in that great city. Will you do that for me?"

Lestrade said that he would.

"Excellent. Dr Watson and I shall return to Baker Street. Send a boy as soon as you have word."

It was the following morning by the time a note was delivered to our door. Mrs Hudson brought up the envelope as Holmes was enjoying the latest in a long line of cigarettes.

Excitedly he called to me. "Watson, we're in luck. A Father Kelleher has fallen sick and is being treated at Bristol Royal Infirmary. Look," he thrust the paper into my hand. "Suspected cholera!"

"I doubt Father Kelleher finds it lucky," my wife commented, not looking up from her needlepoint.

Holmes purposely ignored her. "Don't you see what this means, Watson? Two Catholic priests, both with suspected cholera, but no other cases on record? Tell me, is that likely?"

"Well, if it is the beginning of another epidemic—"

"Of a disease many acknowledge as a disease of the poor."

"Only they are stupendously misinformed. Cholera pays no heed to class or position, Holmes. It kills rich and poor alike."

"True, but statistically the impoverished are more likely to fall prey to its symptoms. Take the last outbreak in London – why the East End and nowhere else?" He continued without pausing for me to answer. "Because work on the sewers had yet to reach the affected areas. Over two thousand dead within eleven weeks, all because they were exposed to untreated water. Now, you saw Monsignor Ermacora... Did he look the kind of man who, despite his calling, lives with the poor and needy? Did he look like the kind of man who regularly consumes untreated water?"

"He looked the kind of man who was very, very sick."

"But not from cholera, and neither is this Father Kelleher. I am sure of it, Watson, as sure as I am that you hurried shaving this morning, and your wife made a catastrophic mistake three rows back but has yet to notice."

On the settee, Mary peered quizzically at her needlework. Holmes meanwhile was in full flow.

"Two men, Watson, both priests; one from the Holy City, one from Bristol. One is dead, one is dying. And why? Because they were poisoned, Watson, and I shall prove it!"

CHAPTER FIVE

SOMETHING ROTTEN

At times like this I often wondered what hold Holmes had over me. Why was I always so willing to go charging off into the unknown with the man, no matter what?

This was especially true during my all too brief time with Mary. If I had known then what I know now, how our life together would be cut so tragically short, I should like to think that I would have stayed at home, to cherish what little time we had left.

Not that she would have let me. Mary knew as well as I that when there was a mystery I would follow my friend to the ends of the Earth.

"Go with him, John," Mary said, as Holmes announced that he was going to Bristol. "Until the repairs are completed we cannot return home, and Dr Mann will look after your patients as he has so many times before. Besides, you will be unbearable until he has returned."

She smiled kindly, and I loved her all the more for it.

"Thank you," I said, rushing to pack the case that the maid had only emptied two nights before.

Before long, we were on a train, heading for Bristol. In London, the snow had all but vanished from the roads, great heaps of slush piled high on the pavements. However, travelling west was like plunging into winter all over again. A thick blanket covered the English countryside, and sheep were huddled in the cold.

The news in the paper was no better. As Holmes studied a map of Bristol, I read of ships lost off the south coast, the death count already in the hundreds. Of particular concern was an American steamer known as the *Suevia*. According to *The Times*, she had arrived at Prawle Point on Monday afternoon only to have a valve of her low-pressure boiler give way. The strong east wind took her straight into the path of the storm. Another steamer, the *Acme* of London, responded to her SOS, but was too small to tow the *Suevia* to safety. Instead the *Acme* transported the chief officer to Falmouth. He set sail again, this time in a powerful tug, but the *Suevia* was nowhere to be found. Fears were growing that she had gone down, taking all hands with her.

I let the newspaper fall into my lap and sighed.

"Watson?" Holmes asked. "Are you quite all right?"

"It's just this damned storm, Holmes. It's brought with it such tragedy—"

"That it makes you wonder why we are charging across country to investigate the death of two men we do not know?"

I nodded, and Holmes smiled, drawing a folded piece of thick paper from his pocket.

"What is this?" I asked, as he handed it to me.

"A papal decree, found nestled in the pages of Monsignor Ermacora's Bible."

I looked at him askance. "You stole it?"

"I liberated it from Lestrade's dunderheaded investigation. While I respect many things about the man, he has already made his mind up about this case. As soon as I recognised the paper stock, I removed the letter while the good inspector was fetching the register."

"And you didn't think to tell me what you were up to?"

"Watson, your talents are legion, but the keeping of secrets is not one of them."

Affronted, I unfolded the paper. Naturally, Holmes was right. The decree bore the crest of his Holiness Pope Leo XIII. I scanned the text, pleased that my command of Latin remained unwithered since my university days. According to the missive, the Monsignor had been given the right of full access in the investigation of the miracle of one Edwyn Warwick.

The name was familiar and I said so.

"I availed myself of the index on our return to Baker Street," Holmes said, referring to the vast catalogue of newspaper clippings and reports that he had carefully curated over the years. "Edwyn Warwick was a philanthropist and merchant, whose great fortune has more than benefited the city of Bristol since his death in 1721, as he died unmarried, his enemies insisting with relish that, despite his many charitable works, no woman in her right mind would consent to be his wife."

"Good Lord," I said. "And did he have many enemies?"

"He was exceptionally wealthy, and the green-eyed monster is a powerful master, especially when the person in question flouts social conventions. A man of means without an heir? To a certain stratum of society, such a thing is unthinkable. Of course, there is also the questionable manner in which Warwick amassed his fortune."

"And that was…?"

"Slavery. Edwyn Warwick was one of the foremost slave traders of his time. Now, a century after his passing, his name is celebrated all across Bristol. There are streets, schools and even a concert hall named in his honour. His legacy is forever assured, thanks to the generosity of his estate."

"Which some claim is tainted money?"

"As General Booth has been known to say, the only thing wrong with tainted money is that *there's jus' taint enough of it*. The people of Bristol have profited nicely from Warwick's riches, that is for sure."

"That's a little heartless, Holmes. So much suffering—"

He waved away my admonition. "Watson, we are not here to debate the morality of Warwick's chosen trade, or for you to judge me. Have you forgotten so easily my efforts to dismantle the slave ring of Bethnal Green?"

How could I? The investigation had nearly cost Holmes his life.

"I speak only of history. My own views on the matter are neither here nor there. What is of interest is the miracle. A senior member of the Vatican's staff is dispatched to Bristol to investigate one of England's most divisive figures. Instead, the priest ends up in a London mortuary, struck down by a disease many hope has been consigned to the history books. And remember his last words, Watson…"

"*Il corpe*," I recalled.

"The body," Holmes translated, his eyes sparkling. "Something is rotten here, Watson; rotten to the core, and I shall discover what it is."

CHAPTER SIX

THE BRISTOL REGENT

Fortunately, our journey was not too heavily delayed by the weather. We arrived at Bristol Temple Meads only forty-five minutes after our due time, and were met by the cab that Holmes had arranged to whisk us to the Bristol Regent Hotel on nearby College Green. I could not help but be impressed as we ascended the short flight of steps to the palatial lobby. It really was as fine a hotel as any I had seen in the capital, the smell of polished mahogany furnishings greeting us as soon as we set foot through the doors.

The grandeur was only slightly spoiled by an argument that was in full flow at the reception desk. A man in his early thirties was giving a handsome woman in a navy dress what for. She in turn listened intently, her hands clasped together patiently, nodding in agreement even though she must have been the angry fellow's senior by a good decade or more.

Not wanting to add to her embarrassment, we hovered by a display of boot blacking and tools advertising the hotel's in-house polishing and repair service, and waited for the disagreement to come to an end. Thankfully, the aggrieved gentleman was soon stomping past us to exit through the revolving doors.

"Mr Holmes," proclaimed the lady in the navy dress as she swept towards us. "I do apologise. That you should arrive when I'm caught in the middle of a… disagreement…"

"The fellow did seem a trifle upset," Holmes noted.

"And that is a trifle of an understatement. A mix-up of dates, unfortunately. Part and parcel of running a hotel. Still, seeing you puts a smile on my face. I'm so glad you have come to stay with us once again."

"And I am glad to be here." My companion turned to bring me into the conversation. "Dr Watson, may I introduce Mrs Mercer, manageress of the Bristol Regent."

"Enchanted," I said. "You have stayed here before, Holmes?"

"Mr Holmes came to the rescue of my husband," Mrs Mercer told me.

"Mr Thomas J. Mercer," Holmes explained. "The former manager of this fine establishment."

"You took over from your husband?" I asked.

"After the dear Lord took him from us, yes."

"Oh my dear woman, I do apologise. You have my sincere condolences."

The manageress smiled sweetly. "Please, there is no need. Thomas passed two years ago now. I miss him terribly, but he lived well, and was a happy man. I am determined to remember him in the same way." She returned her gaze to Holmes. "Now, I have placed you in two of our finest rooms, overlooking the green no less. I think you will be most comfortable, and before you argue, there is no charge."

"Madam," Holmes began, "I must insist—"

"*I* insist," said she with a voice used to being obeyed, "as would Thomas if he were still with us. You served him well. The Regent owes you a great debt."

"Nonsense," Holmes insisted. "Your late husband paid

handsomely for my services, but I thank you for your generosity all the same."

"Whatever you wish, you need only ask."

"Including a peek into your extensive library?"

Mrs Mercer laughed. "Of course. It would be my pleasure."

"You collect books?" I enquired.

"Local history," the lady replied. "It is something of a passion of mine. A hobby. You're a literary man yourself, aren't you, Dr Watson?"

"Oh, I dabble. The odd story here and there."

"Mostly about me, unfortunately," Holmes commented. "But do not concern yourself, Mrs Mercer, Watson always changes the names to protect the innocent."

"Or the guilty?" she asked with a smile.

"There is something you may be able to help us with," I said, remembering the contents of the Pontiff's letter. "Do you know the Church of St Nicole?"

"On Corn Street?"

"Yes. I don't suppose you know anything of interest about the place?"

"You'll find it within the walls of the Old City," she told me, "dating back to either the eleventh or the twelfth century, I believe. I'm afraid I have never visited myself; although it is, of course, the last resting place of old Warwick."

"Edwyn Warwick?" Holmes asked.

"The very same. There is a rather impressive monument; you should see it for yourself."

"An excellent idea," Holmes said with a bow. "An excellent idea indeed."

My room was as sumptuous as Mrs Mercer had suggested. The bed was carved from the most exquisite English walnut and the dressers topped with Sicilian marble. The Bristol Regent was living up to its regal name.

That evening, we dined in the Regent's equally grand restaurant, before making for the lounge to sample the hotel's fine collection of brandies. It was little wonder that, when we eventually retired to our rooms, I slept like the dead.

However, I was awoken at first light by a knock on the door. Thinking it was a maid, I called out that she should come back later.

"I think not," came Holmes's voice in reply.

I went over to the door and let him in, finding my friend fully dressed. He took one look at me and tutted.

"Really, Watson. What would your wife say if she caught you lounging around at such an hour?"

I looked to the clock on the mantel. "It's seven a.m."

"Precisely, and we have work to do. Get yourself dressed and come to my room."

"What about breakfast?" I complained.

"I think you ate your fill last night." He glanced at his watch. "Time is ticking, Watson."

Calling my companion every derogatory name under the sun, and a few of my own creation, I washed and dressed, and made my way across the hall to his suite. He opened the door at my first knock and I was treated to a veritable cornucopia of delights: a food trolley laden with cold meats and cheese.

"You have ordered room service," I said gratefully.

"Well, you know what they say about armies and their stomachs. I assume the same rules apply to retired surgeons."

I pulled up a chair and helped myself to a slice of bread and butter. "So, what's the plan?"

"The plan is that you pay a visit to St Nicole's."

"*Me?* What about you?"

"Unfortunately, I have matters to attend to. As you know, I

was due to return to Paris. There is nothing that cannot wait, but my employer has questioned why I chose to jaunt across England's not-so-green and pleasant land rather than make my way straight to the City of Lights. A few carefully worded telegrams will assuage their concerns, but time is not on my side. We must discover who poisoned Monsignor Ermacora and return to London *tout de suite* or they may well introduce me to Madame Guillotine."

"What do you need me to do?"

"Good man," Holmes exclaimed, clapping me on the back. "As soon as I have dispatched my telegram, I intend to pay a visit to our Father Kelleher. You, in the meantime, will follow Mrs Mercer's advice and visit the final resting place of Edwyn Warwick."

"The Church of St Nicole. But what exactly am I looking for?"

"Nothing, absolutely nothing," Holmes said. "John Watson will not even set foot in the place."

"But you just said—"

"I know what I said. It is time for a disguise!"

In the ten years I had known Sherlock Holmes, I had seen my friend don all manner of disguises. He had stepped out onto the streets of London dressed as pedlars and princes, sailors and heads of state. Once, he had even spent a week as the Bearded Lady of Professor Spindleberry's Gallery of the Grotesque on Hampstead Heath.

I had never expected, however, to don a disguise of my own!

As you can imagine, I did not go quietly into the make-up chair. Even as Holmes later wheeled the depleted room service trolley out into the corridor for collection, I pointed out that I was no actor, and, as he had so recently commented, incapable of keeping secrets.

"Nonsense," said he. "You wear different masks every day,

depending on whom you are with: Watson the general practitioner; Watson the ex-serviceman; Watson the dutiful husband; Watson the Boswell. This is no different. You already inhabit the characters in your stories. Think of it as a writing exercise, a fiction made flesh."

His prattle did little to calm my nerves, even as he went to work on my appearance. Little by little, as I stared into the mirror, John Watson disappeared, to be replaced by a man I did not recognise. My own moustache was joined by a full fake beard, my then-healthy head of hair hidden beneath a bald cap, a few straggly strands combed over my newly barren crown. A large mole appeared on my right cheek while brows almost as bushy as Holmes's own bristled above hooded eyes. The effect was completed by a pair of pince-nez that rested on the bridge of a thick nose. The transformation was incredible, although I still failed to see the point of such blatant subterfuge.

"Like it or not, Watson," Holmes said, revealing the next stage in my transformation, "your name is known thanks to your repeated insistence on bringing us both into the public eye. If Monsignor Ermacora was poisoned in Bristol, he had an enemy in these streets. That same enemy may have known of his fateful journey to 221B Baker Street. Imagine their surprise when who should appear in Bristol but Dr John Watson, associate and friend of the world's greatest consulting detective."

"But, Holmes, half the staff in this hotel know who we are. If you wanted to remain inconspicuous—"

"I have my methods, Watson. Please, do not question them."

"And here I was thinking that only the Lord worked in mysterious ways."

"Well, you should know," Holmes said cryptically. "Or rather, so should Father Morell of the Roman Catholic Church."

With that, Holmes opened the large trunk on his bed to reveal the vestments of a priest.

CHAPTER SEVEN

THE MEMORIAL

To say that I was feeling self-conscious as I walked the cobbles of Bristol's financial district was something of an understatement. This was preposterous. While Holmes would have taken the theatrical world by storm, I would have been booed off the stage. Who in their right mind would believe that I was a man of the cloth?

No sooner had the thought crossed my mind, than a passing gentleman touched the brim of his hat.

"Good afternoon, Father," he said, before continuing on his way.

I was amazed. Perhaps I could carry this off, even with the ridiculous limp Holmes had insisted I adopt. The maniac had gone so far as to place a small pebble in my right boot to remind me which was supposed to be my weak leg.

Before long I had reached the Church of St Nicole. It was a curious building, far smaller than I had expected, and nestled between the quarters of financial institutions on both sides. It was as though the neighbouring buildings were trying to bully the diminutive house of worship for daring to remind the faithful that the love of money is the root of all evil. It certainly looked far from grand enough to house the remains of such an influential figure as Edwyn Warwick. I placed a shaking hand on the ornate wooden door and, fighting the urge to cross myself, pushed it open.

While it had been cold on the street, the temperature in the church itself was positively glacial. My breath misted as I called out, ignoring Holmes's advice to adopt an Irish accent. Enough, after all, was enough. I was having sufficient trouble remembering my *nom de plume*. Surviving a conversation without a slip of my accent would be next to impossible.

"Hello, is anyone there?"

My call echoed around the church and was immediately greeted by the sound of hurried footsteps. A fresh-faced young priest appeared at a door in the north transept. He saw me and a flicker of confusion and surprise crossed his features.

"I'm sorry, I did not hear you come in," he said, striding across the nave to greet me. While consternation was still written across his face, his handshake was considerably warmer than the frosty atmosphere of his church. I felt a twinge of guilt over my deception.

"Father Ebberston," he said. "And you are...?"

I stammered for a minute, hoping that young Ebberston would put it down to the cold.

"Father James Morell, of the *Catholic Herald*."

Ebberston's smile faltered. "The *Herald*? From London?"

"The very same," I replied, appalled to realise that I had subconsciously adopted the Irish accent after all. "It's a pleasure to be here. A pleasure indeed."

Ebberston continued to look unsure. "Well, I enjoy reading your periodical of course, but I'm mystified to know what would bring you to our little church, especially during such inclement weather."

Before I could answer, the door crashed open behind us.

We turned to see a man in threadbare clothes stumble into the vestibule. His body was twisted, and what little we could see of his dirty face beneath a matted white beard, was cadaverous and pinched. The old tramp was wheezing like a grampus, his rheumy eyes wild and staring.

The man took but two steps before his arthritic knees gave way and he collapsed to the floor, striking his head on the cold flagstones.

"Good heavens," exclaimed Ebberston, rushing to the newcomer's aide.

I am ashamed to say that my first reaction was not one of concern for the stranger's health, but annoyance that my investigation had stalled before it even had begun.

However, my training soon kicked in as Ebberston attempted to roll the fellow onto his back. "No, don't move him," I advised, somehow remembering my false brogue. "If he has hit his head…"

The tramp let out a phlegm-filled cough and pushed himself up on shaking arms. "Don't worry about I," he said in a broad West Country accent. "Old Pete's survived worse than a knock on me 'ead." He groaned, and looked as though he was about to pitch forward again before Ebberston grabbed the fellow's arm.

"Help me with him, Father," the young man asked, and I reluctantly deferred to the priest's request, helping the surprisingly heavy man to a nearby pew. The stink from the chap was intense, a heady mix of sweat, gin and other aromas designed to turn a civilised man's stomach. I went to examine Pete's head, but he jerked away as if afraid to be touched.

"Please," Ebberston pleaded with the man, "we only want to help."

"Bless you, Father," the man wheezed. "All I asks is to warm these old bones for a moment, like."

Ebberston placed a kindly hand on Pete's shoulder, and this

time the tramp flinched not at all. "Well, I am not sure I can help with the temperature. St Nicole's is an ice box all year round, but at least we can shelter you from the wind. Jack Frost won't be able to find you in here. Father Morell will stay with you while I find you some blankets."

Before I could stop the earnest young man, Ebberston was striding back to the north transept, and had disappeared through the door again. I was left alone with the vagrant. He stared at me with suspicion.

"Ain't seen thee around 'ere before…"

"Er no, I'm… I'm just visiting." I looked around, trying to make conversation. "It's a lovely old church."

"That it is," old Pete agreed. "Visiting, eh? From Scotlan', by the sounds of it."

I was momentarily confused. "Scotland? Oh, you mean my accent. No, um, Ireland. Yes, definitely Ireland."

The old man was not about to let me off the hook. "Ireland, you say. S'funny. I's travelled the length and breadth of Ireland…"

My heart sank. "You have? Well, they say that travel broadens the mind…"

"And I's never 'eard an accent like thee's."

I wondered if Pete could see my face blanching beneath the make-up. Fortunately, the sound of the transept door halted the interrogation.

"Father Morell, could you lend a hand?"

"Gladly," said I, and meant it. I rushed over to the door where Ebberston handed me a blanket.

"If you could give that to our guest," said he before disappearing again.

"Of course," I said, walking back to the vagrant, who was still peering at me in a worryingly sceptical manner. Yet he seemed grateful enough as he took the proffered blanket.

"Thank 'ee kindly," he said, wrapping it around his narrow shoulders. "Lovely bit of wool that."

"A gift from the League of Merchants," Ebberston announced as he reappeared once again. "You must take it with you. But before you go…"

A glorious aroma filled the church, old Pete eyeing the soup in Ebberston's hands greedily.

"That smells delicious," I commented as the priest passed it over.

"My own take on Scotch broth," the priest explained, smiling benevolently as Pete tucked noisily into his meal. "My father was from Aberdeen."

"You cooked it yourself?"

An embarrassed smile passed over the young priest's face. "It helps me relax. Somehow preparing food brings me closer to the Lord. After all, did he not provide for his flock?"

I fished a notebook and pencil from my pocket. "The cooking curate, eh? My readers will find that fascinating, to be sure."

"Ah yes," Ebberston said, with a hint of a sigh. "Your newspaper."

"A few questions, Father, that's all."

Beside me, old Pete gave a prodigious belch.

"'Scuse me!"

"I'm glad to see you are enjoying it," Ebberston said, smiling benevolently.

I manoeuvred myself so I was standing between the priest and the gauche diner. "It's about the miracle, you see?"

That gained Ebberston's attention. "I beg your pardon?"

"You were visited by Monsignor Ermacora recently, from the Holy City."

The name had a startling effect on the young man. He immediately retreated to the pews on the other side of the nave and busied himself with a pile of already perfectly stacked hymnals.

"I don't think so," he said, examining the spine of the topmost book. "No one has been here for weeks, I'm afraid."

"Are you sure?"

He let out a sharp laugh. "I think I would remember a monsignor walking through those doors."

I felt a pang of disappointment. Perhaps Holmes's hunch had been wrong. Perhaps the reference to St Nicole in Ermacora's notebook had not referred to this church at all.

Behind me, Pete decided to butt his way into the conversation. "This Monsignor of yours. Was 'ee a gurt big fellow, with more chins than 'er Majesty?"

I turned, trying to make sense of the vagrant's peculiar vernacular. "The Monsignor is certainly... rotund, yes."

"And 'ee had a mark 'ere, on the side of 'is face?" Pete tapped his cheek, in the exact location of Ermacora's birthmark.

"That's the man," I said. "Did you see him?"

"See 'im? An angel, that's what 'ee is. Gave me a sovereign, right out there on the street."

"So he *was* here." I turned to Ebberston, my eyebrows raised. The young priest was clutching his crucifix so hard that his knuckles were as white as his ashen face.

"Yes," he admitted, nodding sharply. "He was here. I'm sorry."

I took a step towards the agitated priest. "Then why say he was not?"

"The Monsignor asked me to keep his visit a secret," Ebberston said quickly. "I don't think it was entirely official."

"Official?" I said. "He was carrying a papal decree."

"Was he?" the priest replied, sweat glistening on his brow despite the low temperature. "I'm not sure. I mean, he wasn't here long. An hour at the most. Probably not even that. I'm afraid I couldn't help him."

"About Edwyn Warwick?" I prompted.

"Edwyn Warwick?" Pete parroted behind me, rising from his pew, his blanket still clutched tight. "Buried in this very church, 'ee is. Ain't natural, if you ask I…"

"What isn't?"

"How they found 'im; in 'is grave, see."

"How do you mean?" I asked, intrigued, as Ebberston rushed to bundle the old man back towards the door.

"I pray that the broth will fortify you, but now I must ask you to leave."

"Leave?"

"I'm afraid so. I am about to lock up for the night. But the blanket is yours. As I said, it is a gift from the Worshipful League of Merchants."

"Wait," I said, stepping forward. "What do you mean? How did they find him?"

"You mean you don't know?" Pete asked, stopping short. "You 'aven't 'eard the story of old Ed Warwick? Ain't a miracle if you asks I; it's a curse!"

"Now then," Ebberston said, doubling his efforts to expel the tramp from the church. "Father Morell doesn't want to hear all that stuff and nonsense."

"I assure you I do," I insisted. "Please, we can give Pete a moment, can't we? To tell his tale?"

Ebberston hesitated, looking as if he were about to throw both of us out onto the street. Finally he relented. "Very well, but as I said to the Monsignor, there is no truth in the stories. They are legends, nothing more."

"Legends," I echoed, becoming more intrigued by the second.

"You should show 'im," said Pete. "Show 'im where old Warwick lays in eternal sleep."

Ebberston shook his head. "Very well, but then I must be getting on. I have an appointment with the bishop."

"Of course," I said, eager to continue.

His hands clasped firmly together, Ebberston led us towards a remarkable monument. At its base lay a tomb, on which a marble effigy rested on one elbow, as if lounging at a Roman feast. The statue depicted a man dressed in the garb and wig of the last century, a benign expression etched on its noble face.

"And this is Warwick?" I asked.

"That's 'im," confirmed Pete. "I don't likes 'is eyes. Gives I the creeps, they does."

"Please," snapped Ebberston, his patience clearly wearing thin. "This is a house of worship."

"Then why you got that devil 'ere then?"

"Edwyn Warwick was a pillar of this community," Ebberston insisted, indicating the impressive stone reredos that rose up behind the figure.

"And these are the charitable causes he supported?" I asked, staring up at the list.

"In both Bristol and London," Ebberston confirmed.

"He never married?" I said, remembering Holmes's words.

"So I believe. This memorial was donated by the League of Merchants, one of the many organisations he supported within the City."

"The same body that donated the blanket?"

"They give great support to our work here. Why, only recently, they donated a large sum to assist in the building of a shelter."

"To help poor unfortunates like Pete?" I suggested, drawing a sharp nod from Ebberston.

"Aye, but they do more than just donates money, ain't that right, Father," Pete prompted. "Tell 'im about the body!"

The tramp's words brought back Monsignor Ermacora's chilling epitaph. "No," I said to the old man, "why don't *you*?"

The vagrant grabbed my arm with a bony hand. "It's the work of the devil, I tells thee; Ol' Scratch 'imself."

And with that, Pete began his macabre tale.

CHAPTER EIGHT

THE LEGEND OF EDWYN WARWICK

"Ol' Warwick was an influential fellow, no one doubts that," began the vagrant, "but the curious things was no one, not the business folk, nor the judges, nor even the priests themselves knew where 'ee was laid to rest. Then, some fifty years ago, there was a tremor beneath this very church. The ground shifted, see, and a wall collapsed, over there." He pointed a shaking finger towards the south transept. "It were a door, bricked up and forgotten for I don't knows 'ow many years.

"The priest of the time, 'ee lit a candle, and crept into the 'ole, finding a staircase, the steps crumblin' with age. Ventured down, 'ee did, and found 'isself in a vault, deep beneath the church. Packed with coffins it were, right up to the ceiling. Now the priest, 'ee were a curious sort of fellow. 'Ee started pokin' around, lookin' to see who were interred down there in the darkness. He found one coffin, marked with a name, it was.

"Sophia Warwick.

"'Is heart, it skipped a beat, because young Sophia was the niece of ol' Edwyn. She'd died a young 'un, but like 'er uncle, no one knew where the poor girl was buried. The priest, 'ee started searchin' all the harder, until it found the finest coffin 'ee did ever seen. Right up 'igh it were, near the ceilin'. Solid oak, brass 'andles, the works…

"They bring it out, this coffin, but there's no name, nothing to say who's layin' inside. Askin' God's forgiveness, the priest gets a crowbar and thrusts it into the lid. Grittin' 'is teeth, 'ee 'eaves and 'eaves with all 'is might. One by one, the nails they comes loose, and the priest yanks open the lid to reveal Edwyn Warwick laid out in front of 'im. The priest starts, callin' out to the blessed Mother for protection, because ol' Warwick lying there in 'is coffin is resplendent, see, like a man gone to sleep, not one who's been dead for a hundred years or more."

"What do you mean?" I asked, interrupting the monologue.

"It's nonsense," insisted Ebberston.

"I say it ain't," insisted Pete. "You weren't there, Father, but I were. When I were a boy, I worked in a merchant's 'ouse and I remembers the priest running through the doors, driven 'alf mad with what 'ee found. My master, 'ee rushes over 'ere to sees for 'isself. I came with 'im, and saw it as clear as I sees you now.

"Warwick's skin was soft and flushed, see? 'Is 'air wafting in the breeze. 'Is lips, they were parted, and 'is teeth shone like stars. My skin, it was crawlin' at the sight of 'im. *Any minute now*, I thought, *Ol' Warwick's gonna open those eyes of 'is and stare into thy very soul.*

"Weren't long before the church was 'eavin', mind. Word got round, see, and the good and the great, they came from all around to gawp and gape at Warwick's body. Even 'is descendants, they comes down from London; they wept like babbers, when they saw 'im lying out like that. 'It's a miracle,' they cried. 'A miracle!'"

"It's poppycock," said Ebberston, his arms by now folded across his chest. "That's what it is!"

"Do you not believe in miracles, Father?" I said, losing myself in my role. "Why, the good Lord—"

"I'm sorry," the priest interrupted. "I've heard this story time and time again. That this church would become a carnival is unthinkable."

"And yet they came, mind," Pete insisted. "The lines, they stretched 'alfway down Corn Street, see. And that's not all. The gentry they didn't just come to *see* the body. They wanted to touch it, as if some of Warwick's magic would rub off on them. I've heard that things were taken, the ring from 'is finger for a start; the cross from around 'is neck."

"Rubbish," Ebberston said. "I don't know where you're getting this from."

"I only say what I 'eard, and what I saw with me own eyes. Warwick's body, it was as fresh as the day 'ee died."

"Could this not be the miracle that Monsignor Ermacora was investigating?" I asked. "If the body showed no signs of decay—"

"Of course it was showing signs of decay," Ebberston interrupted, "and I shall tell you what I told the Monsignor. A coffin *was* found in the vault. It was discovered in the spring of 1844. There was no tremor or earthquake, or whatever claptrap the local legends suggest. Restoration work was being carried out, financed by the League. Yes, Warwick's body was found and identified, from a ring on his finger."

"And his remains?"

"Gone to dust. A new lid was secured to the coffin and he was interred here." Ebberston patted the tomb in front of us. "Where he lies to this very day."

"Is that so?" came a voice from behind.

CHAPTER NINE

INSPECTOR TOVEY

So intent was I on Father Ebberston's words that the sudden shout from behind almost had me jumping out of my counterfeit robes.

We turned to see a burly young man march into St Nicole's. He was barely more than twenty years old, dressed in a light brown suit and overcoat, a bowler hat held respectfully in large, hairy hands. Even from a distance I could see that his eyes were sharp and intelligent, so much so that for a moment I was convinced that the fellow was none other than Sherlock Holmes in disguise, bushy beard and all.

Only the fact that Father Ebberston seemed to know the man personally quashed that particular theory. That, and the fact that the newcomer was flanked by a half dozen police officers, two of whom carried crowbars in their gloved hands.

"Inspector Tovey, this is beyond the pale," Ebberston said, stepping forward to intercept the man who, if you have read my *Adventure of the Patchwork Devil*, would go on to become a great friend to both Holmes and me. "I have answered your deplorable questions over and over again. Your allegations are not so much insulting as outright sacrilege."

"Allegations?" I asked, and Ebberston whirled on me. His patience and hospitality had come to an end and he took my arm, intending to lead me to the door.

"I'm sorry that you had a wasted journey, Father Morell, but the only miracle at St Nicole's is that we somehow manage to squeeze in the Lord's work between these constant interruptions. Now, I must ask you to leave. All of you."

"I'd like the Father to stay, if it's all right with you," Tovey said, blocking our path. His voice was as sturdy as his frame, laced with a Bristolian accent that, while less broad than Pete's, was tempered with steel. "He will be our witness. As will that gentleman."

The inspector pointed at Pete, who almost dropped his beloved blanket in surprise.

"Who, me?" the vagrant stammered, his previous bravado evaporating. I suspected that Pete had had many a brush with the law.

"Why would we need witnesses?" Ebberston asked warily.

Tovey flashed an official-looking document. "This is a warrant to open the tomb of Edwyn Warwick." The paper was duly folded and returned to the inspector's pocket. Ebberston, in the meantime, looked set to drop into a seizure at any moment.

"This is an outrage."

"No, Father, it's the law of the land. Come on, boys."

With that, the police inspector barged past the scandalised priest to approach Warwick's effigy.

"But you can't," Ebberston said, lunging for the inspector. "Edwyn Warwick has lain unmolested for fifty years."

The priest was stopped by the nearest policeman, and held back as Tovey used Ebberston's words against him.

"Unmolested, Father. Are you sure about that?" He strode to the effigy and tapped a finger against the top of the marble slab. "Then what are these?"

When neither Ebberston nor I replied, Tovey turned to the old vagrant who stood shivering in his blanket.

"What about you? What do you think, Mr Holmes?"

You could have knocked me sideways. Before my eyes "old Pete" underwent something of a metamorphosis. He straightened, his blanket falling to the floor. His twisted spine was suddenly ramrod straight, the sloped shoulders now held wide. The bewhiskered chin jutted forward, and the once crazed eyes narrowed to slits.

The old beggar from the streets had vanished. In truth, he had never been present. All this time I had been talking to none other than Sherlock Holmes.

"I do not believe we have met," Holmes said, his cultured tones replacing Pete's Bristolian rasp.

Tovey extended a huge hand, which Holmes accepted and shook briskly.

Tovey beamed. "Indeed we haven't, Mr Holmes, although I am a great admirer of both you and Dr Watson here."

"*Dr Watson?*" Ebberston spluttered, his enraged eyes turning on me. "What deceit is this?"

Carefully avoiding the priest's gaze, I too shook Tovey's hand. "Very pleased to meet you, Inspector," I muttered, not sure whether I was relieved or disappointed that my act was at an end.

Holmes moved towards Warwick's monument and examined the spot that Tovey had pointed out. "There are indentations in the stone, Watson, come and see."

Still furious that I had been duped, I joined Holmes as he ran a thin finger across the lip of the tomb. "Yes, very interesting," I sniffed, unable to muster much enthusiasm.

"They are," Holmes insisted. "And recently made too. The edges are sharp, not dulled by time."

"Exactly," Tovey said. "I noticed them the last time Father

Ebberston insisted that my theories were the worst kind of blasphemy."

"You have a keen eye, sir," Holmes commented, obviously impressed.

"Able to see through any disguise, it seems," I added.

"Not all, but I know both your faces. I've read your stories, Dr Watson. Fascinating stuff, absolutely fascinating."

It was clear from the look Holmes flashed me that I was to later enjoy another lecture on how my stories had wrecked his hard-won anonymity.

"You cannot have recognised us from Watson's published works," Holmes said to the inspector. "The illustrator was under strict instructions to alter our appearances."

Tovey rewarded this comment with another wide smile. "Ah yes, but I sent to Scotland Yard for copies of your official files."

The thought appalled Holmes. "We have files?"

"Indeed you do, sir, extremely detailed files. Inspector Lestrade doesn't mince his words."

"I can well believe it, but why go to such trouble?"

"You intrigue me, Mr Holmes, it's as simple as that."

Holmes afforded the man a tight smile. "And you I, Inspector. Tell me more about these blasphemous theories of yours."

"The man's a lunatic," offered Ebberston. "A madman. He believes that somehow Edwyn Warwick's body has been removed from the grave. It is impossible."

"The impossible is my business," Tovey asserted, jabbing a finger at the incensed man of God. "And I shall prove it. Lads, shall we?"

It soon became clear why Inspector Tovey had selected such a brawny bunch of Bristol's finest as his escort. Despite the protestations of Ebberston, the policemen began the Herculean task of shifting Warwick's effigy from his tomb. Even considering their size and obvious strength I was dumbfounded as, with a shriek of marble against granite, the reclining statue seemed to shift easily.

Tovey chuckled as I watched the six men heave what must have been tons of marble to the floor.

"Don't worry, Doctor," the inspector said. "You're not witnessing another miracle." He patted Warwick's bewigged head as a man would pet a dog. "The figure is hollow. Heavy enough to stay in place, but easy to remove when the time is right."

"The time for what?" I asked.

The police officers were already hard at work with their crowbars, prising the genuinely heavy slab from the tomb.

After much huffing and puffing, the slab was laid out on the flagstones next to Warwick's curious statue.

"No!" Ebberston cried out, as Tovey peered into the sarcophagus.

The inspector's face said it all. Triumphantly, he beckoned us to approach. I deferred to Holmes, content for the detective to go first.

Surprised to find itself suddenly bathed in light, a large spider scuttled across the bottom of the tomb as I looked over the side. The arachnid's bewilderment was akin to my own.

Aside from its eight-legged occupant, the tomb was empty. Of Edwyn Warwick's casket, there was no sign.

CHAPTER TEN

TRIUMPH AND DESPAIR

"So my allegations are sacrilege, are they? My questions deplorable?" Inspector Tovey said, whirling to face Father Ebberston. The detective was revelling in his moment, the grandstanding a symptom of his relative youth. Looking back, I should have reminded him of the old saying that pride often pre-empts a fall; a lesson the young firebrand would soon learn for himself.

"I-I didn't know," the priest insisted. "How could I? I would never be a part of this."

Tovey grinned like a wolf, displaying a set of sturdy gapped teeth. "Take him back to the station. I'll question him later."

Ebberston was led from his church still professing his innocence.

"How did you know, Inspector?" Sherlock Holmes asked as Tovey sent one of his men to find the keys to the front door. St Nicole's had become the scene of one of the most repugnant of crimes: body snatching.

"Father Kelleher," Tovey answered.

"The priest with suspected cholera," Holmes stated.

"The very same. He's doing well. They have him in isolation at the BRI. He's dangerously dehydrated, but they're pumping liquids into him as fast as his body's pumping them out."

"Did he meet with Monsignor Ermacora?" I asked.

"He was his aide, assigned by the bishop here in Bristol," Tovey explained. "Word had reached the Vatican of Edwyn Warwick's uncanny preservation." He paused, looking at us both. "I assume you know the stories."

"Oh yes," I said, shooting a look at Holmes. "A fellow of questionable character relayed them to me."

Holmes responded to my barbed comment with an amused nod.

"The Monsignor was dispatched from Rome to ascertain whether a true miracle had occurred. I suspect that what with Warwick's charitable work, the pontiff was wondering whether he should canonise the old goat."

"From what I understand," Holmes said, "there are some in this city who would question Warwick's suitability for sainthood."

"Not enough in my opinion. You gentlemen are acquainted with Monsignor Ermacora, then?"

"Only briefly, alas," I informed the inspector. "The Monsignor died almost the moment he was through our door."

"No! The same symptoms?"

Holmes regarded the young man with interest. "We have been told it is cholera, but like us, you question the diagnosis, do you not?"

"I'm that easy to read, eh, Mr Holmes?"

"You made no comment when I said that Kelleher had been diagnosed with *suspected* cholera. If the thought had not crossed your mind, I daresay you would have questioned my choice of words."

Tovey moved close to Holmes as if concerned that others

were listening. "It's Kelleher. He's started losing his hair. Now, I know that such a thing can happen when the body is under attack, but he's a strong lad, a year younger than me. It just doesn't seem right somehow."

"It's certainly not one of the usual symptoms," I admitted.

"Not for cholera," said Holmes, "but quite common for colchicine poisoning!"

"Colchicine, Holmes?"

"*Colchicum autumnale*, commonly known as meadow saffron or autumn crocus. It grows quite readily in the west of England, producing a vibrant crop of thick leaves in spring, followed by a flower in autumn."

Tovey clicked his fingers. "Naked Ladies, that's what me old ma called them, on account that the flowers appear after the foliage has completely died away. Her garden was blooming with the things every September."

Holmes nodded. "I have often thought that the *Colchicum* bulb would make the most ingenious murder weapon during a cholera epidemic. If ingested, its effects are staggered over a period of days, sometimes even weeks. At first there is an initial stomach upset followed by more serious symptoms, including convulsions, severe cramps, organ failure, and even respiratory or cardiac arrest. In many cases hair loss is also reported. But think of the prevalent symptoms, Watson: stomach pain; vomiting; severe diarrhoea."

"All symptoms associated with cholera," I conceded.

"Which in itself often brings on heart failure. If the poison were administered during an outbreak, the tell-tale symptoms would be misdiagnosed, lost in the wider pandemic."

"But there is no outbreak," I said, "either here or in London."

"Which makes it all the more unlikely that two healthy specimens would go down with the disease in isolation."

Tovey spoke up. "Mr Holmes, Kelleher told me that Ermacora opened the tomb and found it empty."

"Did he not go to the authorities?" I asked.

"He did, Doctor, but the authorities would not listen. Like myself, Father Kelleher has read of your exploits, Mr Holmes. He recommended that the Monsignor go to you, to ask for your help."

"*Il corpe*," commented Holmes.

"But before he left Bristol, Ermacora was poisoned?" I asked. A terrible thought struck me. "Ebberston! He said he liked to cook. He could have administered the bulb. But, Holmes, you ate his broth."

Holmes waved away my concern. "If Ebberston is our poisoner, he would have had little reason to kill a harmless tramp."

"Unless, like Inspector Tovey here, he saw through your disguise."

"I believe I am safe, although I would ask you to keep your eye on my hairline, once I have removed all this," he added, indicating his theatrical appearance.

"So where is Warwick's body now?" I asked.

"That is what I intend to find out," Inspector Tovey said, his eyes gleaming. "Perhaps after you have become yourself again, you could join me at the station, Mr Holmes? You're staying at the Regent, are you not?"

"Good Lord," I said. "Have you been following us, Inspector?"

"I make it my business to know what's happening in this city, Doctor." He gave Holmes another of his gap-toothed grins. "Especially when a celebrity is in town."

I tried not to be insulted that Tovey obviously considered Holmes alone worthy of that title. Even after a decade, my ego had yet to be tamed. Perhaps I too still shared some of Tovey's youth and inexperience.

* * *

A nearby clock tower was tolling noon as we stepped from St Nicole's, and Holmes requested that I wave down a hansom.

"Can't you do it yourself?" I asked, still smarting from his deception in the church.

"Watson, I think a man of the cloth will find it considerably easier to hail a cab than a dweller of no fixed abode!"

Once safely ensconced in a carriage and well on our way back to the Regent, Holmes threw back his head and laughed.

"What sport, Watson!"

"Sport, Holmes?" I spluttered. "A man is dead and another in hospital."

"In a stable condition," Holmes reminded me, and he began to peel off his disguise. "But you should have seen your face. Old Pete was a triumph!"

Once again, my companion erupted into merriment. Despite my best efforts, his glee proved to be as contagious as any plague. Soon, I was sitting back in my seat, tears running down my cheeks.

"It was a consummate performance, Holmes. You had me completely fooled."

"Of course I did, Watson. That was the objective. Well, partly at least. I apologise for the deception, but I wanted to observe rather than question—"

"So you sent me in as your puppet interrogator."

"I knew that whoever you encountered would be wary of a stranger posing questions, so I provided a distraction."

"You certainly did that."

"It was clear that Father Ebberston was guilty of some secret or another, especially when he denied and then admitted to meeting the Monsignor."

"But all that guff about the legend, Holmes." I put on a West Country accent that was as bad as my Irish brogue. "'Warwick's skin was soft and flushed.'" Again we both dissolved into near hysterics. "Where on Earth did all that come from?"

"From Mrs Mercer's library," Holmes explained, pulling the worst of the theatrical gum from his chin, the tramp's beard now resting like a bedraggled cat on his lap. "*Byrne's Annals of Bristol: Volume Thirteen* to be precise, although I may have employed a little poetic licence. You're rubbing off on me, Watson."

Still laughing, we were deposited outside the Regent, the discombobulated cabbie uttering a surprised oath as he laid eyes on the partially transformed Holmes.

"Come, Watson," said Holmes, bounding up the steps two at a time, "before we attract more stares."

As it turned out, all eyes were upon us as we stepped into the lobby. We had barely made our entry through the revolving doors when a man wearing a tweed suit and bowler hat approached us.

"Mr Sherlock Holmes?"

"The same. And you must be a colleague of Inspector Tovey."

The man's eyes narrowed. "You know me?"

Holmes shook his head. "Only that you walk like every policeman I have ever met, and have brought reinforcements to boot."

He indicated a pair of uniformed police officers who were standing patiently by the concierge.

"The name's Hawthorne," the man said, to which Holmes made a show of shaking his hand. "Inspector Hawthorne."

"A pleasure to meet you, Inspector. This is my friend and associate, Dr Watson."

Hawthorne looked me up and down. "Just back from a fancy dress party, are we?"

Holmes gave a polite laugh. "Just a little undercover work. Although I doubt that you rushed your dinner to discuss our sartorial decisions. Was it enjoyable by the way, your chicken broth?"

"Holmes…" I counselled, all too aware that the inspector's irritation was increasing with every second that passed.

But Holmes was unable to help himself. "An excellent choice, incidentally, while recovering from a head cold."

Hawthorne's nostrils flared as he gave a bitter snort. "You think yourself a clever man, don't you, Mr Holmes?"

"There's no think about it," Holmes replied matter-of-factly.

"What is it then? A scrap of chicken caught in my teeth?"

"More the spoonful of broth slopped down your lapel…"

"And the cold?"

Holmes pointed at the inspector's ruddy nose. "The skin is chapped around your nostrils from repeatedly wiping your nose on a handkerchief. I'm sure Dr Watson would be happy to recommend an ointment or cream."

"That won't be necessary," Hawthorne said, a fixed smile beneath his greying moustache. "Can you come this way please, *sir*."

Hawthorne led us past reception and towards Mrs Mercer's private office, the two uniformed officers falling in behind us. On reaching the office, Hawthorne opened the door and indicated for Holmes to enter.

"Will Mrs Mercer not be joining us?" Holmes enquired, turning to the manageress who was standing behind the reception desk, her head turned away from us.

"If you could just come in," Hawthorne insisted. Holmes obliged and I went to follow, until the inspector blocked my path. "Not you, sir." He indicated to the two policemen. "You're with me, Hegarty. Lawrence, you keep the doctor company."

The door was slammed in my face. I tried to listen until Constable Lawrence asked me to move away.

I rushed over to the manageress. "Mrs Mercer, whatever is happening?"

She looked at my disguise with moist eyes. Had the lady been crying? "Is this a joke?" she said, indicating my outfit.

I self-consciously smoothed the front of my faux cassock. "I can explain all this later, but please tell me, what does Inspector Hawthorne want with Holmes?"

"It is not my place to say," the lady replied sharply, her voice catching in her throat. "If you will excuse me."

She stepped away from the desk and disappeared around the corner. Perplexed, I looked around the lobby to find everyone staring at me. As I turned, my fellow guests looked away or muttered to each other.

Enough was enough. I marched back to Lawrence and demanded to know what Hawthorne was after.

Before the constable could answer, the office door opened and Holmes emerged, followed closely by the inspector himself.

"Holmes, what the devil is going on?" I demanded, glancing through the still open door. A great pile of books was heaped on what I could only imagine was Mrs Mercer's desk.

"I'm afraid I shall have to accompany Inspector Hawthorne to the station, Watson," Holmes said, as casually as if he had told me he was off for an evening stroll. "I have been arrested, you see."

"Arrested?" I exclaimed. "On what grounds?"

"Theft," Holmes answered, allowing himself to be led away. "It would appear that I am guilty as charged."

CHAPTER ELEVEN

THE MANAGERESS'S TALE

I have never felt so helpless in my entire life. There I was, standing in the middle of the grand surroundings of the Regent, dressed as a Roman Catholic priest and watching my friend being taken away for a crime he could never have committed. The entire situation would have been laughable in any other circumstances.

I tried to argue with the departing policemen, but was firmly put in my place. I froze, not knowing what to do or where to go. Every eye was upon me. Every mind already made up. My attire only added to my discomfiture. Damn Holmes and his theatrical games.

Rousing myself, I made for the stairs. Of Mrs Mercer there was no sign. I needed to talk to her, but not in this state. I needed to clear my head, to become myself once more.

Bounding upstairs, I flung open the door to my suite and rushed to the sink. I tore at my face to remove the false beard and theatrical gum. It was a hard slog without the proper oils. When I had finished, the face in the mirror was rubbed raw, but it was the face of John Watson, not some half-baked caricature from a second-rate farce.

Before long, I was once again in my customary suit and waistcoat, a stiff collar around my neck and the cufflinks Mary had given me for my last birthday on my sleeves.

Pulling on my greatcoat and grabbing my hat, I hurried downstairs and asked to see Mrs Mercer. At first, the receptionist attempted to feign ignorance concerning the lady's whereabouts, but she unwittingly gave the game away by means of a furtive glance in the direction of the manageress's office.

Ignoring the flummoxed employee's protestations, I rapped sharply on the glass.

"Mrs Mercer, I must speak with you."

There was no reply so I tried again.

"Mrs Mercer, I apologise for the disturbance, but please, I ask but a moment of your time."

I was about to knock a third time when the door opened. Mrs Mercer stood before me, her face pale as mine was flushed.

"Dr Watson, I realise you are upset—"

"Upset? Madam, I have just watched an innocent man arrested. What exactly is Holmes supposed to have stolen?"

Mrs Mercer glanced around the reception area before indicating for me to enter. She closed the door and gestured for me to sit, before taking her own seat behind the desk. Self-consciously, the lady adjusted her cuffs and began her account. "Earlier today, Mr Holmes asked to use my library."

"Yes, I know. To consult the *Annals of Bristol*."

"Of course, I was happy to oblige. I showed Mr Holmes what he wanted to see, and in the process he noticed a number of new additions to my collection."

Her hand rested on a leather-bound book on her desk.

"Is that one of them?" I asked.

"My late husband was devoted to Chaucer," she said, stroking its cover. "How he would have loved to hold this in his hands."

"I assume it is rare."

"Rare?" She let out a gentle laugh. "This is the 1476 Caxton printing."

She looked at me as if that should mean something. When it was clear that I was still none the wiser, she added: "It is the first complete edition of *The Canterbury Tales*, a holy grail for any collector. Mr Holmes asked to see it and, somewhat reluctantly, I agreed. You must understand that I have searched for this book for many years, Doctor. To pass it into the hands of another, even someone I trusted…"

The sentence died in her throat.

"Well, he gave it back, and took his leave. I thought nothing more of it, until I later realised I had left my diary in the library. I returned upstairs, and discovered to my horror that a number of books, including the Caxton, were gone."

"And you suspected Holmes."

"Of course I didn't. He is a friend, or so I thought. I rushed to his room, thinking he may be able to help, but there was no answer. I turned to leave, and that was when I saw it."

"Saw what?"

"A scrap of material, tucked beneath the door. I recognised it at once."

She opened the copy of *The Canterbury Tales* and retrieved a silk bookmark, which she placed in front of me. The slip of salmon-print silk bore the words of Wesley's "Christ The Lord Is Risen Today" and below the hymn, a date: April 6, 1890.

"I'd placed it inside the Caxton on the day I brought the book home," Mrs Mercer explained.

"Then what was it doing beneath Holmes's door?"

"My question precisely."

"It may be a coincidence," I said, knowing full well how desperate that sounded. "Holmes could have one of his own."

She raised a sceptical eyebrow. "And is also in the habit of rubbing his bookmark between his finger and thumb when he reads, as I am?"

She indicated where the silk was starting to fray at one end. I had to admit that it was unlikely.

"I felt sick to my stomach as I realised what I must do," Mrs Mercer continued. "While the privacy of my guests is paramount, there is no door in this hotel that is closed to me. I took my master key and opened Mr Holmes's door to find the books stacked neatly on the dressing table next to pots of greasepaint."

"I don't believe it!"

"Neither did I, Doctor, but there they were, for all to see."

"So you sent for the police?"

"Do you blame me? I was hurt, betrayed. That Mr Holmes would do such a thing was staggering." She replaced the bookmark and closed the book. "Gregory came at once."

"Gregory?"

"Inspector Hawthorne. He was a friend of my late husband since I don't know when."

"And did he find any other evidence to incriminate Holmes?"

"Other than the stolen books, you mean?"

"The *allegedly* stolen books. Do you keep your library locked?"

"Of course. I have the only key."

"And was there any sign of forced entry?"

She shook her head. "Not that the inspector could see."

"May I see the door?"

The question seemed to take her aback. "I beg your pardon?"

"If I could see the door I might be able to ascertain how the thief entered the room. If indeed it was a thief."

"And what does that mean?"

"Doesn't it seem odd to you that Holmes is arrested for a crime the moment we start an investigation, a crime that he would never commit?"

Mrs Mercer bristled. "And what investigation would that be?"

Something in the way she asked the question gave me pause. It was true that she appeared to be the victim here, and yet... If it were true that only she could unlock the library, and indeed any other door in the hotel, could she not have planted the books in Holmes's room, if they were there at all? Someone had obviously tried to pin the blame on my friend, probably the same fiends who had poisoned the Monsignor when he discovered that Warwick's body was gone. Mrs Mercer had known we were going to St Nicole's, and was aware of the church's connection to Warwick.

I countered her question with one of my own. "Does the name 'Ermacora' mean anything to you, Mrs Mercer?"

Again, the lady shifted in her seat. "The name is familiar to me, yes. A Catholic priest of that name stayed here briefly recently."

"Monsignor Ermacora," I said, seizing on the information, "from Rome?"

"I believe so. He left rather abruptly."

Now I was onto something. Was that why Holmes had chosen this hotel? Had he seen something in the Monsignor's notebook that had aroused his suspicions?

"And these books that Holmes is supposed to have taken? Did anyone else see them in his room, other than yourself?"

She shook her head. "I do not believe so."

"So, it is your word against his?"

Her countenance hardened. "I am not sure I like what you are insinuating, Dr Watson."

I held her stony gaze. "I am not insinuating anything, merely... exploring avenues of investigation."

"And that is what you were doing when you returned to the hotel in your... costumes?" she asked. "Exploring avenues?"

Now, it was my turn to shift uncomfortably. "Well..."

The lady shook her head. "I cannot express how disappointed

I am. I welcomed you both as guests, offered you the best suites in the hotel, and this is how I am repaid. My trust betrayed, and my integrity questioned."

"Mrs Mercer—" I began, but she refused to let me finish.

"I must ask you to leave," she said, rising from her seat.

"I beg your pardon?"

"I will have your bags packed and delivered to reception. You may collect them later."

"Mrs Mercer, there is no need—"

"There is every need," the manageress said, showing me the door. "I'm sure you understand."

"I'm sorry to find you so resolute," I said, rising from my chair, "but I remain convinced of my friend's innocence. I shall get to the bottom of this one way or another."

She wished me a good evening and shut the door firmly behind me.

Acutely aware that I was being scrutinised by her staff, I walked calmly out of the hotel with my head held high. I meant what I had said. There had to be an answer to all this, and by Jove, I was going to find it. Striding down the front steps, I hailed a cab.

CHAPTER TWELVE

BLIND EYES

My welcome at the Lower Redland Road Police Station was not cordial.

"You don't understand," I told the gorilla of a desk sergeant. "I must see Inspector Hawthorne immediately."

"The inspector is busy," he replied. "I have logged your enquiry and suggest you return in the morning. There is nothing else I can do for you."

"But—"

"Good evening, sir."

The conversation was at an end. The sergeant turned away from me and stomped back to a desk where a steaming mug of tea awaited him. My stomach gurgled, and I was acutely aware of how long it had been since I had anything to eat or drink myself.

"Dr Watson?" said a familiar voice.

It was Inspector Tovey, walking towards me.

"Inspector, it is good to see you. You'll never guess what has happened."

"Mr Holmes has been arrested. Yes, I know. It's all anyone

can talk about here. For theft, too."

"Tell me you don't believe what they are saying."

Tovey took me by the shoulder and guided me away from the front desk. "I don't like to. There are many who would like to see Holmes brought low, that's for sure."

"But, why?"

"He's an amateur."

"I should like to see you call him that to his face."

"Doctor, it's hard enough to persuade people to trust the police in the first place, especially when the likes of Sherlock Holmes put us to shame. Now, the great detective of Baker Street has been exposed as a common thief."

"But it's not true!"

"I believe you, Doctor, but listen carefully and you'll hear the laughter all the way from Scotland Yard. Remember, I've read the reports. Come on. Walls have ears."

He led me out of the redbrick station and lit a cigarette, offering me his pouch. I declined.

"His arrest does little for my investigation, I can tell you. I've already had the top brass come down hard on me for daring to arrest a priest, not to mention opening a tomb."

"But you had a warrant."

"And you were a reporter for the *Catholic Herald*. Not everything is always what it seems, Doctor. What I waved in front of Father Ebberston was an invitation to last year's Christmas ball."

I could hardly help but smile. "You scoundrel…"

"I do what I need to get the job done. I've played by the rules long enough, and got nowhere."

"How do you mean?"

"This town is rotten to the core."

"Holmes said something very similar."

"Then he is a wise man. Everywhere you look, a blind eye is

being turned. Need to build a factory? Permission granted. Want to demolish a tenement building with no thought for the poor wretches you're chucking out on their ears? Permission granted. Industrial accidents, dodgy deals, even missing persons; the rich get what they want and damn the consequences."

"And there is nothing you can do?"

"Mud doesn't stick around here, Doctor. It washes clean away."

The wind had started to whip up again. I grabbed the brim of my hat to stop it dancing down the slush-lined street.

"I don't see how your current investigation will help."

"The missing body of a man who's been dead for the best part of two centuries?"

"Precisely."

Tovey ground the butt of his cigarette beneath his heel. "Doctor, when Father Kelleher was admitted to the hospital, he was shouting about Warwick's missing body. It was dismissed as the ramblings of a fevered mind."

"A reasonable supposition," I admitted.

"But that's just the thing, they're always reasonable. The excuses. The justifications. Everyone is so keen to sweep the dirt under the rug, but all it takes is one lie to be exposed for what it is and the rug itself will start to unravel. If I can prove that one crime has been covered up, then I know in my bones that others will follow. Besides, if the Monsignor and Father Kelleher were poisoned…"

"Careful," said I. "Holmes came here because he thought Ermacora had been poisoned and look where he has ended up."

Tovey nodded. "There are plenty of folk who wouldn't want a detective of Mr Holmes's calibre wandering free."

"So they framed him? Could Mrs Mercer be in on it too?"

"It's not the first time that strange things have happened at the Bristol Regent, and it won't be the last. All I know is that you and Mr Holmes are key witnesses in my investigation. You were there when Warwick's tomb was opened. Now, Holmes's word has been discredited."

"I could still give evidence," I pointed out.

"Guilt by association, Doctor. As long as Holmes is in custody, you won't be trusted."

"Then help me get him out," I begged him.

Tovey shook his head. "It wouldn't do any good. There's nothing I can do to help Holmes now, in fact any interference on my part would only make matters worse."

He clapped a large hand on my shoulder. "We're not beaten yet, Doctor. We need to carry on as if none of this has happened." He looked up at the darkening sky. "It's getting late."

"Trust me, I have nowhere else to go," I admitted.

"Then come with me, assist this local policeman with his enquiries. Will you do that for me?"

"Come where?" I asked.

"To the Bristol Royal Infirmary. I want to find out exactly where Ermacora dined before he left for London."

"Where he was poisoned, you mean."

Tovey nodded. "Are you a gambling man, Doctor?"

I thought of the chequebook that Holmes had kept for me in our days back at Baker Street, safely locked away to keep me from temptation. "It has been known," I told him.

"Then what's the betting that the Monsignor ate with Father Samuel Ebberston?"

CHAPTER THIRTEEN

THE BRISTOL ROYAL INFIRMARY

Every doctor in the land had heard of the Bristol Royal Infirmary. One of the oldest medical institutions in the country, it had been training medical staff for well over a century. I must admit to experiencing a certain frisson of excitement as I stepped past the imposing columns of the entrance and in through the doors.

Inside was the usual hubbub of hospital life, the sound of wheels against stone, footsteps both shuffling and eager. It felt as much a frontier of medical endeavour as the hospital tents I had experienced in Afghanistan. There, beneath the blazing sun, innovation had been a matter of necessity. Here, it was the lifeblood of the building and those who worked within it. You could taste the history of the place in the air, along with the fresh tang of tomorrow.

Outside the police station, I had felt at sea; far from home and tossed from one wave to the next. Here, in this bastion of medical excellence, my feet were back on solid ground.

Whatever ailed Father Kelleher, be it bacteria or poison, he was in safe hands, I was sure of that.

Tovey led me through the maze of passageways and corridors, acknowledging every nurse and doctor that we passed. Everyone seemed to know his name, and we received a warm welcome wherever we went.

"Just down here, Doctor," he said, having delivered us to the appropriate wing. "Kelleher has himself a private room. Must have had words with Him upstairs."

He paused in front of a recently painted door, and knocked. When there was no answer, he tried the doorknob.

"Father Kelleher?"

A look of dismay came over Tovey's features. "Oh no. No, no, no!"

He rushed into the room, and I saw the young priest lying on his back on a bed. His eyes were open, but there was little doubt that they saw nothing. Dropping my hat onto a chair by the door, I crossed to the bed and felt for a pulse. Tovey went back out into the corridor and called for assistance, but the patient was beyond help. His blue lips were parted, his face a mass of broken capillaries. I bent over and sniffed above his open mouth, only to recoil as the acrid stench of fresh vomit filled my nostrils.

Nurses poured into the room.

"I'm afraid you are too late," I said as I was asked to step aside. "I'm a doctor myself."

The staff ignored me, going straight to work. The pillow beneath the man's head was removed and thrown aside, his head laid back to clear a now redundant airway. There was blood on the pillow. I could scarcely imagine the panic that had set in when the priest realised he couldn't breathe.

"Respiratory failure," I continued. "The poor chap choked on his own vomit. Quite usual, considering his other symptoms."

Now a doctor had joined the throng and repeated my examination, drawing the same conclusion.

A nurse asked if I could wait outside. I did as she asked, leading a crestfallen Inspector Tovey back out into the corridor.

"We were so close," Tovey said, as I shut the door. "All we needed was for Kelleher to tell us what they ate, what killed them both."

"What Holmes *suspects* killed them," I pointed out. There was still no evidence that either priest had been poisoned.

"Is he ever wrong, your Mr Holmes?"

"Rarely," I said with a sad smile.

Tovey let out a grunt of frustration and spun around on his heel. I half expected him to pound the white-washed wall. "One more conversation, that's all it needed. Just one more."

"Inspector Tovey?"

I turned to see a man in his late fifties walking briskly towards us, his cane tapping against the floor tiles. His dark frock coat flapped open as he approached, revealing a rich velvet waistcoat. His silver beard was full but well groomed, its volume a perfect counterpoint to the bald pate of his domed head. As he neared the inspector, the newcomer extended a hand, his face the picture of concern. "Is everything quite all right?"

Tovey had regained his composure as he shook the man's hand. "It's Father Kelleher, I'm afraid."

The bearded man's face fell. "Oh no. You don't mean…"

"We found him ourselves," I said. "Dr John Watson, at your service."

"Lord Redshaw," the man replied, pumping my hand firmly. His grip was strong, but not overbearing. "But this is dreadful. It happened when he was alone?"

"So it would seem."

Redshaw shook his head. "Then there was no one there to read the… oh, what are they called?"

"The last rites?" Tovey offered.

"That's it. Not a Catholic myself, but know how important it is to them. Oh, this is very sad. He was a delightful young man, delightful."

"I didn't realise you knew him, Lord Redshaw."

Now Redshaw's hand was on the inspector's shoulder. "Oh, I didn't. Not well at least. I met him soon after he was admitted."

"You were a patient yourself?" I asked.

"What? Oh, good heavens no. As tough as old boots, me. I do what I can to keep the place ticking over."

"Lord Redshaw is being modest," Tovey told me. "He recently made a considerable donation to the upkeep of the hospital."

"Very decent of you," I commented.

"It's nothing," Redshaw insisted. "A dab of paint here and there."

"Enough paint that they're naming the new wing after him," Tovey said with a smile, despite his obvious frustration.

"You are embarrassing me, Inspector. Anyway, I met young Kelleher as I checked on the renovations. He impressed me, and I agreed to come back when he had recovered to discuss how I could help his work with the poor and destitute."

"Is that why you are here?" I asked. "To visit Father Kelleher?"

My question seemed to surprise the man. "Eh? Oh, no, no. I'm here to see Inspector Tovey."

"You are?" Tovey said.

"I heard a worrying rumour at the League."

"The League?" I asked.

"Of Merchants," Redshaw replied. "A little organisation I belong to."

"You provided blankets for St Nicole's."

Lord Redshaw's face lit up. "We did, yes. You have been there then?" His eyes widened and he snapped his fingers in recognition. "Dr Watson. That's what you said your name was?"

"I did."

"Then you were there with Sherlock Holmes when the tomb was opened."

"As was I," said Tovey, sounding a little peeved to have been left out of the conversation.

"Of course, and that is why I wanted to talk to you. I was visiting the bursar when I heard you were in the building, and felt compelled to see you. Is it true?"

"Is what true, sir?" Tovey said, although the meaning was quite clear.

"Please don't play games with me, Inspector. You know how I abhor games. Old Edwyn's body. They say it is gone."

Tovey confirmed that it was so.

Redshaw took a step back, his hand to his chest. There was something melodramatic about the gentleman.

"Well, this is terrible. One tragedy after another. But how and when did it disappear?"

"That is precisely what I am attempting to find out, Lord Redshaw."

"With the help of Sherlock Holmes and Dr Watson," Redshaw said, bringing me back into the conversation.

"I'm afraid not. Well, I am attempting to assist the Inspector, but my friend—"

"Mr Holmes has been arrested," Tovey explained. I shot the inspector a look. Was it really necessary to advertise Holmes's predicament to everyone we met?

"Arrested?" Lord Redshaw boomed. "On what grounds?"

"There has been a dreadful mistake," I insisted.

"Then you must tell me all about it." Behind Redshaw the door to Kelleher's room had reopened and the nurses were filing out. "First Warwick, then poor Kelleher and now this! Where are you staying?"

"That in itself is a long story. I was at the Regent—"

"The Regent!" Redshaw exclaimed. "A glorified dosshouse with delusions of grandeur. You must stay with me."

The offer took me aback. "That is very kind of you, but—"

It appeared Lord Redshaw's mind was made up. "We will dine tonight and discuss how to liberate your friend. It is clear to me that Bristol needs one man and one man alone. Have no fear: Sherlock Holmes will be free by morning!"

CHAPTER FOURTEEN

JUDGE NOT

Buoyed by Lord Redshaw's words, I allowed myself to be led out into the street once more. Inspector Tovey doffed his hat, and began his long walk back to the station. Redshaw offered him a ride, but the inspector insisted that the fresh air would help clear his head. His disappointment over Kelleher's death was clear for all to see, and he struck a dejected figure as he began the trudge across town.

"Poor Tovey," Redshaw said, as his opulent yellow and black carriage drew up alongside the pavement. "I like the man, but he will find it a struggle to get ahead. Rubs people up the wrong way, you see. Always has. It's a wonder he reached inspector at all." The carriage door opened and a set of steps automatically dropped down in front of us. "Please, after you."

I nodded my appreciation and climbed on board. The interior of the carriage was equally impressive. The seats were handsomely padded, the filling firm but comfortable. Rarely had I travelled in such luxury.

Redshaw struck the roof with his walking stick. "To the Regent, Gordon."

The carriage moved into the road as smoothly as a swan gliding over water.

"The inspector does have… intriguing views," I offered, keen to find out more about the man.

Lord Redshaw seemed keen to oblige. "Let me guess, conspiracies at every turn? Dark secrets in the halls of power?"

I nodded.

"I'm not surprised. From what I have heard, Tovey can see collusion in a Sunday school outing. Not to mention ghosts and goblins."

I laughed, not quite sure what I had just heard. "I beg your pardon?"

"He is a spiritualist, or some such. Believes in all kinds of nonsense, from fairies at the bottom of the garden to the Fishman of Durdham Downs. Most people nod and smile when he starts on one of his crackpot theories, but they try not to be stuck in the same room as him, I can tell you that."

"You seem to get on well enough."

"He's harmless, and a good policeman at heart. Investigated a break-in at my factory a few years back, found the culprits too. Told me that the factory was built on a confluence of… what was it he called them? Ancient sources of power, criss-crossing the land?"

"Ley lines," I suggested.

"That's it. Tovey thinks that is what brought the Templar Knights to Bristol all those years ago. The ley lines. Now, there is no doubting that the Knights were here. Bristol has the highest concentration of temples in the country. Fascinating period of history. That's where Temple Meads got its name, you know. Temple Gate too."

"Are you interested in local history?" I asked.

"Who isn't? And trust me, I like a ghost story as much as the next man. Used to scare the Dickens out of my sister back when we were children. Just prefer facts to fantasy, that's all."

I smiled. "You sound like Holmes."

"I shall take that as a compliment, sir."

We approached College Green and the Regent Hotel. "Have you seen Mrs Mercer's library?" I asked, as we drew up. "I understand it's quite impressive. Second to none."

Redshaw snorted, and wagged a finger at me. "Pah! That's another one to be wary of. Didn't trust her late husband, and don't trust her."

Following our earlier conversation, I was beginning to have doubts myself. I leant forward, eager to learn more. "Anything I should know?"

Redshaw tapped the roof again. "Let's get your luggage out of her clutches, and I'll tell you all about it."

As promised, my case was packed and waiting to be collected. I hated the thought of strangers handling my belongings and always had, ever since my army days. As the porter delivered my luggage to Lord Redshaw's carriage, I wished I had taken the time to pack my own belongings, although my priority had of course been Holmes.

Of Mrs Mercer herself there was no sign, and the Regent staff were courteous and professional. Not that Lord Redshaw took that into account. Standing on the pavement outside the grand building, the outraged merchant made it abundantly clear how disappointed he was with my treatment.

I myself offered no recrimination. My expulsion, unjustified or not, was no more the porters' fault than a soldier could be blamed for the decisions of a deluded general. I tipped my hat to them, and encouraged Lord Redshaw back into his carriage. As he finally clambered on board again, I realised that the scene had attracted something of an audience. A lady walking a small dog had stopped, while a tall African watched our fracas with interest from where he leant nonchalantly against the Regent's railings, smoking a cigarette.

I have never been so grateful to climb into a cab and shut the door firmly behind me.

Lord Redshaw was still complaining loudly as our carriage climbed Park Street towards Clifton.

"I'm sorry, Doctor, but it makes my blood boil. That woman waltzes around the city as if she were Victoria herself. Anyone would think she *built* the Regent, rather than landed on her feet because her husband had the good sense to drop dead."

His words shocked me, despite my misgivings. "That sounds a little harsh," I exclaimed.

My rebuke brought an embarrassed smile from my host. He chuckled, throwing off the last vestiges of his bad humour.

"You sound like my Lucy. 'Judge not, Benjamin,' she used to say."

"'Lest ye be judged,'" I said, completing the quote.

"She was right, of course, bless her soul." He glanced out of the window in an attempt to disguise the fact that his eyes had misted over. His use of the past tense was enough for me not to press the point. The carriage fell silent for a few seconds, and I too looked out of the window, gazing absently at the passing shop displays. We slowed to a crawl, Lord Redshaw's horse struggling to climb the steep gradient of the hill, although the usual pace resumed as we reached the top and the road levelled, as did our conversation.

Lord Redshaw gave a loud sniff and offered me a contrite smile. "You must forgive me, Doctor. I'm getting old in my ways and my opinions. The world is moving so fast, it is hard to keep up, and the old ways… well… younger chaps like yourself, you have your ideas of course, you shape the future, and old men like me should stand aside."

"You are too hard on yourself," I said, wanting to help the man who had already shown me such kindness. "And I would hardly call you old."

Redshaw chuckled. "You hear such stories in town, that is all," he continued, tapping his cane against the floor as he spoke. I could see words engraved on the shaft, yet was unable to make out exactly what they were.

"Stories about the Regent?" I prompted.

"There was a guest, back when the late *Mr* Mercer was manager; a lady of Russian origin. She claimed to be a princess, a cousin of the Tsar or some such. Vladlena Mikhailov, that was her name. And such a beauty. Heads turned every time she stepped into a room. The princess installed herself in the Regent, and by all accounts was free with her riches. Not a porter or maid went by without a sizeable tip. Mr and Mrs Mercer themselves were showered with gifts, tokens of gratitude for their kind service. Weeks turned into months and months into years and still the princess resided at Bristol's most fashionable hotel. But she never showed her face, striking though it was, at social events; never attended balls or galas, keeping herself to herself in her suite of rooms on the top floor of the hotel."

"A woman of mystery."

That drew another laugh, this time a little crueller. "A woman of disrepute, more like."

CHAPTER FIFTEEN

NEVER A VICTIM

"The princess was not what she seemed?" I asked.

"Not in the slightest," Lord Redshaw told me. "Our so-called princess had never even set foot in Russia, let alone the Tsar's court. She was a music hall girl, from Skegness of all places!"

"Good Lord!"

"That is not to knock the girl's talent. Her accent was second to none; her poise and demeanour, while extravagant, convincing enough to fool everyone she met."

"But her riches," I asked, engrossed in the story. "Were they counterfeit?"

"Maybe to begin with, but soon they were genuine enough. The princess's personal riches flourished as she befriended her fellow guests, beguiling them with her exotic charms. Such was her plausibility that often they would take her into their confidence, sharing secrets that she would later use as a source of blackmail. Eventually her sins were found out, and the Mercers claimed not to have known what she was doing, but I ask you… All those gifts? How much of Evangeline Mercer's beloved library was funded by the princess's private enterprise?"

"You believe they were in on it?"

Redshaw raised his hands as if warding off my question. "All I know is that the scandal went away. The princess vanished overnight and the rumours were silenced. Other hotels would have been ruined, but the Regent's doors are still open. There's talk that Her Majesty may even stay there on her upcoming visit. Imagine what she would say if she knew."

I sat back in my seat, flabbergasted. "I should never have guessed. I know the Mercers employed Holmes a few years ago, and that the case was successful. Indeed, Mrs Mercer seemed pleased to see him, and yet… these accusations."

I explained what had happened, how Holmes had been suspected of stealing the books.

"She could barely look at me."

"You think your friend was… what's the phrase? Framed?"

"Of course he was. Holmes is no thief, and his interest in literature in minimal." I leant forward. "You don't suppose Mrs Mercer is behind it? That she wanted Holmes out of the way? What if he found out about the princess?"

"Unearthed a scandal that she thought long forgotten, eh?" Lord Redshaw rubbed his chin. "I'm not sure. Evangeline Mercer is many things, but to make an enemy of a man like Sherlock Holmes? She is no fool. There has to be another explanation."

"Which Holmes would reveal in seconds if he were here," I said with a sigh.

"You know his methods. Could you not employ them yourself?"

The thought made me smile. "I wouldn't know where to begin. Whenever Holmes reveals his thinking to me, it seems painfully obvious, but I can never make the connections for myself."

"We cannot all be giants, Doctor," Redshaw said. "The world needs little people too. But it's good that you know your place."

Know my place? The phrase rankled with me, but he was correct of course.

For now, there was little I could do to help my friend. I vowed to ask my host about it later. Lord Redshaw was obviously a man who liked to know what was going on in his city. He would have connections, associates who might be able to assist Holmes. I had hoped that Tovey would prove a valuable ally, but from what Redshaw had told me, the inspector was not held in the highest regard. Redshaw might be my best, and only, bet. If he could exert some form of influence…

The carriage pulled into pleasant gardens that were still dotted with snow. We proceeded along a well-maintained avenue towards an impressive house, which I assumed was Lord Redshaw's home, a curious mixture of brooding Gothic arches and Tudor beams. The red-tiled roof was a cluster of turrets and chimneys, and ivy smothered the walls as if it were trying to protect the brickwork from the elements.

We came to a halt before a grand entrance to be greeted by a veritable army of footmen, and one immaculate butler.

"Ah, Brewer," Lord Redshaw said as he dismounted from the carriage. "We have a guest, Dr John Watson, visiting from London. He will stay in the Tombo Room."

"Very good, sir," Brewer intoned with an expression that was both attentive and disinterested.

"Don't mind Brewer," Redshaw said as he led me into a surprisingly gloomy entrance, the walls decorated with dark green tiles. "He's a good sort, if a little sullen." He rested a hand on my shoulder, noticing me glance around the cheerless reception area. "And don't worry, the Tombo Room is airier than this old place. Anna is always nagging at me to redecorate, but my father chose these tiles and I am rather attached to them."

"Anna?" I enquired.

"My younger daughter. You will meet her at dinner. Eight o'clock sharp. Don't be late or Brewer will have a coronary. Do you need a man sent up to you?"

I declined the offer, keen to dress myself.

"Well, if you change your mind, just ring the bell. That's what servants are for, after all. Now if you will excuse me, I have business to attend to. Welcome to Ridgeside Manor, Dr Watson. Make yourself at home."

With that, Lord Redshaw disappeared into the bowels of the house. I was led upstairs to a room that, as promised, was far brighter. Gas lamps burned on the walls, illuminating the elaborate teak furniture. Carvings of dragonflies were everywhere, in the panels of the wardrobe and perched on the knobs of the large bed. Paintings of the multi-coloured insects adorned the walls, and a cabinet filled with the creatures themselves, thankfully pinned to a backing board rather than buzzing around, was mounted next to the large bay window.

I sat on the bed, looking at the luggage that had been delivered and opened for me. What in the world was I doing here? I felt like a leaf that had been blown this way and that before being deposited far from the tree.

I stood, and walked over to the window to discover that the house stood at the very edge of the Avon Gorge, that great chasm that runs through Bristol, the river roaring deep below. The moonlit view in front of me was stunning. Isambard Kingdom Brunel's famous suspension bridge spanned the gorge, a wonder of innovation and daring. I remembered reading stories of its construction. Brunel had suspended an iron bar across the gorge and would pull himself from one side to the other using a contraption of his own making, little more than a large basket suspended by a system of pulleys. On one occasion, a wheel jammed, leaving the engineer swinging there, high above the river. Brunel calmly clambered out of the basket and onto the iron bar. Freeing the wheel with no safety net, he continued on his way, whistling a merry tune. What an inspiration the man had been, and what a tragedy that he had never seen his precious bridge completed.

Possessed of a new purpose, I began to dress for dinner. One way or another, I was going to free my friend, and discover why anyone would want to besmirch the good name of the world's greatest detective.

Tovey had been right about one thing; there was something rotten in this city, and I would be the one to expose it.

CHAPTER SIXTEEN

MEET THE REDSHAWS

Determined not to be late, I descended the grand staircase at half past seven, my progress scrutinised by Lord Redshaw's noble ancestors, peering down at me from a collection of magnificent portraits. My frown must have matched theirs as I stopped at an alcove halfway down the stairs. It housed a bronze statue of a semi-naked African girl, her head lowered and her wrists manacled together. I had failed to notice the figure when I ascended, but now that I had seen it, I found myself transfixed.

"Beautiful, isn't she?" said a voice behind me. I turned to see an attractive young lady in her late twenties descend the stairs from the first floor.

"I beg your pardon," I said, caught between standing aside for the lady and continuing on my way. I opted for the latter, not wanting to make her pass me on the stairs.

"No, please," she said. "Stand and look at her if you wish. Father would like that. He's quite proud of her, you know."

"Your father is Lord Redshaw. Then you must be Anna."

She rewarded my deduction with a tight smile. "Anna is my

sister. My name is Marie, and you must be Dr Watson."

She held out her hand, which I kissed, although making introductions on the stairs hardly seemed proper considering our stately surroundings.

As if to spare my embarrassment, Marie Redshaw turned her attention back towards the statue. "They call her the 'Daughter of Eve'. Father had her commissioned from an artist in New York. Apparently they are all the rage over there."

"She is quite striking."

"If not rather disquieting."

I seized upon the word. "That's it. That's it exactly. She makes for uncomfortable viewing in this day and age."

"Which is precisely the point," Marie said. "A reminder of the horrors of slavery, on both sides of the Atlantic. Bristol, of all places, should never forget."

"A reminder also of how far we have come," I suggested.

She smiled, as if I were a child who had unwittingly said something charmingly naive. "Or not, as the case may be."

"And what is going on here? Loitering on the stairs?"

Lord Redshaw's booming voice made me jump. I looked down to see him standing in the hallway in his evening finery. "What would Victor say, eh?"

"He'd say that you shouldn't tease your guests," Marie replied, indicating for me to continue.

I joined my host in the hall and waited for the lady.

"Ha! Watson doesn't mind, do you, old boy?"

"Not at all, Lord Redshaw."

"Please, call me Benjamin. We don't stand on ceremony here at Ridgeside. Come and meet everyone."

Ever the genial host, Redshaw led me to the drawing room, where I was greeted not only by the other members of the dinner party but by the most ostentatious chimneypiece I had ever seen.

It dominated the south wall, a vast column of polished marble covered in an illustrated map. Sailing ships were moored at the harbour, spires reached for the skies and chimneys belched smoke. There was even another reminder of Bristol's more troubling history, with a row of slaves lined up on the harbourside, chained together by the neck.

"What do you think, eh?" Redshaw said, placing an arm around my shoulders as if to hurry me towards the monolith. "Impressive, is it not?"

"I've never seen anything like it," I said, with no word of a lie.

The fireplace itself was set into an alcove at the bottom of the chimneypiece, the resulting space large enough to easily accommodate a pair of full-size settees. A young woman rose from one of these, the resemblance to Marie Redshaw so striking that this could only be Anna. To her side was a man in his twenties, with an apologetic, dough-like face.

"Papa wants you to be awestruck," Lady Anna said, stepping out from beneath the marble colossus.

"Then I'm happy to oblige," I said, kissing her proffered hand.

"That's ten tons of the finest Italian marble," Redshaw explained proudly. "Had it shipped over specially, along with the fellows to carve the blessed thing. Designed the map myself. Bristol in all its glory."

"With the Worshipful League of Merchants' lodge at its heart," Lady Anna said fondly.

"A small conceit on my part," Redshaw admitted.

"The funny thing is," added Lady Marie, "that the fire isn't needed at all. This entire wing is heated through the floor. It's all for show."

"Don't be such a spoilsport, Marie. Allow your father to have his fun," said the final member of the party, a tall, darkly handsome man with piercing green eyes. While the pasty chap with Anna attempted to disguise his poor complexion with enormous sideburns and a rather lacklustre moustache, Marie's companion was clean shaven, displaying a strong jaw and cheekbones my wife would have gleefully described as chiselled.

"Let me make the introductions," Redshaw said, starting with the daughter I had already identified. "This is Anna, the girl who will forever be my babe in arms no matter how domineering she becomes."

"Papa," she scolded.

"And this poor chap is her husband," Redshaw continued. "Harold Clifford, manufacturer of the finest gas lighting this side of London."

Clifford stepped from behind his wife and shook my hand. His grip was as doughy as his face. He went to offer me a greeting, but Redshaw spoke over the fellow, continuing the introductions. "You've met Marie, of course, and this is Victor Sutcliffe, soon to be my other son-in-law."

"Pleased to meet you," Sutcliffe said. His grip was as strong and confident as Clifford's was feeble.

"Sutcliffe's one to watch," Redshaw said, oozing pride that his daughter had managed to snare such an obvious catch. "Thought he'd turned his back on commerce. Off he went, travelling the world, armed only with a damned camera. And then his pictures started coming back, exotic scenes of the Orient. Oh, how my Lucy would have loved them. She adored the East. Never went herself you understand, but collected all manner of trinkets from China and Japan. The Tombo Room, that was her last project before the good Lord took her from us."

"Papa," Anna said, stepping forward to Redshaw to offer comfort, although the large man seemed in little need of it.

"Stop fussing, Anna. I'm perfectly capable of talking about your mother without blubbing. Where was I? I've lost my train of thought."

"The T-T-Tombo Room," Clifford offered, revealing a noticeable stutter.

"The dragonflies are quite beautiful," I said.

"I'm glad you like them," Redshaw said, "although when she put them in I had to ask Lucy what the bloody things had to do with Japan myself."

"*Tombo* means dragonfly in Japanese," Victor told us. "Although the literal translation is 'Victory Bug'. I think it was the Emperor Shōmu who first called Japan 'our precious island of Butterflies'."

"Apparently they were a symbol of courage for samurai warriors," Redshaw added.

"I had no idea," I told him.

"What was it, Victor?" Redshaw asked. "Because they always fly forwards, or something."

"That's right; forwards and never back," Sutcliffe confirmed. "A healthy philosophy for life."

"Yes, f-fascinating," Clifford grumbled beneath his breath, drawing a sharp look from his wife.

Redshaw seemed not to have heard Clifford's comment and so continued to praise Marie's fiancé to the hilt. "Anyway, Victor starts to build up a reputation with these photographs of his. Before you know it, he's importing all manner of Japanese paraphernalia. Art, furniture, fabrics; even teapots. Never seen so many of the blessed things. Before long he'll be richer than all of us."

"You still haven't introduced Dr Watson," Lady Marie pointed out.

"I was just getting around to that, although you have rather stolen my thunder. Anna, Harold, Victor; this is Dr John Watson, known for his association with—"

"Sh-Sh-Sherlock H-Holmes," Clifford cut in, showing more

enthusiasm with those two mangled words than at any other point of the conversation. "I've r-read your stories. Absolutely b-brilliant."

"Thank you."

"We were shocked to hear of your friend's… troubles," said Anna, the insinuation clear in her voice. "What a dreadful business."

News certainly travelled quickly in this city. However, before I could offer a defence, Brewer entered the room and announced that dinner was served.

CHAPTER SEVENTEEN

EXOTIC DELICACIES

Lady Anna led us through to the dining room, fulfilling her late mother's role as lady of the manor, despite being the younger of the two sisters. As we walked Lord Redshaw waxed lyrical about the fireplace. I nodded politely from time to time, although my interest in the behemoth was fading fast.

"Ten tons it weighs," he said again, proudly. "Built directly into the gorge. I added that entire wing; my legacy for the future of this house. There's also a billiard room, you know. Perhaps you'll join me for a game later."

I told him I should be glad to, my eye drawn to a door on the left as we passed. Like the others in the house it was of a dark mahogany, although this one had a Latin motto carved into the wood.

Redshaw followed my gaze.

"*Non qui rogat sed qui rogathur admitto*," he read aloud.

"'I admit not who asks, but who is asked,'" I translated, drawing a chuckle from my host.

"A little joke on my part. The door leads to my study. An Englishman's home may be his castle, but this Englishman needs a private retreat, especially since Anna and Harold moved in."

"They live with you?"

"Made perfect sense," he replied. "No point in them running their own household when Marie and I have all this space to ourselves."

"Especially with the new wing."

He clapped me on the back. "Exactly! Besides, I have little time to run a house this size, while Marie, unfortunately, has little inclination. Anna is happiest when bossing folk around, so I let her handle the household."

The dining room was a more conservative affair, save for the large circular table set out for dinner. Every grand house that I visited had followed the convention of a rectangular table, with a seating arrangement firmly dictated by rank. Not so at Ridgeside. I was seated opposite Lord Redshaw with Lady Anna and Clifford to my left and Marie and Sutcliffe to my right.

Everything else seemed as expected until I looked down to find two thin wooden sticks beside the standard silver cutlery. I resisted the urge to pick them up, but stared so intently that Lady Marie noticed.

"They're called chopsticks," she told me, leaning in. "I'm afraid you've joined us on an evening when father is indulging Victor's obsessions, although to be fair you would be hard pressed to dine at Ridgeside on a night when he doesn't."

"I hope you have an adventurous palate, Watson," Lord Redshaw said as the first course was delivered. A small plate was placed in front of me on which were arranged delicate slices of a thin orange-pink fish on a bed of crisp lettuce.

"You'll enjoy this," Redshaw promised. "What's it called again, Victor?"

"Sashimi," Sutcliffe replied. "Raw salmon."

"Raw..." I repeated. I watched as Redshaw picked up his chopsticks and, holding them in a peculiar pincer movement, plucked a portion of the fish from his plate and popped it in his mouth.

"Delicious," he said, chewing happily. "It's all the rage in Tokyo, you know."

"And has been for hundreds of years," Sutcliffe informed us, keen for an opportunity to show off his knowledge of the Orient. "I first ate sashimi during the Cherry Blossom Festival. Every year, Japan's cherry trees erupt with tiny pink flowers. It's quite spectacular. The Japanese themselves head out to gaze at the flowers in wonder."

"Why would they d-do that?" Clifford asked.

"They believe that spirits live within the tree – the *Kami*."

"And you saw this yourself?" asked Redshaw.

Clifford nodded. "I was incredibly lucky. My host, Mr Arakwana, took me to Mount Yoshino. It's a wonderful place, home to thirty thousand cherry trees."

"Never heard of it," Lord Redshaw admitted. "Where in Japan is it?"

"I forget for now," Sutcliffe said, which I thought odd as the experience seemed to have had a profound effect on the man. "But I can show you on a map after dinner. It was magical. Arakwana's entire family came with us and we dined together under the shade of the blossom, finishing the meal with sake."

Now it was my turn to ask a question. "Sake?"

Redshaw answered for Sutcliffe with a chuckle. "Victor brought a bottle back for me. Strong stuff, I can tell you. Puts hairs on your chest." He glanced at my plate and the salmon, still untouched. "Come on. Tuck in."

I looked down at the starter. While I had no desire to insult my hosts, the thought of raw fish was anything but appetising, and then there was the challenge of the chopsticks. The entire family seemed adept with the peculiar cutlery, although Clifford blatantly refused even to try and used a regular knife and fork instead.

It was a perfectly surreal end to a largely bizarre day. Here I was, sitting in a stately English home, with a stately English family in their stately English finery, eating the most un-English cuisine I had ever seen.

Well, I say I was eating, but in truth I was unable to bring a single morsel of the stuff near my mouth. I tried to replicate the Redshaw clan's dextrous use of the wooden sticks, but had no luck, the salmon repeatedly slapping back to the plate.

Eventually, at Redshaw's behest, I gave in and joined Clifford in using a knife and fork. It has to be said that the fish itself *was* delicious, with a strong buttery flavour unlike any salmon I had ever tasted, although I had little time to savour it before Clifford began firing questions at me.

"So you w-were there, when they f-found that Warwick's body was missing?"

"Harold," Anna chided, placing her chopsticks to the side of her plate on a tiny wooden rest.

"No," Redshaw said, dabbing his mouth with a napkin. "It's a worry to us all. Edwyn Warwick is something of a hero in these parts, Watson."

"Not to everyone," pointed out Marie quietly as she took a mouthful of lettuce.

Redshaw ignored the comment. "That his grave is empty is a concern to many."

"Especially after the b-business with the r-ring," Clifford said.

The temperature around the table seemed to drop several degrees.

"Ring?" I asked.

Redshaw let out a sigh that bordered on irritation. "It's nothing. A mere trifle with which you need not concern yourself." It was less a suggestion than a directive.

"How can you s-say that, B-Benjamin?" Clifford continued,

unperturbed, drawing a glare from his wife.

"The doctor isn't interested, Harold," Sutcliffe said.

"Oh, I should say by his face that he most certainly is," Marie said playfully.

"Really," I said, keen to spare Lord Redshaw's embarrassment. "It is fine. I'm just enjoying this delicious… what did you call it again?"

"No," Redshaw said. "We are being bad hosts."

"There is no need to explain," I insisted, but Redshaw continued anyway.

"As you know, I belong to an… organisation. A guild, if you like."

"The Worshipful League of M-Merchants," Clifford offered, seemingly oblivious to the fact that he was causing both his father-in-law and soon-to-be brother-in-law to squirm in their seats; either that, or I was watching the most subjugated member of the family attempt to score points. There was an air of defeat about Harold Clifford.

However, Lady Marie was correct. My curiosity had been well and truly piqued.

"Are you also a member?" I asked Clifford.

"I am, as was m-my f-father before me."

"And mine," Sutcliffe said, and I was sure Clifford, already pale, lost even more colour for a second.

"Victor is our most recent member," Redshaw explained, raising a glass to Marie's fiancé.

"For his success in the Orient," I said, which Victor acknowledged with a bow of his head.

"Quite so," said Redshaw. "We're a charitable group, following the example of Warwick himself, although we do value a certain level of… privacy."

"Secrecy, more like," Marie commented, returning her chopsticks to their rest.

"We have certain r-relics at the League H-Hall," said Clifford, clearly assuming that I had been welcomed into the circle of trust.

"Relics?"

"Historical artefacts," Victor jumped in. "Such as Warwick's ring and periwig. Bequeathed to the League following Warwick's death."

"As well as most of his fortune," Marie said.

"Did he not leave most of his riches to the poor of the city?" I asked.

"Through the work of the League," Redshaw said. "Which, of course, we are pleased to perform."

"But you mentioned his ring. Has something happened to it?"

"I should s-say so," replied Clifford. "It has been st-stolen from its case."

"Stolen?"

"Mislaid," Redshaw corrected. "It will turn up."

"Maybe faster if we employ the s-services of Mr Holmes and Dr W-Watson," Clifford suggested.

"Mr Holmes is otherwise engaged," Sutcliffe said, glaring across the table. "We don't want to embarrass the Doctor any further than we have already."

"Please, think nothing of it," I said. "In fact, while I cannot thank you enough for your hospitality, I was hoping that you could help Holmes, Lord… I mean, Benjamin."

"As I said on the ride over, there is nothing I should like more," Redshaw said as our dishes were cleared and the next course laid before us; a bowl of clear soup, which Brewer announced as *suimono*, although the look on his face told me that the butler had little stomach for it.

"What exactly are you asking my father to do?" asked Lady Anna as the servants retreated.

"Holmes is innocent," I told her. "I just know he is. Now, a man in your father's position must have a certain influence."

To my right, Victor's eyebrows rose. "Doctor, whatever are you suggesting?"

"I mean no insult, suggest no impropriety on Lord Redshaw's part. I simply mean that, perhaps, Benjamin could have a word with the police, to vouch for Holmes's character."

"Father doesn't even know your Mr Holmes," Anna said, and I could feel the mood around the table rapidly turning against me.

"No, but I know Watson," Redshaw said.

"Benjamin?" Sutcliffe said.

Redshaw raised a hand to quieten the young man. "The doctor seems an honourable sort, and, before you say another word, Anna, I'll remind you that I am usually a good judge of character."

"He had the measure of Harold when you first brought him home," Lady Marie said, drawing a venomous glare from her sister.

"Marie," Redshaw warned, before turning back to me. "I can't promise anything, but I will speak to the Chief Inspector. Remind me, who was the arresting officer?"

"An Inspector Hawthorne," I said.

Redshaw nodded. "Ah. Another good man, and a friend of the League himself. I'm sure they will listen to reason."

"And I'm sure Holmes would be delighted to look into the matter of your missing ring," I offered, wanting to seal the deal.

"As well as investigating Warwick's m-missing body," Clifford said, picking up my train of thought. "We are all eager for his r-return."

"Of course," I agreed. "As you said, we were both present when the tomb was opened."

"In disguise, I believe," Marie asked, raising an amused eyebrow. "How exciting."

I felt my cheeks blush. "That was not my choice."

"But you must tell us of your adventures," Anna pressed, a request that was enthusiastically seconded by Clifford.

"Surely you don't expect Watson to sing for his supper?" Redshaw said.

"I don't mind," said I, my belly warmed by the surprisingly tasty broth and my heart gladdened by my host's promise to intercede on Holmes's behalf. "There was one story that you might find diverting. The mystery surrounding the death of Sir Theobald Maugham was one of the most dangerous cases in our career. I hope it won't put you off your dinner…"

And so I began, falling into my old storytelling ways, Clifford, Marie and Lord Redshaw hanging on my every word. Only two people around the table did not seem entertained. Anna Clifford picked at her meal, as if annoyed that her control of the evening had been well and truly lost, and to my right, I was all too aware of Sutcliffe's emerald eyes upon me, scrutinising my every movement.

CHAPTER EIGHTEEN

IZANAMI-NO-MIKOTO

If you had told my wife that her husband would be licking his lips after an evening of Japanese cuisine she would have laughed, and with good reason. While Holmes had dined in courts and palaces the world over, I was usually content to stick with what I knew: good old-fashioned British food.

However, the night at Ridgeside had been a revelation, with a succession of delicious steamed and boiled dishes, the majority of which possessed names I could barely pronounce. Most seemed to include fish, although one particular dish, which Sutcliffe described as *mushimono*, contained the most succulent chicken I had ever tasted.

The meal concluded with a selection of fruit, although I could barely eat another thing.

"Are you sure?" Redshaw asked, tucking into slices of Bramley apple served in a sweet syrup.

"Absolutely," I replied. "That was delicious. Every last scrap."

"Well, good for you for having a go. Most Englishmen would have balked at the first dish."

"I considered it an education, and a tasty one at that."

The others agreed, although I had a suspicion that Clifford had endured rather than enjoyed his meal.

"Compliments to Mrs Pennyworth," Sutcliffe said, raising a glass.

"Working from the recipes you provided," Redshaw said, returning the gesture.

"Which reminds me," Sutcliffe said, standing up from the table. "If you will excuse me for a moment…"

He left the room, to return a minute later carrying a large rectangular parcel, wrapped in brown paper. Drawing puzzled looks, Sutcliffe walked around the table and presented the package to Lord Redshaw.

"This came in yesterday," he said. "A thank you for welcoming me into your family."

"You're n-not married yet," Clifford muttered, but if Redshaw heard his son-in-law, he failed to acknowledge the fact. Instead, he took the gift gladly and tore the paper away to reveal a framed painting.

"Well, will you look at that?" his Lordship said, turning the canvas towards us. It was a full-length portrait of a woman in what I could only assume was the Japanese style. She was wearing flowing white robes and had long black hair that hung down to her waist. While the picture was certainly not to my taste, Lord Redshaw seemed enchanted.

"Does she have a name?" he asked.

Sutcliffe took his seat. "She does. *Izanami-no-Mikoto.*"

The name had an energising effect on the older man. He looked up at Sutcliffe with wonder in his eyes. "The goddess from the story?"

"What story, Father?" Marie asked.

"One I shared with Lord Redshaw," Sutcliffe explained. "A tale of sadness and terror, but ultimately of joy."

"You should tell them it," Redshaw said, still holding the painting in his hands.

"Are you sure now is the time?" Lady Anna asked. "If the story is a gruesome one—"

Redshaw cut across her. "Where's your spirit of adventure, girl? We Redshaws have strong stomachs. Why, I was saying only this afternoon how I loved telling ghost stories. Isn't that right, Watson?"

"Really, I couldn't," insisted Sutcliffe before I could answer. "Not after Dr Watson has dazzled us with his own stories."

"Nonsense," Redshaw said. "Go on. Tell them."

"Very well," said Sutcliffe, leaning his elbows on the table and lacing his fingers beneath his chin. "According to the Japanese, Izanabi and Izanami were the ancient gods of creation, and their children became the eight great islands of Japan itself: Awaji, Iyo, Ogu, Tsukushi, Iki, Tsuhima, Sado and Yamota."

"R-ridiculous," muttered Clifford, only to be shushed by his father-in-law.

"Please, Victor. Carry on."

"Unfortunately, Izanami became ill, and died. Izanabi wept for his bride, and his tears became the Pacific Ocean. Now, Izanabi could not accept that his beloved was gone, and so he travelled to Yomi, the shadowy domain of the dead. He searched high and low for Izanami and eventually found her, hiding in the shadows. He asked her to step into the light, but she said that she could not. She had already eaten the fruit of the tree of death, and could never return to the land of the living."

To my left, Lady Anna squirmed in her seat, clearly hating every minute of Sutcliffe's tale, but the fellow continued anyway.

"He finally persuaded her to go with him, but only if he agreed never to look at her again. They started the long walk, Izanami shrouded by shadows. All was well, until they stopped to rest in a sacred grove. While Izanami slept, Izanabi lit a torch and held it above his love to gaze upon her beauty. What he saw horrified him. Izanami was nothing more than a rotting corpse, her body riddled with maggots and worms."

"R-really!" Clifford complained, as his wife screwed up her face in disgust. "That is en-enough."

"No, listen," urged Lord Redshaw, revelling in the story. "There is a happy ending, I promise you."

And this from the man who had told me that he preferred facts to fantasy.

"Izanabi fled, and Izanami awoke to find herself alone. She wept bitter tears, thinking that she would never see him again. She could hear the claws of the damned crawling ever nearer, ready to take her back to the underworld, but her husband returned at the last minute and placed a bowl of soup before her. She drank from the bowl and, all at once, was whole again. Her skin was smooth, her hair like silk and her eyes bright. 'What was in the soup?' she asked her love, and Izanabi told her how he had found a new-born lamb, innocent and pure. He had sacrificed the animal and used its blood to make a soup from his own heart. He had given his life so that she could live."

His story at an end, Sutcliffe sat back, as if waiting for applause. Instead we all sat in stunned silence, not quite sure what to say.

All, that is, except Clifford, who had one question: "So, w-what happened to the husband. Did he d-die without his h-heart?"

Sutcliffe was forced to shrug. "I do not know. The legend does not say."

"Doesn't s-sound like a h-happy ending to m-me."

"It was positively beastly," said Lady Anna, standing to leave. "Sacrifice and maggots, at the dinner table? It really is too much."

She swept from the room, saying that she needed air. Clifford went to follow, but Redshaw stopped him.

"She'll be fine, just you wait and see." Then Lord Redshaw's eyes fell on me, and he chuckled. "What must you think of us, Watson? I assure you that not every night is like this at Ridgeside."

"No," said Lady Marie, rising from her seat. "They are usually worse."

CHAPTER NINETEEN

POST-DINNER CONVERSATION

"Go and fetch your sister," Lord Redshaw instructed his elder daughter.

"You expect her to listen to me?" Lady Marie asked.

"We have one last custom to observe," Redshaw told her.

Dropping her napkin on the table, Lady Marie rose to her feet and slunk from the room. "One can hardly wait."

"May the Lord grant you sons, gentlemen," Redshaw chuckled as he too got to his feet. "Let us adjourn to the drawing room. The ladies can join us there."

I must have glanced at Redshaw in surprise, because he clarified his statement. "We don't stand on ceremony in this house, Doctor. We like to do things our own way."

"Th-that's for s-sure," muttered Clifford.

Again Redshaw chose to ignore the barbed comment. "You three go on ahead. I need to fetch a book from the library. I think you'll find it fascinating, Doctor."

I wondered if I were to be treated to more tales of the East. I excused myself to visit the smallest room in the house, which in Ridgeside Manor turned out to be the size of my palatial suite at the Regent.

Suitably refreshed, I returned to the drawing room five minutes later, my head still pleasantly fuzzy from the evening's libations. What I saw, and heard, however, caused me to hover at the doorway, embarrassed to stumble upon a conversation that was obviously intended to be private. Sutcliffe had Clifford backed into that gaudy monstrosity of a chimney breast, the acoustics of the room amplifying their disagreement for anyone to hear.

"What did you think you were doing?" Sutcliffe said. "Matters of the League are private, or have you forgotten?"

"Says a m-m-man who ran from buh-business," Clifford replied. "Your f-father would be ap-appalled."

"Don't you dare bring him into this. He was more a man of business than—"

"What's this?" said Lady Anna, appearing behind me. I stepped aside to let her sweep the length of the room towards the altercation. I became aware of another presence beside me, Marie watching the drama with a cool detachment.

Clifford swiftly grasped the opportunity to shame the other man.

"Victor here was a-accusing me of... actually, what was it, V-Victor? Being indiscreet in front of our g-guest? I should like to know what Dr W-Watson thinks of us now."

I wished that I had turned around and left as soon as I had realised what I had chanced upon. "Perhaps I should return to my room."

"I wouldn't blame you," said Marie, strolling coolly towards a nearby settee. She opened the silver box of cigarettes on a nearby table and lit one as if such ructions were a run-of-the-mill occurrence at Ridgeside.

"You wouldn't blame him for what?" Lord Redshaw asked

as he entered, a weighty-looking tome beneath his arm. I have often heard people talk about wishing the ground would swallow them up, but had never experienced the sensation until now. The situation was mortifying.

My embarrassment did not, however, prevent me from noticing a change in Sutcliffe. The young man visibly relaxed, a look of forced benevolence replacing the fury on his face. "I wouldn't blame Dr Watson for wanting to return to that dreadful hotel," he said, offering a smile that even a blind man would dismiss as disingenuous.

"There is really no need," I offered.

"I think there is," Sutcliffe insisted, striding towards me, seemingly to make amends. "You are a guest in Lord Redshaw's house and I have made you uncomfortable."

"Will someone please tell me what has happened here!" Redshaw blustered.

Clifford was only too ready to oblige, in a desperate attempt to save face. "Victor accused me of b-betraying the League's s-secrets."

"A misunderstanding," Sutcliffe insisted.

"I should hardly call it that," Lady Anna interrupted.

"Incited by high spirits, good sake and Dr Watson's tales of intrigue and derring-do," Sutcliffe continued, not to be subdued. "I hope you will accept my apologies. Here, can I get you something to drink? A brandy, maybe?"

"And there I thought my father was the host," Lady Marie said, taking a pull on her cigarette.

At least that derailed Sutcliffe's attempt at charm. Again I saw anger in his eyes, this time that his intended would dare to scold him so publicly. "Of course," he forced himself to say. "It seems I must apologise again."

"Good Lord," Redshaw said, shaking his great head. "What must you think of us, Watson? I turn my back for a moment and the entire family are at each other's throats. Victor is right, of course, you need a drink. Although I have something other than brandy in mind; Brewer will be bringing it presently."

At that very moment, Brewer entered the drawing room, carrying a silver tray on which lay a curious metal teapot. Behind him came a footman, his own tray laden with china cups and saucers.

"Excellent," Redshaw exclaimed. "Put it down here." He indicated a table to the left of the fireplace.

Lady Anna groaned. "Must we really, Papa? You know I can't stand the taste of it."

"Nonsense," said Redshaw, rubbing his hands as he approached the teapot. "I'll take it from here, Brewer."

The butler bowed respectfully. "As you wish, sir."

"Have you tried green tea, Dr Watson?" Sutcliffe asked as we gathered around the table.

"I don't believe I have."

"A-another ritual Victor's d-dragged back from the Orient," Clifford told me.

"Don't be such a bore, Harold," Redshaw said. "The host brews the tea and pours it himself. I think it's charming."

"I think it's disgusting," Lady Anna said.

"That I would honour our guest in such a way?"

"No, the tea. You don't even add milk."

Redshaw tutted at his daughter and, lifting the lid, stirred the contents of the teapot with a silver teaspoon. He then proceeded to pour the weak liquid into the cups and passed them round. I looked into my own cup and noted that the liquid did indeed have a green tinge to it.

"*Fumeiyo*," said Redshaw, raising his cup to me before taking a sip. The rest of the gathering echoed the strange word, some with more gusto than others.

"Fumeiyo?" I asked Sutcliffe as we sat on the settees.

"It means 'drain your cup,'" Redshaw answered for him.

"Lord Redshaw is my most accomplished student," Sutcliffe said with a condescending smile that Redshaw seemingly failed to notice.

I sat in a rather uncomfortable chair and tried the tea. I soon realised that I agreed with Lady Anna. The taste was earthy and bitter, leaving an unpleasant tang in the mouth. I took another sip to be polite and then sat with the cup and saucer in my lap, letting the contents go cold.

"Well?" Redshaw asked, seeking my approval.

"Lovely," I replied. "This evening has been most illuminating."

"Which reminds me. I fetched you this." Placing his cup on a nearby table, Redshaw handed me the thick book he had brought in with him. I took the opportunity to rid myself of my own frightful brew.

"*The Life and Charity of Edwyn Warwick*," I read from the spine.

"The definitive biography, if you ask me."

The book opened on a portrait of a man I recognised from the monument at St Nicole's. "And here he is," I said. "The man himself. Edwyn Warwick."

"Such an inspiration," Sutcliffe offered.

"Indeed he is, Victor, indeed he is," acknowledged Redshaw.

I seized upon the opportunity to turn the conversation back to the events of the day. Perhaps I could continue to gather information that Holmes might be able to use on his release. "The disappearance of his body must have come as such a shock."

"It has, old chap."

"And then the revelation of Father Ebberston's part in the conspiracy."

"C-conspiracy?" Clifford queried, his curiosity finally compelling him to join us rather than to remain sulking beside the chimney breast.

"He's been arrested," Sutcliffe revealed. "That inspector chap seems to think that he knew the body was missing, and tried to hush it up."

"I'm afraid it's more serious than that," I said.

Lord Redshaw frowned. "How so?"

"Holmes believes that Ebberston poisoned both Father Kelleher and Monsignor Ermacora."

"The Monsignor is dead?" Lady Marie exclaimed.

"I'm afraid so. We believe that Father Ebberston tried to stop the Monsignor from bringing the missing body to Holmes's attention."

"Nonsense," Redshaw said. "I've known Ebberston for years. He is a good and honourable man."

I was too wrapped up in the conversation to stop myself from contradicting my host. "Inspector Tovey agrees with Holmes's assessment of the situation."

"Well, you know what I think about that young man," Redshaw reminded me.

"I do, but the facts seem incriminating."

"I won't believe it."

"Do you th-think Father Ebberston has something to d-do with the r-ring?"

"Harold, not now," Sutcliffe warned, the menace in his voice for all to hear.

"If not n-now then w-when?" Clifford continued, refusing to be silenced. "Surely you can s-see how sus-sus-suspicious this all is. Warwick's ring goes m-missing, and then his b-body v-vanishes. Now M-Mr Holmes finds himself incarcerated in the very same pr-prison as the man he accused of p-poisoning. What else are we s-supposed to think?"

"I think you have read too many second-rate detective stories," said Sutcliffe. "No offence to Dr Watson."

"And n-now he insults B-Benjamin's guest."

"Really," I insisted. "There's no need to—"

Clifford would not listen.

"He b-bullies everyone to get his own way, and when that d-doesn't work the accusations start flying. Well, I've h-had my fill of it. I'm sorry you've had to w-witness this, Dr Watson, but it feels as though Anna and I are being p-pushed out by this cuckoo in the n-nest, or should I say s-snake in the grass."

CHAPTER TWENTY

POST-DINNER CONTROVERSY

Now even Lady Anna joined the chorus of voices against her husband. "Please, Harold, this is not the way…"

"Indeed it is not," agreed Lord Redshaw. "You will be silent, sir, or you will leave!"

Mortified, I offered my apologies and made to leave myself, but still Clifford raged.

"And go where, exactly? You were the one who persuaded me to s-sell the house my father b-built! You were the one who en-ensured that we are f-forever in your debt. And now you expect me to s-stand by when you let Sutcliffe w-worm his w-way through your d-door."

"How dare you!" Redshaw said, his voice ominously quiet. "How dare you embarrass me in front of my guest, in front of my daughters. After everything I have done for you."

"After everything you have d-done *to* me," Clifford snapped back. "If you w-want me gone, then I shall be only too hap-hap-happy to oblige."

"Stop it!" Lady Anna's shout silenced the argument in one. "I can take no more."

Then the lady toppled forward in her seat. Clifford grabbed her, stopping her from hitting the floor.

"Doctor?" Redshaw called to me, but I was ahead of him. I helped Clifford lay his wife out on the sofa, and asked Victor if he could fetch some water.

"Please," came Marie's dismissive voice from the chair she had occupied throughout the conversation. "The last thing we need is Anna's histrionics."

"Your sister is unwell, Marie," Redshaw snapped. "Show some compassion."

"No," Anna murmured from the sofa, her face as pale as a porcelain doll. "I am not unwell. I am with child."

"W-what?" Clifford stammered, dropping down on his knee to take his wife's hand. "My darling, is it t-true?"

The smile the lady returned was almost enough to wipe away the unpleasantness of the last few moments. She grasped her husband's hand in hers. "Yes. Yes, I believe so."

Clifford laughed in amazement and then turned to me, his own smile crumbling into concern. "Doctor, the b-baby? If I had known, I would never have…" Tears started to well in his eyes as he turned back to Anna. "I am so s-sorry. Shall I h-help you to b-bed?"

She stroked his face tenderly. "I am not an invalid, merely a little overcome." Once again I was brought into the moment between husband and wife. "Is that not right, Doctor?"

I took the water that was in Sutcliffe's hand and passed it to the lady. "All will be well, with a little rest. You must try not to excite yourself, that is all."

"In this house?" Lady Marie commented behind me, a strange quaver to her voice.

All the while, Lord Redshaw had stood where he had raged moments before, staring at his youngest daughter as if she were the most incredible creature on God's earth.

She, in turn, looked up at him with beseeching eyes. "Papa? Are you happy for me?" She squeezed Clifford's hand. "For us?"

"Happy?" the older man replied, his face finally breaking into a rapturous smile. "Of course, I am happy!"

He lunged forward, clapping Clifford on the back with such enthusiasm that his son-in-law was in danger of being propelled across the room. Lady Anna rose and let her father embrace her.

"My first grandchild. I can hardly believe it."

A sudden movement caught my eye. I looked up to see that Marie had grasped the edge of her seat so hard that I thought her fingers might disappear into the armrest.

"Marie?" Redshaw said, bringing his daughter to everyone's attention. "Won't you congratulate your sister?"

Anna smiled at Marie, although I could not help but notice that the expression was tempered by a hint of triumph. "You're going to be an aunt, Marie, and I a mother."

Lady Marie's own features were brittle. When she spoke, her voice was as glacial as her demeanour. "Congratulations, sister. I'm sure you will be very happy. Now, if you'll excuse me, I must go to bed."

With that, she rose from her seat and strode from the room without another word.

Sutcliffe made to go after her, but she shut the door firmly behind her, leaving her fiancé with us.

Clifford was quick to capitalise on Sutcliffe's obvious discomfort. "Don't mind M-Marie. You know what a c-cold fish she can be." Then he turned his attention back to his wife. "You will be such a wonderful mother, so kind and warm. We shall be a family, the three of us. And then there will be more; brothers, sisters…"

Anna let out a delighted giggle, touching a hand to her corseted waist. "One step at a time, Harold."

I had stepped back, allowing the couple to share the moment

that would change their lives for ever. Lord Redshaw joined
me, shaking his head in continued disbelief. "Watson, I must
apologise. Dinner at Ridgeside Manor has been more eventful
than I planned."

"Every family has its drama," I told him, but my eyes were on
Sutcliffe. Etiquette forbade him going after his fiancée after she
had retired for the night. He was obviously a man who liked to
be the centre of attention, and to find himself so cruelly set aside
affected him greatly. The balance of power in the house had shifted
in the space of a few minutes. Victor Sutcliffe suddenly looked
every inch the outsider, and I could scarcely help but notice the
resentment that burned in his eyes.

CHAPTER TWENTY-ONE

A VISITATION AT MIDNIGHT

Thankfully, the evening at Ridgeside with its strange concoction of accusation and revelation soon drew to an end. Sutcliffe made his excuses and called for his carriage, while Lady Anna retired to bed.

It appeared for a moment that Clifford was aiming to persuade Redshaw to join him in a celebratory drink, but his father-in-law soon dismissed any thought of late-night revels.

"Tomorrow is fast approaching, and with it a good many meetings in my calendar; I must be off to bed myself. Besides, I shall need to conserve my strength if another generation of Redshaws is to charge through this house."

The disappointment in Clifford's face was painful to see, especially when he piteously commented, "The child w-will be a C-Clifford."

I took the opportunity to return to the Tombo Room, clutching Warwick's biography beneath my arm. Within half an hour I was in my nightgown, attempting to lose myself in the book. I had never been one for biography at the best of times, and this precise time was anything but. I couldn't help but imagine Holmes, lying on a cot in a dirty cell. He would have despised the evening's events, of course, but would at least have been free. Having read enough to make polite conversation the following day, I shut the book and went to bed. My host had meetings in the morning, as did I. I would visit Holmes, both to check on his welfare and to see if he had made any progress on the case. I knew that incarceration would prove no fetter for that magnificent mind of his. Indeed, the isolation and solitude would only focus his deductive powers. The thought of seeing him again raised my spirits as I closed my eyes.

Exhausted by the events of the day, I slipped easily into sleep, only to be awakened seemingly seconds later by a sharp rap at my door. I looked to the clock on the mantel. It was twelve minutes past midnight. Who would be calling on me at this hour?

Pulling on my dressing gown, I crossed to the door and opened it to reveal Clifford standing in the hallway outside, a flickering candle in hand.

"My apologies, D-Doctor," he said, his feeble moustache looking all the more unconvincing in the candlelight. "Did I w-wake you?"

"Is it your wife?" I asked. "Is she unwell?"

He waved away my concern. "N-no, it is n-nothing like that. I m-merely wished to extend an invitation t-to you."

I frowned. "I'm sorry, I don't understand."

"You seemed interested when we spoke of the L-League's collection of artefacts. Of the r-ring and periwig."

"How could I be otherwise? They cause quite a stir."

"Victor is a f-fool, and Benjamin… well, let us just say that, for all that nonsense with d-dinner, my f-father-in-law is a t-traditionalist. Yes, the League operates largely b-behind closed doors, but I think that's wr-wrong, and so do others. The disappearance of the r-ring, and now Warwick's b-body, have caused great c-consternation. The two events h-have to be linked. There is no other e-explanation."

"It would seem a remarkable coincidence if they were not," I agreed.

"Will you c-come with me then?"

"Where?"

"To the L-Lodge."

"Is that allowed?"

"You would be my g-guest. Ideally I would ask Mr H-Holmes to accompany us."

"Ideally he would accept."

"But you know his m-methods. You may see something that Hawthorne has m-missed."

"Inspector Hawthorne is investigating the theft of the ring?"

"If that is what you can c-call it. From what I understand he's barely set f-foot inside the p-place. Will you do it, Dr Watson, will you come with me?"

"It would be my pleasure. But I plan to visit Holmes first thing, so it will have to be later in the day."

"What say I m-meet you on Corn Street at noon?"

I agreed, adding a little mischievously, "And perhaps you could tell me more about Mr Sutcliffe."

"I would t-tell the world if I thought it would r-rid us of V-Victor. So, tomorrow then. M-midday."

"On Corn Street," I said, before bidding him goodnight. Clifford did not wait for me to shut the door before stealing away. As I watched my curious new ally depart, I became aware of a noise drifting through the corridors of the house. I stood there, listening intently. There was no mistaking the sound. Somewhere nearby, a woman was weeping in the dark.

CHAPTER TWENTY-TWO

ALL WILL BE WELL

The following morning, I arose early and pulled back the curtains. The Clifton Suspension Bridge stood out against a crisp, blue sky, carriages already scurrying its length like ants.

Ridgeside Manor was quiet as I descended the stairs, this time passing the 'Daughter of Eve' without stopping.

I found only Lady Anna and Clifford at the breakfast table. Lord Redshaw had apparently left already to go into town, and Lady Marie was still in bed, troubled by a migraine.

"I'm sorry to hear it," said I. "Has she tried soaking her feet in warm water?"

"Somehow I doubt it would do any good," came Anna's reply. "My sister's migraines are less a malady than a convenience. It is extraordinary how easily they come on when she wishes to shut herself away from the world."

"Now, A-Anna," counselled Clifford. "Don't be cruel." It was clear, however, that the reprimand was for my benefit rather than Marie's.

As I sat at the table, I could not help but wonder about the sound of a woman weeping in the middle of the night. Which sister had been so distressed?

"You must think us a most dreadful family, Doctor," Lady Anna said as I tucked into a plate of kippers. "To put you through all that last night."

"Think nothing of it. I am in your family's debt."

"A dangerous place to be," commented Lady Marie as she breezed into the dining room.

I rose, dabbing a flake of fish from my bottom lip. "Lady Marie, it is good to see you. I heard that you were unwell."

"Nothing that strong coffee and the morning papers will not cure," the lady said, taking her seat and waiting for the footman to pour her a steaming cup from the silver pot on the table. "I trust there were no further revelations last night?"

"Only that you left poor Victor adrift," said her sister.

"I sincerely doubt that. He will call on me later." There was little joy in her statement.

We ate our breakfast in silence, Marie perusing the *Bristol Mercury* as I finished off my kippers.

"Is there any news on the missing ships?" I asked, my hunger sated.

"I'm afraid not," Marie replied. "Although the line to Plymouth has reopened." She turned the page and let out a surprised laugh. "Good heavens. Another one."

"W-what is it?" Clifford asked.

Marie's answer was not what I expected. "They've found another monkey."

"Another what?" I asked.

Beside me, Lady Anna rolled her eyes. "Really, do we have to talk about this now?"

Marie ignored her. "A few weeks ago a number of chimpanzees were stolen from Bristol Zoo."

"Chimpanzees?"

The lady's eyes sparkled as she looked at me over the paper. "And that's not all."

"Marie…" Lady Anna warned.

"The monkeys have been turning up one at a time, quite dead."

"Good Lord."

"With their little monkey-hearts missing from their chests."

Anna threw down her fork. "Well, now I don't have any appetite at all. First there was Victor and his horrible stories, and now this. Marie, have you forgotten that I am eating for two?"

The impish smile disappeared from Marie's lips and she returned her attention to the *Mercury*. "As if you would let me forget."

Silence reigned once more, until Clifford was unable to resist adding: "They're not m-monkeys anyway. They're apes."

Growing tired of the familial squabbling, I rose and said that I was going into Bristol. Clifford caught my eye and I confirmed our meeting with a nod before leaving the dining room.

Lord Redshaw had left instructions that I should avail myself of one of his many carriages, so I recovered my hat and greatcoat and braved a morning that was considerably warmer than the atmosphere between the Redshaw sisters.

As we rattled through Clifton village, I had a smile on my face, due in part to the telegram that had arrived before I left Ridgeside Manor.

TELL SHERLOCK ALL WILL BE WELL STOP
AM ON MY WAY TO BRISTOL STOP HIS
LOVING BROTHER STOP

I cannot describe the joy I experienced on reading the message. Although I had met Mycroft Holmes but a handful of times, I trusted the man implicitly. While the affection displayed in the telegram was surprising – neither of the Holmes brothers was what one would call sentimental – the thought that Mycroft was *en route* was encouraging. If any man alive could extract Holmes from prison it was Mycroft, who held a position of great influence at Whitehall. With the telegram safely tucked in my jacket pocket, I was convinced that Holmes would be free by the close of day.

With a renewed sense of optimism, I dismounted outside Lower Redland Road Police Station to be greeted by a familiar voice.

"Travelling in style, eh, Doctor?"

Inspector Tovey was walking towards me, although his handsome face showed little sign of his usual geniality.

"I am staying with Lord Redshaw," I informed him, although it appeared my movements were already known to the man.

"So I heard." He shot a look at the driver, who was already parking the yellow and black carriage on the other side of the road in preparation for my return journey. "Tell me, is it the madhouse that everyone says?"

"You have no idea."

"Redshaw's an odd one, but his heart's in the right place. Look how he took in his son-in-law…"

"Mr Clifford."

Tovey nodded. "Poor sod's had no end of troubles since he took over the family business."

"Lord Redshaw persuaded Clifford to sell his home, I understand."

"Persuaded? From what I heard he had little choice in the matter."

While this was all very interesting, I had other things on my mind.

"How is Holmes?" I asked.

"Do you want to see him?"

"Is that allowed?"

"No, but seeing I have nothing else to do…" He winked at me and smiled. "Come on."

He led me into the station and past the desk sergeant, who was again nursing a cup of tea.

"Have you heard about Ebberston?" Tovey asked as he opened a door for me.

"No. Has something happened?"

"You could say that. I was forced to let him go."

"But the poisoning…"

"*Suspected* poisoning," Tovey reminded me. "We have no evidence and Father Ebberston, it appears, has no garden."

"I beg your pardon?"

"No Naked Ladies. It's a convincing theory, but unless Ebberston found the damned flower growing on the downs, how did he get hold of the bulb? With both Ermacora and Kelleher gone, we don't even know if he broke bread with them in the first place."

"What has Ebberston said?"

"He's denying everything."

"As you would expect."

"Trouble is, no evidence—"

"No case!"

Tovey nodded. "And with no case I have no way of keeping him under lock and key. I've been told to forget about the entire thing."

"By whom?"

"By those who could have me out on my ear for insubordination. They've had me rounding up beggars. 'A better use of my talents', apparently."

"But two men are dead!"

"Of cholera. Or so the death certificates say."

I was unable to credit what I was hearing. "So all this was for nothing."

We were now in the bowels of the building, little in the way of light reaching the white-tiled walls.

"Have you seen Holmes?" I asked.

"Briefly," Tovey said, holding another door open for me. "He seems in high spirits. The other prisoners aren't so happy though."

"Why not?"

"Since Mr Holmes has been here, he's provided enough evidence to hang three of his fellow inmates, all from the confines of his cell. He even located the body of a prostitute by the way her murderer coughed after breakfast. I don't know how he does it."

"He's a remarkable man," I said. "But surely if he's bringing killers to justice…"

"He'd be acquitted of his own crime? You would think so, but Gregory Hawthorne is a stubborn beggar. He's not going to let Holmes off the hook that easily."

"He may not have a choice. Holmes's brother is on his way from London."

"A force to be reckoned with, eh?"

"Trust me, Inspector, it runs in the family."

We were now in the station's cell block. I followed Tovey along the passageway, ignoring the jeers aimed at me.

"I've a visitor for you, Mr Holmes," the inspector said, as we approached the end of the gloomy corridor. He opened a small window in the last door and his eyes widened. "Oh my God! Mr Holmes!"

"What is it?" I asked as Tovey fumbled for the key and flung open the door. He darted inside and I followed, only to stop short on the threshold.

Sherlock Holmes lay on the floor in a pool of blood.

CHAPTER TWENTY-THREE

TO A PULP

"Let me see," I said, pushing Tovey aside.

The cell was a mess, blood splattered up the walls, but Holmes was in a worse state. His face was almost unrecognisable, a swollen mass of contusions.

I fell on my knees beside him, my hands shaking. I had seen him injured before, but never like this.

I heard Tovey call for assistance. Footsteps thundered towards the cell in response. I checked for a pulse, finding it slow but steady. Holmes groaned at my touch and tried to turn his battered head towards me.

"Holmes, can you hear me? It's Watson."

His only answer was a gurgle of thick phlegm. His right eye was completely swollen over, his left open a crack, but it was clear he was unable to focus. He grabbed for my arm, his knuckles caked in gore. Holmes had obviously put up a fight. I clutched his hand, holding it tight. It felt so thin and weak, not like Holmes's hand at all.

He moaned again, his split lips forming indecipherable words.

"Don't try to speak, old man," I told him. "We'll sort you out, I promise."

Yet, even as I checked the extent of his injuries, a gruff Scottish voice growled behind me, "Step away from the prisoner."

I looked up to see a man in his fifties glaring down at me. A fine set of whiskers bristled across his face as he stared at me through wire-framed pince-nez.

"Didn't you hear me, man? Let me see my patient!"

He shoved me rudely aside as I got to my feet. A hand touched my elbow. It was Tovey.

"Don't worry, Dr Watson. Mr Woodbead is the police surgeon. Holmes is in good hands."

"Very kind of you to say so," said the surgeon from the floor beside Holmes. "Now, everyone out!"

"I can help," I said, as Tovey tried to guide me towards the cluster of policemen gawping at the door. "I'm a doctor myself."

"I'm very pleased for you," Woodbead said. "But the last thing I need is a well-meaning sawbones beneath my feet."

"Sir, I'll have you know—"

"Get him out of here, Abraham, unless you want this man to die."

"Please, Doctor," Tovey pleaded, his grip now forceful on my arm. "Come with me."

I attempted to struggle, but Tovey was having nothing of it. Clearing the policemen out of our way, he dragged me from the cell.

"But you don't understand, I'm his doctor. I'm his friend."

"Which is exactly why you need to let Mr Woodbead do his job. You're too close."

I wasn't having that. I shouted into the cell, "Everything is going to be all right, Holmes. Do you hear me? Your brother Mycroft is on the way. He sent a telegram this morning."

My words were drowned out by Inspector Hawthorne's angry

voice. "What the hell is going on here?"

The inspector was marching towards us.

"Tovey?"

"It's Holmes. He's been beaten."

For the second time in ten minutes I was pushed out of the way as Hawthorne barged past.

"How has this happened?" he demanded, only to be given the same short shrift by Mr Woodbead.

"What is wrong with you people? Get out!"

Tovey pulled Hawthorne from the cell and Hawthorne whirled around, his fist raised.

"Gregory, calm down," Tovey snapped.

"Calm down? What have you done to my prisoner?"

"This was how we found him!" I insisted.

"In his cell?"

"The door was locked," Tovey told him.

"That's impossible!"

"Is it? Wouldn't be the first time."

Hawthorne took a step towards Tovey. "What are you insinuating?"

I was incensed at what I had heard. "What? He's done this before?"

"I haven't done anything," Hawthorne insisted, jabbing a finger towards me.

Tovey had no intention of giving up. "This isn't your handiwork?"

"I never laid a hand on him," said Hawthorne. "More's the pity."

"Then who did?"

"Holmes's knuckles," I realised. "They're red raw."

"So?" Hawthorne asked.

"He's an accomplished boxer," I told the man. "Whoever did this to him would bear the marks."

"Who was on watch last night?" Tovey asked the two policemen who were loitering nearby.

"Hanson, sir," replied the taller of the two, a red-haired constable with a flat nose.

"And where is he now?" Hawthorne asked.

"Gone home I think. Not feeling well."

"Well, there you have it," I said, triumphantly.

"You know where he lives?" Tovey asked.

"I do," the other policeman replied. "Has a place down Temple Back."

"Then get round there, both of you," Tovey ordered. "See what's wrong with him."

The constables did as they were told, hurrying out of the cell block. Hawthorne, meanwhile, had spotted something on the floor.

"What's this?"

He bent down to retrieve from the floor a small length of metal.

"A file of some kind?" I guessed.

Hawthorne turned it over in his hand. "It's a lock pick." He looked at the floor again, finding another near the wall. "This too."

"What are they doing out here?"

Hawthorne rubbed his fingers through a stain by the door. They came back red. "Blood out here too."

He stood, shaking the picks in front of me. "Recognise these, Doctor?"

"Why would I?"

"Could they belong to your friend in there?"

"He has a set; I'll not deny it."

Tovey took the tools from him. "What are you suggesting?"

"I'm suggesting that Holmes tried to escape in the night, but came up against Hanson."

He turned back to the door. There were traces of footprints across the threshold, trodden in blood.

"Hanson saw to it that the prisoner was in no state to get away, and dragged him back inside the cell."

Hawthorne looked up and saw the incredulity on my face. "Don't look so surprised, Doctor. Holmes isn't the only one who can find clues."

"I was more surprised that you seemed to see no problem in the fact that an innocent man has been beaten to a pulp and dumped in a cell."

Hawthorne's lips drew back in a snarl. "Hanson was only doing his job."

"Or what he was told," Tovey said.

"You'd better watch that mouth, Tovey," Hawthorne snarled, squaring up to him. "It'll get you in trouble."

"Like Holmes, you mean?"

"I'm warning you…"

"If you two are quite finished," said Woodbead from where he had appeared at the door, his hands smeared with Holmes's blood.

"Come to rescue your boy, eh?" Hawthorne sneered.

"Only one man needs rescuing around here," Woodbead replied. "Abraham, go to the surgery. Get me towels, water and morphine. You'll find a bottle in the cupboard above the sink."

"What is your diagnosis?" I asked, as Tovey hurried away.

"My diagnosis is that the prisoner is bloody lucky to be alive, no thanks to any of you."

I was about to retaliate when he finally answered my question.

"Lacerations to the face, severe bruising and a jaw broken in at least two places."

"His jaw?"

"Not badly by any means, but enough to cause problems. I'm going to wrap his head for now, to keep the teeth in alignment."

"Wrap it? Surely it needs pinning. Only the other day I was reading about a new technique of rigid stabilisation—"

"Yes, thank you, Doctor. I know what I'm doing."

"You're taking him to the hospital, then? The Royal Infirmary?"

"He stays here," growled Hawthorne.

"You can't be serious."

"He's tried to escape once—"

"There's no evidence—"

"And I'm not about to give him the opportunity to try again," Hawthorne insisted, talking over me.

Woodbead raised a bloody hand. "Have no fear, Doctor, I will care for Mr Holmes personally. He'll be quite safe."

"And secure," Hawthorne added.

Somehow, this failed to put my mind at rest.

CHAPTER TWENTY-FOUR

RECRIMINATIONS

"Is that it?" I asked Tovey as we stepped outside the police station half an hour later. "Surely there is *something* you can do?"

Holmes had been transferred to Woodbead's police surgery and was being treated at that very minute. Not even to be allowed to assist was unbearable.

"Clarence Woodbead is one of the best, Doctor. He'll do whatever he can to help Holmes."

"Holmes should be in a hospital," I insisted.

"And if it comes to that, Clarence will transfer Holmes himself, I have no doubt. You said Holmes's brother is on his way?"

"Mycroft, yes. He didn't say at what time he would be arriving." I checked my watch, realising that it was not yet ten o'clock. Another two hours before I had arranged to meet Clifford.

"Perhaps I can meet the gentleman. If he's something in government, then perhaps he'll be able to exert some pressure around here, get those charges against Mr Holmes dropped."

I frowned. "How did you know Mycroft is in government, Inspector? I'm sure I didn't say."

Tovey rubbed the back of his neck. "I've done my homework. I'm afraid I've rather made it my business to know all there is to know about your friend."

I was impressed. Tovey was certainly thorough, but to find out anything about Mycroft was something of an achievement. No matter what Lord Redshaw thought of the man, Tovey was obviously not the kind of fellow who took no for an answer.

It came as no surprise therefore when he told me that he was making a return visit to St Nicole's to see if he could discover anything else from Father Ebberston. "Do you fancy tagging along?"

"I thought you were off the case?"

"I am. But confession is good for the soul. I want to give Father Ebberston one more chance."

Yet, when we arrived at St Nicole's, the front door was bolted shut. No sanctuary would be offered today.

"Could he be at home?" I offered. "Or visiting his congregation?"

"Or suddenly decided to whisk himself off on a pilgrimage."

"Do you think that's likely?"

"As likely as anything in this case. Perhaps I should pay a visit to the bishop."

"To enquire as to Ebberston's whereabouts?"

"Or whether they have another key. Although after my stunt with the warrant, somehow I think my prayers will go unanswered."

Now it was Tovey's turn to check his watch.

"Do you need to be somewhere else?"

"The vagrants won't clear themselves, more's the pity. Are you going back to Ridgeside Manor?"

"Not yet," I replied, keeping my cards close to my chest. "I didn't sleep well last night. A walk will do me the world of good."

"Hardly surprising, considering everything that's happened."

The inspector touched his hat and took his leave.

"You'll send word if there is any change in Holmes's condition?" I called after him.

"Of course," he replied, and strode away. I consulted my watch. My appointment with Clifford was still over an hour away. Alone in the city, I had no choice but to make good on my lie to Tovey. I strolled down to the river that flowed through the heart of Bristol. It was a veritable hive of activity. Tugboats and steamers chugged up and down, while labourers unloaded crates and barrels onto the harbourside.

I looked into the murky water, wishing that I were standing beside the Thames rather than the Frome. Why had Holmes insisted we come here? Why could he not have gone back to France? Whatever dangers he faced on the continent could hardly be worse than being beaten to within an inch of his life in a stinking police cell.

I looked up from the water towards College Green on the far side of the river. There stood the towering walls of the Regent.

Before I knew what I was doing, I had crossed the river and was marching up the steps of the hotel.

Once inside, I saw a female silhouette through the glass of Mrs Mercer's office door. This time I would not be sent away. This time I would have it out with the woman once and for all.

My mind made up, I strode over to the door and, not stopping to knock, grasped hold of the handle.

"Sir? Sir, can I help you?"

Ignoring the receptionist, I pushed open the door and barged into the office. Mrs Mercer was already on her feet. She looked at me in amazement, as did the elderly gentleman with whom she was in conversation.

"Dr Watson," she exclaimed. "What is the meaning of this?"

"I wish to speak with you," I told her, uncertain who was more taken aback by my impudence, the manageress or myself.

"I am in a meeting," she pointed out, stepping around the desk to show me the door. I had no intention of leaving.

"And I apologise," I said, acknowledging the hunched gentleman in the starched collar who was glaring at me in outrage. "But I am afraid this can't wait."

"It will have to," Mrs Mercer insisted. "You can make an appointment at reception—"

I was having none of that. "Do you have any idea what you have done?"

The manageress turned to the elderly gentleman. "I am sorry about this, Sir George."

"Perhaps I should leave," he said in a thin voice, already pulling grey gloves onto his gnarled hands. Then he turned upon me a needle-like gaze. "This is most irregular."

"Sir George!" Mrs Mercer exclaimed as the old man hobbled from her office without another word.

"That was intolerable," the lady snapped, turning to face me.

"Intolerable?" said I. "Shall I tell you what is intolerable? Sherlock Holmes was found in his cell this morning, beaten half to death!"

At least the lady had the decency to raise a hand to her mouth. "I had no idea. Will he—"

"Will he live? If he does, it will be no thanks to you."

"Me?"

"You are the reason he is there in the first place. If not for your lies, he would be a free man."

She went to close her office door, but I blocked the way.

"There's no hiding this time, Mrs Mercer. The truth will out, about you and this hotel. The sordid little secret you have worked so hard to protect. If you have a shred of decency you will go to the police right now and tell them that Holmes didn't steal that book. Because if you don't, so help me God, I shall see to it that you pay for what you have done."

"Are you threatening me, Doctor?" she said, tight-lipped.

"I'm warning you. Someone wanted Holmes out of the way, and for reasons I have yet to ascertain you were only too happy to oblige. In my eyes, you are just as culpable as whichever thug broke his jaw."

Her jaw dropped open at this, a chink in her armour finally showing. "They broke his jaw?"

But I was not fooled. This was concern not for Holmes, but for her own reputation.

"I'm so sorry."

"I hope you are, madam, because by the time this day is out I shall see that everyone involved in this travesty is brought to justice, one way or another."

CHAPTER TWENTY-FIVE

BLINDFOLDED

Yes, it was an overreaction; and yes, I should not have said such things, but I cared not a jot, even as I stormed out of the hotel.

However, as I headed for Corn Street my temper cooled. Maybe it was the late morning air. Maybe it was concern over what my outburst would mean for Holmes's case.

At the time of our altercation, I had been unable to see beyond my own anger. Now, I worried how it would look to others.

The friend of an accused man, threatening the woman who had condemned him.

I groaned at the thought. What an idiot I had been. I paused in the street. Should I turn back? Should I apologise?

No. My outburst, while hardly good manners, was justified. Mrs Mercer had set everything in motion when she called the police. Even if we believed her story, why the devil had she not confronted Holmes instead, so that he could prove his innocence? I stood by what I had told her. She was as responsible as whichever villain had attacked Holmes.

I continued on my way with a renewed belief in the rectitude of my actions. Holmes may have been incapacitated, but I would make damned sure that he had every scrap of information he needed upon his recovery.

Harold Clifford was waiting for me on Corn Street, standing beside one of Lord Redshaw's carriages. I felt a tug of pity for the fellow. There was a proud man beneath that fleshy face, despite the best efforts of his father-in-law. Was that why he had offered me the tour of the Lodge? Was this all a secret act of rebellion?

"Dr Watson," he said as I drew nearer. "I thought p-perhaps you would not come."

"You piqued my interest, Mr Clifford," I admitted, shaking his hand.

"Please, call me H-Harold."

We clambered into the carriage and, at a rap of his knuckles against the roof, were off.

"As you d-discovered last evening, we're a secretive bunch," Clifford told me, "which is why I must ask you to w-wear this."

He held out a blindfold.

"You're joking."

"I'm afraid not. I'm breaking enough rules simply taking you to the Lodge. I can't r-risk giving away the exact location as well."

"But the League's existence is well known."

"As is our official address…"

"But that's not where you are taking me."

"No. The *real* business of the League goes on behind very secret doors."

"Surely you can trust me?"

"If I didn't trust you, you wouldn't be here."

He held out the blindfold again. It was only when I took it that I realised that the man's stutter had all but disappeared. It wasn't only his speech impediment. Clifford seemed a different man out of his family's presence. More assertive; more in control. Perhaps I was seeing – or at least hearing – a little of the fellow's true nature before whatever troubles had overwhelmed his company.

Reluctantly, I tied the blindfold around my head. With the material in place, I was as blind as the proverbial bat.

"Thank you," Clifford said, tapping the roof one more time.

The carriage lurched to the left.

Remembering how Holmes had foiled Professor Attercop in the Limosonian Diamond Affair, I set about memorising every aspect of the journey. I listened for the rattle of manhole covers, the thrum of machinery, even the shout of a newspaper salesman revelling in the grisly discovery of more missing apes found without their hearts.

Of course, the fact that I knew so little of Bristol's landscape was something of a disadvantage. During the course of our journey I heard the blast of not one but four boat whistles, and was aware that we clattered across at least one bridge.

My frustration grew with every corner taken. I would have struggled were I in London, let alone in a city I barely knew.

The process was made no more straightforward by Clifford, who babbled away, apologising over and over again for his behaviour at dinner the night before.

"Think nothing of it," I assured him, wishing the man would be quiet. "As I told Lord Redshaw, every family has its own peculiarities, especially with a stranger in their midst."

Clifford laughed. "Peculiarities? You have a talent for understatement, Doctor."

"Not according to Holmes."

"Of course, I shouldn't rise to Sutcliffe's nonsense, but the man r-riles me. Always has."

"Have you known him long?"

"We n-never had much to do with each other as children, but then he took up with Marie on his r-return from the Orient. He's after Benjamin's money, of course, that much is obvious. He can't have as much as Benjamin thinks."

"What makes you think that?"

"The fellow lives in P-Portland Square," Clifford said, as if that should be answer enough.

"I don't follow you."

"Well, I f-for one can't see why anyone would choose such an address. No wonder he couldn't wait to p-pop the question. No one expected her to say yes."

"Why?"

"Marie's tastes are… slightly more earthy. They haven't even s-set a date for the wedding."

"Maybe she won't go through with it?"

"I can't see Benjamin allowing that. All those books of spells and w-whatnot Victor's brought back from Japan. It's as if he's put a hex on the old man."

"Spells?"

"You heard him the other night. The story of Izanami and… whoever it was."

"Izanabi," I provided.

"That's the fellow. Victor's full of that stuff. Well, he's full of something anyway, and Benjamin l-laps it up. He used to be such a rational man. An engineer, like me."

"And Victor's changed him?"

"I caught them m-meditating the other day, in the drawing room. Meditating, a m-man like Benjamin. It sickens me that in an age of science like ours, men can still be so damned superstitious."

I chuckled. "You sound like Holmes."

"I would like to m-meet him."

"That may be difficult."

"Because of his bother with the police, you mean?"

I told Clifford what had happened in the police cell, and

the man seemed genuinely distressed.

"That's d-dreadful. Absolutely dreadful. I'm sorry to hear it. You should have a word with Benjamin tonight. He'll have to speak to the police now."

"He has said he would…"

"And you must make him. My f-father-in-law is a man of influence. Trust me, I should know. If anyone can help your friend, it's Benjamin. I'd head down to Redland Road and have it out with them myself, for all the good it would do."

I smiled and let the conversation die. I needed to concentrate on the sounds and odours of the streets. We had travelled up a number of hills, of that I was sure. Then ahead there was a sudden clamour, a cry of "look out", followed by an almighty crash, like tiles smashing on the road.

"What was that?" I asked as the carriage lurched to the right.

"N-nothing to worry about. Here we are."

We came to a halt and I pitched forward. I threw my hand out and it found Clifford, who steadied me before I could fall.

"Whoa there."

"Can I take this thing off now?"

"Not until we're inside, I'm afraid, but not long now." I heard the carriage door open.

"You cannot expect me to walk in the street like this. Besides, how inconspicuous will a man in a blindfold be? Surely you don't want to draw attention to your mysterious lodge?"

I was trying to keep my voice light, but was incapable of disguising my frustration.

"I cannot apologise enough, Doctor, but we are nearly there. Here, let me assist you."

The carriage shook slightly as he stepped onto the pavement, and I felt a hand grab my own. The thought of being helped out of a carriage like an invalid was abhorrent and I considered pulling my hand free. However, as I would no doubt end up sprawled across the pavement, I let myself be led from the carriage, one tentative step after another. Never have I felt so vulnerable.

"Wait here," said Clifford, disappearing for a moment from my side. It was all I could do not to rip the mask from my eyes there and then. I heard feet on steps, followed by a key turning in a lock and a door opening, the hinges in desperate need of oil. Then, Clifford took my arm again, as one would a blind man.

"There are steps ahead," he said, leading me forward. "Careful."

I proceeded gingerly, stepping down... one, two, three. We passed through what I could only assume was the open door into a cool space. The sounds of the outside world grew muffled and then disappeared altogether as Clifford closed the door behind us.

"I assume we have arrived at our destination?" I asked him, cocking my head to the side in the darkness. There was a hiss of gas followed by the sound of ignition, and I saw a soft glow through the blindfold. I sniffed. The air was redolent with the stink of damp and animal droppings. The smell certainly indicated that Clifford had brought me to a somewhat insalubrious location.

"You may remove the blindfold," came his reply. At last! "But please don't judge us by your surroundings. I've been forced to bring you in through the t-tradesman's entrance, as it were."

I made no reply. I was too busy trying to disentangle the knot. I had tied it too well.

"Shall I—"

"I can do it," I snapped, as the knot came apart in my fingers. With another tug the blindfold was free.

CHAPTER TWENTY-SIX

THE WARWICK ROOM

I blinked as my eyes became accustomed to the dull glow of the gas lantern that swung from Clifford's hand.

We were standing in a dank, claustrophobic corridor, the crumbling brick walls devoid of decoration. I put the blindfold to my nose to protect myself from the foul reek of the place.

"As I said, you're not exactly seeing us at our best."

"That much is certain," I agreed, to be rewarded by another well-meaning chuckle.

"This way then. Let's get you back to civilisation."

He walked ahead, holding the lantern high. The yellow glow of the flame cast strange shadows on the mould of the wall, and I jumped at the sound of tiny feet scampering away. Where had he brought me?

Clifford reached a simple door that was bolted from the inside. He threw the bolt and pulled the door open. Light streamed out, and I was led into such luxury that it was as though I had been transported from the tenements of Whitechapel to the grandeur of Buckingham Palace. The deep shag of a plush carpet was beneath our feet and velutinous purple flocked wallpaper covered the walls. Ornate light fittings blazed bright compared with Clifford's lacklustre flame. He extinguished the lantern and, stowing it back in the squalid corridor, closed the door. Our curious entrance all but disappeared into the wall. If one did not know it was there, one would have passed the hidden door without question.

"Welcome to our *sanctum sanctorum*," Clifford said in a theatrical whisper.

Our footsteps muffled by the thick carpet, we walked deeper into what I could only imagine had once been a grand house in the middle of the city. As at Ridgeside, I found myself scrutinised by the eyes of countless portraits as we passed. Each showed a knight of old draped in a white robe with a single red cross on his chest. They held swords in their hands and a look of zealous faith upon their faces.

"Templar Knights?" I asked.

"You know their links to Bristol?"

"Only what Lord Redshaw has told me," I admitted. "Is there anyone else here?"

"In the Lodge? I shouldn't think so, not at this time of day, but it's better to be safe than sorry."

He put his finger to his lips and tried an internal door. It opened to reveal an immense library split over two storeys, the walls lined with solid oak bookshelves that ran from ceiling to floor. Dust motes hung in the air, illuminated by the same gas lighting as the corridor outside, a necessity as I realised there was not a single window in the vast room.

"The accumulated knowledge of Bristol," Clifford said proudly. "My father was the librarian in his day. History, commerce, law; it's all here."

"It's incredible," I said, and meant it. While I read little other than the odd adventure story or my growing collection of medical journals, I could scarcely help but be impressed. If not for the lack of ventilation I could imagine myself spending hours exploring the bookshelves. As for Holmes, well, we would lose him for days at a time as he added to his vast repertoire of mental bagatelles, one of which would some day turn a case on its head.

Clifford ran a hand along a row of precious spines. "Father told me there is even a ledger here that contains the name of every poor soul sold by Warwick at the harbourside."

"Surely not," I said.

"I've never seen it myself, and I know there are others that would gladly see the book burn. Anything to forget how Warwick really made his money."

"It doesn't worry you then?"

"Don't get me wrong, Doctor. Such enterprises were abominable, but it was a different time. I'm a firm believer that one must understand the mistakes of the past, to ensure that history doesn't repeat itself."

"Very wise," I said, noticing a section of medical books. I turned my head to read the titles on the spines, and was excited to see treatises from the likes of Doctors Hervey, Vesalius and Pretorius. "This is a treasure trove."

Clifford smiled at my enthusiasm. "Don't worry, Doctor. I'll be sure to bring you back this way."

He opened a door on the other side of this Aladdin's cave and reluctantly I followed. We were in another splendid passageway. More portraits graced the walls, the subjects of more recent years, each wearing an identical chain of office around his neck. As we approached the large double doors at the end of the corridor, I found a face I recognised.

"This man," I said, stopping in front of the portrait. "We have met, although I cannot say where."

Clifford glanced up at the gaunt features, perfectly captured in oils. "That is S-Sir George Tavener, our Grand M-Master."

Shame washed over me as I realised where I had encountered those small penetrating eyes. Sir George was the understandably aggrieved gentleman who had been in conference with Mrs Mercer when I burst into her office this morning.

"So all these men were Grand Masters?" I asked, covering my embarrassment with the question.

"Yes," Clifford replied. "Right back to the League's foundation in 1322."

"Impressive," I said.

Clifford smiled. "Not compared with what lies through here."

He led me to the doors, which bore a large coat of arms, the device being split between the two of them. A shoal of fish swam in the centre of the crest, which was supported by two braying unicorns. Beneath them ran a motto: *vade et tu fac similiter*.

"'Go and do thou likewise,'" I translated. "From the parable of the Good Samaritan. The motto of the League?"

"No," replied Clifford. "Of Edwyn Warwick. This is the Warwick room."

He pushed open the doors and we entered a room not unlike a chapel in both size and decoration. Stained-glass windows shone from the walls, each portraying a different aspect of the philanthropist's life: Warwick the businessman; Warwick the orator; Warwick the crusader for justice; and Warwick the saint. Yes, one would have thought, due to his depiction in the last window, that the man had already been sanctified. He was standing in the centre of Bristol surrounded by the poor, who reached up to touch his robe as if the fabric alone could deliver them from destitution.

As for Warwick the crusader, he was seen breaking the chains of the oppressed. Considering Warwick's history, even his most apologetic of supporters must have found such a portrayal in rather poor taste.

There was something else odd about the windows. The light behind them flickered, as if each image were lit by a dozen candles.

"What do you think?" Clifford asked.

"Words fail me. The light behind the windows? It's not natural..."

"We are at the heart of the building. The windows are illuminated by a series of gas lamps, installed by my own father."

"He worked hard for the League, by the sounds of it."

"He dedicated his life to its work. We all do."

I turned on my heel, surveying what could only be described as a shrine. Banners hung between the windows, each representing a different aspect of Bristol's economic history. There was boat-building, trade between nations, heavy industry and the arts. Of slavery and piracy there was no sign, both ugly stains on Bristol's collective soul scrubbed clean.

The prosperity of the city, however, was clear to see. The pillars that supported the ornate plastered ceiling were smothered in gold leaf. Silver goblets and ornamental plates were displayed on plinths around the walls, each embellished with a glittering array of jewels. It was a temple of affluence, offering praise not to the Almighty, but to profit and gain.

"Are you ready for the greatest riches of all?" Clifford led me along the central aisle, rows of extravagantly carved pews to our right and left. Ahead, where one would expect an altar, was a cabinet containing but one item. A bust of Warwick watched our approach, the man's own periwig on the effigy's marble head.

"H-here it is," Clifford said, with awe in his voice. "Edwyn's wig."

I was unsure exactly what to say. In all honesty, I felt a little underwhelmed after the majesty of the shrine itself. The wig was surprisingly modest, and obviously of great age. So I said the first thing that came into my mind.

"Is it ever worn?"

"Good heavens, no. It remains in the cabinet at all times, for all to see."

"Who sees it though? What is this place for?"

"Reflection, and contemplation," came Clifford's considered reply. "Members often come in here and simply sit, hoping to soak up a little of Warwick's industrious nature."

"And his charitable heart?"

"Of course. And there are l-lectures. Sir George gives an annual address on the anniversary of Warwick's birth, usually anyway."

"Usually?"

"The next was due on Saturday, but it has been cancelled because Sir George is away on business. Caused a bit of a stir when it was announced. The League hasn't missed a W-Warwick address for decades."

"What about the ring?" I asked, keen to guide the conversation to the reason for our presence here.

"Ah yes. It was k-kept in this display case here."

He moved towards the kind of cabinet usually to be found in museums or galleries, containing the accumulated knick-knacks of our ancestors. This was no different. The cabinet held a pearl letter opener as well as various wax seals and quills.

"These all belonged to Warwick?" I asked.

Clifford nodded. It was a curiously humdrum assortment for such grand surroundings, like entering the Great Pyramid only to find the Pharaoh's nit-comb and a paperclip.

Perhaps I was being unfair. This worship of a mere mortal, no matter how altruistic he may have been, disturbed me, my initial wonder giving way to distaste. Still, I had a job to do.

"It sat there?" I said, pointing at a bare cushion in the middle of the collection.

"For decades, yes."

"And it was taken from Warwick's finger, when the body was displayed at St Nicole's?"

"I'm afraid so," Clifford confirmed, proving once and for all that the legend Holmes had related as old Pete was indeed true. "Ghoulish when you t-think about it. The ring was removed, as were the cross from around his neck and his shoes."

"His shoes?"

Clifford gave a skittish laugh. "Yes, I know. Ridiculous, isn't it? They used to be displayed here too, on one of the plinths, so we could 'imagine walking in Warwick's footsteps'. Now they are in storage, as is the cross. The ring is a m-mystery though. It vanished overnight, just two weeks ago. There was uproar as you'd expect, suspicion all round."

I examined the cabinet, finding it locked.

"And who has the key?"

"The Grand Master, and Benjamin, of course."

"Lord Redshaw?"

"He's the High Warden, second only to Sir George. The two have been friends for years."

I did what Holmes would do, checking for any sign of forced entry, but there was none.

"There's currently an amnesty," Clifford continued. "The League has announced that the culprit may return the ring without fear of indictment. As long as he also makes a sizeable donation to the poor fund, naturally."

I stood again. "What does the ring look like?"

"Gold with an emerald set into the band," Clifford told me. "There'll be a picture in the library. You wait here. I'll g-get it."

Before I could argue, Clifford hurried out of the room. Left alone in the shrine, I was suddenly aware that Warwick's bust seemed to be glowering at me.

Scolding myself for such whimsy, I turned my back on the

effigy and wandered down the aisle as I waited. I looked up, gaping at the ostentatious ceiling. I failed to hear the door opening behind me, or the scrape of a candlestick being removed from a plinth. I didn't even hear a step on the flagstones until it was too late.

I turned, at the last minute, as something hard came down on the back of my head and the world went dark.

CHAPTER TWENTY-SEVEN

CAUGHT IN THE ACT

"Dr Watson?"

The voice was familiar, but I was unable to place it, or indeed to identify my whereabouts. A hand was on my shoulder, trying to rouse me, the voice urgently repeating what I could only assume was my name.

"Dr W-Watson, can you h-hear me? Are you awake?"

I groaned, not so much in answer to his question but because it seemed the only rational thing to do in the circumstances.

"Steady now," the voice said, as I examined the back of my head with a shaking hand. My fingers met inflamed skin and I flinched, the sharp pain bringing me halfway back to my senses.

"Here, let me help you up."

"Never move someone who's suffered a blow to the head," I muttered, my words slurring, "unless it's absolutely necessary."

"We can't have you lying there."

I attempted to get to my feet, my knees buckling almost immediately. I did not crash to the floor but was supported like a drunken man in another's arms. I looked up, but my vision was blurred. Eventually, a fleshy face came into focus.

"Clifford?"

"That's it. Let's s-sit you down."

He lowered me onto one of the pews. "What happened?"

"I was about to ask you the s-same question. I was only g-gone for a m-moment, and returned to find you laid out on the floor."

I made another tentative examination of the egg that had sprung up on the back of my head. My fingers came back red.

"Oh Lord, you're b-bleeding. Let me see." Clifford went to grab my head, but I swatted him away.

"He came up behind me…" I realised, trying to focus on the front of the shrine. There was a door, next to the cabinet I had examined. "What's through there?"

"I d-don't know," Clifford admitted. "N-never been in there. A store room I t-think." He walked over to it. "Do you think that's where he c-came from?"

He tried the handle, finding the door locked.

"Someone could have been waiting inside."

"But f-for what reason? To attack you?"

"Why was Holmes arrested? Why is St Nicole's locked? Someone is trying to cover up what is happening here. First the body and now the ring."

"It doesn't m-make sense."

"Words I seem to say most days around Holmes. Perhaps we disturbed an intruder and he hid. Does it lead anywhere?"

"I don't think so. As I s-said—"

"You've never been in there."

I massaged my temples. My head was throbbing uncontrollably. Two blows in two days would do that to a man. Or maybe it was more. I couldn't even remember how long we had been in Bristol. I needed to think straight. I needed to think like Holmes!

I looked up and locked eyes with the bust of Warwick.

Something was wrong, but my muddled mind was incapable of working out what.

And then realisation hit me. "The wig," I exclaimed. "It's gone."

Clifford whirled around. "No. That's not p-possible."

And yet it was true. The bust was completely bald, the musty old periwig nowhere to be seen.

Clifford rushed forward, trying to open the cabinet. Its hinged door was locked as tight as the storage room.

"Is anything else missing?" I asked, trying to stand, only to find that sitting was far preferable.

Clifford looked around. "I don't think so. Everything seems in order." His eyes fell upon an empty plinth to the right of the shrine. "Except for this. There should be a candlestick there, from Warwick's house in London."

"Big enough to knock a chap out?" I asked.

Clifford hurried back to me. "Doctor, I'm s-so sorry."

"This isn't your fault."

"I should n-never have b-brought you here."

"Trust me, this kind of thing happens with alarming regularity. I'm surprised my skull is still in one piece. Now, help me up before—"

My sentence was cut off by a cry behind us. "Harold? What the devil has happened?"

Thankfully there was no need for me to turn in order to identify the owner of the voice. Victor Sutcliffe charged into the shrine, appearing at my side.

"Dr Watson?"

Even in my weakened condition, I could hardly help but notice the change in Harold Clifford. In the presence of Sutcliffe, the man sagged, as if collapsing in on himself. His stutter even returned with full vigour as he babbled an explanation, telling Sutcliffe about my assault and the missing wig.

"This is terrible!" At first, I thought Sutcliffe was talking about my cracked head, but it soon became clear he meant the theft. "What were you doing here in the first place?"

"I w-was showing Dr W-Watson the ring, or rather the l-lack of it."

"Is that right?"

"Absolutely."

"You weren't stealing the wig yourself?"

Clifford's mouth dropped open. "Y-you think it was m-m-me?"

Sutcliffe's arms were crossed over his chest. "You are the only ones in the building, against Benjamin's wishes!"

"Mr Clifford wasn't even in the room when I was attacked," I said, pointing towards the storage room door. "Whoever did this to me came out of there."

Sutcliffe ran across to the door.

"You won't b-be able to open it," Clifford told him. "It's locked."

Sutcliffe turned to face him. "How did you get in here? Did you take Benjamin's keys?"

"So w-what if I did?"

Sutcliffe held out his hand. "Hand them over."

Shame-faced, Clifford fished a set of keys from his pocket and proffered them to Sutcliffe, who snatched them without another word and set about finding the right one for the job.

"You could have opened the door?" I asked, incredulous.

"I d-don't know which is w-which, only the s-side entrance."

"Luckily I do," Sutcliffe said, pulling open the door. I pushed myself up from the pew and staggered over. As Clifford had suggested, the door opened onto a narrow cupboard. Shelves built into the walls were filled with dust-covered boxes and files. One particular item above all attracted my attention.

"Is that the candlestick?" I asked, pointing at the nearest shelf.

Sutcliffe picked up a large silver candlestick that lay on its side. "What's this doing in here?"

"Someone tried to hide the evidence," I said. "May I see?"

He passed the candlestick to me and I turned it over in my hand. Sure enough, there were traces of blood on the base. My blood.

"This makes no sense. How long did you say you were gone?"

"Only a f-few minutes. Th-three at most?"

"And yet my attacker had time to knock me senseless, hide the candlestick and get awa—"

The room shifted again, and I pitched forward, only for Sutcliffe to catch me.

"We need to get him back to Ridgeside."

It appeared this was finally something upon which both men agreed. "We can send for M-Melosan."

"Who?" I asked.

"Family d-doctor. He'll see you right."

"S'no need," I slurred.

"There is every need," Sutcliffe insisted.

"But what about the w-wig?" Clifford asked.

"We'll deal with that later. Now, help me get Watson outside. I have a cab waiting."

Sutcliffe's arm wrapped around my back.

"I have the b-b-blindfold here," I heard Clifford say as I took an unsteady step forward.

"At least you showed a little sense," Sutcliffe replied, before grabbing my arm. "Watson, sit over here and we'll put it on you."

"I don't think that will be necessary," I slurred, before collapsing to the floor.

CHAPTER TWENTY-EIGHT

A MEETING OF THE LEAGUE

I remember little about the journey back to the manor. I sat sandwiched between the two men, fading in and out of consciousness. I caught snippets of their conversation, but was unable to put much of it into context. There was something about an admiral and an anonymous tip-off about a break-in that had sent Sutcliffe running for the Lodge. It was also clear that if Sutcliffe had his way, Clifford would face expulsion from the League for his actions.

By the time we reached Ridgeside, I had regained enough of my senses to be led rather than carried to the Tombo Room. I was deposited on the bed and Lord Redshaw sat with me himself until the family doctor arrived. Dr Melosan was a fussy man who had been fetched from the Royal Infirmary in town. However, by the time he had shone lights into my eyes and prodded the painful lump on my head I was sensible enough to have performed my own diagnosis.

I could not be completely sure that my skull was not fractured but both Melosan and I doubted that permanent damage had been done. The swelling was already going down, and I was responding well, despite collapsing earlier. That was put down to pain, and I was offered an opiate, but refused. I wanted to remain as alert as possible for the arrival of Mycroft Holmes, whenever that might be.

Dr Melosan bid me good day and I was left alone to sink into a deep sleep. By the time I opened my eyes again, the sun had vanished behind the gorge.

Ignoring the pounding in my head, I sat on the edge of the bed, working up the courage to stand. Holding tight onto one of the dragonfly-topped bed-knobs I rose unsteadily. An onrush of dizziness almost had me falling back onto the mattress, but I leaned against the wall and the world steadied itself again. My mouth was dry, but a jug of water had been set by the bed. I poured myself a glass with a shaking hand, and sipped gratefully.

My thirst quenched, I looked down and realised I was still in the clothes I had worn earlier that day. I changed, taking longer than usual, but managed both my buttons and necktie on the first attempt, which I took as a small victory. The walk to the stairs was slightly more fraught, but I was able to reach the ground floor without tumbling head over heels, and paused in the hall to catch my breath.

I heard the sound of raised voices nearby, and realised they were coming from the direction of Lord Redshaw's study. Feeling bolder than I had any right to, I edged towards the door and placed my ear to the wood. While the voices were muffled, I could make out the tones of Redshaw himself, poor stuttering Clifford, the loathsome Sutcliffe and another gentleman possessing a thin, reedy voice that I recognised from our brief encounter in Mrs Mercer's office. It could only be the Grand Master himself, Sir George Tavener.

"Well, it has to be found…" That was Sutcliffe.

"Obviously," said Sir George. "In the meantime, we will

replace the wig with one from my private collection."

"You mean there's another?" Sutcliffe asked, sounding shocked. "I thought ours was unique."

"You think Warwick had only one wig? His sister gave one to my grandfather as a memento. I shall happily donate it to the League in our hour of need."

Sutcliffe seemed in no hurry to let the matter go. "This changes everything—"

"I don't see why," Sir George snapped. "And you are distracting us from the main issue – why Clifford was at the Lodge in the first place."

"And g-good th-thing I w-was," Clifford replied, the man's stutter more distinct than ever. "Otherwise w-we'd never even have kn-known it was g-gone."

"What of this Watson fellow?" asked Sir George. "Could he have taken it?"

"And then knocked himself out?" Redshaw said, echoing my own thoughts. "Besides, he wasn't even in Bristol when the ring went missing."

"Or so we are led to believe," Sir George suggested. "From what the Mercer woman has told us, Holmes delights in deviousness. Look at how he and Watson disguised themselves to visit Warwick's memorial. How do we know they weren't sticking their noses into our affairs before they announced their presence?"

"You are seeing conspiracies where there are none, Grand Master," Lord Redshaw said, jumping to our defence once more. A good job too, as I had been about to burst in and tell the assembly exactly what I thought of their scurrilous accusations, no matter what words were inscribed above Redshaw's study door.

"You should never have taken him in, High Warden," Sir George told my host. "It's too much of a risk."

"I did what I thought right."

"As d-did I," stammered Clifford.

"You have only made matters worse," Sutcliffe insisted, but the rest of the conversation was lost to me as I heard someone approach. I stepped quickly away from the door, and continued on my way just as Brewer appeared around the corner.

"Dr Watson?" he said. "We did not expect to see you out of bed."

"I needed a change of scenery," I replied. "Thought I might sit in the drawing room for a while, catch up on the newspaper perhaps."

"Can I get you anything, sir?"

"No thank you, Brewer. I'm sure you have duties to perform."

"Very good, sir," he said, bowing just enough to be respectful. I waited for him to continue on his way, but he stayed rooted to the spot. The man was obviously waiting for me to stop lurking around his master's study.

"Yes, well… the drawing room," I said, smiling weakly and turning to leave. Brewer watched me go for a moment, before carrying on about his business.

I had half a mind to sneak back to the study door when I heard something nearby, the same sound that had so intrigued me in the thick of the night. Someone was crying nearby. Abandoning my eavesdropping, I followed the noise to find Lady Marie sobbing piteously in front of the dining-room fireplace.

I hesitated at the door, caught between an urge to offer assistance and a reluctance to intrude upon a lady's grief. Either way, I was caught out. Lady Anna appeared behind me, making me jump as she addressed me by name.

"Dr Watson, are you well enough to be out of bed?"

Flustered, I looked at Marie, who met my gaze with red-rimmed eyes.

"I am fine," I stammered as Lady Marie rose swiftly from her seat and exited through a door beside the chimneypiece. I guessed it must have led to Lord Redshaw's much-prized billiard room. Somehow I doubted she was rushing to set up a game.

I called after her, but she did not stop.

"Leave her," Anna said, her tone sharp.

"But she is upset."

"My sister is always upset. It is her preferred condition, especially when others are happy."

It seemed to me that no one in this house was particularly happy, myself included.

"Anna?" said Clifford behind her, appearing at the door. The meeting in the study had clearly come to an end. "Is s-something wrong?"

"Oh, not a bit of it. Just Marie throwing one of her tantrums."

It had hardly seemed a tantrum to me, more like a heart breaking.

Now Sutcliffe was in the drawing room too, asking after his fiancée.

"She went through there," I told him, and he set off to find her, almost shoving me out of the way in his haste.

"No, please," I declared with more sarcasm than I intended, "excuse me!"

"Watson?" Lord Redshaw exclaimed as he too entered. "What are you doing up?"

"I asked the very same thing, Father," Lady Anna told him. I raised a palm to ward off the concern.

"I'm fine," I lied. "Really I am, save for a slight headache."

"You were lucky you weren't killed. On behalf of the Worshipful League of Merchants, I offer you a heartfelt apology."

"No, Lord Redshaw, it is I who must apologise. I betrayed your trust. I should not have gone to the Lodge."

"You only went because you were invited," Redshaw stated, shooting a look at his son-in-law, "by someone who should know better."

Clifford looked suitably contrite. "I am s-sorry to have d-dragged you into this, D-Doctor."

"Please. I became involved as soon as Ermacora set course for Baker Street. What of the periwig?"

"The Grand Master is to launch an internal investigation," Redshaw said. "Oh, and he sends his apologies for not greeting you in person. He wanted to return to the Lodge as soon as possible."

For this I was grateful. I had little wish to renew our acquaintance. "What have the police said?"

"They will not be involved."

"Really? But if the periwig has been stolen—"

"This is an internal affair—"

"In which I was assaulted!"

"In which you were trespassing!"

Redshaw's indignation took me by surprise. He regained his composure immediately.

"I'm sorry. This is a stressful situation, and personally embarrassing seeing as Harold was involved."

"You can't blame him?" exclaimed Anna.

"Blame him? I staked my entire reputation on him! The Grand Master was all for expelling your husband for his actions."

"He did nothing wrong."

"I b-broke the r-rules," Clifford admitted. "Your f-father stood up for me. I am in his d-debt… once more."

Redshaw sighed, rubbing the bridge of his nose. "I don't know what this city is coming to. It's becoming harder and harder to make an honest living. Strikes. Workers' rights. Just today I had a meeting with the damned unions, wanting more money for the men. How are we supposed to keep afloat with all these demands left, right and centre? Wasn't like it in Warwick's day. Back then they let you get on with things. Business was allowed to be business, none of this namby-pamby welfare rubbish. Harold knows it as well as I. Profits are going down, industry is moving elsewhere and no one will raise a finger to help. And then, after all that, I come home to this. Thieves in the Lodge. Watson nearly killed. The world's going to the dogs."

My head was throbbing uncontrollably now. All I wanted to do was escape from this house with its secrets and quarrels. If not for Holmes, I would have set off back to London there and then.

I must have swayed on my feet, because Lady Anna was at my side in a heartbeat, guiding me towards a chair.

"I am quite well, I promise you," I maintained, although I felt nothing of the sort.

"Nonsense," said Lord Redshaw. "Harold, get the man a brandy. Watson, sit down for God's sake."

I did as I was told and gratefully accepted the drink a moment later.

"I'm sorry to hear about your friend being beaten in custody," Redshaw said as I sipped the oaky liquid. "Harold told me about Holmes. It's a terrible business, all of it. I doubt you will ever want to see Bristol again."

The thought had occurred to me.

"I have had a word with Dr Melosan," Redshaw continued. "He is going to see what he can do about securing Holmes's release into the Royal Infirmary."

His words felt like a sudden ray of light on a cloudy day. "Thank you."

"It is the least we can do, after everything you've been through. Do you want another?"

I looked down at my glass, realising that I had drunk the lot. "No, thank you. One is enough."

"Well, I know *I* need one," said my host, crossing to the drinks cabinet. "What a day it has been, eh?"

As Lord Redshaw poured himself a glass, he had no way of knowing that the day would very nearly be his last.

CHAPTER TWENTY-NINE

A VISITOR

Lord Redshaw's glass had barely reached his lips before the front door bell chimed.

"What now?" his Lordship asked, as we waited to see who would present themselves.

Within a few moments, Brewer appeared at the drawing-room door, haughty as ever.

"A Mr Holmes to see Dr Watson, sir," he intoned.

I jumped to my feet so fast that my head was almost sent into another spin.

"Mycroft?" I asked, expecting to see Holmes's rotund brother waddle through the door.

"I am afraid not," came an unfamiliar voice. I stopped in my tracks, momentarily confused. A tall, lean figure had appeared behind Brewer, dressed in a smart blue suit. That he was related to Holmes there was no doubt. He shared the same hawk-like nose and bushy eyebrows, but was a good many pounds lighter than Mycroft, although not as thin as Holmes himself. His hair was grey and sparse, a tidy angular beard perched on his chin, and he wore a monocle in one grey eye.

When he spoke again, I realised that his voice was deeper than Sherlock Holmes's own, a rich baritone that seemed to belong to a larger man.

The newcomer bowed his head in our host's direction. "Lord Redshaw, my name is Sherrinford Holmes, and I should like to thank you for accommodating Dr Watson during my brother's troubles."

"I beg your pardon," I said, holding onto the back of the chair to stop myself from pitching over. "I do not believe we have met."

"Indeed we have not." Sherrinford Holmes walked towards me to extend his hand and I noticed he was limping on his left foot. "I apologise that I am not the man you were expecting. Brother Mycroft rarely ventures out of his chambers, let alone the capital."

He shook my hand warmly, cupping it between both palms.

"And as for Sherlock, I doubt he has ever mentioned my name."

"I'm afraid not," I admitted.

"I thought as much. Regrettably, the Holmes brothers are less close than once we were. Both Sherlock and Mycroft were keen to fly the ancestral nest, whereas I stayed at home to manage the estate. I am sorry to say that I share little of their sense of adventure."

"Will you have a drink, sir?" Lord Redshaw asked, his own glass still in his hand.

"Is that brandy?" Sherrinford asked.

"Indeed."

"Then yes, that would be most pleasant, thank you. It has been quite a journey."

"Where have you come from?" asked Lady Anna, indicating that Sherrinford should take a seat.

"Sussex. I came as soon as I could."

"How did you know?" I asked.

"What had happened to my brother, you mean? I received a

rare message from Mycroft, asking me to intercede on his behalf."

I wanted to ask more, but was forced to wait until Lady Anna introduced her husband.

"It is a pleasure to meet you all," Sherrinford said graciously. "If only it could have been under better circumstances."

"I shall take you to see Holmes in the morning," I promised.

"There is no need," Sherrinford replied as Redshaw handed him a glass. "I have already seen him."

"You have?"

Sherrinford nodded, taking a sip of the drink. "I came directly from the police station. Quite a mess." He shook his head sadly.

"How is he?"

"Stable, although he had been drifting in and out of consciousness. The surgeon…"

"Mr Woodbead," I provided.

"He has Sherlock trussed up like a spring chicken, but at least he seems not to be in too much pain, all things considered."

"My father is going to have him moved to the hospital," Lady Anna told Sherrinford.

"Is that so?"

"That's certainly the plan," Redshaw told him, standing with one thumb tucked into his waistcoat pocket.

"Very kind I'm sure, although I should prefer Sherlock to stay where he is."

"At the station?" I asked, flabbergasted.

"In Mr Woodbead's surgery. He is in good hands, Doctor, have no fear. And besides, my solicitors are looking into these scurrilous charges that have been levelled against Sherlock. They believe it would be better for him to remain in custody."

"Who are you using?" Redshaw said.

"McCarthy and Turner," Sherrinford replied. "Perhaps you have heard of them?"

Redshaw shook his head. "Can't say I have."

"Ah. Well, they are a local firm, but quite competent."

"Do you think they can help?" I asked.

"Think?" Sherrinford scoffed. "I *know* they can. My brother is many things, Doctor, but a thief he is not. This woman, Mrs…"

"Mercer," Redshaw snarled.

"Thank you. She is obviously mistaken. I'm sure we will be able to convince her to have the police drop the charges, as long as she does not feel intimidated in any way."

"Ah…" I said.

"Ah?" Sherrinford echoed.

"I, er, may have paid a visit to the Regent myself."

"You did?"

"I was so angry, especially after what had happened to Holmes…"

"That you had it out with Mercer."

"I'm afraid so."

Sherrinford dismissed the concern easily. "Your reaction is quite understandable. I am sure it will be no problem. And if it is, we shall make it go away."

"That's the ticket," Redshaw said with a laugh. "A man after my own heart."

Sherrinford Holmes was certainly sure of himself. Having seen Holmes and Mycroft together I could imagine the clash of personalities when all three Holmes brothers were in the same room. No wonder Holmes kept his distance.

"You must stay with us, of course," Redshaw announced. "I will have Brewer prepare a room."

"You are most kind, and yet I must respectfully decline. I am staying with friends near Bathampton, the Jarrett-Pettingales. Do you know them?"

Lord Redshaw shook his head. "I've never had the pleasure."

"I am not surprised. They are a quiet couple, keep themselves to themselves. I plan to travel back and forth until we have Sherlock safely back in London. And Dr Watson of course."

"You two must have a lot to talk about," Lord Redshaw realised. "We should leave you to it."

I stood as he began ushering both Anna and Clifford from the room. "Lord Redshaw, please. I have inconvenienced you enough."

"Nonsense," came the reply. "Take as long as you need, and please help yourself to another drink. I'll be in my study if you need me."

And then the door was closed, and I was alone with a brother of Holmes I had never even known existed.

"It is good to meet you finally, Doctor," Sherrinford said, rising to limp across to the drinks cabinet. "I have read your stories with great interest. You are a talented storyteller, sir."

I felt myself blush. "I'm not sure your brother would agree."

"Sherlock? Oh, what a philistine my brother can be."

"I wouldn't say that."

"Then you are either a loyal friend, or a saint." He poured himself a second brandy. "Sherlock wouldn't know culture if he was battered around the head with the *Complete Works of William Shakespeare*. Talking of which, how is your injury?"

"My injury?" I said, raising my hand to the back of my head.

"A-ha, I thought so," Sherrinford said with glee. "I could tell you were unsteady on your feet, and your pupils are slightly dilated, suggesting a blow to the head. The fact that you reacted by reaching for the affected area only proves my suspicion."

I laughed. "You're definitely a Holmes."

"Because of the guessing games? That is all they are, and don't let my brother tell you otherwise." He replaced the stopper on the crystal-cut bottle. "The three of us were brought up by an ogre of a nanny and survived only by tormenting her mercilessly. Who would have thought that our childhood games would provide Sherlock with a profession?"

He limped over to the drawing-room door and opened it a crack, peeking outside. What the deuce was the man up to? A smile flickered across his lips and he closed the door again, turning back to me.

"Tell me honestly, Watson, what do you think of my brother?"

The question flummoxed me.

"He's my closest friend."

"Of course he is, but there must be times when you want to take that service revolver of yours to his head."

The suggestion appalled me. "I would never do such a thing."

"I would hardly blame you if you did. All those infuriating habits of his. Is he still as untidy as ever?"

"Holmes is always immaculately dressed."

"Of course, but so slovenly at home. All that mess and confusion everywhere you turn. And then there are the mood swings, and the inappropriate demands on one's time. Tell me, did he actually ask you to accompany him to Bristol, or merely assume you would follow?"

"I was happy to accompany him."

"As I said, a saint. As is your wife. Mary, isn't it?"

He limped towards me, but paused to bounce up and down on his heels. "Oh, that won't do. No, not at all."

I looked at him quizzically. Was the man right in the head?

Sherrinford held his glass out to me. "Doctor, would you be so kind as take my drink for a moment?"

I accepted the glass and watched as this remarkable brother of Holmes perched on the edge of a sofa and undid his left boot. As I watched in bewilderment, he pulled out his stockinged foot, turned the boot over and gave it a shake.

A small round pebble fell to the floor, and bounced once before rolling over to my feet.

"That's better," said Sherrinford, his eyes sparkling with mischief. "As you know, Watson, it is always best to keep a stone in your boot…"

"To remind yourself on which leg you are limping," I said, dumbfounded.

"Quite so. But between you and me, it's damned uncomfortable all the same."

He smiled, and I saw in an instant that the monocled man in front of me was none other than Sherlock Holmes himself.

CHAPTER THIRTY

THE LONG-LOST BROTHER

I nearly dropped the brandy in amazement. "Holmes, is it really you?"

"Keep your voice down, Watson," Holmes whispered as he pulled on his boot and retrieved the pebble, slipping it into his jacket pocket. "When I checked outside, the corridor was empty, but you can never be sure, hence all that nonsense about Nanny."

"But I don't understand…"

"Evidently."

"I saw you. In the cell. Your injuries…"

Holmes took the glass from my hand and sat on one of the settees in front of the fireplace. I sat opposite him, still stunned by the revelation.

"I was never injured," Holmes explained, taking another sip, "just as this brandy is not half as good as Lord Redshaw thinks it is."

"But your face, your jaw."

"The poor fellow in my cell was Jamie Miller, a tramp from these parts. He's a similar height to myself, I grant you, although in desperate need of a good meal in his belly."

I remembered the skeletal hand, so unlike Holmes's own. Suddenly it made sense. How could I have been so stupid?

"But how did you do it?"

"We swapped places in the middle of the night," Holmes said, removing the monocle from his eye and placing it on the sofa beside him, "Miller changing into my clothes and vice versa. Then, by the light of a candle, I got to work."

"I don't understand."

"With the make-up, Watson. Please do try to keep up. I have to say, even I was impressed with the final result. Most life-like."

"So every bruise and scrape…"

"Were as fictitious as the brother who sits before you now. The reason you have never heard of Sherrinford Holmes is that Sherrinford Holmes does not exist. Another brother? Heaven forfend. But the people of Bristol aren't to know that. As far as everyone is concerned, Sherlock Holmes lies near death in Lower Redland Road Police Station—"

"While his devoted brother walks free."

"I should think so. Sherrinford has done nothing wrong… yet."

I shook my head, struggling to take it all in. "But this Miller character?"

"How did I employ his services?"

I nodded.

"You really need to pay more attention, Watson. Did Inspector Tovey not tell you he was clearing tramps from the streets?"

"Tovey's in on it?"

"It is always good to have a man on the inside. He found a fellow who could pass for me and we went from there."

"But the blood?"

"Pig's blood. Tovey's sister is married to a pig farmer in a delightful village called Hanham. As for the other evidence, the lock picks in the corridor and so on, those were Tovey's idea. He got quite carried away, although why he permitted you to come down and find the body I shall never know. If you had realised what we were up to…"

"Miller batted my hands away," I remembered, "when I tried to examine him."

"And a good job too. While the make-up was impressive, there was no way it would fool a medical man like yourself, especially if you attempted to wipe away the blood."

"But it fooled Mr Woodbead," I said with a chuckle. "Ha. Serves him right, the old fool."

"The old fool who happens to be Inspector Tovey's uncle."

My face fell. "His uncle?"

"On his mother's side. And, it would appear, a fine actor to boot."

I slouched back on the sofa. "He knew it wasn't you."

"Of course he did. Although I am glad he didn't take your advice and have poor Miller's jaw pinned. I wasn't lying when I said that the fake me is trussed up. You have never seen such an elaborate frame of bandages and gauze. Inspector Hawthorne is utterly convinced that Sherlock Holmes is in there."

"You've seen Hawthorne?"

Holmes grinned. "When I visited myself in the police station. He took me into the surgery himself. It's a peculiar feeling to gaze upon your own broken body."

"You're unbelievable," I declared quietly, shaking my head. "Just when I thought… I was really worried about you."

Now Holmes laughed out loud, which only irked me all the more.

"I'm sorry, Watson, but if it is of any comfort, you have played your part wonderfully."

"My part?"

"You have helped convince everyone that Sherlock and Sherrinford Holmes are two separate people, from your dismay in the cell to your excitement over the telegram from London."

My brow furrowed. "Of course. The telegram. How on Earth did you send that?"

Holmes took a sip of his drink. "A delightful young lady by the name of Mary helped me. Do you know her?"

"Mary? You've involved her in your scheme as well? Oh, Holmes, this really is the limit."

"A man must have his sport, Watson. Surely you can't deny me that? Although I truly am sorry for duping you again."

"What is that old proverb?" I said with a rueful sigh. "Fool me once, shame on you."

Holmes smiled. "Fool me twice, shame on me."

"Exactly."

"I expect you wish you'd had another drink now," Holmes said, draining his glass and placing it on the table between us. "But enough of this. Tell me what has been happening since my incarceration. I need to know everything."

"Well, I am a talented storyteller, after all," I said with a grin of my own. "Your brother told me."

Before long I had recounted the full events of the last couple of days. When I had finished, he shook his head.

"I'm sorry to hear about Father Kelleher."

"I know. It was very sad."

"No, you misunderstand me, Watson. I should have liked to see the corpse for myself."

"You say the strangest things, Holmes."

"Describe it to me."

"His corpse?"

"Watson, please."

I did my best, although Holmes naturally had more questions.

"And you say he choked on his own vomit?"

"I could smell it on his breath, not that he… well, you know what I mean."

"And tell me, was there blood on his lips, or around his nose?"

"Blood? No. But there was some on the sheets."

"The sheets? Are you sure it wasn't the pillow?"

"Actually yes. You're right. The nurse removed the pillow and there it was. How did you know?"

"Because Kelleher didn't choke on his vomit. He was smothered, the pillow held over his face, hence the blood."

"Are you sure?"

"The signs were all there, although you failed to see them. You say his lips were blue and that the blood vessels in his face were broken. Classic signs of asphyxia."

"And the vomit?"

"Not to put too fine a point on it, the fellow was sick as he was smothered, but the vomit collected in his throat as it had nowhere else to go, thanks to the pillow pushed over his mouth."

"Good Lord," I said. "I had no idea."

"And why would you? You have an innocent mind, Watson, which is what makes you so useful."

"So Kelleher was murdered."

"Twice. Once by poison and next by suffocation, only the latter was more successful."

"But if he was murdered to cover up the fact that Warwick's body wasn't in its grave…"

"Why kill the priest after the tomb was opened? To stop him talking to Tovey perhaps?"

"But none of this makes sense, Holmes. Why go to all this trouble to steal a corpse one hundred and seventy years old?"

"And then make off with his periwig and ring? It is an intriguing problem."

"Could it be revenge? For the man's involvement in the slave trade."

"Descendants of those he sold?" Holmes steepled his fingers in front of his lips. "An intriguing idea, Watson. It would have to be a person of influence. None of this has reached the morning papers."

"Except for your imprisonment."

"For a crime which I did not commit."

"I'm glad to hear it."

Holmes's hands dropped from his mouth. "You doubted my innocence, Watson?"

"Not for a moment. I simply can't see why Mrs Mercer would blacken your name."

"Fear that I was getting too close, maybe?"

"But she was your friend."

"She was my client, and a grateful one, I believed. She has a fascinating family history, you know?"

"In what way?"

"Her great-grandfather was originally from Africa."

"He was a slave?"

He nodded. "Apparently so. Transported first to the Caribbean, then to Bristol, where he was given his freedom."

"So she could have a grudge against Warwick." I snapped my fingers. "The library in the Lodge. According to Clifford it holds a ledger containing the name of every slave on Warwick's books."

Holmes dismissed the thought. "I find that hard to believe. Why would he take the trouble to record their names?"

"It's the only lead we have. If Mrs Mercer has a copy in her own library..."

"She is hardly likely to show us after your outburst, and we have no idea where this Lodge actually is."

"*Sanctum sanctorum.*"

"I beg your pardon?"

"That's what Clifford called the place."

"The holy of holies," Holmes mused, before checking his watch. "Well, it's getting late. I shall return tomorrow and request a visit to the Lodge."

"You're heading back to Bathampton then?"

"Of course not. I have rented a room near Temple Meads. My driver is another of Inspector Tovey's tramps, only too glad of a few shillings."

I found myself chuckling. "I just can't keep up with you, Holmes."

Holmes rose to his feet, but before he could reply a terrible scream echoed through Ridgeside Manor.

CHAPTER THIRTY-ONE

A GRISLY DISCOVERY

Holmes and I ran with all speed from the drawing room. The cry had come from the hall, where we found Lady Anna standing at the open door to Lord Redshaw's study. Her hands were at her mouth as she stared straight ahead. Holmes brushed past her, entering Lord Redshaw's private retreat.

I followed him in and gasped in horror.

Our host was lying on his side by a large writing desk, blood already soaking into the carpet.

"Let me see," I told Holmes, as my friend turned Redshaw onto his back. The man was out cold, a vivid gash on his temple.

"There's blood on the edge of the desk," said Holmes, using Sherrinford's voice. "He must have hit his head when he fell."

However, it was not the head wound that worried me. The front of Redshaw's waistcoat was slick with blood, and I removed it quickly to find his shirt similarly drenched.

Holmes watched as I unbuttoned Redshaw's shirt to reveal two stab wounds in his abdomen, fresh blood pumping out like water from a spring.

"Good L-Lord," said Clifford, who had appeared behind his wife. "W-what has happened?"

"Get the lady away," Holmes ordered.

"B-but—"

"And call for the driver," I added. "We'll need to get him to the hospital."

Clifford hovered where he was, paralysed with shock.

"Do it, man!"

"Y-yes, of c-course."

Lady Anna cried a plaintive "Papa" as Clifford pulled her away from the doorway, only for Sutcliffe to arrive in their stead. He rushed into the study, but I had no time to worry about an audience.

"We need to staunch the wounds."

Holmes had already removed his jacket and was unbuttoning his waistcoat.

"Do you have bandages?" he barked at Sutcliffe.

"I don't know…" the man stammered in reply.

"Then ask the servants!" Holmes said, Brewer having also appeared by the door.

They disappeared, but Holmes was already pulling at the seams of his waistcoat to use the material for dressings. Finding the stitching too tough to break he surveyed Lord Redshaw's desk, yanking open drawers to find a pair of scissors.

"Hurry!" I urged, as Holmes sliced the front panels from the waistcoat's silk back, and folded the navy material into squares.

He dropped to one knee beside me and whispered, "Let me see the wounds first. We need to know what the weapon was."

"There's no time!" I hissed back, snatching for the fabric. He held it tight for a second, his eyes locked on Lord Redshaw's torso, before finally releasing his hold.

I pressed the makeshift wadding over the wounds and pressed down hard as Brewer appeared by my side with bandages.

"Excellent," said I, instructing Holmes to keep pressure on the wound while I dressed Lord Redshaw's head. Clifford returned to tell me that Redshaw's driver Gordon was waiting outside. A crowd had gathered around the study door now, both family and servants, Lady Marie at the back, looking on with wide eyes.

With Holmes's help, I tied the wadding in place and buttoned up Redshaw's jacket to hold the dressing in place. Now came the real challenge.

"We're going to have to carry him to the carriage without aggravating the wound. I'll take the left arm, Sherrinford, you take his right. Sutcliffe and Clifford, you take his legs."

"You give the word, Doctor," Holmes said as everyone took their positions.

"Clear our path please, Brewer," I instructed the butler, before nodding towards my accomplices. "Everyone ready? Right, on three. One… two… three."

We moved as one, heaving Redshaw from the floor. The old man groaned, the pain rousing him.

"Brewer, take his head," I ordered, and the butler hurried around us to support his master's neck.

"Steady now," I said, as we carried Redshaw through the open door, his body a dead weight. "One step at a time."

The servants parted as we bore Lord Redshaw from his study into the hall. He started to move, squirming in our grip as we hurried as fast as we could to the front of the house.

Gordon had the carriage door open for us, and I asked him to take Lord Redshaw's arm as I jumped inside to guide my patient into the vestibule.

"Lay him on the floor," I advised.

"He won't fit," Sutcliffe argued. "We should sit him up."

"We need to keep the wounds level. Easy now."

Getting Redshaw on board was no easy task, but we managed

it. He moaned again, more weakly this time. I removed my jacket, folded it into a rough approximation of a pillow and slipped it beneath his bandaged head.

"I'll come with you," said Sutcliffe, jumping in beside me.

"Shouldn't you stay with Lady Marie?" I asked.

"We're coming too!" Lady Anna insisted.

"I shall bring the ladies in my carriage," Holmes said, gently adjusting Lord Redshaw's legs so he could shut the carriage door. "Get his Lordship to the hospital. We'll be right behind you."

Lord Redshaw made not a sound as the carriage pulled away from the front of the manor.

"Will he live?" Sutcliffe asked, staring down at the old man.

"He will if I have anything to do with it," I replied.

But as we sped through Clifton, Lord Redshaw arched his back and cried out in pain.

"No!" I shouted, dropping down beside him. "Lord Redshaw!"

"What's happening?"

"Myocardial infarction. His heart's giving up. Come on, Benjamin, stay with me. Not far to go now."

With Sutcliffe yelling for Gordon to speed up, I manoeuvred myself behind Lord Redshaw's head. I had to keep him breathing, although the only method I knew would play merry hell with his injuries.

Grabbing Redshaw's wrists, I drew his arms up to expand his chest, pressing them back down to his sides to compress the lungs again.

"What are you doing?" Sutcliffe asked.

"The Silvester Method. It draws air into the lungs."

"But his wounds…"

"Best not to think about what it's doing to them!"

What worried me most was that Redshaw, having again fallen silent, remained so even as I repeated the process over and over again. Was I going to lose him before we even reached the hospital?

Sutcliffe looked out of the window. "Why is it taking so long?"

"We'll get there when we get there," I said, more to calm myself than to comfort the young man. I was unable to shake the feeling that it was already too late and I was wasting my time trying to save Redshaw.

The driver called for help as we arrived at the hospital, and a gaggle of medical staff rushed out, led by none other than Dr Melosan.

"Dr Watson?"

"I hope you are not going to tell me I should be in bed," I told him as two porters lifted Lord Redshaw out of the carriage and put him on a stretcher. I jumped down, following them through the front doors. Melosan made no comment as I told him what I had done, merely thanking me before asking me to wait outside as Redshaw was whisked into the operating theatre.

I looked down at my hands, which were stained with blood. Had I done enough to save the man who had taken me in?

My hands screwed into fists as I made a decision. I was sick of having doors slammed in my face.

Holmes was rushing up the corridor towards me when I pushed my way into the operating theatre.

"Dr Watson?" Melosan exclaimed.

"I can help," I insisted, before my eyes went wide. Dr Melosan was standing in front of some kind of mechanical pump, a length of rubber tubing in his hand. "What on Earth do you think you're doing?"

"Says the man who bursts in unannounced on my theatre. I am preparing to make a transfusion, of course. Lord Redshaw has lost a lot of blood."

I could barely believe what I was hearing. Looking back, my horror seems strange, but you must understand that at this time, blood transfusions had fallen out of favour in most hospitals; the risks to patients were simply too great. The previous two decades had seen all manner of experiments: Germans had transfused pig's blood into humans, while the Americans had even tried cow's milk. Even when human blood was used, patients usually failed to survive the operating table.

"Shouldn't you be using a saline solution?" I suggested.

"Not in my hospital," Melosan insisted. "I must ask you to wait outside."

"I have no intention of doing that," I told him, rolling up my sleeve. "If you're going to do this, then you can use my blood."

"That's out of the question," Melosan argued. "You are suffering from concussion."

"B-but I am n-not," came a voice from behind. Clifford had entered the operating theatre and was already removing his jacket. "Whatever I t-think of Benjamin, he is my f-father-in-law. I would g-gladly donate the last drop in my veins if it would save him."

"Oh, very well," Melosan agreed. "Nurse, prepare Mr Clifford, but I must have silence."

Behind us Anna had followed her husband into the theatre and was sobbing uncontrollably.

"Lady Anna," I said, stopping her from rushing to her father. "You must wait outside."

"I can't," she cried.

"We must," said Holmes.

"Thank you," said Dr Melosan as we ushered her out into the corridor. I glanced back to see a needle being inserted into Clifford's arm.

The doors shut behind me and we were led by a nurse to a hard wooden bench where we waited. Lady Anna sobbed quietly into her handkerchief the whole time, while her sister sat a little way off with a face like flint. She had shed not a single tear since her arrival, and she shrugged off every attempt Sutcliffe made to comfort her.

"Leave me alone," Marie finally snapped, standing abruptly. "What are you doing here at all?"

"I am to be your husband," he reminded her.

"No longer," she barked back. "Get away from me. I don't want to see you ever again."

The man stood, trying to grab her arm, telling her that she was hysterical. She pulled away angrily, nearly barging into the nurse who was rushing forward to calm the situation.

"Please," the nurse said. "This is a hospital. If you cannot act with decorum, I must ask you to leave."

"Then leave I will," Lady Marie said, storming away. Anna rose, calling after her sister, but Marie refused to stop.

"Go after her," I told Sutcliffe, but Marie's spurned suitor had obviously had enough.

"No, she has made her decision. If you need me, I will be at the club."

"What club? Sutcliffe, wait."

Anna put a hand on my arm. "No, leave them, Dr Watson. They deserve each other. Father is all that is important. If anything should happen to him, and to Clifford too..."

The tears returned. I comforted her as well as I could and after a while she grew calm.

There we sat, until Holmes drew me aside under the pretence of giving the lady some room.

"A curious turn of events, Watson," he whispered when he was sure we were in no danger of being overheard.

"Is that all you can say? The man will probably die."

"You did your best for him, I am sure. But the real question must be why?"

"Why I tried to save him?"

"Why he needed saving at all. Tell me, who would want Lord Redshaw dead?"

CHAPTER THIRTY-TWO

SUSPECTS

"Surely you don't suspect Lady Anna," I said, as Holmes stared at Redshaw's daughter through his monocle. Anna looked so vulnerable as she sat on the bench alone, desperately trying to compose herself.

"Until the murderer is found, everyone in the house is a suspect, Watson."

"She is devoted to her father," I insisted.

"And her husband?"

I considered this. "There's certainly something between Clifford and the old man. When we were away from the manor, Clifford's stutter all but vanished, and yet as soon as he was in Redshaw's presence, not to mention that of Sutcliffe…"

"Interesting, although the stutter might have been amplified by the stress of being discovered breaking you into the Lodge."

"We hardly broke in. Clifford had a key."

"Which he stole from Redshaw. No wonder there would be a level of awkwardness."

"No, it goes deeper than that. Redshaw puts Clifford down at every opportunity. Their relationship is fraught to say the least."

"Enough to commit murder?"

"The thing is, Holmes, why stab the man and then put yourself through a blood transfusion?"

"A guilty conscience? Regret?"

That made sense, at least. Clifford had made the snap decision to take me to the Lodge. What if he had acted on impulse in the study?

"His wife would be set to inherit a small fortune," I said.

"Surely the majority of the estate would go to the elder daughter."

"Marie? She's a troubled one, that girl."

"Evidently."

"I caught her crying in the drawing room, just before you arrived."

"An unhappy love affair, perhaps? The relationship between the lady and her intended is far from a healthy one."

"I have seen little warmth between them since Lord Redshaw took me in. Or between the lady and her father for that matter."

"Another suspect, then?"

"His own daughter?"

"And what of this Sutcliffe?"

"I'm not fond of the man, I can tell you that."

"But was Lord Redshaw?"

"There's certainly a bond there. Redshaw respects the young man's business."

"Importing curios from the Orient."

"The late Lady Redshaw was a devotee of all things Japanese, apparently. And then there's the business about the spells, although that is all stuff and nonsense, if you ask me. Clifford is obviously a trifle jealous of the attention Redshaw lavishes on Sutcliffe."

"Jealous or not, it is an intoxicating mix. Mysticism and murder from the Far East."

I raised an eyebrow at the detective, still in disguise. "And you say that *I* am the melodramatic one."

"Either way, it seems that Sutcliffe and Lord Redshaw are as thick as thieves."

"Yes, but he did become quite animated at the suggestion that Redshaw should try to have you released from prison."

"Did he now? So it could be any of them."

"But what I don't understand is why we heard nothing until Lady Anna screamed."

"The door to the study is thick and might have muffled the sounds of a struggle."

"True. I could barely hear through it earlier."

"Snooping around, Watson? I have never been more proud. The window in the study was locked from the inside, so the attacker must have come through the door, surprising Lord Redshaw. He turned, rising from the chair, and received the first blow to his stomach. The attacker pulled out the weapon and stabbed again; Lord Redshaw fell, knocking himself senseless against the desk. The attack must have been swift, the assailant leaving the way he came in. On the journey here, Lady Anna told me that she noticed that the door was ajar, which is not her father's custom. She went to close it and saw him sprawled on the floor. Either that, or she committed the crime herself and merely backed out of the room before screaming."

"It was all an act, you mean."

"The flaw in that theory is that the lady had no trace of blood on her. None of them did. Without the weapon itself, I am reduced to conjecture, but at first glance I could see no sign of it, either in the room or the hallway outside."

"It could be outside, if the assailant escaped through the window."

"Indeed. I checked briefly before the carriage left, but could see nothing by moonlight. And of course, there is every chance the attacker took it with him. Not every villain is so considerate as to leave bloodstained evidence lying around. However, we do have the wounds."

"What about them?"

"On the second blow, the knife was thrust with sufficient force to bury the blade to the hilt."

"How can you tell?"

"The bruising around the wound."

"Suggesting an assailant of considerable strength."

"Unless the blade itself was exceptionally sharp, which is a distinct possibility."

"But if it isn't, you're saying that the attacker had to be a man."

"I'm saying nothing of the sort. They may be *called* the fairer sex, but there are plenty of physically adept women in this world, especially in service. However, I concede that neither Marie nor Anna would appear at first glance to possess the required strength."

"But Lord Redshaw could have been attacked by a servant?"

"Quite possibly. Indeed, the shape of the wounds is of interest."

Holmes pulled a notebook and a stubby pencil from his pocket and drew the wounds from memory. They looked like two teardrops running horizontally along the page.

"See the corners, Watson. One rounded, while the other has a distinct point. That suggests a one-sided knife; one edge sharp and the other dull."

"A kitchen implement?"

"Possibly. If only I had stayed behind to check the kitchens."

"Sherrinford Holmes is supposed to be a landowner," I reminded him, "not a detective."

"Come now, Watson. All it would take is to become lost in the house and end up below stairs by accident."

"Would you even know what you were looking for?"

"I shall remind you that I am not the one who suffered a blow to the head today. Even allowing for the elasticity of Lord Redshaw's skin, the blade must be only two inches wide."

Our conversation was interrupted by the reappearance of Dr Melosan, rolling down his shirtsleeves. Lady Anna rose as he approached.

"Papa?" she said, steepling her fingers in front of her mouth as if beseeching the Almighty. "Is he—"

"Alive, and as stable as can be expected, thanks largely to the ministrations of Dr Watson."

I acknowledged the compliment and asked after my host's injuries.

"The knife wounds were deep, but clean," came the reply. "Both have been stitched, and we will monitor for infection or signs of internal bleeding."

"And his heart?"

"Lord Redshaw's pulse is weak but steady. We've given him morphine for the pain, and must now wait and see."

"But he will live?" Anna begged him.

The grey-haired doctor turned to the lady and gave her a sad smile. "We will do everything we can. I suggest you go home and try to rest. Your husband will need to recover following the transfusion."

"May we speak with Lord Redshaw?" I asked, eliciting a frown from Melosan.

"He is sleeping…"

"Which is understandable, but we need to know who did this to him."

"I'm sure the *police* will want to speak to him when he wakes."

"And when will that be?" Anna asked.

"Impossible to tell, I'm afraid. He is still very weak, so it may be some time, but rest assured that we will take good care of him. Now, if you have no other questions?"

"I do," piped up Holmes.

"Yes?" said Melosan, peering at my friend, the only member of our small group whom he did not know.

"Your tattoo. Where was it done?"

"I beg your pardon?"

"The tattoo on your forearm. I spotted it as you were rolling down your sleeve, a narrow band encircling your arm like a cuff. Most striking."

"I hardly think this is the time to be discussing tattoos," Lady Anna said, gathering her things. "I must go to my husband."

"Quite so," replied Holmes. "I apologise. It's just that I have been thinking about having one done myself. They are quite the fashion now that the Prince of Wales has visited the tattooist's chair. Eddie is such a trendsetter, always has been."

Melosan was staring in confusion at my friend, rubbing his forearm as he replied, "An associate of mine dabbles with the inks, but I'm afraid his is not a public enterprise."

"Ah well, thank you all the same," Holmes said. "Maybe next time I am in London."

Taking his leave of us, Dr Melosan called over a nurse to take us to Clifford.

"What was all that about?" I hissed as we followed her.

"What was what?" Holmes replied, innocently.

"All the nonsense about tattoos and what-not? Prince Edward hasn't really got one, has he?"

"His Majesty? Why yes. A Jerusalem Cross. His mother is not amused. And where the Prince of Wales goes, the aristocracy follow, although I was surprised to see a Bristol doctor following the trend. And as for Lord Redshaw..."

"Redshaw?"

"I spotted it as he was being prepared for the transfusion, on his left arm. Two rings this time, compared with the doctor's one. Definitely the work of the same artist."

Ahead of us, Lady Anna had quickened her pace, reaching her husband who was slumped in a chair in the corridor ahead. The poor chap looked drained, quite literally.

"Oh, Harold. What you did for Papa. So brave."

"Yes," I agreed. "Well done, old chap."

Clifford smiled at me weakly. "N-not used to being the h-hero. I quite l-like it."

"Let's get you home," I said.

"Are you sure we should leave Papa?" Anna asked.

"There's nothing else we can do here. Your father needs rest, as do you."

"That may not be an option," Holmes commented, nodding down the corridor.

We turned to see Inspector Hawthorne marching towards us.

CHAPTER THIRTY-THREE

UPSTAIRS AND DOWNSTAIRS

The police inspector insisted on accompanying us all back to Ridgeside Manor, Holmes included. It was amusing to see him treating my disguised friend with such respect, unaware that he was the very same man he had falsely imprisoned.

Lady Marie had already left for the house, having hailed a hansom. Of Sutcliffe there was no sign, so the rest of us bundled into our carriages and returned to the manor.

Back at the house, Hawthorne gathered us all in the drawing room, taking statements and asking questions. He then asked me to show him where the body had been found and I, of course, obliged, Holmes dogging our footsteps.

"What a shame my brother is not here," Holmes commented as the inspector examined the now dried blood on the desk and the carpet. Hawthorne ignored the jibe, running through the course of events once again. As I answered his questions, I could see Holmes wandering around the study, hands thrust in pockets, feigning a casual interest in the maps and paintings on Lord Redshaw's walls. I knew all too well that it was an act, and that those sharp eyes would be sweeping the room for clues.

The inspector closed his notebook and, slipping it into his inside pocket, rattled the window in its frame.

"Locked, from the inside," he commented. "Meaning the attacker must have struck from within."

"You should interview the staff," Holmes commented, turning to smile at Brewer. The butler had been waiting patiently in the corridor outside with a look of disgust that strangers were abroad in his master's private refuge.

"That's exactly what I intend to do, Mr Holmes," Hawthorne replied.

"My apologies," Holmes said. "I'm teaching my granny to suck eggs. You don't read Chinese, do you, Inspector?"

Hawthorne looked confused at the sudden change of subject. "I beg your pardon?"

"Chinese," Holmes said, pointing at a small frame at the wall. It contained two ornate letters in an oriental language, painted impeccably in black on yellow paper.

Hawthorne looked at the calligraphy and sniffed. "I'm afraid I don't, not that it would help. That's Japanese."

"Japanese?" Holmes exclaimed. "I'm impressed. Do you know what it says?"

"I'm afraid not. Now, if you'd excuse me…"

"Yes, you have work to do, of course," Holmes said, indicating that Hawthorne should take the door.

"No, please," replied Hawthorne, standing his ground. "After you!"

Holmes smiled politely as he was ejected from the study, stopping to address the butler. "Mr Brewer, the hour is late and I fear that my hosts in Bathampton will have retired already. Might I trouble you for a bed tonight?"

"I will check with Lady Anna," the butler intoned, before leading the inspector away.

"Did you hear that, Watson?" Holmes whispered as we watched them go. "He'll check with Anna, not Marie."

"I told you. Anna does seem to run the household. Marie shows very little interest."

Holmes waited for the coast to become clear before he quickly reopened the door closed by Hawthorne moments before.

"What are you doing?"

"Stop gaping and come in," I was told, Holmes shutting the door behind me.

"What if we're caught?"

Holmes removed one of his cufflinks and tossed it across the room. "I'll say we were looking for that."

He began stalking around the room, pointing at the oriental writing in the frame as he passed. "Interesting that Hawthorne could identify that as Japanese."

"I'm surprised you didn't know the difference."

Holmes sighed. "Of course I did, Watson. The question is, how did Hawthorne? Everyone seems obsessed with the Land of the Rising Sun around here."

"What does it say then?"

"*Saisei.*"

"And what is that?"

"Rebirth, or the return to life."

"Resurrection, you mean. Like Christ."

"Most cultures have resurrection myths, gods springing back to life."

"Like Izanami and Izanabi for the Japanese."

Holmes looked at me in amazement. "Watson, I am impressed. I had no idea you were such a scholar of Eastern mythology."

"Oh, I'm not. Sutcliffe told us the story over dinner, Izanabi venturing into the Underworld to rescue his wife."

"Did he now? Perhaps he is less familiar with the legend than he thought."

"How so?"

"It is Izana*gi* not *bi*. Izanagi-no-Mikoto."

"Anyone can make a mistake, I suppose."

"And my mistake was letting everyone in here," Holmes commented, hands on his hips as he looked down at the carpet. "This room has seen more footfall than the Great Exhibition this afternoon, with the world and his wife tramping in and out."

He crouched down by the door and pointed towards a minute stain on the carpet. "But look at this!"

"What is it?" I said, joining him. "Soil?"

Holmes rubbed a finger across the stain and then brought it to his nose. He took one decisive sniff.

"No. Boot blacking."

He stood, scanning the rest of the carpet. "But no trace of it elsewhere. This is where it would have happened, Watson, the struggle between Lord Redshaw and his assailant. If the fellow had blacking trapped in the treads of his shoe, it might have been ground into the carpet as they tussled."

Recovering his discarded cufflink, Holmes went to the door and, opening it, stepped outside.

"No sign of it out here either."

I followed him into the hall and he closed the door behind me.

"Could it not have come from Redshaw's own shoes?"

"Lord Redshaw was dressed for dinner. He was wearing black shoes. That shade of blacking could only have been intended for brown shoes. Now, correct me if I am wrong, but no one in the house was wearing brown footwear tonight."

I was forced to admit that I had no way of confirming or refuting his statement.

"Because you see, Watson, but never observe. Now, I admit it is hardly compelling evidence, but it does spark a thought."

Holmes said no more, but set off in the direction Hawthorne had gone, disappearing through the door that led below stairs.

"Where are you going?" I hissed after him, giving chase. I found him at the foot of the stairs, surprising a footman.

"Sir, may I be of assistance?"

"Who repairs the boots in this house?" Holmes asked.

"I beg your pardon, sir?"

"It's a simple enough question. Lord Redshaw's boots, who repairs them?"

The kerfuffle drew Brewer out of his office, where he was being interviewed by Inspector Hawthorne.

"What's going on here?" The butler's eyebrows nearly shot through the roof to see guests of the family in the domain of the servants. "Mr Holmes? Dr Watson?"

Holmes raised a placating hand. "I'm sorry, Brewer, I didn't mean to disturb you. My right shoe is in need of a little repair, that's all."

"The hall boy can see to that when you've gone to bed, sir," Brewer said, Hawthorne appearing behind him to peer at Holmes in puzzlement.

"No need to trouble him," said Holmes. "Cobbling is an occasional hobby of mine. My own man at home is appalled, but what can I say, it relaxes me. Just show me to the lad's tools and I can help myself. I promised Dr Watson I would show him how to trim a sole, you see."

"This is most irregular—" Brewer began, until Hawthorne interrupted him.

"Mr Brewer, I still have questions. If the gentleman wants to mend his own shoes, let him do so, for heaven's sake."

Looking as if he were living through the end days, Brewer

ordered the footman to show us where the hall boy kept his tools.

We were guided to the workroom by the equally perplexed footman. Holmes thanked him cheerfully and closed the door behind him. Once we were alone, he crossed over to the table that housed the hall boy's stash of dubbin and brushes. Holmes rummaged through the various pots and bottles, discarding them one by one.

"No, not that one. Nor that."

"What are you looking for?"

"The right shade, of course."

"Isn't it just black?"

Holmes looked at me as if I had just questioned his parentage. "Watson, have you not read my monograph, *The Difference in Shade and Texture of 170 Brands of American and European Boot Blacking*?"

"I can't say that I have."

"Remind me to provide you with a copy when we return to London. The blacking found in the study is obviously the product of Cole and Company of Fetter Lane, London."

"Obviously," I said, as if such a fact should be clear for anyone to see.

"Cole's Blacking is a popular brand, sold as a paste in a pot, whereas this household prefers the wares of Robert Burrows of the Strand, sold as liquid in a bottle."

"So the blacking did not come from Ridgeside Manor?"

Holmes paused, tapping a finger against the table. "I wonder how Mr Sutcliffe has his boots polished?"

His eyes fell on the hall boy's tools of the trade, a series of knives and scrapers. He first picked up a wooden knife, much like a narrow spatula.

"I wonder..." he repeated.

"What?" I asked, as Holmes continued his exploration of the

work area. I picked up the wooden implement that Holmes had already discarded. "You don't think Lord Redshaw was stabbed with something like this?"

"Not the wooden knife. That is used for scraping excess polish from a boot, the wood soft so there's no danger of damaging the leather. As you can plainly see, the shape is quite wrong. And besides, the pressure required to puncture skin with such an instrument would be immense."

"You did say the knife was embedded to the hilt."

"A hilt which that knife does not possess. No, I believe we are looking for something such as this."

He presented me with a second implement, this one boasting a metal blade and a handle carved from beech. "Single-sided, for the trimming of leather."

"Single-sided like the knife that stabbed Lord Redshaw!"

"Clearly," said he, taking back the tool. "The point has been clipped from the tip of the blade, which is sharpened on only one edge. Four and a half inches, which means that Lord Redshaw's additional girth around the waist saved his life. Had he been a lean man the blade would have struck an internal organ. And before you ask, this is not the murder weapon. The only stains upon its hilt are those of grubby fingerprints rather than Redshaw's lifeblood."

I raised a hand to stop him. "But wait a minute. You're saying a cobbler stabbed him?"

"I'm saying it is a possibility. The wound matches the weapon."

"Then why the bootblack? A cobbler wouldn't be polishing shoes. That's the work of children, not skilled men."

"Any cobbler worth his salt will polish the shoes after a repair or have a boy to do it for him. All it takes is a smashed pot, the paste ground into the tread of the cobbler's shoes by accident."

"It seems rather a stretch to me."

"And yet it is all I have to go on. For now, at least."

There was a knock on the door. Holmes slipped the knife back into its box.

"Yes?"

The door opened to reveal a sour-faced Brewer. "I was wondering if you would be requiring any supper, sir. Inspector Hawthorne has been called away, and the ladies are retiring to bed."

"That would be splendid, Brewer," Holmes said cheerfully in Sherrinford's deep voice. "I'm positively famished. Watson, what say you?"

I shook my head. "I wouldn't have the stomach for it, not after everything that has happened."

"I shall dine alone then, Brewer," said Holmes, breezing past the butler. "Some sandwiches would be splendid. Ham if you have it, with a dash of pickle. Delicious. I shall be up in the drawing room."

Offering Brewer an apologetic smile, I followed, leaving the bottles of blacking on the table behind me.

CHAPTER THIRTY-FOUR

A BITTER BREAKFAST

The rest of the evening proved uneventful. Holmes's request to stay had little to do with his imaginary hosts; he wanted to search for more clues. With the rest of the family gone to bed, he had ample opportunity, although I myself was struggling to keep my eyes open. The combination of my exertions with Lord Redshaw and the injury I had suffered at the Lodge had sapped what was left of my natural resources. I made my apologies as Holmes tucked into his supper, and retired to the Tombo Room, falling into a deep sleep the moment I crawled into my bed.

My sleep was restless, however, beleaguered by dreams in which I ran through an endless maze of stained-glass windows, only to find Lord Redshaw at the heart of the labyrinth, liquid blacking oozing from deep wounds in his belly.

I woke early and descended for breakfast to find that I was first to the dining room. I was ravenous, a good sign after my trauma, and so was tucking into a plate of scrambled eggs when Lady Anna and Clifford joined me. I rose as they entered, noting a certain redness around Anna's eyes, understandable given the circumstances.

Clifford looked better, the colour returning to his podgy cheeks.

Before long, Holmes also joined us, dressed as his apocryphal brother. He loaded his plate high with kippers and set about his breakfast with enthusiasm.

"Will Lady Marie not be joining us?" he asked, his mouth full of salted fish.

Anna made no attempt to disguise her scorn. "Why should she? She has made her feelings abundantly clear. She is probably lounging in bed, waiting for Papa to die."

"Anna!" Clifford said, looking more than a little abashed. "You're em-embarrassing our g-guest. Such talk at the b-breakfast table."

Holmes dismissed the concern with a wave of his fish knife. "It is only natural that passions are running high." He paused, chewing thoughtfully. "Of course, if your father were to die—"

"Holmes!" I interjected, confounded by his tactlessness. He looked at me as if *I*, not he, had crossed the line of decency.

"At times of crisis, one needs to remain pragmatic, Doctor. I was about to say that if the worst were to happen, Lord Redshaw's fortune would pass to Lady Marie."

Lady Anna's tired eyes were wide as saucers. "What are you suggesting?"

"Nothing at all," Holmes insisted. "I am merely stating facts of business. I apologise if I have caused offence. It is the landowner in me, I suppose. Marie is the elder child, is she not?"

"She is."

"Then I would be not at all surprised if young Mr Sutcliffe were to come a-calling today."

"I th-think we've seen the last of him," Clifford insisted, taking a sip of coffee.

Holmes continued to needle away. "I wouldn't be so sure. He seems a tenacious young man, and his betrothed is about to become an exceedingly wealthy woman."

That was the last straw. Anna rose abruptly, her chair skidding back. "How dare you! My father is lying in hospital and you talk as if he is already gone. You must think me exceedingly foolish not to know the measure of Victor Sutcliffe. He has sniffed around my sister like a dog foraging for scraps, but if the worst happens – and I pray to God that it does not – he will not see a penny."

Now Clifford chimed in. "It's true that Marie hasn't l-lifted a finger to help r-run the house since Lucy passed away. It has been down to my w-wife."

"Which Lord Redshaw clearly knows," I said, desperate to smooth the troubled waters. "He is exceptionally proud of you."

"I should hope so," Anna said, throwing down her napkin. "Now, I suggest you enjoy the rest of your breakfast, and leave."

Clifford's mouth dropped open. "My d-dear, after everything Dr Watson d-did for your f-father last nuh-night…"

"I am not talking about the doctor," Anna replied, her eyes positively boring into Holmes, before she stormed from the room. Clifford apologised and chased after her like a loyal puppy.

The dining room was quiet except for the scrape of Holmes's knife and fork on his plate.

I stared at him, astounded. "How could you, *Sherrinford*?"

Holmes dabbed at his lips with a napkin. "I appear to have outstayed my welcome. The lady has made her feelings known and I must abide by them. I shall leave at once."

"And go where?"

"To the prison of course, to visit my dear brother. You will accompany me, Watson?"

I should have refused, but the thought of remaining in such a poisonous atmosphere was unbearable.

Half an hour later, we were rattling towards the gates of the estate in Holmes's carriage. Holmes sat staring ahead, at least showing the decency to wait until we were out of the grounds before throwing back his head and roaring with mirth.

"I don't see what there is to laugh about," said I.

"You should have seen your face, Watson. The very picture of outrage."

"I should think so. I've never been so mortified in all my life. What were you thinking, man?"

"I was wondering how far I could push the Cliffords before they told me what I wanted to know. Did you see the way she was standing, Watson?"

"It was difficult to ignore!"

"A hand over the child she is carrying. The legacy of the Redshaw line. She knows all too well that by rights the house should go to Marie, but as long as Marie remains unmarried and without child, the cards are stacked in Anna's favour."

"But you discounted both Lady Anna and Clifford as suspects."

"I did no such thing, I merely said that it was unlikely. I doubt it was Sutcliffe, however. Whether he was angry that Lord Redshaw was considering coming to my aid or not, if he is the gold-digger that Lady Anna suggests, surely he would wait until the ring were on Marie's finger?"

"Unless he hoped to hurry Marie on. She has yet to set the date for their wedding."

"A wedding that you said Lord Redshaw supports wholeheartedly, almost as if Sutcliffe has him under a spell…"

"You think she's being forced into it?"

"It would explain the antagonism she displayed to both her father and her betrothed. From what you have told me it is clear that Ridgeside was an unhappy house long before Lord Redshaw was attacked."

"But what of the blacking on the study carpet? How does that fit with your theories?"

"That, my dear Watson, is a very good question."

"And where shall we find a good answer?"

"At our destination, I hope."

"The police station?"

Holmes smiled. "Oh my dear chap, you of all people should be able to tell the difference between fact and fiction. We are not bound for the station."

"Then where are we going?"

Holmes made no reply. Instead he leaned forward and removed his right shoe. I watched in perplexity as he turned the shoe over and, producing a penknife from his pocket, proceeded to prise off the heel.

"Whatever are you doing, Holmes?"

"One question at a time, Watson. You asked where we are going. Why, to the scene of my crime, of course."

CHAPTER THIRTY-FIVE

ST JUDE'S

"Have you gone quite mad?" I spluttered, as the carriage pulled up outside the Bristol Regent Hotel. "I thought I, not you, had taken a blow to the head."

"Come now, Doctor," said my friend as he slipped the now ruined shoe back onto his foot. "Sherrinford Holmes has nothing to fear in this particular establishment."

Jumping from the cab, Holmes hauled himself up the front steps, his affected limp more pronounced than ever thanks to the heel that flapped away from his sole. I myself paused, remembering all too well my last visit to the Regent. I could imagine the reception I would receive, but Holmes was already inside. Taking a deep breath, I proceeded after him.

Mrs Mercer spotted me the instant I was through the revolving doors. Her face paled and it looked as though she was caught between the urge to fight and the desire to flee. I would have preferred the latter, but instead she strode from the reception desk towards me, bustling past the disguised Holmes.

"I am surprised to see you here, Dr Watson," she said *sotto voce* as she stopped me in my tracks, "but unless you have come to apologise, I must ask you to leave. I have no desire to engage in more unpleasantness."

"Nor do we, dear lady," said Holmes in his false baritone. She turned quizzically.

"I beg your pardon?"

Holmes bowed his head. "My name is Sherrinford Holmes, and while I understand you have a quarrel with my unscrupulous brother, I hope to throw myself on your mercy."

As she looked upon him, dumbfounded, Holmes simply lifted his right foot to display the heel flapping like a dog's tongue.

"As you can see, my shoe has suffered some unfortunate damage. As we were passing, Dr Watson mentioned that the Regent employs its own cobbler. I was wondering if your man could save my sole."

Mrs Mercer shook her head as if her ears were deceiving her. "Dr Watson brought you here, of all places?"

Holmes nodded. "He did. He is too proud to say it, but the poor chap is consumed with regret for his past actions."

I opened my mouth to complain, before a sharp glare from Mrs Mercer persuaded me to shut it again. "So he should be; but while I have no argument with you, Mr Holmes, I'm afraid I must disappoint you. There are plenty of cobblers in Bristol. The concierge will be more than delighted to furnish you with a list."

"I am willing to pay for the inconvenience. I would not expect your man to work for nothing."

"I'm glad to hear it, but my answer remains the same. I'm afraid Powell isn't in today."

"Powell? Is that your cobbler?"

"He is, yes."

"Then perhaps you could provide me with his address? Perhaps he undertakes private commissions?"

"He does nothing of the sort," Mrs Mercer replied, her temper threatening to boil over. "And even if he did, he is at home, quite unwell."

"Oh, I'm sorry to hear that. Cobbler's femur?"

"I beg your pardon?"

"I read about it in *The Times*. Something to do with the constant pounding of leather on one's lap. I'm sure Dr Watson could explain it better?" He looked to me, his eyes shining with amusement.

I shook my head, reluctant to be drawn into the conversation. Fortunately, Mrs Mercer brought the debate to a swift conclusion.

"Nelson is suffering from influenza."

"Your cobbler."

"Yes. Now if you would excuse me—"

Mrs Mercer was interrupted by the sight of a young lady rushing through the reception area towards the doors.

"Lady Marie?" I said, as Lord Redshaw's daughter dashed past. The lady made no response, not even turning at her name. Instead she plunged through the revolving doors as if running for her life.

Mrs Mercer regained her composure and attempted to guide Holmes and myself towards the concierge. Holmes, however, had other plans.

"Come, Watson," he said, limping towards the exit. "Mrs Mercer is quite correct. There are plenty of cobblers in town. Thank you kindly, madam."

"What the blazes?" I asked when we were both safely through the doors.

Holmes whistled for his carriage and, after a word with his tramp-turned-driver, we were off.

"Well?" I demanded, as the cab rocked to and fro.

"Cole's Blacking," he replied.

"The stuff from Lord Redshaw's study? What about it?"

"It's the brand favoured by the Regent. Pots of the stuff were on display alongside the advertisement for Mr Powell's services to the Regent's patrons: 'Shoes repaired and polished. A complete service.' Surely you recognised the label?"

"Why would I?" I exclaimed. "Besides, did you not say it was a popular brand?"

"Indeed I did."

"So surely it must be favoured by boot-blacks on every street corner. Why make your way straight to the Regent?"

"Because every investigation has to start somewhere. And besides, if we hadn't visited the Regent we would not now be following Lady Marie Redshaw."

"We are?" I said, thrusting my head out of the window. Sure enough, another of Lord Redshaw's carriages with its recognisable yellow trim was speeding ahead. Holmes's driver kept a safe distance, so not to alert Marie's man to the fact that we were in pursuit. "Where the devil is she heading?"

"To the wrong side of town," Holmes said, removing the heels from both shoes to balance his gait.

The road narrowed as we descended into the dark heart of Bristol, crumbling tenement buildings clustered together as if crowding for warmth.

"St Jude's," Holmes explained as I covered my nose with the back of my hand. As in all great cities, the physical boundaries between rich and poor in Bristol were wafer thin. We had travelled no more than two miles and already the cobbles had become uneven beneath the carriage's wheels. Ragged children stood on every street corner, their eyes hollow with hunger, holding out bunches of wilting cress or matchboxes, desperate to earn a few pennies.

We sped on, passing not only the destitute, but also Lady Marie's carriage.

"Holmes, she has stopped."

"And so shall we; although Rawnsey knows better than to come crashing to a halt behind a quarry, even if you do not. Really, Watson. You must learn to engage that brain of yours! How you survived a war I shall never know."

Trying hard not to take offence, I fumed as the driver brought us to a stop. Holmes was across the road before I had even exited the carriage. I did likewise and saw Holmes slip a shiny coin into the palm of a street urchin.

"What was that?" I asked, as the girl scampered into a nearby porch.

"That was a child," Holmes replied. "Your powers of observation decline by the second."

"The money," I growled.

"A transaction. According to my grubby-faced informant, Lady Marie vanished into Parson's Close."

"Are you sure?" I said, eyeing the cesspit of an alleyway with suspicion. "Why would she come here, of all places?"

"Why indeed?" Holmes said, disappearing into the gloomy lane.

My boots squelched in thick mud as I followed Holmes into Parson's Close. At least I chose to believe it was mud. As we ventured deeper into the maze of passageways, tenements all but blocked out the sun on either side of us.

"She came this way," Holmes insisted, following a path through the muck that only he could see.

"How do you know?" I asked, having long since lost my sense of direction.

"Her dress has left a clear trail in the mud."

"I'll take your word for it."

But I could see for myself the tableau that greeted us as we turned a corner. Lady Marie was pinned against a wall, a blackened hand around her neck.

CHAPTER THIRTY-SIX

BOYLE'S COURT

The thug with his hand around Lady Marie's throat glared at us as we froze in place. He was a big man, in a jacket and trousers that had more holes than one of my theories. His face was unshaven, a patch across one eye and a deep scar where a left ear should be.

I have no doubt that Holmes would have sprinted to Marie's aid, if not for the knife the villain held in his other hand, its point at her belly.

"Let her go," I demanded, but the man's palm remained locked around Marie's thin neck. The miscreant stared back at us like a cornered fox. He looked as though he were uncertain whether to run or stand his ground. We too hesitated. There was no way of knowing what the man would do to Lady Marie if we made the wrong choice.

"Now listen," Holmes said, one hand raised towards the fellow while the other clutched his cane. "No one wants any trouble…"

"S'at right?" the brute growled in reply, showing a mouth largely untroubled by teeth. His one good eye flicked between Holmes and me. "Leave us be then. This ain't got nuffink to do with you."

"You know we can't do that," Holmes said. "Besides, what would stop us going straight to the authorities?"

The monster laughed, a thick ugly sound. "Authorities? You mean the police? Police don't comes round here. No one comes round here; not fancy folk like thee, nor pretty things like this. And even if they does, they'll never find I, not in a million years."

What the rascal said may well have been true, but they would certainly have heard his howl of pain and surprise as Lady Marie brought her knee up sharply into his unmentionables. He stumbled forward, but not far enough to send him sprawling into the mud as Marie tried to push him aside. Instead he turned, and for a moment I thought he was about to drive the knife into her side. He would have done so too, had Holmes not launched his cane at the degenerate with all the skill and strength of a Greek athlete. It soared through the air like a javelin, its rounded head hitting the scoundrel in the temple. He cried out, dropping his knife. Holmes sprang like a wildcat, barging the man away from Lady Marie. The two of them crashed to the ground in a mass of splayed limbs and clenched fists. The thug gained the upper hand and was on top of Holmes in an instant. He raised his block-like fist, ready to slam it into Holmes's face, but he had forgotten about my presence. I hooked the crooked end of my own cane's handle around the fiend's elbow and pulled hard. He lost his balance and tumbled back, giving Holmes the opportunity to grab a fragment of brick from the mud, cracking it hard into the side of the man's head. The blow toppled the brute to the side, but such was the thickness of the lout's skull that still he made a grab for Holmes as he fell. Holmes delivered a well-aimed punch to the man's jaw and the thug lay still.

Breathing heavily, Holmes straddled his fallen foe, arm raised to deliver another blow, but when it was clear that the man was staying down, he turned to Lady Marie.

"We need to get you out of here," he said, wiping his hands together as if that could clear half the muck that smothered him from head to toe.

"No," she replied, taking a step back as if Holmes were her attacker rather than her saviour.

"Lady Marie, I don't think you understand the danger you are in," I said, shooting a glance at the unconscious brute to make sure he was not already coming around.

"What are you doing here?" she said, looking at us from one to the other.

"A question we might also ask you," Holmes said.

"You must leave," she insisted.

"We shall do nothing of the sort," I told her. "Unless you come with us."

"I cannot," she said.

"Then we have reached something of an impasse," observed Holmes.

Marie looked to us and then to the man who had assaulted her. It was clear she realised that she could neither persuade us to leave her nor escape our protection, so instead she chose the third option.

"Can I trust you?" she said finally.

"With your life," I assured her.

She opened her hand and we saw for the first time that there was a piece of paper crumpled in her palm. She handed it to me and I read the words written in the clear, neat handwriting of an educated woman.

Mrs Protheroe, 3 Boyle's Court,
off Parson's Close, St Jude's

"This is whom you have come to see?" I asked, and the lady nodded. "But why?"

"Will you come with me?" she asked.

"Of course," Holmes said, "but I suggest we hurry before our friend awakes."

We hurried away from the unconscious villain. The turn of a corner had us walking through a low-roofed passage. A couple of washerwomen approached from the other direction, regarding us with understandable suspicion.

"Excuse my appearance, ladies," Holmes said, as if the state of his coat were any worse than the threadbare clothes on their own hunched backs, "but I wondered if you could direct us towards Boyle's Court."

The broader of the two women, her grubby face a cluster of hairy warts, sniffed. "Boyle's Court? Just round the corner, sir."

"Thank you," said Holmes, slipping her a coin.

"Much obliged to you, sir," she said, tugging at her scarf and hurrying on, no doubt to tell her entire brood that strangers were abroad. I gripped my cane all the more tightly, convinced that a pack of wolves were about to descend upon us, ready to relieve us of the contents of our wallets.

The crone's word had been good, however. Boyle's Court was exactly where she had said, a square of abominable land between four imposing buildings. The few windows that pitted the rough walls were caked with grime, brown paper and rags stuffed roughly into cracks in the glass to keep as much warmth as possible within the tenements. If the stink of the alleyway had been bad, the fetid reek of the court was unbearable. A privy was situated beside a water pump, and my stomach lurched as I spotted that some industrious soul was using the foul space to smoke kippers. Across the way, a fellow looked up from where he was turning wooden handles on a lathe, masses of the things piled up in baskets by his side.

"We're looking for number three," Holmes called out merrily, as if we belonged and were in no danger of being garrotted at every turn.

The wood turner pointed to the nearest doorway and returned to his work without a word.

"Much obliged," Holmes said, leading us across the threshold and up creaking stairs. The stairwell echoed with the sound of every soul that lived and worked in the building. There were shouts and laughter and singing and the shrill cries of a new-born babe. So many voices crammed into one place. Eventually we found the correct door, a faded "3" stencilled into wood that had barely seen a lick of paint in its entire life.

"Are you sure this is the place you wished to visit?" Holmes asked Marie, giving her the chance to change her mind, but the lady merely stepped up to the door and rapped loudly.

It was yanked open by a large man with fierce whiskers whose surprise when he found us at his door equalled our own at seeing him.

"Yeah?" he asked, looking us up and down. "You from the landlord? Rent's not due 'til Monday."

"We are looking for Mrs Protheroe," Marie told him.

"Who?"

"Mrs Protheroe," Marie repeated, trying to look into the room beyond. There was little to see. The room contained two beds, a chair and a pile of rags, which its occupant was in the process of turning into garments for market. "Does she live here?"

"Never heard of her," the bewhiskered tailor replied.

"Perhaps she recently moved out," I suggested, remembering stories of the swift turnover of tenements such as these, families evicted if they missed only a single week's rent.

"Not from here she didn't. Lived here three years, and never missed a payment. What is this?"

"A mistake, it seems," Holmes offered. "I apologise for

disturbing your work." His eyes fell upon a heap of shoes the man was patching up for sale and he added: "I don't suppose any of those are a size twelve?"

A quick exchange of coins later and Holmes was furnished with a pair of boots that, while of dubious quality, were still sturdier than the shoes he had vandalised himself. The door to 3 Boyle's Court slammed shut.

It was then that Lady Marie let out a heartfelt sob.

She stumbled back and I went to grasp her, only for the lady to steady herself against the wall, raising a hand to ward off my offer of assistance.

"I am fine, thank you, Doctor," she said, curtly.

"Then perhaps you will tell us what brought you to this den?" Holmes asked, cutting straight to the point. "Who is this Mrs Protheroe?"

Lady Marie Redshaw looked him straight in the eye and said, "She is the woman who took my baby."

CHAPTER THIRTY-SEVEN

MARIE'S STORY

I had never been so glad to be away from anywhere as St Jude's. Retracing our steps through the mud we were relieved to see that the blackguard who had attacked Lady Marie had crawled away to whatever hole he called home. Word had spread through the back-to-back buildings, however, and the narrow passages were lined with slum-dwellers curious to see the gentlefolk who had wandered haphazardly into their domain. I gripped my cane as I accompanied Marie Redshaw out of Parson's Close, the lady's arm slipped through my own and her head held high. She really was a remarkable woman. For all her obvious distress over the last few days, she had a seam of steel running through her soul. One would have thought we were strolling through the park as we passed a succession of filthy tykes and toothless hags. Still, as we stepped back out onto the main thoroughfare, I realised that I had been holding my breath, and not only because of the stink.

"There you are, my dear," I said, patting her gloved hand. "Out, safe and sound."

I turned to tell Holmes that I would take Lady Marie to her

carriage, but he was not there. Fear gripped my heart. He had been walking behind us through that Stygian passageway, his newly purchased boots squelching in the mud. What had happened to him? Had the lowlife in the eye-patch returned to bury his knife in Holmes's back?

"Go to your carriage, and get away from here," I told Marie, slipping my arm free. "I shall meet you at Ridgeside."

"No," she said. "I can't go there."

This was no time for an argument. "Then go somewhere safe, and I will find you after I've located Holmes. A coffeehouse or some such."

"A capital idea," said a deep baritone from the gloom. Holmes appeared at the ingress, smiling broadly. He held his cane in his hand, although his mud-stained long coat and top hat were missing. "I for one would love a warm brew."

"Holmes!" I said. "What the devil happened to you?"

Holmes's eyebrows were raised in mock befuddlement. "What happened? Nothing happened, Doctor. I merely stopped off to chat to some of those delightful people. It always strikes me as curious that poverty and community go hand in hand."

"But your coat and hat?"

"You saw the state of them. Besides, I found a couple of fellows whose need was greater than mine."

"You gave them away?"

"I donated them, in exchange for information…" His sharp eyes turned to Lady Marie. "… about Mrs Protheroe."

Marie gave a little gasp. "And what did you learn?"

"Absolutely nothing," Holmes admitted. "No one has heard of her, which is a near impossibility in a warren such as St Jude's. Life in the slums makes everyone's business one's own. I even talked to the shopkeeper, Mr Finch, he of the kippers. Again, Mrs Protheroe's name drew only a blank stare, and shopkeepers are the eyes and ears of a tenement; they know exactly how much every family earns. How else can they know how much credit to offer when a poor soul asks to put a slice of bread on tick?"

"Then I am quite lost," Lady Marie said, fighting back tears.

"Not if you tell us everything," Holmes insisted. "Problems can never be solved if they are kept secret. You have trusted us once today. Will you not do so again?"

I had become acutely aware of numerous sets of eyes staring at us, but knew that it would be rash to hurry the lady into giving a hasty answer. Instead, we waited as Marie studied Holmes's face with such intensity that I feared for a moment that she would see beyond his disguise. How could she trust a man whose very existence was a fiction?

It appeared that I was worrying in vain. "Dr Watson mentioned coffee. I know a coffeehouse nearby which is discreet and serves an excellent macaroon. Would you gentlemen care to join me?"

Beaming, Holmes held out his arm. "If the establishment will forgive my attire, it would be a pleasure."

It was becoming abundantly clear that life with Lady Marie Redshaw held one revelation after another. I should hardly have been surprised. After all, this was a lady who thought nothing of walking into one of Bristol's most notorious slums armed only with an address written on a scrap of paper.

At her request, we followed her carriage through a quarter known as Old Market to a street called Laurence Hill. It was a bustling thoroughfare lined with shops and stalls. Bakers, butchers, confectioners and fruiterers rubbed shoulders, their wares perused by Bristolians of all classes and creeds. We alighted from our carriages next to the Packhorse public house and followed the lady up a narrow paved alleyway, this one a thousand times more sanitary than Parson's Close. Marie stopped at an archway and pushed open a door to an iron staircase that curled down to what can be only described as a subterranean street. I could scarcely believe what I was seeing in the glow of gas lamps that burned bright. There stood a row of shopfronts, complete with windows and hoardings running into darkness at either end of the cobbled street, on which a number of arched cellars had been built.

"This is incredible," I said, which drew a smile from Marie.

"The original Packhorse Lane," she explained, leading us to a shop beside a near duplicate of the pub on the street above. "It was entombed when the road was raised to accommodate new railway lines a decade or more ago. Only certain folk know it still exists."

"But you do," Holmes commented as he looked up at the arched ceiling that formed the new road, dust falling like snow with the passing of every carriage.

"I have friends in low places," she said with a sad smile, opening the door of the shop to let us enter.

We found ourselves in a gas-lit coffeehouse, the odour of freshly ground beans washing over us as we walked in from the curious street. The place was surprisingly clean considering its subterranean nature, sawdust covering the floor around wooden tables lit by flickering lamps on the wall.

"Poor Clifford would be proud, if he only knew about it," she said, ushering us towards an empty table. "His father's lamps still burning."

Holmes and I sat beside each other on a wooden bench, the remarkable girl nodding to the other patrons as she joined us to sit opposite. They were a mixed bunch of both men and women, with clothes nowhere near the cut and class of Lady Marie, but they smiled happily as she greeted them.

"You are known here?" I asked.

"I would hope so," she replied. "Father has his retreat at Ridgeside. This is ours."

"Yours?" Holmes asked.

"Mine," she corrected herself.

"Marie," said a welcoming voice, and we turned to see a portly fellow with a stained brown apron approach from a small bar at the back of the shop. "Now this is a pleasant surprise, a pleasant surprise indeed."

His accent indicated that he hailed from the East End of London, rather than the West of England, and his many chins were unshaven, his hair a mane of curls that the strongest of combs would struggle to tame.

"Jacob," she said, her tone warmer than I had heard yet. "I've brought some new customers. I hope you don't mind."

"A friend of Marie Redshaw is a friend of mine. No Nelson today?"

Marie's smile faltered. "I'm afraid not."

Jacob scratched his jowl. "Haven't seen him myself for best part of a month. Was starting to worry that you'd forgotten about us." The chubby man's eyes fell upon Holmes. "Looks like you've taken a tumble. Need to clean yourself up?"

Knowing Holmes as I did, the desire to rid himself of the mud of St Jude's must have been very great. Holmes was like a cat in his personal grooming, not a hair out of place, no lint on his sleeve. To be in so dishevelled a state must have been hell, and yet he declined the offer, no doubt worried about smudging his disguise in the process.

"Just three cups of your finest brew," Holmes said cheerfully, and Jacob tapped a podgy finger against his nose.

"Right you are."

The shopkeeper returned a few minutes later to deliver cups of the strongest and most satisfying coffee I have ever tasted.

Across the table, Lady Marie sipped from her cup and looked at us both with curiosity.

"You seem to be taking all this in your stride, gentlemen."

"Dr Watson has lived a full life," Holmes replied as Sherrinford, "which I have observed from afar, but I pride myself in possessing an open mind. We all have our secrets, Lady Marie. We all wear masks."

"Some more than others," I muttered, shooting Holmes a look.

"You do not approve, Doctor?" Marie asked, misunderstanding my comment.

"Oh no, my dear. I did not mean you. From the moment we met you struck me as a young lady who marched to a different drum from the rest of her family."

There was that smile again. It was a shame she wore it so seldom. "I hope so, Doctor."

She took another sip of her coffee, delaying the explanation she had promised us.

Holmes had waited long enough. "Lady Marie, you mentioned a baby."

She nodded, replacing the cup. "I did. My baby."

"Which was conceived out of wedlock," Holmes said.

"Holmes, really!" I admonished, but Lady Marie jumped to my friend's defence.

"Mr Holmes is correct. I took a lover, and we were... unfortunate."

"Could you not marry?" I asked.

She laughed, and shook her head. "Not exactly, no."

"The joining of the houses of Redshaw and Powell," Holmes said, causing me nearly to choke on my coffee. "A lady of the manor and a hotel bootblack."

"A cobbler," she corrected him. "And a proud one. But you are correct once again. My father would never have been ready to welcome Nelson to Ridgeside."

"Because of his station?" I asked.

"That, and his heritage," she replied. "Nelson's family came to England on the slave ships. Father was furious when he found out."

"He is African," Holmes said. "Yes, I can see how that might cause problems in a family such as yours. How did the two of you meet?"

"At the Regent, while I was attending one of the League's tedious balls."

"The Regent?" I commented. "That surprises me. Your father is hardly fond of the place, or its manageress."

"I don't think he has a choice in the matter. Business is business as far as Sir George is concerned. Besides, the hotel bends over backwards to accommodate the League's wishes. The balls are lavish affairs."

"But not to your taste?" Holmes asked.

"No," came the reply. "Of course, Anna is in her element, preening on Clifford's arm as if he were the catch of Bristol. Usually I play along, ever the dutiful daughter, but that night, I could take it no longer. I felt suffocated by the hypocrisy."

"How so?"

"Everywhere I looked I saw the same faces, so arrogant and pietistic. The great and good of Bristol, drinking the finest wines, stuffed like prize geese with more food than was decent. They stood there, wallowing in their own benevolence, while not half a mile away the poor they sought to rescue starved in their hovels. It made me sick to my stomach."

"So you left?"

She nodded at Holmes. "I had promised myself I would stick it out to the bitter end. Anna never wastes an opportunity to remind Father of what a failure I am, both as a lady and a daughter. Why give her more ammunition? And Father had even been more attentive than usual, until I realised why. It was no society ball; it was a cattle market, and I was the stock."

She put on a rough approximation of her father's voice. "'Poor Marie, still unmarried at her age. Never mind, we'll find her the right man, for the right price.' I could see him, talking with his cronies, lining up deals. Soon a parade of bachelors would appear at Ridgeside, invited to dinner and seated beside me. Young or old, it would be of no concern as long as their prospects were good, and new alliances could be made. We had played the game for so many years, and I had disappointed Father time and time again, but he never learned, he never realised that the more he pushed me into something – or someone – the more I ran. Mother understood, and when she was alive, she protected me, God bless her. Now she is gone, he thinks my life and my future are his to do with as he pleases."

Her words were uncomfortable. I did not want to believe such things of Lord Redshaw, who had shown me such kindness. Nor was I so much of a fool, however, that I did not recognise the truth of it. It seemed to me that the very rich and the very poor had a great deal in common. Both were born into their respective states and could do little to alter them; they were governed by preordained destinies. The wretches in the slums were caught in the never-ending grind of day-to-day survival with no hope of escape; while Marie lived a life of privilege and wealth, she too had been set upon a track from the moment she was born, governed by expectations and etiquette. How lucky was I to be born in neither stratum. I, like Holmes, could make my own way in the world. However, when ladies such as Marie attempted to take control of their own destiny, only disgrace and dismay loomed large in their future.

"I chose my moment," she continued, "and slipped out of the ballroom, not caring whether I was missed or not. I found myself outside at the back of the hotel, and there he was, leaning against the wall, smoking a cigarette."

"Nelson Powell," Holmes said.

She smiled again, as if the memory were both sweet and sorrowful. "He was more of a gentleman than anyone in that ballroom. He apologised and went to take his leave, but I said no. I was the one intruding on his world, not he on mine. Not that I would have minded. I had never seen such a handsome man. When he smiled..." She paused, embarrassed. "I am not a romantic soul and never have been, but he made my heart soar. Nothing happened that night; of course it didn't, how could it? We talked for no more than five minutes at most, but a connection was made. I went back to the ball, and I played my part, dancing and laughing and wearing the masks you mentioned earlier..."

"But thought of nothing but Mr Powell," Holmes said softly.

"He consumed me, both that evening and the day that followed. I found myself drawn back to the Regent, taking tea in the lobby, longing to see a glimpse of the only man who had ever made me feel alive. And I know what you are thinking, that it was an infatuation, the lure of the exotic, but it was more than that; it *is* more than that to this very day.

"Before long we were meeting, tucked away from what is laughably called polite society. He brought me to places like this and told me so much: how his grandfather had been brought to Bristol by the traders; how they had won their freedom, despite such odds; how they had persevered and survived.

"Nelson had learnt a trade in the slums, fixing shoes like the tailor we met. He fought his way out, finding a sponsor in Mrs Mercer. She set up his workshop in the hotel, promised him a better life, and delivered on her promise, becoming almost a second mother."

"You sound exceptionally fond of the lady," I said.

"She found out about us, but kept our secret. For that I will be forever grateful. Nelson loves her. He would do anything for her, of that I am certain. The way she is treated by the League, the contempt she faces every single day, is scandalous."

"How so?" asked Holmes.

"I know only what Nelson has told me. The Regent has something of a chequered past."

"That business with the Russian princess, you mean?" I asked, to which Holmes shook his head.

"I am still amazed that Mrs Mercer has managed to keep such a scandal out of the public record. I had no idea." He turned back to Lady Marie. "But we digress; please continue with your story. Mrs Mercer kept your secret, but I imagine your father was less than pleased when he discovered you were with child."

"He was furious," replied the lady. "I was confined to my bedroom for the whole time, the servants and the outside world informed that I was suffering from brain fever. Only Dr Melosan was permitted to see me. Sworn to secrecy, he delivered the child himself – a boy, so beautiful, so much like his father."

"And Mrs Protheroe?" Holmes asked.

"She arrived soon after and whisked the baby away. I was told that she was a private nurse, taken on by my father, who would find a home for my son. From that day forward, Father watched my every move, and then Victor appeared, a surprise guest at dinner one evening, seated beside me at table. Once again, my life was not my own, my engagement a contract drawn up behind Father's study door. There was nothing I could do. I even told Victor my secret."

"About the child?"

She nodded. "I cared nothing what anyone thought of me by that point. I believed that if Victor knew what had happened, he would call off the engagement."

"But he did not."

"He said he would stick by me, come what may. I had only trapped myself further."

"What of the Protheroe woman?" Holmes asked, steering the conversation back to the baby's birth. "Can you describe her to me?"

"Well, my mind was on other things when she arrived," Lady Marie said, gracing us with another tight, knowing smile. "But she looked respectable enough."

Holmes fell easily into questioning, no matter what voice he used. "How old was the lady?"

"In her forties, I would say, maybe a little older."

"Or younger, if she lived a tough life in the slums."

"But you see, that is why I was surprised..."

"When you found the address in your father's study?"

"How did you know?"

"The paper in your hand was torn from a ledger in his desk. I noticed it when I searched for a pair of scissors following his attack. The rule and weight of the paper is most distinctive, the product of Barlow's of Finchley. You copied down the address from his papers after the stabbing."

"After?" I asked.

"The journal was at the top of the pile in the drawer, meaning that it was constantly in use. Lord Redshaw would have noticed a torn page."

"You share some of your brother's talents," observed Lady Marie.

"More than you know. So you were shocked when you learned Mrs Protheroe lived in the slums. Why?"

"Because of her clothes. They were neither threadbare nor worn. In fact, I would say they were of this season, the styles modern but respectable. Don't ask me to describe them, except for her boots. It's odd the things you remember, is it not? Her boots were patent leather with a row of white buttons up the left-hand side. In my delirium, I remember thinking that I would like a pair of boots like that!"

"You would place her in the middle classes then?"

"She was certainly educated, and well spoken."

"Curious then, although the fact that no one in Boyle's Court knows of her existence points to the fact that she gave a false address. Why your father would hire a woman from St Jude's, however, is a mystery."

"He was desperate. I believe he found Mrs Protheroe in the *Mercury*, through an advertisement."

"An advertisement? Interesting."

"There was a receipt amongst his papers. Ten pounds. That's what he paid for her to take away my child. Ten pounds."

"And your father told you nothing else about the woman?"

Marie shook her head. "No one in the house was allowed to talk about what he so delightfully described as 'the sorry affair', myself included. I couldn't see Nelson. I feared what my father would do to him."

"You mean physically?"

"There are more ways to hurt someone in this city than violence, Mr Holmes, and my father knows them all. He is not the man you think he is."

"Then who is he?" asked I.

"My gaoler." The words were delivered with no venom, but as a statement of fact. "At least he was."

"Before you went to see Powell at the Regent this morning."

"That's right. After everything that has happened…" She paused, her voice wavering. "I can live a lie no longer."

"But Mr Powell wasn't in his workshop?" I asked.

"Nor in his room."

Holmes frowned. "He lives at the hotel?"

Marie nodded. "Mrs Mercer provides him with a room as part of his terms of employment."

"But she said he was at home," I remembered.

"Maybe she was protecting him?" Holmes said.

"From what?" Marie asked.

"From arrest." Holmes had lowered his tone as he levelled his accusation. Marie's eyes widened.

"For what crime?"

"For the attempted murder of your father."

"What?" Marie gasped.

"If I am correct," Holmes revealed, "and I believe I am, Lord Redshaw was stabbed with a shoe knife."

"And we found blacking on the carpet of the study," I added. "The same brand that is used at the Regent."

"No," she insisted, her voice dropping to a whisper. "That is impossible."

"Is it?" Holmes countered. "The father of your child kept away from you. Is it not likely that he would want to take revenge on the man who took away his son?"

"But Nelson didn't know," Marie insisted. "I never told him about the baby. That's why I went to the Regent this morning, to tell Nelson everything that had happened and to ask him to go with me to St Jude's."

"To find your child?"

"To get him back. To escape from all this, just the three of us."

"To start a new life," Holmes said.

Marie's eyes were hard. "Let Anna have the house, with her perfect family and her perfect husband. Let Father die for all I care. I hope he does. He deserves it!"

CHAPTER THIRTY-EIGHT

REVOLUTION

"Marie, is everything all right?"

It was Jacob, hovering behind us. It was obvious what he was thinking, that Holmes and I were somehow threatening the lady. Perhaps that was indeed the effect of Holmes's questioning, as he slipped easily from confidant to interrogator.

Opposite us, Lady Marie regained her composure. "Everything is fine, Jacob. Thank you. It has been a tiring morning, that is all."

"And it's not over yet," the owner of the coffeehouse said, still viewing us with poorly disguised suspicion. "Would you like more coffee?"

"No. Just the bill, thank you."

"It's on the house," Jacob said. "It's good to see you again. Don't leave it so long next time, eh?"

"Most kind of you," Holmes said, laying on the Sherrinford charm, before turning back to Marie. "I apologise if I upset you."

"I thought you wanted to help me," she retorted.

"And we will."

"By accusing Nelson? He would never hurt Father, no matter what he's done."

"I'm sure you are correct, but for now we shall never find Mrs Protheroe if we lurk underground. I suggest you return to Ridgeside. Dr Watson and I will proceed to the police station to look in on my brother. We can take the opportunity to avail ourselves of Inspector Tovey's assistance and see what light he can shed on your mysterious midwife. If only my brother were awake. He would see through this mess in a moment."

If only, indeed. We accompanied Lady Marie back up to the street and waited for her to depart in her carriage.

"What do you make of it, Holmes?" I asked as we set off back to town in our own conveyance.

"I think that I need to get out of these clothes."

"Of the case, Holmes!"

"Lady Marie is a curious beast, Watson, adept at hiding what she is really thinking thanks to years spent in high society. She is also a woman who lives to break rules, and to shock. There are over a hundred cocoa and coffeehouses in Bristol; why take us to Jacob's singular establishment?"

"Because it was a safe place to confess her shame?"

"Because of the pregnancy, you mean? Tell me, Watson, does Lady Marie strike you as a woman who feels shame? She is angry, that much is certain. Angry enough to conspire to kill her own father?"

"I'm not sure about that, Holmes. You saw the way she reacted when you accused her lover."

"I saw shock, yes, but how are we to know that it was not an act? I would suggest she took us to old Packhorse Lane *precisely* because it was a singular experience; a theatrical one. Think of it, Watson. Bored with her old life, she throws herself into an affair with a man below her station, a man with an exotic heritage, a taboo in her father's eyes. Forbidden trysts in forgotten streets? They obviously frequented the place as a couple, away from prying eyes. Her notion of class structure is breaking down. A lady brought up in a stately home, sitting at the next bench to anarchists and revolutionaries."

"Anarchists? Surely not."

"You have eyes but you do not see, Watson. The fellow at the next table had three cups of coffee in the time we had one. If the broken veins in his nose tell us anything he has swapped one addiction for another, from gin to caffeine. Coffee palaces, be they above or below the ground, are a breeding ground for radicalisation. Reformers and agitators are known to induct their followers into coffeehouse culture. Why?"

I was unsure whether Holmes's questions were rhetorical or not, but I had no answer, either way. Holmes answered for me, as I knew he would. "Because coffeehouses do not serve alcohol, which, as every reformer knows, is the bane of the working class. How can the downtrodden masses revolt against their oppressors if they are sunk in a drunken stupor? No, keep them alert, and keep them sober, so they can read pamphlets promoting social upheaval such as that which was sticking out of our red-nosed friend's jacket pocket."

"Yes, yes, Holmes, you've made your point."

"Have I? Lady Marie has begun to question the privileges and perils of her social station. You heard her talking about the Worshipful League's charitable works. You saw her walk into a slum, with no thought of the dangers that might befall her. She is railing against her breeding, and against the man who is the very personification of her place in society."

"Her father," I answered reluctantly.

"Her father. A man who now lies dangerously wounded in hospital. Watson, I checked every door and window I could in

Ridgeside Manor. They were all locked, with no way of opening from the outside, especially on the side of the house that looks over the gorge. And yet somehow our attacker got in and out, with no one noticing."

"Maybe he had a key?"

"Maybe he had an accomplice."

"Lady Marie?"

"She is grieving for her lost child, trapped in a house with a family she despises. Her future is not her own. To make matters worse, her sister announces that she is with child. Tell me, Watson, how did Lord Redshaw respond to the news?"

"With joy," I said, remembering the scene all too well. "As one would expect."

"A man celebrating his first grandchild. But it wasn't his first, was it? The heir to the Redshaw fortune had already been born, of the wrong stock, and, dare I say it, the wrong colour. What else could Redshaw do? Present his mixed-blood bastard of a grandson to his peers?"

"Holmes, really!"

"And there you have it, in your own reaction, Watson. Embarrassment. Shame. This is the world that Redshaw's class has created and which the rest of us maintain."

"The 'Daughter of Eve'," I said, struck by a memory.

"What's that?"

"Something I said to Lady Marie on the night we first met. I was admiring a statue of a slave girl in chains. I suggested it was a reminder of how far we have come as a society."

"And what did she say?"

"'Or not, as the case may be.' The look in her eyes, Holmes. She was haunted."

"By what she had lost, and maybe by the realisation that the chains placed upon us by society are equally binding today."

"But invisible."

"Ever the poet, Watson. Is it too much a leap of the imagination to suggest that such grief and anger would boil over to hatred? Perhaps she had met with Powell after all to concoct their own revolution."

"That Jacob fellow said he hadn't seen either of them for some time."

"As I have observed, there are other coffeehouses in which to plot a murder. On the night of my arrival, Powell came to Ridgeside Manor and found a door left open as planned. His prey was in the study and the rest of the house occupied. Powell slipped in, surprised Lord Redshaw in his sanctuary and, the deed done, disappeared back into the night. As for Lady Marie, she had the perfect alibi. She was with her soon-to-be-estranged fiancé."

"But why, Holmes? What would they gain from such a barbaric act?"

"Revenge. Revenge against the man who stopped them being together. Revenge against the man who forced Marie into an engagement she neither wanted nor could stomach. Revenge against the man who took away their son."

"A son Powell knew nothing about, remember."

"We have only Lady Marie's word for that. Either way, it's a son she now wants back." A shadow passed over his face. "That is the most tragic aspect of all, Watson. If my suspicions are correct, Lady Marie's baby may well be long since dead."

CHAPTER THIRTY-NINE

AN EVIL BUSINESS

Looking back, I find it incredible that Holmes would have the gall to condemn another for displaying a flair for the dramatic. It was as though he had planned the timing of that last comment perfectly, delivering it on the instant that we drew up outside Lower Redland Road Police Station. He had opened the door and bounded out onto the pavement before I could ask him what on Earth he meant. Neither did he wait for me before he marched up the steps to the large blue doors and entered, demanding to see Inspector Tovey.

"How is my 'brother'?" Holmes asked as the inspector led us into a private office.

"Still doped up to the eyeballs on laudanum," came the reply as Tovey closed the door carefully behind us. Then he turned to me and smiled an impish grin. "I see you've met Sherrinford, Dr Watson."

I did not return the good humour. "I have, and I cannot believe what you two put me through."

Tovey eyed my disguised colleague. "By the looks of things, Sherrinford shares his brother's nose for trouble."

"It is a long story, which Watson will be more than pleased to share."

"Will I?"

"You cannot expect me to walk around like this for much longer, Watson. The inspector has very kindly agreed to hold on to some luggage for me in case of emergencies, sartorial or otherwise."

Tovey chuckled. "Evidence room two, down the corridor to the left. Here." He passed Holmes his keys. "And be quick about it."

With Holmes gone, I explained all, feeling more than a little guilty for breaking Lady Marie's trust, whatever Holmes thought of her.

"But what I don't understand is Holmes's suggestion that the baby might already be dead," I admitted as I finished the tale.

Tovey scratched his cheek. "There's little proof, I'll grant you, although I can see why he has his suspicions."

"You can?"

The inspector sighed, leaning on his desk. "Have you heard the term 'baby farmer', Doctor?"

I told him I had not.

"They're women who care for unwanted children on behalf of others, or, in some cases, find new homes for the infants, families willing to take them in. At least that's the theory."

"And in practice?"

"Most of the time they do as they're asked, taking care of the children and saving the mothers from shame. However, where there's money to be made, there are devils ready to make deals. We've encountered a few over the years, more's the pity."

"Devils? How so?"

Tovey sat back, tucking his thumbs into his waistcoat pockets. "A few years back, I came across a woman by the name of Margaret Percival. She was paid to find new homes for unwanted children, and find a home she did, in a dirty back room in Bedminster. She'd slip them morphine to keep them quiet, and leave them in the dark, until they wasted away, poor little mites. Soon her doctor, well, he became suspicious writing so many death notices for one woman, so she moved her entire operation to Lewin's Mead, changing her name and even her appearance. She couldn't risk being discovered again, so instead of letting nature take its course, the old harpy took matters into her own hands. She strangled the babbers and dumped their bodies in the Frome, wrapped in old newspaper and weighed down by rocks."

"Good Lord," I said, horrified. "That's… evil. Pure evil."

"Not to women like Margaret Percival. It's business, plain and simple."

"You brought her to justice, though?"

"She got careless; didn't weigh the bodies down well enough. Dock workers found them, floating on the surface. And the thing is – and Mr Holmes, he'd like this – I realised that the knots were the same. Each and every one. My father was a fisherman, see, and I recognised them in an instant: gunner's knots. Turns out Margaret's old man was a fisherman too. So I knew that the babes were being killed by the same hand, and from where they were coming up, I knew where they were being dumped."

"So you lay in wait."

Tovey nodded. "On the third night she appeared, a bundle beneath her arm. I jumped out before she could drop it in the water, knowing all too well what I'd find when I cut those knots and peeled back the paper. I cried that night, I don't mind admitting it, seeing the marks around that little one's neck. I was too late to save that child, but she never killed again. They hanged her, and I was pleased to see it. Trouble is, scum like that, they're like the head of a hydra, you know, from the old legends. Cut one down, and two grow back in its place. This city's lousy with folk profiting from the misfortune of others."

"But we have no reason to believe that this Protheroe woman is of the same ilk?"

Tovey raised his eyebrows. "Don't we? You said yourself that she gave Lord Redshaw a false address. Most legitimate baby farmers I know don't need to do that. Why would they? If you ask me, the very fact that she lied casts a shadow of suspicion over her. You say Redshaw found her in the *Mercury*?"

He crossed to a desk that was piled high with folded newspapers, and took one at random from the heap. He started flicking through its pages, checking the small advertisements until he found what he was looking for.

"Here we go."

He stood aside so I could see.

Married couple with no family would adopt healthy child, nice country home.
Terms £10 – Gardiner, care of Ship's Letter Exchange, Stokes Croft, Bristol.

Tovey looked at me as if I should see something in the words.

"What do you think, Doctor? Does it look plausible enough to you?"

"Well, yes. A family is willing to pay ten pounds to adopt a child."

"Ah, but that's not how it works, see. The ten pounds is paid by the *mother*, given over with the baby, to help pay for the child's upkeep. More often than not, the mother is even given a receipt, to keep everything above board. We found out, too late, that Margaret Percival was doing the same thing, placing adverts to attract desperate folk, accepting money and then… well, you know the rest."

"But how can you tell which ones are false, and which are

genuine?" I asked, my head spinning from the revelation.

"That's the problem. You can't," Tovey said, flicking through another edition. "Here's another, see? 'Grieving family seek adoption of healthy baby boy or girl. Well-appointed Gloucester home. Terms £10 – Stanton, care of 7 Wilbur Court, Midland Road, Bristol.' The pattern is always the same; similarly worded advertisements, all asking for ten pounds to care for the child. The trouble is, we can't follow up each advertisement just in case there's foul play at work. The newspaper's full of the damned things, all with different names and addresses. Turns out Percival used four or five pseudonyms in her career."

"You could trace who is placing the advertisements?" I suggested.

"Even if I could get the *Mercury* to co-operate, there's no guarantee it's the women themselves. They often have lads working for them. I tell you, Doctor, it's impossible."

"I thought the impossible was your business, Inspector?" Holmes said, opening the door to the office. He had changed into a fresh suit and shoes, his face finally free of dirt.

"The inspector has just been telling me about this baby farmer business," I told him. "I can't believe it."

"That is because you are an innocent, Watson."

"Let me see what I can do," Tovey said, as I showed Holmes the advertisements from the papers. "Perhaps someone's heard of a woman matching the description of this Protheroe character. It's not as if I have anything better to do."

"The investigation is not going well, Inspector?"

Tovey perched himself on the side of his desk. "Surely you don't mean the Warwick investigation, Mr Holmes?" he asked, his eyes twinkling. "As you know, I've been taken off the case."

"Of course you have," Holmes said. "Officially."

"And unofficially?" said I.

"Unofficially, I'm getting nowhere fast, Doctor. No one's seen hide nor hair of Father Ebberston since his release, and St Nicole's is locked up tight. I did manage to talk to one of Ebberston's congregation, a Mr Garrett. Apparently, this isn't the first time the doors of St Nicole's have been unexpectedly closed this year. Not four weeks ago, Ebberston had Tavener's stonemasons in."

"Tavener?" I asked. "You mean Sir George Tavener?"

"The very same. Do you know him, Doctor?"

"I met him briefly at Ridgeside. The Grand Master of the Worshipful League of Merchants."

"Is he now?" said Holmes, tapping a long finger against his lips.

"Apparently there was a problem with an arch above the church entrance," said Tovey.

"The narthex," Holmes offered.

"That's it. Crumbling mortar by all accounts, but Garrett, he's a retired mason himself. He says the archway was repointed a year or so back. Should have lasted for years."

"How long did the work take?" Holmes asked.

"No more than a day or so."

"Long enough to remove a body from a tomb."

"My thoughts precisely, Mr Holmes."

"But why steal it in the first place?" I asked.

"From what you have said, the League of Merchants is rather preoccupied with Warwick's relics."

"Some personal effects, yes, but his corpse?"

"The work would give them ample cover," Holmes said. "The marks you discovered on the top of the tomb, Inspector, the evidence that led you to believe that it had been prised open recently?"

"The crowbar marks?" Tovey replied. "What about them?"

"That is the point, Inspector. I doubt very much that they were made by a crowbar. If they had been, the indentation would have been shaped like a wedge. These marks were arched as if the end of the tool were curved, like a brick jointer, used for repointing mortar."

"So Tavener *was* involved," I exclaimed.

"It is a distinct possibility."

Tovey stroked his beard. "Then we'll have to tread carefully. Sir George is an influential man."

"Fingers in many pies, eh?" I asked.

He nodded. "Let me do some digging."

"Capital," said Holmes. "In the meantime, Watson and I are to return to College Green."

I groaned. "Back to the Regent? Mrs Mercer will have us turned out the moment we walk through the front doors."

Holmes produced a small leather pouch, which I recognised immediately as his lock-pick kit. "Then we shall just have to make sure she doesn't see us, won't we?"

CHAPTER FORTY

THE SILVER FRAME

There was no locked door in all of England that could stop Sherlock Holmes. In the years when I shared lodgings with the detective, we would regularly take delivery of boxes packed to the brim with padlocks and latches sent from reclamation yards the length and breadth of the country. Of an evening, while I sat with the newspaper, Holmes would be hunched over the dining table, dismantling the blasted things like a mortician performing one autopsy after another. Manufacturers would even bring locks of innovative new design to see whether Holmes could break them. They would enter our sitting room convinced that they had invented the holy grail of locksmiths everywhere – the unpickable catch – only to leave despondent after Holmes had opened it with ease.

I had lost count of the times that Holmes had put his questionable skills to good use on a case. All I knew is that I made for a nervous accomplice every time the lock picks came out of his pocket. I would stand there while he went to work, convinced that we would be sprung before the lock. Even then, as we stood in a narrow alleyway around the side of the Bristol Regent,

Holmes crouching in front of a door, I glanced nervously about. Holmes had already been arrested for theft once this week. On that occasion he had been innocent, but now, as I heard the lock spring open, we were both guilty as charged.

Holmes bundled me in and led me down a corridor until we reached a stairwell leading high into the building.

"How do you know where to go?" I asked as we climbed the stairs.

"You forget that I have been here before. The late Mr Mercer hired me to trap a thief. It turned out that the Regent had a light-fingered maid who was hiding the proceeds of her thievery beneath a loose floorboard."

"In the servants' quarters?"

"The very same." Holmes reached a door at the top of the stairs and pushed it open a crack, checking the corridor on the other side. With no one to be seen, I followed him through, finding myself in a passageway full of doors, empty except for a trolley laden with laundry.

"How will we know which room belongs to Powell?" I asked.

"Only a few employees live on site," he said, darting from one door to the next, examining each door handle in turn. "Fewer since the business of the larcenous maid. And here we have it." He stopped, at the far end of the corridor. Out came the lock picks once again.

"Are you sure?"

The lock was opened in less time than it took for Holmes to answer. "Look to the handle, Watson. Even you can hardly miss the fingerprints."

He was right. I could see them, dark smudges on the dirty brass. "Cole's blacking?"

Holmes opened the door and slipped inside. "You're learning, Watson. You're learning."

The room beyond could scarcely have been more distinct from the palatial suite I had stayed in during my brief time at the Regent, or even the Tombo Room at Ridgeside Manor. Illuminated by what little light pushed its way through a single grubby, narrow window, the meagre furniture consisted of a single bed with a thin mattress and coarse blanket, an empty clothes rail, and a small wooden table complete with one drawer. The surface of the table was bare and as I closed the door behind me, Holmes eagerly pulled open the drawer, to find it empty.

"Has our bird flown his cage, Watson?"

"It looks that way to me, unless he lives an extraordinarily frugal life."

Holmes turned his attention to the bed and flipped the flimsy mattress with ease.

"A-ha," said he, as he revealed a delicate silver picture frame more suited to a lady's dressing table than a cobbler's room. I knew whose face would be gazing back at me before Holmes held the frame up to the candlelight. Lady Marie Redshaw smiled from the photograph.

I looked around the dismal cell, wondering whether Marie had met with Powell here. Holmes read my expression in an instant.

"Watson, you are an insufferable snob."

"I am not!" I blustered, offended by the accusation.

"I can see it in the way your nose wrinkles. Where do you think they met for their romantic assignations? You, a married man. Shame on you."

I was about to offer a suitably witty rebuke when footsteps sounded in the corridor outside.

"Someone's coming," I hissed.

"A man who looks after his boots," Holmes whispered as we took up position beside the door, so that it might shield our presence if opened. "In a hurry, too."

I held my breath, willing the owner of the cared-for boots to continue past Powell's door. Instead, he was halted by a sudden female voice.

"Nelson?" It was Mrs Mercer. "Nelson, I thought you were gone."

"And I will be," came a deep reply, "if you let me get on. I forgot something, that's all. Something important to me."

I glanced down at the silver frame in Holmes's hand.

"I've had folk asking for you," Mrs Mercer told Powell.

"The police?"

"No. That brute of a doctor, and the brother of Sherlock Holmes."

Brute of a doctor?

"What did you tell them?"

"That you are unwell."

"And they believed you?"

"I think so. And that's not all. Lady Marie was here earlier."

"Marie?"

"Elsie found her in your room. You told me she would stay away. I can't have the Regent mixed up in all this. If Redshaw dies…"

I glanced up at Holmes, who was listening intently.

"I was careful," Powell assured the manageress. "There's nothing to link what I did to the hotel, and soon I'll be gone too. You need never see me again."

There was a pause before Mrs Mercer said, "Nelson, I'm sorry."

"That it ended like this, or that Redshaw didn't die?"

"Nelson, please…"

I could hear the consternation in Mrs Mercer's voice. She was worried that Powell would be overheard, and with good reason.

"He deserves everything he got," Powell told her. "You said so yourself. Now, let me fetch what I came for and I'll be away. My train leaves in an hour."

"Where are you going?"

"It's best you don't know, but thank you. Thank you for everything you've done for me."

"No," Mrs Mercer replied. "Thank you."

Thank you for what? For attempting to kill Lord Redshaw? My mind was spinning with the revelations. Framing Holmes was one thing, but colluding in the murder of a man was another.

The conversation in the corridor outside was at an end, Mrs Mercer's heeled footsteps fading as she walked briskly away.

Powell entered the room, and Holmes was crushed against me between the door and the wall. Powell moved quickly to his cot. I dared to peer around the door and realised that I had seen the man before, leaning against the railings when Lord Redshaw collected my luggage. The African was tall, with shoulders as broad as I had ever seen. As I watched he felt beneath the mattress and, finding the photograph gone, pulled the bedding up to search for his missing treasure.

Letting out a cry of dismay, he flung the mattress aside as if it were made of cardboard. I gasped and Powell wheeled around, his eyes widening as he saw us in our hiding place. He sprang towards the open door but Holmes slammed it shut. There was a nauseating crunch as Powell was caught between door and doorframe, but he pushed back with considerable force, and ran into the corridor.

Holmes and I took off after him, back towards the stairwell. Holmes ran ahead, throwing himself towards the cobbler. Wrestling, the pair tumbled to the ground, but I raced forward and, grabbing Powell by his jacket, hauled him off Holmes. My assistance did not go as planned. Powell used the momentum against me, pushing back, slamming an elbow into my chin. I crashed to the floor, throwing up my arms to stop my head smacking against the wall. Powell was already running for the stairwell when Holmes pushed the laundry trolley into his path.

Unable to stop, Powell crashed into the trolley and ended up on the floor, draped in sheets. Holmes was upon him like a shot.

"It's no good, Powell," Holmes said, pinning the large man down. "We know what you've done. Call for a policeman, Watson. Tell them we have captured Lord Redshaw's would-be murderer."

"I wouldn't if I were you, Doctor," said a voice, "unless you want me to put a bullet in the head of Sherlock Holmes."

Mrs Mercer stood behind us, and I would find it impossible to tell you what was more terrifying; the look of fury on the lady's face, or the pistol in her hand, pointed straight at Holmes.

CHAPTER FORTY-ONE

DESPERATE ACTS

Holmes stood slowly, his arms raised.

"So you have seen through my disguise," he said, looking past Mrs Mercer's gun to stare her straight in the eye.

"I admit that you had me fooled," she replied, her pistol following Holmes as he got to his feet. "But your voice betrayed you."

Holmes acknowledged his oversight with a wry nod. It was only now that I realised that he had commanded Powell to remain still in the strident tones of Sherlock rather than Sherrinford Holmes.

Powell finally freed himself from the cat's cradle of sheets. He threw the linen aside and backed away to stand beside his partner-in-crime, rubbing the back of his thick neck.

"So what now?" Holmes asked, acting with such indifference to the situation that one might think he was held at gunpoint every day. Looking back, that was not so far from the truth. "We seemed to have reached stalemate in this little game. I am a fugitive from justice, while you, Mrs Mercer, are harbouring a felon wanted for attempted murder."

"A felon with whom you colluded," I added, no longer able to hold my tongue.

Mrs Mercer looked at me in shock. "You think I was involved?"

"We heard you in the corridor, concerned that the hotel would be tarnished by Powell's crime, the crime you yourself sponsored. No wonder you made up that nonsense about Holmes stealing those damned books. You had this planned all along. The last thing you wanted was a detective of my friend's calibre staying beneath your roof while you were colluding with Powell to murder Lord Redshaw."

"Mrs Mercer did nothing of the sort," Powell insisted.

"There's no good denying it," I retorted. "I saw the way you looked at us when we collected my luggage, the contempt for Benjamin in your eyes."

Powell laughed bitterly. "*Benjamin?*" He jabbed a finger at me. "You have no idea what you're talking about."

"We know more than you think. We know about you and Lady Marie." That silenced him. "We know about your affair, about the child you fathered."

Powell took a step towards me, but I was in no mind to be intimidated.

"We also know how she left a door ajar," I continued, "so you could steal into Ridgeside Manor and attack her father."

Of course, we knew nothing of the sort for certain, but I had seen Holmes pull this trick many a time, trapping a suspect by presenting a suspicion as a statement of fact and watching the reaction.

"She did not," Powell responded, clearly flustered. I had him on the ropes now.

"Is that so?" I continued. "She had ample opportunity that night, not to mention motive."

"Watson."

I raised my hand to silence Holmes, never taking my eyes from the cobbler. "For all we know, Marie came to you; she told you that Redshaw was planning to speak out in Holmes's defence, to have those ridiculous charges dropped."

"Watson!"

"That forced your hand. Lord Redshaw had to die, and Holmes would remain in gaol. The perfect crime."

I stopped, feeling rather lightheaded. Neither Mrs Mercer nor Nelson Powell was interrupting me now that their entire plan had been laid bare. Mrs Mercer's gun had even dropped to her side, the manageress staring at me in amazement.

I glanced at Holmes. Why had he not seized the moment and sprung forward to overcome Powell once and for all?

Finally, he acted, but not in the way I expected. As Mercer and Powell gawped at me, Sherlock Holmes raised his hands and applauded.

"Bravo, Watson. Bravo."

I felt a swell of pride in my chest. While I had no desire to glory in the moment, the recognition from Holmes did me good.

I raised my hand modestly. "Please, it was nothing."

"Nothing?" Holmes echoed. "You have done spectacularly well. To misconstrue the facts so *thoroughly* shows talent worthy of Scotland Yard."

My face fell. "What?"

"That Mr Powell stabbed Lord Redshaw there is no doubt," Holmes continued. "But what on Earth led you to the conclusion that he was sent by Mrs Mercer?"

I could feel my cheeks flushing as I looked at Holmes in sudden confusion. "Their conversation. She admitted it."

"I did no such thing!" Mrs Mercer insisted, an assertion that Holmes immediately upheld.

"Quite right. You and I heard the same thing, Watson; that

Mrs Mercer shared Mr Powell's belief that Lord Redshaw deserved his fate. That she was concerned that the Regent would be linked to the act."

"Exactly," said I.

"Neither of which is a confession. If Mrs Mercer is guilty of anything, it is protecting a valued member of staff, of not turning him over to the police when she discovered what he had done."

"And of false testimony against you, Holmes. She had you arrested for a crime you did not commit!"

"Because she was forced to, Watson, against her will."

"What?"

"It's true," Mrs Mercer insisted. "I never wanted to say those things, but he made me."

"Who did?" I asked, feeling my argument start to crumble.

"Sir George Tavener," Holmes announced.

"The Grand Master of the League?" I said.

"The very same. The pieces of the puzzle were in front of me and yet I was unable to see them until now. As Lady Marie told us, scandal has dogged the Regent of late. There were the robberies that led to Mr Mercer seeking my employ, not to mention the exploits of Princess Vladlena."

The very mention of the name brought an angry flush to Mrs Mercer's face. "We were the innocent party in both cases. Thomas never recovered from the shock; he would lie awake at night, worrying that it would all come out and ruin us."

"And yet Watson told me that the Vladlena scandal went away. That is an impressive achievement in a city this size. You need friends… influential friends… like the Worshipful League of Merchants. We know you have had dealings with Sir George of late. Watson interrupted your meeting, of course, and on the day I was arrested I couldn't help but notice your diary open on your desk. The morning of the eleventh, the day I was arrested, was clear, save for one meeting: 'G.T. at 11 a.m.'"

"George Tavener," I realised.

"Perhaps he was meeting with you about the League's ball, or perhaps he was alarmed that you knew the detective who was investigating St Nicole's Church. If our suspicions are correct, the last thing Sir George wants is for anyone, let alone Sherlock Holmes, to investigate Edwyn Warwick's missing body."

"Warwick's body is missing?" The shock on Mrs Mercer's face appeared genuine. "Why would anyone take his body?"

"Revenge," I told her. "For the enslaving of one's ancestors, perhaps."

"Do you mean my great-grandfather?" Mrs Mercer said. "Why would taking Warwick's body put that right?"

"Precisely," Holmes agreed. "Although why Sir George would want the corpse is still a mystery."

"He is a vile excuse of a man, that's all I know," Mrs Mercer admitted. "Yes, he came to us after the Vladlena affair, offering to help. Little did I know what that help would cost in the long term."

"Blackmail?" Holmes asked.

"Poetic justice, some would say. I must accede to his demands to this day. If the League wants a room for a function, the League must have it, no matter what. It doesn't matter if the room is already booked, Sir George and his cronies can waltz in at the last minute and demand that we cancel everything in their favour."

"Your disappointed guest," Holmes recalled.

I raised an eyebrow. "What's that?"

"On the day we arrived," Holmes reminded me. "A young man was telling Mrs Mercer exactly what he thought of her establishment."

"So he was," I realised. "I had quite forgotten about it. A mix-up of dates, you said."

Mrs Mercer nodded. "If I refuse his demands, Sir George

soon reminds me of what he has done for the Regent, and how damaging it would be for the truth to come out."

"Surely if you revealed how you were being intimidated…" I suggested.

Mrs Mercer snorted in derision. "You think I would be believed? Sir George holds all the cards, Doctor, and who am I? The woman who has unwittingly harboured a thief of a maid, a faux princess, and now a despoiler of ladies."

"Mrs Mercer!" Powell protested.

"You know it is not what I think, Nelson, but it is how *they* think. Sir George *is* the Worshipful League of Merchants, and the Worshipful League of Merchants make the rules in this city; they always have, and they always will. They think they can do what they want for one good reason: they can. They even forced me to lie about Mr Holmes, to accuse an innocent man. I had no idea why at the time—"

"But you could not refuse," Holmes said. "And now Sir George has even more leverage against you."

"I am sorry," Mrs Mercer said, taking a step towards Holmes. "So very sorry. After everything you have done for the Regent…"

"Then why point a gun at us?" I asked.

"Because the lady lives in fear, Watson," Holmes said, displaying more empathy than I. "And she is at the end of her tether. She knows Tavener can bring her business crashing around her at any moment. Fear makes us irrational. Once it has us in its grip, we find it impossible to trust anyone, even a friend." He turned to face the manageress. "There is no need to apologise."

"Oh, believe me there is. If I could be free of that man…"

"Then why have Powell attack Lord Redshaw?" I asked, still reeling from her revelations.

"She didn't," Powell interjected. "It was nothing to do with her."

"I believe you," said Holmes, crouching down to retrieve

something from the sheets at his feet. It was an envelope, and I could tell by the way that Powell's hand suddenly went to his left breast that it had fallen from his jacket pocket during his struggle with Holmes.

The detective opened the envelope to reveal a wad of banknotes.

"Payment due?" Holmes asked. "For the attack on Lord Redshaw?"

"Blood money," I said, bitterly.

"Yes, but not from Mrs Mercer…" He removed the money and held the envelope up to the light. "There's a watermark. Come and see, Watson."

I did as he asked, and saw the mark for myself, a vertical row of elegant symbols. They were Japanese.

"Sutcliffe?" I asked in wonder.

"The very same. You see, Watson, during your earlier tirade, you missed something of note. When you blurted out that we were aware of the existence of Lady Marie's child, Mr Powell showed no sign of shock. Angry, yes, but not surprised. He already knew."

"And yet Marie said she hadn't told him," I realised.

Holmes nodded, before turning to Powell. "I assume we can take the lady at her word?"

"You can," the cobbler confirmed, sadly.

"Then we can also assume that she was telling the truth about why she came to the hotel this morning," Holmes continued. "To break the news. Now, only a handful of others knew Lady Marie's secret."

"Lord Redshaw," I said.

"Who, I'm sure you will agree, is unlikely to organise his own assault. There is Dr Melosan, of course, but, as far as I can see, he would have nothing to gain from Lord Redshaw's death. Which leads us to the third person who knew. The fiancé she attempted to shock into leaving her."

"It was his idea," Powell admitted. "All of it. He came to me and told me about the child, about what Redshaw had done. Then he offered me the money, telling me when to come to the manor and how to get in.

"I knew I couldn't be with Marie, her father would never allow that, not now. Sutcliffe offered me a way out. I could take the money, make a new life for myself and let her live hers."

"But, like Mrs Mercer," Holmes said, "there was a price to pay for Sutcliffe's 'kindness.'"

"He said he needed the old man out of the way, that things had gone too far. He seemed... I don't know... desperate."

"He must have been," I commented, thinking how Lord Redshaw had assented to free Holmes. "Do you think he's in on it, Holmes? With Sir George I mean?" Sutcliffe had certainly been unhappy at the thought of anyone from outside investigating the robbery at the Lodge.

Holmes had no chance to reply. Powell lurched forward and for a moment I thought he intended to attack Holmes. Instead the cobbler merely seized my friend's arm. "I did it for her. You see that, don't you? I wasn't going to leave her with Sutcliffe. How could I? But the money..."

"You were going to use it to find Marie's baby," Holmes said, making no attempt to pull his arm free. "To seek out Mrs Protheroe, and pay her to tell you who had adopted your child, maybe even buy your son back."

"Mrs Protheroe?" the manageress asked.

"The woman Lord Redshaw paid to take the baby, if that is her true name."

"Why would it be otherwise?" Powell asked.

"She gave a false address," I told him. "We went there ourselves, and yet there was no sign of her. No one even knew of her. Holmes fears that she is not what she seemed to be."

"It is a theory," Holmes pointed out. "Nothing more."

"I've read of such things in the papers," Mrs Mercer said, wringing her hands together. "I wish to God I hadn't."

"What things?" Powell demanded, desperation colouring his voice.

"Of women who accept money to care for unwanted children," I explained, "and then betray that trust, in the most horrific way possible."

Powell's eyes widened. "You mean they kill them, don't you? That's what you're saying. These women kill the babies."

"And from what Inspector Tovey shared with me earlier, it is almost impossible to prove one way or another." I told the pair about the advertisements, and how they were often used to deceive those in need.

"Often, but not always?" Powell said. "Just because this woman gave a false address doesn't mean she used a false name, or that the names in the paper are not genuine."

"True," I replied. "The names are common enough, that's for sure. Oh, what were they, Holmes? Garden?"

"Gardi*ner*," Holmes confirmed. "Gardiner and Stanton."

"Protheroe, Gardiner and Stanton…" Mrs Mercer said, lost in thought for a moment.

"You recognise something about them?" Holmes asked.

She looked at him decisively. "Can I trust you, Mr Holmes, even after all I have done?"

Holmes smiled. "You know my secret as I know yours. It appears that the four of us have become ensnared in a web of deceit and intimidation, Powell included."

"Then perhaps we can still salvage some good from this unholy mess," Mrs Mercer said. "Come with me, please. I have something to show you."

CHAPTER FORTY-TWO

THE HIGH SHERIFFS OF BRISTOL

Finally, after having heard so much about it, I was standing in Mrs Mercer's now infamous library. While it was certainly impressive, it paled into insignificance compared with that I had seen in the League's secret lodge.

Mrs Mercer's collection was housed in the attic of the Regent Hotel, curtains pulled across the large windows to protect the precious tomes. Holmes was in his element, whereas I was still uncomfortable standing alongside a man who had admitted to attacking Lord Redshaw. Whatever the motives for his crime, there was no evading the fact that he had tried to kill a man who had helped me in my hour of need.

"Here," said Mrs Mercer, bringing a thin leather-bound book to the reading table at the centre of the room. "*The High Sheriffs of Bristol from 1373 to the Present Day*."

"How does this help?" I asked.

"Let me show you."

Placing the slim volume on the table, she began carefully turning the pages. "Bristol has had High Sheriffs since medieval times."

"What do they do?" asked Powell.

"The office has existed in Britain for one thousand years or more," Holmes explained, "its holder being the sovereign's representative in matters of law."

"Indeed," said Mrs Mercer. "However, some names from our more recent history may be of interest."

She stopped at a page tallying the High Sheriffs from 1800 onwards. "For the first half of the century two men shared the position, each pair taking office every September." She ran a finger down the list of names. "Here we are."

Holmes looked where her finger had stopped. "1804 – Levi Amis Junior and Philip Protheroe."

"And now here," Mrs Mercer said, indicating another name. "1819. James George and John Gardiner."

Now Holmes was scanning the names himself. "A-ha! 1826 sees Daniel Stanton taking up the post."

"The names from the advertisements," Powell said.

"A coincidence?" I asked.

"Possibly. Mrs Mercer, I assume the hotel supplies its guests with newspapers if required?"

"Of course."

"Then perhaps you would be so kind as to have someone gather as many copies of the *Mercury* as you can lay your hands on."

The order was sent out and in due course a member of staff returned with a bundle of newspapers, which were deposited on the reading table. Holmes went to work, rifling through the small advertisements.

"But can the names help us find the woman?" Powell asked.

"Maybe, maybe not," Holmes replied. "But they can help us identify a pattern. Here we are, another one. A Mrs Castle, wanting to adopt a quiet baby."

"Michael Hinton Castle," Mrs Mercer said, checking the list of sheriffs. "1832."

Out came another paper, and another name was found. "Mrs Hillhouse?"

"Abraham Hillhouse, 1817," Mrs Mercer announced.

Now we were all at it, rifling through the newspaper to find one advertisement after another. Soon the names were piling up: Mrs Walker, Mrs Haythorn, Mrs Hassell, each and every one taken from the distinguished company of royal representatives.

"The coincidence grows with every passing page," Holmes said, "unless someone is indeed choosing pseudonyms from the ranks of the High Sheriffs of Bristol. We've seen such habits before, have we not, Watson?"

"We have?"

"Of course. Remember the Strangler of Birdcage Walk. He used a long line of nom-de-plumes to arrange rendezvous with his unfortunate victims, each and every one an Archbishop of Canterbury."

"I don't think I was involved in that case, Holmes."

"Were you not? Then I must furnish you with the details when this business is over. I think you will find it diverting. I identified the culprit by means of a stuffed squirrel."

"But why use a list of names at all?"

"Because the constant creation of new identities is a drain on the imagination, Watson. Far easier to plunder an obscure list that no one will notice, unless they are an expert like Mrs Mercer."

It was just as Tovey had said. Hardly an edition went by without the inclusion of a similarly worded advertisement, all with the same fixed terms of ten pounds per child.

"Surely there can't be that many unwanted children in the world, let alone one city," I said.

"Try not to be naive, Watson," Holmes said sternly. "Besides, not every advertisement would bring success."

"But you are sure they are the same woman?" asked Powell.

"The similarities in content are too great to be a coincidence, as are the assumed names. Always mention of her home, always ten pounds; the same amount paid to Mrs Protheroe. This is the woman who took your child, I am sure of it."

"So if we find her, we can find my son?"

"Possibly, if he is still alive."

"Surely he has to be, Holmes," I said. "If the woman is harming such a large number of children, wouldn't the police—" I stopped myself, glancing at Powell.

"Wouldn't the police have discovered any bodies?" the man said matter-of-factly.

"One would hope so, unless our High Sheriff of baby farmers has found a way to stay one step ahead of the authorities. Inspector Tovey is a good man, an intelligent man; but like all his breed, he is hampered by resources if not vision."

"Still, he could help us all the same," I said.

"If you can trust him," Mrs Mercer added.

Holmes regarded her with interest. "You are thinking of our mutual friend, the loathsome Inspector Hawthorne."

"He is in the pocket of Sir George," Mrs Mercer said.

I shook my head again. "Sir George again. He had everything worked out, didn't he? St Nicole's. Your arrest…"

"Well, he had failed to take Inspector Tovey into account. Tovey is an honest man, dedicated to the pursuit of justice. Besides, one only has to look at the cut of his jacket to see that Tovey survives on very little, while Hawthorne wears a suit of the finest quality, far beyond the means of a police inspector. Most of what Tovey earns goes to his sister in Weston-super-Mare."

"Then we should go to him," Powell insisted before I could ask how Holmes could possibly know about Tovey's family situation. "And explain everything that has happened."

"Nelson, you'll be arrested on the spot," Mrs Mercer pleaded with the young man.

"So be it," said Powell. "Which matters more? My freedom, or the fate of my child?"

CHAPTER FORTY-THREE

THE COWARD'S WAY

Perhaps I had done Powell a disservice. The man certainly showed more honour than I would have imagined as he marched into Lower Redland Road Police Station and declared his guilt. He was taken away by a sergeant, but of Inspector Tovey there was no sign.

"What do you want with him?" said Inspector Hawthorne on hearing of our enquiries. "Come to see your brother, Mr Holmes?"

"I am understandably concerned," said Holmes in Sherrinford's deep timbre, "although I gather from Mr Woodbead that there is little change in Sherlock's condition."

Nor would there be, until Woodbead stopped administering the sedative. The thought of doping an innocent fellow rankled with me, but Holmes had assured me that the vagrant who had taken his place would be remunerated generously for his troubles. Better for him to be drugged than only feigning sleep.

"I hear you brought in Lord Redshaw's attacker," Hawthorne said. "I thought your brother was the detective."

"Dr Watson tracked the fellow down," Holmes lied. "Using Sherlock's methods. I have to admit that I was quite impressed.

Perhaps the doctor is the brains of the partnership after all."

He laughed, but neither Hawthorne nor I joined in the merriment.

"Still," Holmes continued, playing the buffoon, "do you know where I can find Inspector Tovey? You see, I understand that he has an interest in the folklore of the region."

"Folklore?"

"I have discovered something that he might find interesting."

Hawthorne snorted. "You're welcome to him. Last thing I heard he was called down to the gorge. Another jumper."

"Jumper?" I asked.

"A suicide," Hawthorne growled. "They throw themselves from the bridge. Waste of time and manpower if you ask me. If the idiots want to do themselves in, so be it. The coward's way out – the world's better off without them."

Hawthorne's harsh words ringing in our ears, we took Holmes's carriage down to the Avon Gorge. We found Tovey and the flat-nosed constable from the police station already on the mudflats. Like the Thames, the River Avon was tidal, and the murky water had retreated. Tovey was instructing the policeman, who in turn was trying to haul a body from the silt without being dragged in himself.

I looked up at Brunel's majestic bridge suspended high above the gorge. The coward's way? Surely not. To throw oneself from such a height spoke to me only of despair and anguish.

"He was spotted when the tide went out," Tovey said as we approached. "Poor fellow. Pockets full of rocks to weigh him down."

"But no coat," Holmes commented. "The body is in his shirtsleeves and waistcoat."

"Guess he didn't think he'd feel the cold where he was going."

The constable slipped and landed noisily in the mud. Tovey

struggled down to lend a hand. I went to follow, but Holmes stopped me.

"Let the police do their work, Watson. In the meantime, tell me, what do you think of the case now?"

"Which one? What the devil have we got ourselves wrapped up in, Holmes? First the Monsignor and then Father Kelleher dead."

"Poisoned," Holmes reminded me.

"And then a missing corpse, a stolen ring and wig, and a stabbing, not to mention my own assault in the Lodge, wherever that is."

"And now our mysterious baby farmer so hard at work in Bristol's streets."

"It's a mess, Holmes. A damned mess."

"And yet, all interlinked. Monsignor Ermacora and Father Kelleher, silenced to halt the investigation of Warwick's missing body. Inspector Tovey taken off the case, I incarcerated and you knocked senseless. All to protect those guilty of removing Warwick's mortal remains."

"Sir George Tavener..."

"And, it seems, Victor Sutcliffe. He told Powell that things had gone too far. Because he was endeavouring to free me from the clutches of the law, maybe, or the man Sutcliffe believed was me?"

"What of Clifford? Do you think he is part of the conspiracy?"

"He is certainly a man under a great deal of pressure, if that stutter is anything to go by."

"It vanished almost completely when he took me to the Lodge."

"Because for once he was being his own man, not kowtowing to the wishes of Sir George and the others."

"There is certainly animosity between Clifford and Sutcliffe. Clifford can hardly look the man in the eye."

"From what little I've seen, his stammer increases in Sutcliffe's presence, as does Clifford's tendency to tuck his chin into his chest when they converse."

"He does what?"

"It's quite natural. Just as an animal will flatten itself or curl up in a ball to protect itself in the presence of a predator, Clifford's body attempts to make itself smaller when Sutcliffe is around. Such ticks are commonplace; a defence mechanism triggered by anxiety. You, for example, massage the thenar musculature of your left hand when under stress."

"I do not!"

Holmes's only response was to glance at my hands. I followed his eyes to find myself rubbing the web of flesh between my thumb and index finger just as he had described. I pulled my hands apart, annoyed with myself.

"There's nothing to be ashamed of, Watson. Mrs Mercer rubs the inside of her wrist, a pacifying gesture similar to that of a mother soothing a child. Either that or she points a revolver at people, it seems. One or the other."

"And what of you, Holmes?" I asked. "What do you do to calm yourself?"

"Torment you, mostly," came his reply as he took a cautious step forward. "The rest of our conversation must wait for now. It appears that Inspector Tovey has his man."

Both Tovey and the constable were pulling the dead weight of the suicide victim up the bank. We joined them, unable to resist our own morbid curiosity.

"Let's turn him over and see who we've got," Tovey told the policeman, who manhandled the corpse onto its back.

I could not help but gasp when I saw whose lifeless eyes stared up at us. It was Victor Sutcliffe.

CHAPTER FORTY-FOUR

EXAMINATION BY THE RIVER

"Like father, like son," Tovey commented, as Sutcliffe's body was loaded into the back of a police cart.

"I beg your pardon?" Holmes asked, a cold wind whipping the length of the gorge to cut through our coats.

Tovey took another pull on the cigarette he had lit while the constable and the cart driver dragged Sutcliffe's body onto a stretcher.

"Sutcliffe's father, Ernest, threw himself from that bridge not four years ago. Fell to his death at low tide. A horrible business."

"Do we know why he did it?" I asked.

"The Sutcliffes were in the tanning business, had a place down by the docks. There was a fire, a bad one. The roof came down, trapping the workforce inside."

"Was there much loss of life?" Holmes asked.

Tovey finished his cigarette and ground it into the road with his heel. "Only a few men got out. It was terrible. Sutcliffe was ruined. Two weeks later, he walked onto the bridge and threw himself over the side."

"And Victor?"

"Disappeared. We discovered later that he'd gone travelling, taking what little money the family had left. There was just Ernest and Victor, see. Ernest was a widower, his wife having died when Victor was a boy."

"Tovey, will you let Watson examine Sutcliffe before he is taken away?"

The inspector was taken aback by the request. "Here?"

Holmes took a step closer. "We cannot trust that evidence would not be tampered with back at the station."

Tovey frowned. "What are you suggesting, Mr Holmes? Mr Woodbead—"

"Your uncle is an honourable man, Inspector, of that I am sure, but the same cannot be said of others at Lower Redland Road. We have reason to believe that Inspector Hawthorne is at the heart of a conspiracy."

The words piqued Tovey's interest and he moved closer to Holmes. "It would never surprise me. I've caught Gregory taking bribes on more than one occasion. He has a flexible interpretation of justice, that one."

"Then why have you done nothing about it?" I asked.

"Because Inspector Tovey's superiors share Hawthorne's view of the natural order of things, I suspect," Holmes suggested, to which Tovey nodded.

"I only wish it wasn't so. This conspiracy, then?"

Holmes told Tovey what we had found at the Regent, how Mrs Mercer had admitted being coerced into incriminating Holmes and how Sutcliffe had paid Powell to kill Lord Redshaw.

"Good Lord," Tovey said as he listened to Holmes's litany of indictment. "I had my suspicions, of course, but to hear it from your lips… You think Sutcliffe was driven to the bridge by remorse, then?"

"That is why we must inspect the body."

Behind our huddle, the driver had taken up the reins and the constable was already on the back of the cart, sitting beside the corpse. "Ready to go, Inspector?"

"Hold on a minute, Hegarty," Tovey said. "Dr Watson is going to take a look at the body."

Hegarty's eyebrows shot up beneath his helmet. "Here, sir?"

"Before rigor mortis sets in. It's what they're doing up in London; examinations at the point of discovery, less chance of contamination of evidence," Tovey said, clutching at several straws at once. "Shift yourself out of that wagon."

"But what evidence, Inspector?" Hegarty argued, jumping from the back of the cart. "The fellow jumped—"

"Enough of that," Tovey berated Hegarty, even though the constable must have been ten years his senior in age if not rank. "Dr Watson, if you will?"

"I shall need an assistant," I blustered, thinking on my feet. "Mr Holmes, I realise this is a dreadful imposition—"

"Nonsense," said Holmes. "It will be a pleasure to watch a master at work."

I hauled myself up onto the cart and, shuffling along beside Sutcliffe's body, sat on one of the two benches.

"Give the doctor room," I heard Tovey say as he led the constable a short distance away, before calling over to the driver. "You too, Bert."

Grumbling, the driver dismounted. I leaned forward and made a show of examining Sutcliffe's body.

"First thoughts, Watson."

"What is there to tell? The man drowned."

"Is that so?"

"It's obvious, isn't it?"

"What's obvious is that you cannot see what is in front of your eyes. Look to his face. Pale skin, with no sign of bruising."

"Why would there be?"

Holmes ignored my question and turned to shout across to Tovey. "Inspector, Dr Watson would like permission to remove the victim's shirt."

"Remove his shirt?" Hegarty complained. "Why in God's name—"

Tovey placed a hand on Hegarty's arm, silencing him. "Whatever the doctor thinks best, Mr Holmes."

Holmes waved in acknowledgement and returned his attention to me.

"What are you waiting for, Watson? You heard the inspector. Undo the man's shirt."

"This is hardly respectful, Holmes."

"Death seldom is," he replied, as my fingers fumbled with the wet buttons to reveal a thin, pale chest. "Well?"

"It would help if I knew what I was looking for."

"Bruising."

"There is none."

"Exactly. Now, let's turn him over."

Acutely aware that Hegarty was glaring at us, I helped Holmes manhandle the body onto its front. The detective quickly removed Sutcliffe's cufflinks and peeled the wet shirt away.

"As I thought," Holmes said, pressing his fingers against Sutcliffe's mottled purple shoulders.

"That's not bruising," I pointed out.

"Of course it isn't," retorted Holmes. "Livor mortis. Blood has settled at the lowest part of the body, but what does that tell you?"

"That death occurred at least two hours ago."

"Yes. And?"

"And…" I repeated, not knowing what else to say.

Holmes sighed in frustration. "It tells you that Sutcliffe died on dry land. In cases of drowning, signs of livor mortis are found on the face, chest, lower arms and calves, sometimes even on the hands and feet due to constant movement in the water.

"Also, the lack of bruising is most peculiar." Holmes glanced up at Clifton Suspension Bridge. "Sutcliffe fell at least two hundred and forty-five feet. Putting his weight at around ten stone, he must have hit the water within four seconds, travelling at a speed of thirty-eight to forty miles per hour. Bruising would have been inevitable."

"Do you think he jumped at all? If you are right and he was killed…"

"Maybe the perpetrator simply dumped the body in the river?"

"Exactly."

"Check his spine."

"What?"

"Do it, Watson!"

I ran a hand up Sutcliffe's back, checking each vertebra, until I came to a fracture obvious even through the clammy skin.

"Well?"

"He broke his back."

"So, yes, Sutcliffe fell from the bridge, or rather his body was thrown over the side to make it look like a suicide."

"Like father, like son," I said, remembering Tovey's earlier words.

"Precisely."

"So how did he die?"

Holmes had me help him return Sutcliffe onto his back.

"There are no visible signs of violence, neither stab wounds nor blows to the head, but if you would be so kind as to open his eyes?"

Carefully, I pulled back Sutcliffe's right lid to reveal a milky, sightless eye.

"Excellent. And now the other one?"

I obliged, and Holmes peered closer still.

"As I thought. Do you see the marks on the conjunctiva, Watson? Like tiny pinpricks."

I leant in and said that I did. It was as if a crimson rash had spread across the white of Sutcliffe's eyes.

"*Tardieu ecchymoses*, first identified by the eminent French doctor Auguste Ambroise Tardieu. A clutch of burst capillaries…"

"Like Kelleher," I realised.

Holmes nodded. "Often found in victims of violent asphyxia, but rarely seen in drowning."

"So he was strangled then?" I glanced at Sutcliffe's throat. "But there's no bruising around his neck."

Holmes leant forward and pressed both sides of the body's neck, abandoning all pretence of being an observer alone. "Both fingertips and ligatures would leave marks," said he, "but the crook of an elbow is a different matter."

"A chokehold? He was attacked from behind then?"

"If one compresses the carotid arteries, one's victim will fall unconscious within fifteen to twenty seconds."

"And death follows within a couple of minutes."

"If the killer is strong enough, yes," Holmes confirmed, moving to slip a hand into Sutcliffe's trouser pocket.

"I'm sorry, but enough is enough!" We looked up at the shout. It was Hegarty, stepping towards us angrily. "Having the doctor make an examination is one thing, but rifling through a fellow's pockets is another. That's tampering with evidence, that is!"

"Hegarty, I told you—" Tovey began, but Holmes leapt from the back of the wagon, talking over them both.

"No, Constable Hegarty is correct, Inspector. I was merely seeing if the deceased had left a note in his pocket, to explain his actions. As Dr Watson has confirmed, this is undoubtedly a case of suicide."

"Didn't need a doctor for that," Hegarty grumbled as I climbed down from the cart. "Even old Bert could have told you what did him in."

Holmes pulled Tovey aside as Hegarty clambered back up beside the corpse, shaking his head.

"Well?" Tovey asked, expectantly.

"There is foul play afoot, that is for sure. Tell me, do we know where the not-so-dear departed lived?"

"Sutcliffe? I'm afraid I don't."

"I do," I realised. "Clifford mentioned it. Oh, what was it? Port something. Portman Square?"

"Portland," Tovey corrected me. "Portland Square, near St Paul's Church."

"That's it. A less than desirable address from what Clifford suggested."

Tovey stroked his beard. "That's a little uncharitable, but the place has seen better days, that's for sure."

"Then that is where we must go, Watson, without delay."

"Why, Mr Holmes?" Tovey asked.

"Holmes believes Sutcliffe was murdered," I told the inspector.

"Then I must come with you."

"No, Inspector," Holmes said. "You must follow protocol to the letter. Go back to the station, make whatever report you will, but mention none of my suspicions. I would know more of Sutcliffe before his death becomes public knowledge."

"If you say so, Mr Holmes, but report back as soon as you find something. If what you said about Hawthorne is right, he'll be keen to cover this up."

We bade the inspector farewell, and waited for him to clamber onto the back of the cart and trundle away, Bert at the reins.

As soon as he was out of sight, Holmes and I returned to our own carriage and instructed the driver to take us straight to Portland Square.

* * *

Our destination turned out to be exactly as Tovey had described. The once grand Georgian buildings surrounded a muddy patch of parkland, many of the houses converted from homes to business premises, largely manufacturers of boxes or bottlers of ink. Indeed, the malodorous reek of heated solvents permeated the air from the ink works. I found it hard to imagine anyone willing to wake each morning to such a mephitic atmosphere, let alone a man with such pretensions as Sutcliffe.

Holmes crossed the road, pausing only to let a rag and bone cart rattle by, before addressing a number of ragged boys on the street. As I watched, coins exchanged hands and the lads scampered off.

He returned to me a satisfied man. "Sutcliffe lives at number two," he said, showing me a row of houses, the once light stone blackened and stained.

"Are you sure? The place looks like a factory."

"A shoe factory," Holmes told me, obviously amused. "Perhaps Powell should have sought employment there, instead of at the Regent. Sutcliffe rents rooms at the top of the building, in the attic no less."

"He is obviously not the man of means we believed. Does he have servants?"

"So one would assume. Shall we find out?"

We made our way to the factory and, on making enquiries, were pointed in the direction of a stairwell that led up the side of the building. The stairs were filthy, and creaked ominously beneath our tread as we climbed to the top floor and found a modest doorway in a cobweb-infested hall. There was no number, nameplate or knocker, and so Holmes rapped on the wood, waiting patiently.

No one came as we stood listening to the cacophonous sounds of industry below. Holmes tried again, with the same result.

"If the man does have servants they are either absent or deaf," he suggested.

"I'm surprised they can hear anything over that racket."

"Well, I'm sure Sutcliffe won't complain if we let ourselves in."

"Your lock picks?" I asked.

Holmes fished something from his pocket and held it up for me to see. "No need for that, Watson; not after Sutcliffe so kindly furnished me with this."

In his hand, Sherlock Holmes held a long metal key.

CHAPTER FORTY-FIVE

TRUTH AND LIES

"You took it from Sutcliffe's body?" I asked as Holmes slipped the key into the lock.

"He had no more need of it."

"You can be a terrible ghoul at times, Holmes."

"And you, Doctor, are a hypocrite."

"I beg your pardon?"

"Did you respect the man in life?"

"You know I did not."

"Then why concern yourself with how he is treated in death?"

"Common decency."

"Foolish sentiment," concluded Holmes and opened the door. We paused at the threshold, peering into the dark corridor. The only sound was the hammering and whirring of machinery below. Satisfied, Holmes entered, beckoning for me to follow.

"No servants then," I commented.

Holmes closed the door behind me. "When a man cannot afford carpet on the floor he has little need for maids and footmen."

The walls were covered with faded wallpaper, the light fittings disconnected. What little light there was spilled through the three doors that opened from the main passageway, one on the left and two to the right.

The first revealed a sitting room of sorts, although one in complete disarray. There was a threadbare sofa, its cushions discarded on the floor. Books were scattered across the untreated floorboards, a tin bath upended in the corner. A mirror hung at an odd angle above the bare hearth and the thin curtains that had once covered the dirty windows were torn from their fittings.

We rushed from one room to the next. All three were in a similar state.

The second had been Sutcliffe's bedroom. A clothes rail was toppled over, jackets and shirts ripped from their hangers. The bed itself was shoved beneath another grimy window, the sheets hanging loose. The only furniture to be found in the third room was a large empty chest. One hardly needed to be a detective to know that it had once housed the tangle of exotic silks that was now strewn across the floor.

"The place has been ransacked."

"And yet there is no sign of forced entry," replied Holmes, returning to the front door. He dropped into a crouch, and ran his fingers across the floorboards. "Yes. This is where Victor Sutcliffe died."

"How can you be sure?" I asked.

"Sutcliffe opened the door and was attacked. The dust beneath our feet has been disturbed, probably by the same struggle that left scuff marks on the skirting board; there and there, do you see? Sutcliffe kicked the wall before submitting. Once he was dead, his assailant searched his rooms."

"Looking for what?" I asked, following Holmes back into the sitting room. "There is little of value here, save for those silks and Sutcliffe's clothes. I don't understand it, Holmes. How could Lord

Redshaw not have known that Sutcliffe was living like this?"

Holmes snatched up a book and flicked through its pages. "His clothes were of good quality. If Redshaw never ventured to Portland Square, how would he know?"

"But what of his business? Was that also a lie?"

"Not according to these records," Holmes said, showing me the ledger in his hand. "What Lord Redshaw told you was true. Sutcliffe rents a warehouse in the docklands, trading in fabrics from the Far East. However, the enterprise is nowhere near as successful as Redshaw suggested. Sutcliffe's income barely covers the rent of the warehouse and what little he pays for this place. He is surviving on a knife-edge, making just enough to maintain the illusion of prosperity and wealth, but enjoying none of the benefits."

"Except acceptance into Lord Redshaw's family."

"And the Worshipful League of Merchants. See, he makes a regular donation to their good works, probably as a condition of his membership."

Holmes handed me the ledger and continued to examine the rest of the scattered books as I flipped through the pages. "There is something else here," I said, finding an outgoing payment month after month. "'The Admiral'. Holmes, I've heard Sutcliffe speak of this admiral before. He mentioned him to Clifford in the carriage on the way back from the Lodge on the day I was attacked. Who do you think it is?"

"Not who, but what," Holmes said, fishing something out of his pocket and holding it out to me without looking up from the books. I took the tiny object from his hand. It was a cufflink, monogrammed with the letters T.A.C.

"Is this…?"

"One of the cufflinks I removed from Sutcliffe's body."

I was unable to suppress a shiver. "Holmes. If that constable had spotted you…"

"He didn't," said Holmes, picking up another book, this one with a red cover. "And in case you are wondering, the initials that have so spectacularly failed to pique your interest stand for 'The Admiral Club'. Sutcliffe was obviously a member."

Sutcliffe's words from the previous night came back to me: *If you need me, I will be at the club.*

"Look at this," Holmes said, showing me the book in his hands. "*Punter's Travels in Japan: A Journey through the Land of the Samurai*." He opened the pages at random. "Fascinating."

"What is?"

"Sutcliffe has made extensive notes in the margins." He turned to a bookmarked page and began to read: "'As spring approaches, nothing can prepare the traveller for the glory of Japan's cherry blossoms.'"

"Ah, yes," I said. "Sutcliffe mentioned the blossom. Some kind of festival."

"Apparently so," Holmes said. "He has underlined the entire passage: 'For thousands of years, the Japanese have left their homes to gaze in wonder at the vibrant colours of the pink flowers that adorn the *sakura* trees, and to pay their respects to the *kami* spirits who reside within the wood. My host, the honourable Arakwana-san, was keen—'"

I interrupted him. "What was that name?"

"Arakwana-san," Holmes repeated. "Why?"

Discarding the ledger, I took the book from Holmes's hands. "Sutcliffe said his guide in Japan was a Mr Arakwana, who took him to see the cherry blossom."

I found the passage and continued: "'My host, the honourable Arakwana-san, was keen for me to experience the festival myself, and arranged a visit to Mount Yoshino, home to more than 30,000 cherry trees.' Holmes, Sutcliffe claimed the exact same thing; that this Arakwana fellow took him to see the trees at Mount Yoshino."

I ran my finger down the page, reading on. "It's almost to the letter. He visited with his family and they shared sake under the shade of the blossom, *exactly* as it says here. But the odd thing was that he couldn't remember the location of the mountain itself..."

"Almost as if he had never been there..."

"He lied about his time in Japan as well?"

"He certainly amassed quite a library about the place. History, geography..." Holmes plucked another book from the floor. "Mythology."

He opened the book, turning to a page that was folded down at the corner. "Well, well, well; the legend of Izanagi and Izanami."

"The woman in the painting. But, if all Sutcliffe's knowledge of the Orient comes from books..."

"Has he ever been to the Far East at all? Watson, go and fetch those silks from the trunk, will you? I want to see if they are genuine."

"Or as fake as Sutcliffe himself. Right you are."

I hurried to the other room and gathered the brightly coloured fabrics into my arms. As I did so, a folded paper dropped from the silks.

"What's this?" I asked out loud.

"Watson?" Holmes asked from down the corridor. "Have you found something?"

I scooped up the paper and unfolded it. "It's a bill of sale. Holmes, you'd better see this."

He appeared at the door, a small brown book in his hand. I passed him the receipt. "Another lie to add to the list. The silks are genuine, but Sutcliffe didn't import them from Japan."

"Instead he purchased them from a Farler and Mackenzie of Liverpool, 'purveyors of the finest Japonisme'. Watson, there are numerous entries in that ledger marked 'F&M'. Sutcliffe wasn't importing goods at all—"

"But buying them from these Farler and Mackenzie folk.

SHERLOCK HOLMES

Holmes, check to see if the painting of Izanami is in the ledger. He said it had just come in."

"I shall make a detective out of you yet, Watson," Holmes said, turning once more towards the sitting room, when he paused and bounced up and down on his heels.

"What are you doing?" I asked.

"This floorboard is loose."

"Hardly surprising. Look at the state of the place."

But Holmes had dropped to his hands and knees. "No, the nails have been removed. Remember what I said about the light-fingered maid at the Regent? Loose floorboards make for good hiding places."

He pulled out his tools and, removing a pick from the pouch, used the implement to ease up the floorboard. Working his fingers beneath it, he pulled the board free, revealing a pile of papers secreted below. As he grabbed a handful, I noticed something glinting in the weak light.

"What's that?"

Holmes reached into the gap and retrieved a small gold band set with a large green emerald. I knew what it was at once.

"Warwick's missing ring!"

CHAPTER FORTY-SIX

THE SAISEI RITUAL

"Are you sure it is the same one?" Holmes asked as he held Warwick's ring to the light.

"I have never seen it myself," I admitted. "But it's how Clifford described it. A gold ring with an emerald stone."

"Then it appears we have found our thief."

"No wonder he didn't want anyone investigating the disappearance of the ring. Not when he took it himself."

"And what else, I wonder?" Holmes said, reaching into the hole once more. "A-ha—what is this?"

With a flourish, he pulled out a tattered old hairpiece.

"The periwig too!" I exclaimed. "It was *Sutcliffe* who knocked me out…"

"Only to double back on himself and 'catch' you and Clifford at the Lodge, the first on the scene."

"Because he was already in the building!"

"Indeed," said Holmes, tossing the wig to me. I dropped the horrid thing as if it were alive. Holmes's arm was again searching below the boards. "There's something else down here too."

"I dread to think," I said, wiping imaginary hairs from my hands.

Holmes drew out a long leather pouch.

"More relics?"

Holmes sniffed the leather. "The pouch is new."

"But what's inside?"

Holmes rolled the leather out flat on the floor to reveal three wooden rods, each roughly the length of a pencil.

"What do you make of that?" he asked, handing me one of the sticks.

"Some kind of stylus?" I asked, taking the implement. It certainly felt like a pen, but instead of a nib, five tiny needles were strapped to the end. I went to try them on my finger.

"I wouldn't, Watson."

"Why?" My eyes widened as a thought occurred to me. "They're not poisoned, are they?"

"Nothing so melodramatic. The needles are hollow, designed to prick the skin and deliver ink from a reservoir in the bamboo handle."

"For tattooing," I realised. "Like Lord Redshaw's?"

Holmes took the pen back from me. "The traditional Japanese method. Quite painful by all accounts."

"You think Sutcliffe did them himself?"

"A distinct possibility," Holmes said, looking at the parchments he had recovered from the floor. "Someone here was quite the artist."

I looked at the pictures on the papers. Most were unfinished sketches, somewhere between the anatomical diagrams of a medical textbook and the Japanese art that Sutcliffe had presented to Redshaw. They all showed the body of a man lying naked on his back. His chest was open to expose the heart for all to see. In some pictures he was alone, while in others he was surrounded by a ring of small animals, each linked to the man by thin red lines that ran from their hearts to his. It was both grotesque and beautiful at the same time.

"What does it all mean?" I asked.

Holmes held the paper up to the light. "The stock is Japanese, similar to the envelope we found on Powell, but the ink isn't right." He fished around in the hole again, retrieving bottles of black and red ink. "As I thought," he said, examining the labels. "Manufactured by Williams of Portland Square."

"Here?"

Holmes shrugged. "Why buy expensive Japanese inks when you have a fresh supply on your doorstep?"

"So these are all the work of Sutcliffe. Forgeries for his business?"

"Possibly." Holmes sorted through the papers. "All the same subject, gradually becoming more complex. Hullo…"

"What is it?" I asked.

Holmes pulled a sheet to the top of the pile. This one had the addition of Japanese writing running down its side, including a couple of characters I recognised.

"Those are the ones from Redshaw's study, aren't they? I recognise the symbol for rebirth."

"*Saisei*," Holmes confirmed, "and what is this?"

He had found a sheet covered not with Japanese but English. He held it up to read, his brow creasing.

"Watson, what was it Clifford told you about spells?"

"That Sutcliffe brought books of the things back from the Orient. Why?"

"Listen to this: 'The Saisei Ritual. Death is not the end. A body preserved in death can rise anew. Follow the example of Izanabi the re-creator. Give a pure heart as he gave his. Take the completed body to the sacred grove on the day of his first birth. There, under the deceitful eyes of the damned, restore with the blood of innocent lambs. He who was lost will rise again on the day for the glory of all.'"

"What absolute twaddle," I said.

"And yet, here it is, translated into Japanese on these drawings, although what it has to do with the legend of Izanami I don't know."

I told him what Sutcliffe had told us around the dinner table.

"But that's not how the story ends," Holmes said, on hearing about Izanagi's life-giving broth. "Izanagi is so repulsed by his wife's decaying flesh that he seals her in Yomi for all time. Furious at his betrayal, Izanami promises to slay one thousand of the living each and every day, to which Izanagi responds that he will give life to over a thousand more to make up the difference."

"So he doesn't raise her from the dead?"

"Not at all. I've no idea where Sutcliffe found his version of the tale, or this spell. It certainly features in none of these books, but I tell you what else I have found..."

He held up the spine of the small brown book he had brought with him.

"*Byrne's Annals of Bristol*," I read.

He nodded, flicking through the pages. "Volume thirteen, with the passage about Warwick's body lined and annotated. Look."

"The *saisei kanji*," I said, seeing the now familiar characters scrawled in the margin.

"Think of it, Watson. 'A body preserved in death'? Does that sound familiar to you?"

"Edwyn Warwick! You don't think Sutcliffe believed all this hocus-pocus, do you? That he was planning to bring Warwick back to life?"

"It's a possibility we need to explore, if only to eliminate it from our investigation. All I know for certain is that the theft of Warwick's body has left murder in its wake; first the priests, and now Sutcliffe himself."

"Not to mention Lord Redshaw."

"A man Sutcliffe wanted dead. And I think it is about time we found out why."

CHAPTER FORTY-SEVEN

AN EMPTY ROOM

"I thought it was obvious why Sutcliffe wanted Redshaw dead," I said, as we made our way back to the Bristol Royal Infirmary. "He didn't want Benjamin releasing you from prison."

"Watson," the detective replied, "although it pains me to say as much, not everything in the world revolves around Sherlock Holmes. We have already established that Sutcliffe's accomplice has considerable influence in this city. If the malignant George Tavener wants me to rot in jail, could Benjamin Redshaw overrule such a demand? 'Things have gone too far.' That is what Sutcliffe told Powell, but what things? What was so far along a road that death was the only answer?"

The carriage screamed around a corner, forcing me to cling onto my seat. "But why the hurry?" I asked. "Sutcliffe is dead."

"But Tavener is very much alive. Sutcliffe's instructions state that the ritual must take place on the day of the dead man's first birth. When is Edwyn Warwick's birthday?"

"Tomorrow," I realised. "Clifford told me that the lecture for the anniversary of Warwick's birth was meant to be this Saturday, but had been cancelled because Sir George had to be elsewhere."

"Raising the dead?"

"Surely you don't believe that?"

"Whether I believe it is neither here nor there, Watson. The question is whether *Sir George* believes it!"

The carriage pulled up outside the infirmary and Holmes jumped out. When he was in such a mood, I found it hard to keep up, both with the pace of his thoughts and his feet. He burst into the reception area and accosted a passing nurse. "Lord Redshaw. Where would I find him?"

The bewildered woman looked at Holmes in confusion. "I'm not sure, sir."

"Come on, you must know. In his late fifties, stab wounds to the abdomen, an over-sentimental attachment to the past?"

"I'm afraid I haven't the first idea of whom you're talking about," the nurse insisted. "If you ask at the administrator's office—"

She was cut short by the approach of a wasp-faced matron, thin hands clasped in front of a narrow waist.

"Is there a problem, Nurse Robbins?"

"This gentleman is looking for a Lord Redshaw."

The matron inspected Holmes quizzically. "He is in room forty-eight on the third floor, but—"

Now it was the matron's turn to be interrupted. Holmes thanked her for her help and positively sprinted for the stairs. I took off after him.

"What did you mean about Redshaw's attachment to the past?" I asked breathlessly as we bounded up the stairs.

"Isn't it obvious? Redshaw's cane, engraved 'with love from Lucy' on its side, has been repaired not once but twice, and according to the amount of ink on his fingers he persists in using a Japanese fountain pen that leaks profusely rather than the three perfectly good pens still in their boxes in his desk drawer."

"A present from Sutcliffe?"

"Due to its age I would suggest it was another gift from the late Lady Redshaw."

"So it's not so much sentimentality for the past, but for his wife."

"It's more than that. Think of all the framed maps on his walls; Bristol as it used to be at the turn of the century or before. And as for that damned chimneypiece, celebrating the city's past glories…"

I considered this as we barrelled onto the third floor. "And there are the tiles, I suppose?"

"Tiles?"

"All over the house. Lady Anna wants him to redecorate, but Benjamin can't bring himself to get rid of the things as they remind him of his father."

"He is a contradiction, your Lord Redshaw. Sentimental about the past, yet progressive in so many ways. The lack of segregation after dinner—"

"And the choice of menu. He has certainly embraced his wife's love of the Orient."

"That is the problem with people, Watson. Try as I might, they constantly rail against categorisation. How I wish they would merely accept the labels I place on them and be done with it."

We passed door after door, eventually coming to room forty-eight. Holmes rapped once and opened the door without waiting for an answer.

The room was empty.

"Holmes, you don't think…" I began, as my companion took a step towards the bed.

"Lord Redshaw is still alive, not dead. If he had died, the bed would have been stripped and remade. No self-respecting nurse would leave a sheet like this."

He pulled back the cover and placed his palm on the mattress.

"Cold. Wherever he is, Lord Redshaw has not been in this bed for quite some time."

"So where is he?"

"Exactly what I want to know," said Marie Redshaw, appearing at the door.

"Lady Marie!" I exclaimed. "I thought you were returning to Ridgeside?"

"I couldn't go back there after what had happened. I went to the *Mercury* to see if they could tell me who placed that advertisement. I even asked to see Mr Lacey."

"And he is?" Holmes enquired.

"The editor," Marie replied. "A dreadful snob of a man whom unfortunately I know from League balls. He wasn't there and no one could help me, so I went to the Admiral."

"The Admiral Club?" I asked.

"He's a member there, but apparently he has not been seen since last night, when he was with Victor of all people."

"Was he now?" Holmes commented.

"No one has seen him since, so I came here, hoping that Father could tell me more about Mrs Protheroe. He owes me that at least."

"But you found him gone."

"Yes, and I can't find Dr Melosan either. I found another doctor on his rounds, and he said that Father hasn't been discharged. He is doing well by all accounts, but was to be kept in for observation."

"Holmes," I said, "could he have been taken?"

"Taken? Why ever do you ask that, Watson?"

"Perhaps he found out what Sutcliffe and Tavener were planning?"

"Victor?" Marie asked, but Holmes was too busy discrediting my theory to acknowledge her question.

"Found out? From his hospital bed?" Holmes strode over

to the wardrobe and pulled open the doors to reveal that it was bare. "Besides, if he has been abducted, would they also take his clothes?" He returned to the bed and flipped over the pillow to reveal a neatly folded hospital gown. "Or tidy up after him. No, his Lordship left of his own accord."

"You mentioned Victor," Marie said, refusing to be ignored this time. "What has he been doing?"

Holmes sighed and turned to the young woman. "I'm afraid this will come as a shock to you. Your fiancé paid Nelson Powell to stab your father."

Marie took a step back. "No. He can't have."

"He could and he did. Mr Powell has given himself up."

"And Victor?"

"I'm afraid he is dead, my dear," I said.

"Dead?"

"He took his own life," Holmes stated flatly, and I looked at him sharply. We both knew that was untrue. "In the manner of his father."

"But why?"

"He left no note, so we shall never know. Maybe it was remorse for what he had done."

Marie was visibly shaking. I went to touch her arm, but she pulled back. "How could he involve Nelson?" she said. "And how could Nelson agree?"

"Sutcliffe told him about the baby," I said. "Mr Powell accepted the money to find your son."

"And now everyone will know my shame. Good. Let them all know. Let them know how I was treated." She pointed angrily at the bed. "This is his fault. He caused this. All of it."

"Lord Redshaw thought he was doing what was best," I argued.

"For him. Not for me. Not for my son."

"Lady Marie," Holmes said. "I realise this is all very distressing, but there are other forces at play. Whatever you think of your father, he may be in danger. Your sister made it clear that I am not welcome at Ridgeside, but if you would grant me permission…"

"Do what you want," Marie snapped. "Everyone does. I can't stay here any longer. Not after this."

She went to leave, but I called after her. "Lady Marie, I'm sure the scandal will pass. People will forget."

She turned to me, her eyes flashing with anger. "You think that is what I care about? Let them think what they will. I'm not leaving for them. I'm leaving for myself."

Marie swept from the room and I went to follow, but Holmes held me back. "Let her go, Watson. You will see her soon enough."

"Why? Where are we going?"

"Back to Ridgeside. We need to find Lord Redshaw, and tell him everything."

CHAPTER FORTY-EIGHT

TO MAKE AMENDS

The sun was setting as we arrived at Ridgeside Manor. Brewer opened the door to greet us with an expression of abject disappointment.

"Back again, like a bad penny, Brewer," Holmes said in the guise of Sherrinford. "We were hoping to see Lord Redshaw."

The butler frowned. "He is not here, sir. He is still at the infirmary."

"I beg to differ. Lord Redshaw has flown that particular nest. And yet he has not come home to roost? Interesting. Mr Clifford then. Is he home?"

"No, sir. I haven't seen Mr Clifford since breakfast. Lady Marie has just returned, but—"

"Is taking no visitors. No, that is to be expected. Lady Anna?"

"In the ornamental garden. However—"

"Capital. I owe her an apology so I shall deliver it now."

Holmes did not wait for the butler to respond, but stepped back out of the door. We walked around the house to find Lady Anna sitting on a bench in a high-walled garden. As we approached, it was clear that she had been crying.

She looked up, her expression hardening when she saw Holmes. To his credit, he was quick to put her at ease.

"Lady Anna, I owe you a sincere apology. My words at breakfast were tactless and insensitive. I pray that you will forgive me."

For a moment, it looked as though Anna were about to tell Holmes what to do with his apology, before she thought better of it. "Thank you, Mr Holmes. Emotions were running high this morning. It would appear they still are, in my sister's case."

"You have seen Lady Marie then?"

"Oh yes," Anna said. "She came in like a whirlwind, as always. Father has discharged himself from hospital and I am welcome to him, apparently. She says she is going to America."

"America?" I asked.

"We have family over there. Distant cousins. We barely know them, but that won't stand in Marie's way. Nothing ever does."

She looked away, putting a gloved hand to her mouth.

"Dear lady," I said.

"Please, Dr Watson," she said, firmly. "I do not need to be fawned over. You know, I honestly thought things were improving." She placed a hand on her stomach. "With the baby on the way, and Marie set to marry."

"Clifford made it seem that you didn't approve of Sutcliffe."

"Oh, she could have done a lot better, but I hoped that she would be happy all the same. We were close once, when we were children. Now, everything is changed." She paused before adding, "Marie says Victor is dead."

"I'm afraid so," I said.

A tear ran down her cheek. "Then that is sad. Now Harold will be unable to make amends."

"Your husband?" Holmes asked.

The lady stood. "It is growing cold. We should go inside."

"Lady Anna," Holmes said. "What do you mean? Why would

your husband need to make amends to Victor Sutcliffe?"

She turned to the detective and looked him straight in the eye. "I didn't know, not until this morning. Harold has kept it from me all this time, but it finally came out. I was saying that I hoped we would never see Victor again, but Harold said that I shouldn't be so sure, that Victor would be unable to resist lording it over him after all that had happened. I told him that he needed to stand up for himself, not to let the likes of Victor bully him. 'Imagine what your father would do,' I said. And that was it. Something snapped in him."

"What did he say, Lady Anna?"

"He told me what had really happened to the Sutcliffe family business."

"There was a fire," I said, "in the tannery."

She nodded. "They put it down to the alcohol used in the tanning process. That's what we believed for years, that Josiah Sutcliffe – Victor's father – was cutting corners and the fire would never have happened if he had followed the right procedures. Do you know what happened to Josiah, Dr Watson?"

"He took his own life."

She nodded. "The Sutcliffes were ruined and Victor disappeared on his travels. But all the time Clifford knew the truth."

"Tell me, Lady Anna," Holmes asked. "Did your husband have his stutter when he was young?"

She shook her head. "Not when we were children, no. It came later in life, but I didn't care. I've loved him since I was a girl, for all his faults."

"Was it around the time of the fire?"

This she considered. "Yes it was, and I suppose now I know why."

"Because of what your husband has told you."

"Two weeks before the fire, Josiah had new lighting installed throughout the tannery. *Gas* lighting."

"From your husband's company."

"It belonged to his father then, Richard Clifford, although Harold worked there, of course. Things had not been going well for a while. The business was in trouble. I don't know all the details…"

"Except that Josiah Sutcliffe was not the one who cut corners," Holmes prompted.

She shook her head. "The fire was caused by the new lamps. If the news had been made public, Richard would have been ruined. Clifford's Lighting was struggling as it was."

"Which is why your husband ultimately sold his family home."

"Richard passed away soon after the fire, leaving Harold a company to turn around."

"Which he did with your father's help?"

This time Lady Anna was incapable of holding back the tears. She sat down on the bench again so fast that I feared she was going to miss the seat and end up on the ground.

I crouched beside her and took her hand. "Lady Anna."

She could hardly bear to bring herself to look at me. "Father helped more than I thought. Harold's father was an important member of the League of Merchants."

"The librarian," I recalled.

She nodded. "The other members rallied around him, my father included. Josiah Sutcliffe was told that he must take the blame for the fire, to protect Richard."

"He was to be a scapegoat," said Holmes.

"Harold didn't find out until his father died, but by then it was too late. Josiah had taken his own life and Victor was gone. When he came back, Harold wanted to tell the truth, but Father wouldn't let him. It would throw the League into disrepute. He promised he would see Victor right…"

"Which explains why he so welcomed Sutcliffe into your family," Holmes said.

"But Victor knew, Harold was sure of it. He would make comments that made no sense to me, but Harold understood all too well. Father kept telling him to take it on the chin, reminding Harold what the League had done for him, what they had done for his father. All this time, I had no idea what was going on in my own home."

"My dear, I'm so sorry," I said, patting her hand. "Where is your husband now?"

She shook her head. "He went out, saying that he could stand it no longer, that he was going to put things right."

"How?" I asked, wondering for a minute if he had gone to have it out with Sutcliffe.

"I don't know," she admitted. "I think he was going to see Sir George."

"Sir George Tavener," I said, looking up at Holmes sharply, but my friend appeared not to be listening. Instead he stood looking intently at one of the flowerbeds. "Sherrinford, did you hear that? Clifford went to see Sir George!"

Still he ignored us, asking a question of his own instead. "Lady Anna, did Monsignor Ermacora visit Ridgeside?"

She looked up at him in confusion. "Why, yes. The Monsignor stayed here, as Father's guest."

"Stayed here?" I asked. "But I thought he was a guest at the Regent."

"Father wasn't going to have that when he found out. He insisted that the Monsignor come here."

"Which is why he suddenly left the hotel," I realised, remembering Mrs Mercer's words.

"And what of Father Kelleher?" Holmes pressed. "Did he come to Ridgeside?"

"They took tea with Father many times. Why?"

"Why did you not tell me, Watson?" Holmes snapped at me.

"I didn't know!" I admitted, before a recollection of my first night at Ridgeside resurfaced. "Wait. Lady Marie was shocked when she heard that the Monsignor had passed away…"

"Meaning that she knew him. Watson, I was relying on you to be my eyes and ears."

"I can't be expected to remember everything, Holmes. I am not you!"

Lady Anna was looking between us now, visibly perplexed. "What do you mean by eyes and ears? Doctor, were you spying on us?"

"No," I said quickly, realising that we were in danger of uncovering Holmes's disguise. "Sherrinford has been trying to build a picture of recent events, to help his brother's case."

"And exactly what picture have you built, Mr Holmes?" the lady asked, rising to face my friend, her tears replaced by anger.

"That we have intruded too long on your hospitality," Holmes said, maintaining Sherrinford's voice. "Dr Watson will come to stay with me."

"I will?"

"Perhaps that would be for the best," Anna agreed. "Considering everything that has happened."

"I shall help him pack," Holmes said, escorting me from the garden.

"What was all that about?" I hissed as we climbed the manor's grand staircase.

Holmes waited until my dragonfly-encrusted door was closed behind us before answering.

"Watson, when did you first meet Lord Redshaw?"

"In the Royal Infirmary."

"When he was about to visit Father Kelleher?"

"That's what he said."

"What else did he say? How well did he know Kelleher?"

"Not well at all. He said they'd only met…" Sickening realisation dawned once again. "… after Kelleher was admitted to hospital."

"Which we know was not true. Kelleher came to Ridgeside on numerous occasions."

"But why lie?"

"Isn't it obvious, Watson? Benjamin Redshaw murdered them both. The blood of Monsignor Ermacora and Father Kelleher is on his hands!"

CHAPTER FORTY-NINE

IN PLAIN SIGHT

"I refuse to believe it," I said.

Holmes clapped his hands together. "What are you waiting for, Watson? You need to pack."

"Just because Redshaw lied about knowing Kelleher, doesn't mean he killed the Monsignor."

"No," Holmes admitted. "But the fact that his ornamental garden is overflowing with *Colchicum autumnale* is certainly of interest."

"Autumn crocus," I said, eyes wide.

"The very same. I wonder if Ermacora and Kelleher took tea with Lord Redshaw before the Monsignor left for London?"

I thought of Redshaw's ritual, pouring green tea for his guests.

"*Fumeiyo*," I muttered.

"What's that?"

"Something Redshaw said before he took tea. A custom Sutcliffe brought back from Japan."

"But Sutcliffe has never been to Japan," Holmes argued. "Otherwise he would know that the Japanese say *kanpai* before taking a drink, meaning 'drain your cup."

"No, but that's what he said *fumeiyo* means. Something else he got wrong."

"Did he? Watson, *fumeiyo* means disgrace or dishonour in Japanese. Sutcliffe had Redshaw and Clifford raising their glass and saying 'disgrace' every time they drank tea together."

"He was playing a joke on them?"

"I wonder if it's more than that. Either way the epithet fits, for Redshaw at least. Think about it. Why were you visiting Kelleher at the hospital?"

"So Tovey could ask where he and Ermacora had eaten."

"And the answer would have been Ridgeside Manor. But Father Kelleher is silenced before he can tell Inspector Tovey. Lord Redshaw's secret is safe, but to make doubly sure he greets you and the inspector, taking you in – in every sense of the word."

"You think he killed Kelleher too?"

"He lied about knowing the priest. Why not lie about why he was in the hospital in the first place? It was certainly convenient that he was so quickly on the scene, like Sutcliffe in the secret lodge. Now, if you are not going to pack your clothes, may I suggest that you at least bring your service revolver?"

"My revolver? Why? Where are we going?"

"To find Lord Redshaw."

I did as he asked, slipping my gun into my coat pocket and following Holmes downstairs. Without a second thought, he marched into Redshaw's study, much to the dismay of Brewer, who called after us.

"Sir? Sir, what do you think you're doing? That is Lord Redshaw's private study!"

"We're looking for the location of the League of Merchants' Sacred Grove."

"Whatever do you mean?"

"'Take the completed body to the Sacred Grove,' Holmes

said, reciting the Saisei ritual even though the reference would obviously be lost on Brewer. "The Lodge. Clifford called it their *sanctum sanctorum*. All I need is the address." He looked at the bemused butler in anticipation.

"It is on Stephen Street, sir."

"No, not the official address, the private one. The secret one."

Holmes opened the drawers to Redshaw's desk, searching through the contents. Brewer had already called for assistance from the footmen.

"No need, Brewer," Holmes said, stalking out of the study. "There's nothing here. But what about the drawing room? All those maps on the walls."

"Mr Holmes!"

The detective ignored the butler and strode into the drawing room to perform a swift circuit of the walls. "There has to be something here. No, not this one. Nor this."

"What are you looking for, Holmes?" I asked.

"I shall know when I see it," Holmes replied, stopping in front of the great marble chimney breast. "That's odd."

"Odd? It's a monstrosity, that's what it is."

"No, I mean the map, carved into the marble. It is slightly askew, with much of the old city to the right. Why position it like that?"

"Because the League's headquarters are at the centre. Redshaw told me so himself."

"But they are not." Holmes peered closer. "Look, there is Stephen Street, to the right. It is not central at all – but *that* is." He pointed towards a small lane.

Holmes hurried over to a framed map on the wall, finding the same lane on the yellowed parchment. "Lye Close," he announced, with a chuckle. "How very appropriate. That's where the League really are, just off Canynge Square in Clifton."

"The secret lodge," I realised.

"I knew you would get there in the end, Watson."

Holmes's triumph was short-lived. Brewer stepped forward, his expression telling us that enough was enough, as did the presence of several large footmen standing behind him.

"I'm afraid I shall have to ask you to leave, sir."

"No need. We are on our way. Watson will send for his things later. Be a good fellow and pack them up for him, will you?"

Lady Marie was struggling down the stairs with a large suitcase as we approached the front door.

"Lady Marie," Holmes said, skipping up the last few steps to help her with her luggage. "Let me assist. We are going into town, quite near to Temple Meads Station, if you require a lift?"

"Thank you, Mr Holmes, but I can take one of my father's carriages. I have relied on others for too long."

"A wise decision," the detective said, placing the suitcase at the bottom of the stairs. "Then we shall bid you farewell. Don't worry about us, Brewer. We can see ourselves out."

Holmes rushed ahead of the now beetroot-faced butler and yanked open the door to find Inspector Gregory Hawthorne about to ring the doorbell.

"Ah, there you are," the inspector said with a tight smile as he laid eyes on my disguised friend.

"Good to see you, Inspector," Holmes said, trying to step around the policeman. "If you wish to see Lady Marie, there she is. She already knows the fate of her late fiancé, I'm afraid, if that is what you have come to tell her."

Hawthorne moved to block Holmes's path.

"I haven't come to see Lady Marie," he said, his smile becoming savage. "I've come to see you. You're under arrest... Sherlock Holmes."

CHAPTER FIFTY

ALL IN THE WRIST

"So, it appears the game is up," Holmes said, dropping Sherrinford's voice without argument.

Hawthorne's grin bordered on a snarl. "You can run if you want to. I'd like that."

Behind him Constable Hegarty was standing by a carriage, driver Bert at the reins. Behind us were Brewer and his footmen.

There was no escape.

"Don't worry. We shall come peacefully, won't we, Watson?"

"*We?*" I exclaimed, surprised by the comment.

Holmes turned to face me. "Aiding and abetting a fugitive of the law, Doctor? Surely you didn't think you would escape justice?" The detective returned his attention to Hawthorne and held out his wrists. "I assume you will be wanting to use cuffs."

Five minutes later, we were both cuffed and sitting in the carriage, hands behind our backs. Hegarty sat in with us, my confiscated revolver in his hand. Hawthorne was up front with Bert, every inch the conquering hero.

"So my double was discovered," Holmes called up to the inspector.

"Mr Woodbead forgot to administer his morning morphine," Hawthorne replied. "The fellow was still asleep, but talked in his sleep – with a broad Bristolian accent. Luckily one of my men was passing and heard it, Mr Holmes. I have to applaud you on the make-up. An excellent job. Most life-like."

"And I assume Mr Woodbead is already in custody?"

"I wouldn't worry about him, Holmes. He'll be keeping you company in the cells, where you'll stay this time."

"Well, to lose me twice would be embarrassing, would it not, Inspector?"

Hawthorne's only reply was a mirthless laugh.

"But less embarrassing than having it revealed that you were complicit in my initial false imprisonment, not to mention all the bribes you have accepted from Sir George Tavener..."

This time Hawthorne remained silent.

"Or the murder of Harold Sutcliffe?"

Finally the words drew a response. "Be quiet, Holmes."

"Are you sure you don't intend to force me, as you did with Sutcliffe? By clamping your arm around his throat until he died?"

All the time, Holmes was looking straight at Hegarty, who in turned looked straight ahead, not making eye contact.

"It must have been a struggle, him writhing about on the floor, until the life was squeezed out of him. And then, after all that, you left empty handed, didn't you? Couldn't find the ring or the wig? Sir George must have been furious. Where did you tell him, Hawthorne? At the Admiral's Club? And when? After you threw Sutcliffe's body from Clifton Suspension Bridge?"

That caught Hegarty's attention. He tried to resist, but at the mention of the bridge he could not help turning his head to watch Holmes.

"You're talking rubbish, Holmes," Hawthorne growled.

"Am I? It's all in the wrist, you see, Inspector. All in the wrist."

This time there was no opportunity for Hawthorne to respond. The horses whinnied and the carriage lurched. There was a cry from the inspector, followed by the heavy crunch of a body hitting cobbles.

I slammed into Holmes as we came to an abrupt halt, and looked up to see the doors of the carriage being thrown open.

"Inspector Tovey," exclaimed Hegarty, as he saw who was standing outside.

"Stay where you are, Bob," Tovey said, clambering inside the carriage. "I need to get Holmes and Watson out of here."

"No you don't," roared Hawthorne, grabbing Tovey from behind. He hauled Tovey back and the two inspectors landed hard in the road. Holmes went to lunge from the carriage, but was stopped by the sight of my own service revolver pointing at him. Hegarty had the gun in his hand, and looked ready to fire.

"In your seat," the constable ordered, and Holmes complied.

Outside, the two policemen were fighting fiercely. Hawthorne was a big man, but Tovey was larger still. He delivered a punch that made my teeth ache in sympathy. Hawthorne went down, and Tovey loomed over him, grabbing his rival by the lapels to drag him back to his feet.

"I'll see you go down for what you've done, Hawthorne!"

"You'll never see again!"

Hawthorne reached up and grabbed Tovey's face. There was a thick, wet sound and Tovey screamed. He staggered back, clutching his face. Blood gushed through his fingers and I knew at once that Hawthorne had put his thumb through one of Tovey's eyes.

Hawthorne swung a foot around, taking Tovey's legs from beneath him. Tovey fell, and Hawthorne was on his feet, towering above the fallen policeman. He pulled back a booted foot, ready to plant it into Tovey's side, when there came the crack of a gun. Hawthorne lurched, gaping at his chest in amazement as the front of his waistcoat turned red. He looked up, mouth slack, to see Hegarty, my smoking revolver still in his hand. The inspector coughed once and fell to his knees before toppling forward onto the cobbles.

Holmes leapt from the carriage and rushed to Tovey's side. The policeman was on his back, still clutching his face.

"Watson!" Holmes yelled up to me, as he tried to prise Tovey's hands from his ravaged eye. Only then did I realise that Holmes was no longer wearing handcuffs. When had he slipped out of those?

"Constable?" I said pointedly, turning so that my own cuffs were towards Hegarty. The policeman gave no argument, but went to work with the key.

I was out of the carriage as soon as the iron slipped from my wrists. Tovey was in a bad way, his left eye completely destroyed. "We need to get him to the hospital straight away," I said.

The inspector passed out from the pain as Holmes and I lifted him into the carriage.

"You take him, Bert," Hegarty said, after we had made our injured friend as comfortable as possible. "I'd better stay with Hawthorne."

The driver flicked the reins and the carriage was off, speeding to the infirmary. A crowd had already formed, Hegarty advising them rather forcibly to go on their way.

"You'll be needing this," the constable said, holding the butt of my revolver towards me. I took it gratefully.

"Thank you for trusting us, Constable," Holmes said.

"A lot of what you said made sense," Hegarty replied. "A little too much for my liking."

"Perhaps this city is less rotten than Tovey believes. Now, which way to Canynge Square?"

Hegarty pointed up the road. "Back up Regent Street and onto Clifton Down Road. Keep straight ahead on to Canynge Street and it's on your left."

Holmes checked his watch. "Seven o'clock. Five hours to Warwick's birthday. Come on, Watson."

"Wait a minute," I said, crouching beside Hawthorne's body. I pulled back the dead man's sleeve to reveal cufflinks bearing the monogram T.A.C., plus a dark ring tattooed around his forearm. "All in the wrist, eh?"

"You mean you failed to notice when Hawthorne was slapping on the Darby cuffs? You really need to pay more attention!"

Holmes grabbed Hegarty's hand and pumped it furiously. "Thank you again, Constable, and good luck."

"And to you, Mr Holmes," Hegarty called after us as we raced up the hill.

CHAPTER FIFTY-ONE

AN INNOCENT'S CRY

The dash to Canynge Square took fifteen arduous minutes, running mostly uphill. Holmes raced ahead while I struggled on, my old war wound giving me merry hell. The Georgian square was quiet as we raced around the central garden looking for the entrance to Lye Close.

"There!" I said, pointing ahead. One of the townhouses was caged in scaffolding, its roof under repair, no doubt from storm damage. "I heard a shout and a great crash when blindfolded. It might have been that roof coming down."

"A distinct possibility," said Holmes. "Perhaps I am too hard on you."

"Frequently," I replied, as we turned at the far end of the garden. Lye Close lay off to the right, nothing more than a tiny dark alleyway. A wall ran along the right side of the lane, while warehouses were situated to the left.

I counted four separate buildings in the moonlight. "But which is the Lodge?"

"Think, Watson. When you were brought out of the carriage,

can you remember anything else about your surroundings? Any particular smells or noises?"

"Steps! We descended three steps to reach the door. Clifford said we were going in by the tradesman's entrance."

Holmes ran the length of the lane, stopping outside the third warehouse. "This has to be it," he told me as I caught him up. "It's the only building with steps leading down. Excellent work, Watson."

The building itself looked unoccupied, its windows shuttered. Could the League's opulent headquarters really lie behind such a modest façade?

Holmes had already bounded down the steps and was examining the lock on the door by the time I joined him.

"Shouldn't be too much of a problem," he said, pulling his picks out of his pocket. Sherrinford's monocle came with them.

"I shan't be needing that again," he said, tossing it away.

"Holmes!" I scolded him.

"Really, Watson," he replied, going to work on the lock. "I am on the run from the police for the second time in a week. Littering is the very least of my worries."

The door clicked open to reveal the foul-smelling corridor I remembered from my previous visit. Holmes ushered me in and shut the door firmly, plunging us into darkness.

"How far to the internal door?" he asked.

"I'm not sure. Only five yards or so."

Holmes led us through the gloom, feeling against the wall as he went. I tried to estimate how far we had walked, but was disorientated by the darkness. My foot kicked something that clattered loudly.

"Watson!" Holmes hissed.

I bent down to stop the noise, my hand touching metal. "It's Clifford's lamp."

"And here is the door."

I heard Holmes's picks in the lock and light spilled into the narrow passageway as he pulled the door open.

"Bring the lamp with you," whispered Holmes as we crept into the corridor lined with portraits of the Templar Knights. "Which way to the shrine?"

"Up here," I said, creeping towards the library door. I opened it a crack to find the room empty. "This way."

Holmes followed me through the library without pause, although I could see his eyes sweeping over the bookshelves as we passed.

The next corridor was clear, the doors to the Warwick Room to our right. I was about to lead Holmes past the portraits of the Grand Masters when we heard something.

The cry of an infant.

I looked at Holmes in surprise, ready to dive back into the library, but the detective followed the noise. He walked away from the Warwick Room, his footfalls muffled by the thick carpet. I followed and we came to a single door, slightly ajar. Holmes looked through the gap and, satisfied, opened the door to step inside.

I could scarcely believe what we found. It was a reception area of some kind, shutters closed on the windows and a second door directly opposite us, presumably leading to another room. The floor was packed with wooden cots, each containing a small, sleeping baby. Holmes moved to the child who was grizzling, a tiny infant so swaddled in blankets that it could barely move. He – or at least so I chose to assume; there was no telling given that it was so tightly wrapped – wriggled in his cot as Holmes stepped aside for me so that I could examine the child. The baby looked healthy enough, and quietened as I placed the little finger of my right hand to his lips. Soon the only sound from the crib was contented sucking.

"Holmes," I whispered. "What are they doing here?"

The detective's face was grim. "I have a terrible suspicion,

Watson. 'Restore with the blood of innocent lambs.'"

"The ritual?" My stomach clenched as I realised what he was saying. "You don't mean…?"

Holmes moved to a side table, from which he picked up a small bottle. "'Mrs Winslow's Soothing Syrup'," he read from the label. "'The mother's friend', no less."

"Used to quieten babies, yes."

"Not surprising, as it includes laudanum amongst its ingredients."

"I didn't say I approved!"

There was a sound from the corridor outside and Holmes quickly replaced the bottle. Someone was coming. Holmes indicated the second door, and we raced towards it. We had hardly made it into the adjoining room when the door to the strange nursery opened.

We stood with our backs to the wall, listening as someone walked into the room. I heard a tut, followed by the scrape of the bottle of syrup being fetched from the table. More footsteps, presumably taking the newcomer back to the distressed baby; a few seconds later, the crying stopped, the child lulled by the solution. It was all I could do not to burst out from our hiding place. If Holmes were right, the fate that awaited these children was abominable. I thought of all those adverts in the *Mercury*, all the women who had put their trust in this monster. By my reckoning there were twenty cots in the room, maybe more. Twenty lives not yet lived.

My impulse was halted only by the sound of someone else entering the room.

"Mrs Nell." The name was spoken in the reedy tones of Sir George Tavener. My skin crawled all the more.

"Grand Master," a woman replied.

"How are the infants?"

"Sleeping soundly. All will be well."

"We are bringing the ceremony forward to midnight. We have waited long enough."

"Of course."

"You will show the League down when they arrive?"

"As you wish, Grand Master."

"Excellent. I shall be in my office if I am needed, preparing for the ritual."

"Would you like tea?"

"That would be splendid, thank you."

"I shall bring it up."

"You will be remembered for your part in this, Mrs Nell. That I promise you."

I made my own promise as the two conspirators left the room. They would be remembered all right, for their sins. Drinking tea like civilised folk when preparing for deeds of such depravity? It made me sick to my stomach.

The door clicked shut, but Holmes indicated that I should stay where I was. We waited for a few moments to make sure that neither Tavener nor Nell returned, slipping back into the reception room.

"We need to get these children out of here, Holmes," I insisted.

"Not just yet. We should see the full extent of the ritual before we spoil Edwyn Warwick's birthday celebrations." He checked his watch. "It is a quarter to eight. We still have time. Tell me, Watson. Did you see any stairs leading to an upper storey when you were last here?"

"No, but there must be. Nell said she would take Tavener's tea up to him."

"And that the League's members would need to come down when they arrived."

He moved to the door and checked the corridor outside. "No one around. Watson, show me this shrine."

Retrieving the lantern, I took Holmes down the corridor

to the double doors. The Warwick Room was deserted and we slipped inside, shutting ourselves in. I showed Holmes where I had been attacked.

"And this is where Sutcliffe was hiding?" Holmes asked as he tried the storage room door.

"So we think. The candlestick was hidden inside."

"Meaning that he went back into the storage room after knocking you insensible…"

Holmes's picks made short work of the door and he was in the room in a jiffy. "Give me the lantern."

I passed it over and he lit the lamp, turning around in the cramped space.

"When you described your attack, I thought it bizarre that your assailant had the time – or indeed the inclination – to hide the candlestick, lock the door and then make an escape before Clifford returned from the library."

"I said the same myself at the time. Unless Clifford was lying about how long he was away."

"Or there is another way out of the cupboard…"

Holmes walked to the back of the storage room and tapped the wall. It sounded hollow.

"A secret door?"

Holmes ran his fingers along the brickwork in search of an opening mechanism. "My favourite kind. But how to open it?"

I looked up, seeing a long narrow window above his head. "We're in the middle of the house," I stated. "Clifford told me. That's why they have lamps behind the stained-glass windows."

"So why have a ventilation window in a store room?"

He reached up and grabbed the window's latch. There was a dull click within the brickwork. Holmes gave the wall a shove and it swung away from him, revealing a spiral staircase of red stone.

Without another word, Holmes descended into the gloom.

CHAPTER FIFTY-TWO

THE TEMPLE

The staircase was narrow, the steps barely wider than our feet. We followed it down, the air chilling with every turn. Holmes held up the lantern as we reached the bottom and walked through an arch to find ourselves in a vast underground chamber.

The space was roughly octagonal in shape, lit by large candelabras against the plain stone walls.

"A Templar chapel," Holmes said, pointing towards the large Maltese cross that dominated the domed ceiling. "The League's very own 'sacred grove.'"

"And that's not all," I said. Two altars lay side by side in the middle of the room. One was empty; on the other was a large wooden coffin. A number of rubber tubes ran from holes drilled in the side of the casket, each snaking to twenty or so small cribs arranged in a circle, like spokes in a wheel.

Holmes stepped over the tubes and, placing the lamp on the empty altar, tried the lid of the coffin. "It's not nailed down," he said. "Give me a hand, will you?"

I did as I was asked. The lid came away easily, revealing its prize. The body of a mummified man lay before us. His eyelids were closed, his skin like old leather. The lips were parted to show long yellow teeth, the nails on his fingers also unnaturally long.

"Warwick?" I asked.

"Less fresh than the legend would have us believe, but still remarkably well preserved. He must have been dried out by the cold air of St Nicole's crypt, the thick wood of his casket slowing decomposition. A miracle of nature rather than the divine."

"Or the satanic," I added, glancing around the temple in disgust.

"They have found a replacement gem," Holmes said, pointing out the ruby ring on a long grey finger.

"And a periwig too," I said, assuming that the hairpiece framing Warwick's sunken face was Sir George's prize relic.

"The ritual stated that the body needed to be completed. It was essential that Warwick's property be returned to him."

Holmes was right. Even the cross Clifford mentioned, stolen from the corpse, was once more around the mummy's neck.

Holmes pulled aside the dead man's shroud.

"Good heavens," I said as I saw the gaping hole in Warwick's grey chest. "The heart's been removed."

"To make room for a pure one, again as per the ritual. I wonder, Watson, all those poor chimpanzees, stolen from the zoological gardens. They were found without their hearts, were they not? Trial runs maybe. I wonder if the Worshipful Merchants have made any sizeable donations to the zoo recently."

As he spoke, Holmes fiddled with the nest of rubber tubes that surrounded Warwick's body. They were attached to needles already inserted into the corpse's dry veins.

Holmes traced the path of a tube through the wood to a pump and then out to one of the cradles. The meaning was clear, and it sickened me.

"They're going to drain those babes…"

"To pump new life into Warwick."

"It's obscene."

"And beyond the laws of science, not that that seems to worry the League."

I examined the pump, recognising the design. "This is the work of Melosan. When I offered to give blood..."

"Melosan shares a tattoo with Redshaw and Hawthorne," Holmes said. He approached an iron cage that hung from the ceiling near the back of the chamber. "Here's another relic from an earlier age."

I had seen similar objects depicted in some of the more esoteric books Holmes liked to read. It was made of iron, the bars curved to form the outline of an adult man.

"A medieval coffin cage," I said.

"In which blasphemers were hung to be pecked at by birds." He turned, looking at the unholy machine the League had constructed. "How lucky we are to live in more enlightened times, eh, Watson?"

"But what's the cage for?"

Holmes made a motion for me to be silent.

"I was only asking..."

"I mean it, Watson. Be quiet."

He darted across the chamber, leaping over the mess of rubber tubing to disappear through another arch.

"Watson, quick!"

I rushed after him, finding Holmes stooped over two figures, both bound and gagged.

"Clifford!" I exclaimed, recognising Anna's husband.

"And Father Ebberston too," Holmes pointed out, working the gag from the priest's mouth.

"Oh, thank God," Ebberston gasped. "You have to help us."

"It's B-Benjamin and the others," Clifford said. "They've

g-gone m-mad. Some kind of r-r-r—"

The last word proved too much for him, so Holmes completed the sentence for the terrified man.

"A ritual, to raise Edwyn Warwick from the dead."

"But why?" Ebberston said.

"To provide leadership?" Holmes theorised. "To lead them into a golden age?"

"Or r-return us t-to o-one," Clifford said as Holmes worked on the knots that bound him. "B-Benjamin and Sir G-George have talked about it b-before."

"A time before workers' rights," I said, remembering Redshaw's words in the drawing room. "When business was allowed to be business."

"They were going to sacrifice Mr Clifford," Ebberston gabbled, shivering both from the cold and from abject terror. "And make me watch from that cage."

"'Under the deceitful eyes of the damned,'" Holmes said, quoting the ritual. He leant across to where I was trying to free the priest, and inspected Ebberston's arms. "No tattoo for you."

"What do you mean?" Ebberston asked.

"The participators in the ritual have been marked by Sutcliffe."

"V-Victor?"

"You are a pawn in their game, Father. Your face betrayed you when Warwick's body was discovered missing. You already knew it was gone."

"Tavener told me not to tell anyone."

"Why? What does he have on you? He blackmailed Mrs Mercer. What secrets is he using against you?"

Ebberston shook his head. "No, that's not it. He promised support for St Nicole's, for our work in the city, the opening of a new shelter for the poor and destitute."

"And you went along with it?" I said.

"He was offering a small fortune. Told me it would be bad for the city if the truth of Warwick's tomb were known. Even when you came to the church, asking questions, and the tomb was opened... I went to him, begged him to let me tell the truth..."

"But the deed has already been done. He has made a liar of you, sir," Holmes said, "and you have damned yourself by your silence. Your deceitful eyes must bear witness so that the ritual will work."

"And w-will it?" Clifford asked.

"Of course not," I insisted, unable to loosen a single knot of Ebberston's ropes.

"No one will ever find out, one way or the other," Holmes insisted, working on Clifford's restraints. "I shall see to that."

"Will you indeed?" said a voice from the other side of the arch.

We wheeled around to find Lord Redshaw standing behind us, flanked by Dr Melosan, Tavener, a prim-faced woman whom I could only assume was Mrs Nell, and a large man with a crop of red hair whom I didn't recognise. Mrs Nell was wearing an austere black dress, with boots of patent leather, fastened with white buttons. So *this* was the mysterious Mrs Protheroe. The men were all dressed in the same way, wearing black breeches and loose cotton shirts rolled up at the sleeves. Like Redshaw's and Melosan's, Tavener's wrinkled arm was tattooed, a single black ring to Redshaw's two.

I was unable to see whether the red-haired man's arm was inked. I was too concerned about the shotgun he pointed in our direction.

Holmes went to stand.

"Stay where you are," the flame-haired man said.

"Now, Lacey," Redshaw said. "We're not savages. Let the fellow get to his feet."

Another piece of the puzzle fell into place. Mr Lacey, the esteemed editor of the *Bristol Mercury*. He was in on it too.

"Thank you," said Holmes. "I assume I no longer need to maintain my disguise?"

"We know who you are," sneered Redshaw. My former host was slightly hunched over and I could see bloody dressings through the fabric of his shirt.

"Benjamin, you don't have to do any of this," I pleaded with him. "Those babies upstairs. They don't have to die."

"You are right," Redshaw nodded. "Of course you are. Clifford was to be our pure heart. So naive. So guileless. But no longer. Not compared to you. Dr Watson, who has seen the evil of the world time and time again and yet still clings to good; railing against injustice, defending those who cannot protect themselves. You are a perfect candidate. "

He nodded in Melosan's direction and the doctor stepped towards me. Holmes moved to intercept, but was halted by a warning from Lacey and a wave of the gun. Melosan tried to grab my arm and pull me forward, but I resisted. He was no match for me. But then Redshaw joined the fray. He pulled at my free arm, and blood splattered against his shirt as the stitches in his side burst. He was unperturbed, even as he buried his fist in my stomach.

I doubled over, winded, and Redshaw shoved me to the floor. Before I knew it, he was kneeling on my chest, his large hands around my throat, pressing down hard. Melosan held one of my arms, leaving my other free to batter Redshaw, but my strength was deserting me, Redshaw's grip too tight. I gagged, trying to call Holmes's name, but my friend was unable to move without risking a shot from Lacey. There was a flash in the corner of my vision; Mrs Nell had something in her hand. Was that a syringe? I had no fight in me. She bent forward and I felt the sharp scratch of a needle before everything went dark.

CHAPTER FIFTY-THREE

FIVE MINUTES TO MIDNIGHT

I had no idea where I was. I was unable to move, hardly able even to breathe. Something was in my mouth. I bit down with what little strength I could muster. It was hard against my teeth. I coughed. Something tickled the back of my throat, a hair or a thread, I couldn't tell what.

I tried to open my eyes, but they refused to respond; I wanted to move my arms but they were strapped down. The air was cool against my chest. Where was my shirt?

I groaned, and heard my name echoing from far away.

I turned my head, finally able to open my eyes a crack.

There was my name again. *Watson*. Nearer this time.

I was unable to see properly. There were lights, dancing in front of me like will o' the wisps, tiny specks that became flickering candles. There were figures too, standing around me. White shirts. Black trousers. Blurred faces. Movement. Hushed voices.

And my name, over and over again.

Watson.

Watson.

Wat-son.

Suddenly, everything came into focus. I knew where I was. I knew what was happening.

I turned my head, seeing Warwick's coffin on the slab beside me. I railed against the leather straps that bound me to the altar, yelling Holmes's name, my voice hoarse and desperate.

Holmes hung in front of me, in the coffin cage, hands bound behind his back. A rope gag hung loose around his neck, identical to the one clamped between my jaws. He had worked his loose, but I could not do likewise, the gag was too tight.

All around was silent activity, the anticipation in the room palpable. Mrs Nell inspected the cots. Oh God. That meant the babies were in place. To my side, Dr Melosan was arranging a line of scalpels on the edge on the altar. I looked down, realising to my horror that the skin across my naked chest was smooth, devoid of hair. They had shaved me while I slept.

"Watson," Holmes shouted. "Watson, listen to me. You're going to be all right. Do you hear? We're going to get you out of this."

I could see the muscles of his arms twitching through the sleeves of the jacket. He was working at whatever they had used to tie his wrists together. He would be free soon, of that I had no doubt, just as he had escaped the cuffs in the police carriage, but what of that cage? It was fastened with two huge padlocks, which looked strong enough to confound even the greatest escapologist, let alone Holmes.

A shadow fell across me. I looked up to see Benjamin Redshaw.

"It is nearly time, Watson," he said, a manic look in his eyes as he stared at his pocket watch. "Five minutes to midnight. It is fitting that you wake to see what you would have halted."

"We *will* halt it," Holmes yelled from his cage. "Do you hear me, Redshaw? This plan of yours, this ungodly rite; it's insane. You know that, don't you? It won't work. It can't. Sutcliffe made it up, all of it. The legend of Izanami. It doesn't end the way he told you. She isn't restored, Redshaw. She is left rotting in hell. You will do the same if you go through with it. If you hurt a hair on Watson's head you will hang, and Warwick will still be dead."

"Says the damned from his cage, watching all, but unable to act," Redshaw shouted back, his voice echoing around the chamber like a mad evangelist. "As it was written."

"As *Sutcliffe* wrote. One man, consumed with revenge. Do you not see, Redshaw? He was going to trap you, to shame you all as you shamed his father. That's why he had to die, wasn't it? Why you sent Hawthorne to throttle him? He had met with Lacey, in the Admiral's Club. Offered him the scoop of the century. The Worshipful League of Merchants performing a blasphemous act of black magic. How he must have laughed when you swallowed his occult claptrap. You fell for it hook, line and sinker, didn't you, Redshaw? All the lies that you wanted to believe, the spells written on ancient parchments thousands of miles away. But they weren't. They were written here, in Bristol, by a man who hated you, who hated what you had done to his family."

"The damned man lies," shouted Tavener from his place beside Redshaw, "as deceitful now as when dressed as a vagrant, or as his non-existent brother. You don't know what is true. This organisation has practised rites for centuries. We have protected this city and we will do so again."

"The hour has come," Redshaw said, snapping his watch shut. "Midnight. Gather around, brothers. The ritual must begin. Warwick will rise."

I looked around frantically as the members of the Worshipful League formed a circle around the chamber. There must have been twenty of them or more, one for every cot, one for every life that was about to be snuffed out.

"Dr Melosan?" Redshaw asked. "Are we ready?"

Melosan checked his surgical implements once again, his eye twitching violently. "Yes, yes we are."

Redshaw looked down at me, rapture written all over his face. "Your heart will become his, Watson, and then the blood of the innocent lambs will bring new life."

How much of this was mania, or the painkillers he had been given for his wounds? I bucked against my restraints, but they held.

"You will play your part in our restitution, Watson," he said, saliva flecking his lips. "Our innocent heart."

"Innocent?" Holmes jeered from his cage. "Watson? Now I have heard everything. If you wanted innocent you have chosen the wrong man. Should have stuck with Clifford."

"Silence!" Redshaw bellowed. "We must begin."

"And you will fail!" Holmes promised, even as Melosan picked up a scalpel from the slab. "Think about it, Redshaw. If Sutcliffe's parchments contain the truth, if you *can* raise Warwick from the dead, can you risk that John Watson is the man you think he is?"

Redshaw ignored Holmes's jibes and nodded at Melosan, who leant across my chest, scalpel in hand. He was about to open me up alive!

CHAPTER FIFTY-FOUR

THE PERFECT SPELL

"Do not listen to him!" Redshaw boomed. "He is the damned."

No, listen to him, I begged silently as the scalpel brushed my chest. *Please, listen to him!*

"Yes, I am the damned, but so is Watson," Holmes insisted, as he pulled his hands apart behind his back.

"He is free!" Tavener yelped in panic, only to be hushed by Redshaw.

"He will never escape the cage."

Holmes twisted, barely able to move, and reached a hand to one of the padlocks. All the time, he shouted down at the doctor. "Listen to me, Melosan. I've seen your work, the precision of the pumps, the craftsmanship. It will all be for nought, because John Watson is no innocent."

Above me, Melosan faltered just for a moment, as Holmes continued both with the assassination of my character and on the locks.

"Think of it. He is a doctor who has killed, time and time again. Not on the operating table, not by accident. But in anger, a gun in his hand. He is a gambler too, unable to stop himself from risking everything. So much so that I have to lock his money away, so that he is unable to squander every last penny he has."

"Shut him up," Redshaw raged.

Lacey moved to the cage, shaking it in an attempt to silence Holmes, even as the detective abandoned the first padlock for the other.

"He could have stayed at home with his wife," Holmes continued, "the honest and decent thing to do. But he left her alone to come away with me, and I am a devil after all. He is no more innocent than any man in this room. He will fail you as he has failed everyone, time and time again."

The harsh words stung me, but they drove Redshaw into a fury.

"Don't listen to him," roared the peer, moving around the altar to shake Melosan as one might rouse a man from slumber.

"But…" Melosan began to argue.

"Idiot," Redshaw raged, grabbing the scalpel from the doctor's hand and pushing him to the ground. Redshaw whirled about, and I realised that he meant to cut my heart out himself. Melosan scrambled up, trying to stop him.

"Benjamin, wait. If he's right…"

Redshaw answered by bringing his elbow back into the doctor's nose with a nauseating crunch of cartilage.

"Holmes is lying to you," he spat. "He's lying to everyone."

"No," shouted a voice from across the room. "He's telling the truth. No man is innocent, especially here."

There was the sharp retort of a gun, the acoustics of the underground temple magnifying the sound to that of thunder. Redshaw let out a guttural cry and froze like a statue for a second, before the scalpel slipped from his fingers. The life draining out of him, he toppled forward to land heavily across my chest. His body slid to the floor as all hell broke loose in the subterranean chamber. The members of the League ran in panic as blue-uniformed constables swarmed down the staircase, passing the figure of Inspector Abraham Tovey, his gun still raised and a bloody patch across his left eye.

Dr Melosan ran beneath the coffin cage just as it snapped open and Holmes dropped down on him. The surgeon let out a cry of terror and Holmes delivered a punch that sent him sprawling across the floor.

"On the stroke of midnight, Inspector!" Holmes panted, standing over the unconscious doctor. "That's what I told Hegarty. I thought policemen could tell the time!"

Tovey let his gun drop and staggered back to sag against the temple wall.

"Inspector Lestrade's report was right, Mr Holmes. You really *are* impossible."

"Then it is fortunate that the impossible is your business," Holmes replied.

In the relative quiet of the Lodge library, I rubbed the sore skin of my wrists. After Tovey and Holmes had stopped bandying words, someone had remembered me, strapped to a stone altar like a sacrificial virgin. Holmes had released me, whereupon I leapt from the slab to check on the infants. They were alive, each and every one drugged to the eyeballs with laudanum, but breathing all the same.

I felt a hand on my shoulder. It was Mr Woodbead, asking if I could assist in carrying the babies upstairs. Word had been sent to the Bristol Royal Infirmary and help would be on its way, but in the meantime we had much to do. I was happy to oblige, anything to avoid thinking about the scalpel discarded on the temple floor.

Now, sitting alone, I was content to let the others clear up.

Tovey's men were everywhere at once, and a team of nurses had arrived to take care of the children.

"How are you feeling?" said Holmes, breezing into the library as if he had just spent an evening playing whist.

"How do you think?"

He perched himself on the side of the reading desk. "Tovey's been taken back to hospital, where he should have remained. He couldn't bear not to see things through to the bitter end, no matter what the cost. I can appreciate that."

"But how…" I stopped myself and laughed. Here I was, once again asking for an explanation from Sherlock Holmes. This truly was my lot in life.

Holmes spared me the indignity. "I was out of the cuffs before we had even left Ridgeside Manor. All I needed to do was to reach into my back pocket to retrieve my notebook and pencil. While I kept Hawthorne talking, I wrote a note to Hegarty…"

"Behind your back?"

"Behind my back. I admit, the handwriting was not my neatest, but you can't have everything. It was clear from Hegarty's face that he was uncomfortable with our arrest. I had observed him in the short time I spent in Lower Redland Road Police Station. He is a good policeman, like Tovey. And he made his choice, ending Hawthorne's corruption once and for all."

"But when did you give him the note?" I asked, before realising. "When you shook his hand so vigorously. Of course."

"The note contained the address we suspected to be the headquarters of the Lodge…"

"Lye Close…"

"And instructions to look for a monocle, which I would leave on the street outside the correct building."

"Well, I'll be blowed…"

"Of course, I had no idea what we would find. So, in case

everything went wrong, I instructed our friends in blue to raid the Lodge at midnight sharp, which they did… more or less."

"Which is why you tried to keep Redshaw and Melosan talking."

"Of course, when I wrote the note, I had no idea that you would be under the knife or that I would be suspended like a bird in a cage."

"Yes, about that. Broadcasting my failures as a man and a husband…"

Holmes waved my complaint away. "I would have said anything to delay the inevitable and give Hegarty's squad the time they needed to burst in."

"But you had no idea they were coming, or that Hegarty could find enough honest policemen to mount a raid."

"You are not the only man who likes a flutter, Watson."

"You gambled with my life, and never thought to tell me what you were planning… again."

"Hegarty was insurance, that is all. A back-up plan. I hoped it wouldn't come to that, but it did and for that I apologise. Nobody's perfect, Watson."

"Not even you?"

Holmes considered this. "I am the damned, after all."

I rubbed my chest where the scalpel had rested. "I believe you."

We sat in silence for a moment. "So all this," I finally said. "All this madness…"

"Was part of Sutcliffe's plan to discredit Redshaw and the others, a trick that went horribly wrong." Holmes stood and perused the bookcases. "Tavener was right. If some of the texts in this library are anything to go by, the League have performed rituals and magic for generations, whatever Redshaw claimed about Inspector Tovey's 'mumbo-jumbo'. Sutcliffe saw an opportunity to exploit both the League's superstitions and their worship of Warwick."

"Providing the perfect spell."

"One thought that they would have done some research of their own, discovered that Sutcliffe's rites were a load of hogwash. But he played to their hubris, and they swallowed it all. They were so desperate to retain power at any cost that they believed every word he said. Little did Sutcliffe know how far they would take it; the murders, the babies... Mrs Nell has been bleating her innocence to all and sundry, not that anyone believes her. It turns out that she *was* arrested for her past crimes, by Inspector Hawthorne no less. He was going on a description given by Lord Redshaw, who realised what a boon a baby farmer would be for the ritual. Nell was given a choice; face the noose, or procure innocent blood for the League. She chose the latter."

"So when Sutcliffe found out that they meant to go through with it all..."

"He must have panicked, trying to stop what he had started. First he steals the ring and then the wig, without which they would be unable to perform the rite he had created."

"Unaware that Tavener had relics of his own."

"Then he attempts to have Lord Redshaw killed. From what we have seen tonight it is obvious that Redshaw is the true power here, not Tavener. But you saved him, Watson, because no matter what I said in the cage, you are a good doctor."

I thought of Sutcliffe jumping into the carriage with me, asking if Redshaw would live.

"With Warwick's birthday approaching, Sutcliffe returned to his original plan, taking the story to Lacey in the Admiral's Club."

"Unaware that Lacey was in on the conspiracy."

"How else could the League have kept so many atrocities and scandals from the papers?"

"But Lacey didn't have a tattoo, like the others."

"Because Sutcliffe was unaware he deserved one." Holmes

found the book he was looking for. "Here we go – *Punter's Travels in Japan*, a more recent edition than Sutcliffe's. Unfortunately, Punter didn't recount the true story of Izanami and Izanagi, but he does delve into some fascinating criminal history."

Holmes brought the book to the reading desk and, checking the index, flicked it open to a page that featured photographs of men's forearms, each with its own tattoo.

"Traditional Japanese tattoos from the Edo period," Holmes explained, reading the caption, "used to brand criminals."

"Criminals?"

"I suspect that Sutcliffe told Redshaw and his cronies that they were badges of honour or power…"

"Just as he told them that *fumeiyo* meant good health rather than disgrace."

Holmes closed the book. "Of course it worked, in the end. The League of Merchants is no longer Worshipful. Not even Lacey will be able to sweep this ignominy beneath the carpet. Their sins will be the talk of the city."

How wrong Holmes was. The League was disbanded, that much is true, but the true nature of their crimes was never made public. The following day, after we had resided as guests of Mrs Mercer once again, we were greeted by an unexpected figure in the lobby of the Regent Hotel.

Mycroft Holmes had come to Bristol after all.

We were ushered into Mrs Mercer's office, where Mycroft laid down the law. The true details of the case could never be known. The Worshipful League of Merchants' interests spread far beyond Bristol. There were red faces in Whitehall, who wished for the scandal to go away.

We were sworn to secrecy, as was Inspector Tovey, who could

never explain the true story of how he had lost an eye. He would be rewarded in time, and given a new post in London alongside Inspector Lestrade, investigating cases that other policemen would not touch. I never discovered what happened to Nelson Powell and Marie Redshaw. They vanished, hopefully to start a new life together. Harold Clifford sold his business and moved away with Anna and their new-born daughter, also to start afresh, far from his past.

As for Lye Close, Mycroft confided to us that it would be demolished, the temple filled in. It would be as though the little street had never existed, other than as an anomaly on old maps of the city.

Holmes brooded all the way back to London. Soon he would be on a boat back to France, and I was not to see him again until he walked into my surgery one fateful evening looking pale and drawn and told me of a man by the name of Professor James Moriarty. Once more, as terrible events overtook us, Sherlock Holmes would keep me in the dark.

But did I mind?

No, not really.

After all, as the man reminded me himself, nobody is perfect.

ABOUT THE AUTHOR

Cavan Scott is the author of *Sherlock Holmes: The Patchwork Devil*, published in 2016, which was described as "an intriguing puzzle" by *Publishers Weekly* and as "a thrilling tale" by *Sci-Fi Bulletin*. He was also a contributor to Titan Books' anthologies *Encounters of Sherlock Holmes* and *Associates of Sherlock Holmes*. Beyond the world of Arthur Conan Doyle, he has written over ninety books and audio dramas including the UK no. 1 bestseller *Star Wars: Adventures in Wild Space—The Escape*. He has written for such popular series as *Doctor Who*, *Star Trek*, *Vikings*, *Torchwood*, *Warhammer 40,000*, *Pathfinder*, *Judge Dredd* and *Highlander*. Find out more by visiting www.cavanscott.com, or follow him on Twitter @cavanscott.

ACKNOWLEDGEMENTS

First of all, thanks to historian Eugene Byrne for first bringing the curious discovery of Edward Colston's body to my attention. It's found in Latimer's *Annals of Bristol*, if you fancy a read.

Thanks also to George Mann, for bouncing the plot around on a walk around sunny San Diego and back at home; to my editors Miranda Jewess and Gary Budden for poking holes in the self-same plot to make sure it worked; to Titan's wonderful publicists Lydia Gittins and Philippa Ward for working so hard on this and *The Patchwork Devil*; and to my brilliant agent, Jane Willis for being, well, brilliant.

And, as always, thanks above all to Clare, Chloe and Connie for all their love and support in the writing of this book. You make it all possible.

SHERLOCK HOLMES
THE PATCHWORK DEVIL
Cavan Scott

It is 1919, and while the world celebrates the signing of the Treaty of Versailles, Holmes and Watson are called to a grisly discovery.

A severed hand has been found on the bank of the Thames, a hand belonging to a soldier who supposedly died in the trenches two years previously. But the hand is fresh, and shows signs that it was recently amputated. So how has it ended up back in London two years after its owner was killed in France? Warned by Sherlock's brother Mycroft to cease their investigation, and only barely surviving an attack by a superhuman creature, Holmes and Watson begin to suspect a conspiracy at the very heart of the British government…

"Scott poses an intriguing puzzle for an older Holmes and Watson to tackle." *Publishers Weekly*

"Interesting and exciting in ways that few Holmes stories are these days." **San Francisco Book Review**

"A thrilling tale for Scott's debut in the Sherlock Holmes world." **Sci-Fi Bulletin**

TITANBOOKS.COM

SHERLOCK HOLMES
THE THINKING ENGINE
James Lovegrove

It is 1895, and Sherlock Holmes is settling back into life as a consulting detective at 221b Baker Street, when he and Watson learn of strange goings-on amidst the dreaming spires of Oxford.

A Professor Quantock has built a wondrous computational device, which he claims is capable of analytical thought to rival the cleverest men alive. Naturally Sherlock Holmes cannot ignore this challenge. He and Watson travel to Oxford, where a battle of wits ensues between the great detective and his mechanical counterpart as they compete to see which of them can be first to solve a series of crimes, from a bloody murder to a missing athlete. But as man and machine vie for supremacy, it becomes clear that the Thinking Engine has its own agenda…

"The plot, like the device, is ingenious, with a chilling twist... an entertaining, intelligent and pacy read."
The Sherlock Holmes Journal

"Lovegrove knows his Holmes trivia and delivers a great mystery that fans will enjoy, with plenty of winks and nods to the canon." **Geek Dad**

"The concept of an intelligent, self-aware Thinking Engine is brilliance itself." **The Book Bag**

TITANBOOKS.COM

SHERLOCK HOLMES
GODS OF WAR
James Lovegrove

It is 1913, and Dr Watson is visiting Sherlock Holmes at his retirement cottage near Eastbourne when tragedy strikes: the body of a young man, Patrick Mallinson, is found under the cliffs of Beachy Head.

The dead man's father, a wealthy businessman, engages Holmes to prove that his son committed suicide, the result of a failed love affair with an older woman. Yet the woman in question insists that there is more to Patrick's death. She has seen mysterious symbols drawn on his body, and fears that he was under the influence of a malevolent cult. When an attempt is made on Watson's life, it seems that she may be proved right. The threat of war hangs over England, and there is no telling what sinister forces are at work…

"Lovegrove has once again packed his novel with incident and suspense." **Fantasy Book Review**

"An atmospheric mystery which shows just why Lovegrove has become a force to be reckoned with in genre fiction. More, please." *Starburst*

"A very entertaining read with a fast-moving, intriguing plot." **The Consulting Detective**

TITANBOOKS.COM

SHERLOCK HOLMES
THE STUFF OF NIGHTMARES

James Lovegrove

A spate of bombings has hit London, causing untold damage and loss of life. Meanwhile a strangely garbed figure has been spied haunting the rooftops and grimy back alleys of the capital.

Sherlock Holmes believes this strange masked man may hold the key to the attacks. He moves with the extraordinary agility of a latter-day Spring-Heeled Jack. He possesses weaponry and armour of unprecedented sophistication. He is known only by the name Baron Cauchemar, and he appears to be a scourge of crime and villainy. But is he all that he seems? Holmes and his faithful companion Dr Watson are about to embark on one of their strangest and most exhilarating adventures yet.

"[A] tremendously accomplished thriller which leaves the reader in no doubt that they are in the hands of a confident and skilful craftsman." *Starburst*

"Dramatic, gripping, exciting and respectful to its source material, I thoroughly enjoyed every surprise and twist as the story unfolded." **Fantasy Book Review**

"This is delicious stuff, marrying the standard notions of Holmesiana with the kind of imagination we expect from Lovegrove." **Crimetime**

TITANBOOKS.COM

SHERLOCK HOLMES
THE SPIRIT BOX
George Mann

German zeppelins rain down death and destruction on London, and Dr Watson is grieving for his nephew, killed on the fields of France.

A cryptic summons from Mycroft Holmes reunites Watson with his one-time companion, as Sherlock comes out of retirement, tasked with solving three unexplained deaths. A politician has drowned in the Thames after giving a pro-German speech; a soldier suggests surrender before feeding himself to a tiger; and a suffragette renounces women's liberation and throws herself under a train. Are these apparent suicides something more sinister, something to do with the mysterious Spirit Box? Their investigation leads them to Ravensthorpe House, and the curious Seaton Underwood, a man whose spectrographs are said to capture men's souls…

"Arthur Conan Doyle was a master storyteller, and it takes comparable talent to give Holmes a second life… Mann is one of the few to get close to the target." *Daily Mail*

"I would highly recommend this… a fun read."
Fantasy Book Review

"Our only complaint is that it is over too soon." *Starburst*

TITANBOOKS.COM

SHERLOCK HOLMES
THE WILL OF THE DEAD
George Mann

A rich elderly man has fallen to his death, and his will is nowhere to be found. A tragic accident or something more sinister? The dead man's nephew comes to Baker Street to beg for Sherlock Holmes's help. Without the will he fears he will be left penniless, the entire inheritance passing to his cousin. But just as Holmes and Watson start their investigation, a mysterious new claimant to the estate appears. Does this prove that the old man was murdered?

Meanwhile Inspector Charles Bainbridge is trying to solve the case of the "iron men", mechanical steam-powered giants carrying out daring jewellery robberies. But how do you stop a machine that feels no pain and needs no rest? He too may need to call on the expertise of Sherlock Holmes.

"Mann clearly knows his Holmes, knows what works... the book is all the better for it." **Crime Fiction Lover**

"Mann writes Holmes in a eloquent way, capturing the period of the piece perfectly... this is a must read." **Cult Den**

"An amazing story... Even in the established world of Sherlock Holmes, George Mann is a strong voice and sets himself apart!" **Book Plank**

TITANBOOKS.COM

SHERLOCK HOLMES

THE ARMY OF DR MOREAU
Guy Adams

Dead bodies are found on the streets of London with wounds that can only be explained as the work of ferocious creatures not native to the city.

Sherlock Holmes is visited by his brother, Mycroft, who is only too aware that the bodies are the calling card of Dr Moreau, a vivisectionist who was working for the British Government, following in the footsteps of Charles Darwin, before his experiments attracted negative attention and the work was halted. Mycroft believes that Moreau's experiments continue and he charges his brother with tracking the rogue scientist down before matters escalate any further.

"Succeeds both as a literary jeu d'esprit and detective story, with a broad streak of irreverent humour." *Financial Times*

"Deftly handled… this is a must read for all fans of adventure and fantasy literature." **Fantasy Book Review**

"Well worth a read… Adams is a natural fit for the world of Sherlock Holmes." *Starburst*

TITANBOOKS.COM